The Other Garden
and
Collected Stories

From 1964 to 1980 Francis Wyndham was
a feature writer on the staff of the *Sunday Times*.
He is the author of a collection of essays, *The Theatre of
Embarrassment*, as well as *Out of the War, Mrs Henderson
and Other Stories*, and *The Other Garden*, which won
the 1987 Whitbread First Novel Award.

Francis Wyndham

The Other Garden
and
Collected Stories

With an Introduction by
Alan Hollinghurst

PICADOR

This collection first published 1992 by Vintage

This edition first published 2008 by Picador
an imprint of Pan Macmillan Ltd
Pan Macmillan, 20 New Wharf Road, London N1 9RR
Basingstoke and Oxford
Associated companies throughout the world
www.panmacmillan.com

ISBN 978-0-330-45720-0

Out of the War first published 1974 by Gerald Duckworth & Co., Ltd
Mrs Henderson and Other Stories first published 1985 by Jonathan Cape Ltd
The Other Garden first published 1987 by Jonathan Cape Ltd

A CIP catalogue record for this book is available from
the British Library.

Typeset by SetSystems Ltd, Saffron Walden, Essex
Printed in the UK by CPI Mackays, Chatham ME5 8TD

Visit **www.picador.com** to read more about all our books
and to buy them. You will also find features, author interviews and
news of any author events, and you can sign up for e-newsletters
so that you're always first to hear about our new releases.

Contents

Introduction

The three books collected in this volume were written over a period of more than forty years. The stories in *Out of the War* date from Francis Wyndham's late teens, when he was waiting to be called up, and when he was convalescing after being invalided out of the army with TB. Astonishingly he was unable to get them into print, and they were put away, along with the principal ambition that they represented, of being a writer. He went into publishing instead; then into journalism: he became a reviewer of unusual subtlety and scope, and also a master of the interview, often of a non-literary figure – a form to which he brought something of the melancholy hilarity and quirky verisimilitude of his fiction*. Then in 1972 Wyndham rediscovered the manuscript of *Out of the War* and a couple of years later it was published. 'The stories seemed to have been written by someone else', he said at the time, ' – and, in a sense, I suppose they were.' In a sense, of course, they weren't; and part of the fascination of having them together with the two subsequent books that their success seems to have freed or precipitated – *Mrs Henderson and other stories*, published in 1985, and *The Other Garden* (1987) – lies in tracing the enduring preoccupations in a small but exceptionally accomplished body of work.

* Some of these pieces were later collected in *The Theatre of Embarrassment* (Chatto & Windus, 1991).

Each book has its own tonality: *Out of the War* is marked by a sense of bitterness and futility, with an intense, discontinuous, almost absurdist vision, reminiscent at times of the contemporary work of Denton Welch; *Mrs Henderson* is more spacious, ironic and funny; *The Other Garden* more luminous and elegiac. Only *The Other Garden* is a novel, but one cannot help being struck by the inner coherence of the books of stories. *Out of the War* is unified by time and place – the war years in a market town in the south of England – and linked by the parallel predicaments of characters who recur, a minor figure in one piece often becoming the protagonist of the next. It is like a novel that has been decentred and fragmented: a kind of formal slippage has taken place. In *Mrs Henderson* the viewpoint is more stable: the stories follow the curve of a single narrator's life from prep school to late middle age; after three short fast movements comes the expansive andante of the story 'Ursula', which takes up half the book and brings us away from the period of the war towards the present, where it is capped with a prestidigitatory finale, 'The Ground Hostess'. The comparative sobriety of 'Ursula', a moving record of love, loyalty and idealism, prepares us for the return in *The Other Garden* to the war years and the poignant and unconventional friendship which lies at the novel's heart.

The paradox of the war, which plays its part in all three books, is that the action is all taking place elsewhere: the people in these stories are left behind in villages, country towns, a convalescent home, a half-deserted Oxford, as if in a state of suspended animation, the prey to boredom, deprivation and a mood of unfocused expectancy. And the paradox obliquely dramatizes their very inactivity. In *Out of the War* they are almost all young women, living with repressive mothers in an atmosphere of misunderstanding and ennui. Their only escape is through the fantasy of songs, films and magazines; they are full of longings, but any attempt to translate them into reality is likely to generate anxiety, panic and even revulsion. There is a magnetic oscillation between longing and dread, a sense of expectation being sweeter than fulfilment, of activity being a disagreeable transition between the pleasures of looking forward and of looking back: 'The fun has stopped and the more enjoyable period of looking back on, thinking about and discussing that fun is beginning.' The teenage Wyndham was already a connoisseur of these emotional contrarieties, developing, as the narrator of *The Other Garden* puts it, 'a taste for boredom and inaction, which like a drug habit formed in youth, I was never to succeed in conquering'. 'What I've always wanted to do in fiction', Wyndham has said, 'is to write about the hours and hours and hours, the enormous proportion of life which is spent in a kind of limbo, even in people's active years. It seems to me that it isn't sufficiently celebrated.' That it should be a matter for celebration may come as a surprise, yet the reader of these fictions will find how consumingly interesting that limbo can be in Wyndham's witty and disconcerting account.

The narrator of *Mrs Henderson* is an elusive figure, whose principal irony is the deprecation of himself and the knowing, tactical absorption of our curiosity about his affairs into his own fascination with those of others. The first-person narration is favoured not for confession, but for its life-like acknowledgement of how little it is possible to know about others, their thoughts and motivations. The protagonists of these stories are distinguished from the passive narrator by their glamorous irrationality, the baffling firmness of their views, the certainty with which they act in response to the call of their destinies. Often they are escapees, moving from the domestic world of the story into a wider realm of danger and determination; their inscrutable fates take on the lineaments of family myth.

They are not figures who communicate: they are too

caught up in their own obsessions – the schoolboy in 'Mrs Henderson' who believes his mother to have a penis; Lady Fuller, in the story called 'Obsessions', who holds out hysterically for the right to drink her after-dinner coffee at the table and not in the hotel lounge; the blindly oppressive egotism and altruism of the narrator's two friends in 'The Ground Hostess', perhaps Wyndham's funniest as well as his most painful story. Their egos and manias run riot in torrents or spasms of language that are caught with uncanny truthfulness by Wyndham's attentive ear, and which, with typical ambivalence, seem comic, pathetic and disturbing by turns, or all at the same time. Their habits are echoed, it is true, by a mild faddishness of the narrator's own; but where he fills the apparent vacancy of his days with passions for popular music and detective novels, they are prone to more pointless and demanding crazes, snobberies and superstitions. Wyndham places his period detail with graphic exactness – clothes, cars, songs, forgotten light novelists. They are offered as the random and amusing tokens of what fills up the limbo of a life, but by a masterly sleight of hand are also shown to be the dwelling-places of obsession.

In *The Other Garden* the narrator's temperament finds its match in the morbid passivity and moral paralysis of his friend Kay, with her hapless and obscure affairs, her problems in getting, much less holding down, a job, her sense of being an outcast and at the same time a prisoner in the conservative, titled world of the village where they live. The two of them are joined by a sympathetic feeling for the absurd and the original and a slightly luxurious sense of hopelessness. She is twice his age, but no less defenceless and childlike than he is. They share various enthusiasms – for the stirring defeatism of torch songs, for instance – and Kay has drolly vigorous views on films and film stars. But the novel ingeniously shows up Kay's cruel parents as pathological types of a fiercer kind, her father a violent bully, pushed into asocial touchiness by his deafness, her mother, Sybil Demarest, with her fatuous serenity and domineering monologues, surely one of the most brilliantly rendered bores in literature. Like the society of *Emma* this is one a good deal more amusing to read about than it would be to live among. Kay and the narrator both in the end make their escape from it, but where Kay's escape is triggered by desperation and overshadowed by an air of doom, that of the narrator is more subtle and equivocal.

Subtle is a word one is forced on time and again in describing Wyndham's work, and it is indeed one of his own most characteristic adjectives. He belongs in a tradition of social comedy going back through Henry James to Jane Austen; but he brings to it a peculiarly paradoxical sensibility, at once commanding and self-effacing, vigorous and passive, high-spirited and intriguingly withdrawn. It is no surprise that it should be one so keenly attuned to the paradoxes of pleasure and pain, the perverse satisfactions of frustration, the mercurial mood-swings which reveal experience as at one moment wretched and at the next irresistibly funny. 'At last the conversation degenerated once more into a grumble, and the shortage of food, petrol, and, above all, servants, was examined in all its aspects with a hopelessly indignant, impotent and yet vaguely comforting thoroughness.' That is a sentence written in youth, but the innate elegance, the concision, and the comic but startling emotional accuracy of the closing phrase are typical of Wyndham's writing.

If much of the pleasure it gives comes from this precision, the certainty one has of being in the hands of a writer who never wastes a word or puts one wrong, then much of its power and ability to haunt the memory lies in a larger subtlety of structure and treatment. Wyndham's ironies are always oblique, his stories are never moralities. 'C'est ce que j'ai d'inhabile, d'incertain, qui est bien moi-même', runs the epigraph to 'Obsessions': 'It is in my awkwardness, my uncertainty, that I am most myself'. Wyndham's stories, for all their wit and shapeliness, are really concerned with the acknowledgement of something more inward and unsure, with states of mind, hidden harmonies and discords that lie not in things themselves but in the mysterious relationship between them. 'The Half Brother' ends with a financial calculation, a mathematical puzzle which wryly ties up the anecdotal content of the story whilst leaving us with the sense of some far deeper puzzle about life, whose terms have been subtly established, but to which no answer is possible. 'Obsessions' is made up of discrete and inconsequential events, of absurd little episodes in lives which coincide but never communicate; but its truthfulness and force lie in a recognition which the story itself will not directly express: that these moments of maladroitness and inconsequence, the fervour of the characters' obsessions with valueless things, are the vital symptoms of our psychopathology.

Readers will find that Francis Wyndham's fiction has modesty and tact; but it resonates and is a world.

Alan Hollinghurst

MRS HENDERSON
& OTHER STORIES

FOR JAMES LYTTLETON FOX

Acknowledgements

The title story in this collection appeared in the *London Magazine*, 'Obsessions' in the *New Review*, 'The Half Brother' and 'The Ground Hostess' in the *London Review of Books*. My thanks are due to their respective Editors: Alan Ross, Ian Hamilton and Karl Miller. I am especially grateful to Karl Miller for his encouragement during the writing of this book, and to Susannah Clapp, Assistant Editor of the *London Review of Books*, for her help and advice.

Mrs Henderson

Henderson's people lived in London. For that reason he was pitied, even despised, by most of the other boys, but to me it made him an object of envy. A snobbish assumption prevailed in this seedily conventional prep school that anything urban was somehow common; to 'live in the country' was the desired norm, while the grandest thing of all was to come from Scotland. (The school itself was situated on the outskirts of Oxford.) Henderson and I knew better. I associated London only with rare, ecstatic treats and could hardly imagine such a glamorous place being somebody's home. For his part, Henderson revealed an intimate knowledge of the Underground Railway and certain bus routes with a slightly proprietary air, as if his connection with them might be more privileged than that of a mere passenger. His father worked in the Civil Service, and Henderson had inside information about such matters as the latest designs for postage stamps and banknotes, in which he took a sober and responsible interest. I cultivated his company because I loved to hear him talk about the various monuments in Kensington Gardens and the new cinemas in Leicester Square; gratified and mildly surprised to find himself commanding any kind of audience, he tolerated mine. At the time of our friendship, we were both ten. Henderson was big for his age, with a very white skin and hair the colour of Quink.

Everybody at school was hungry all the time. On summer

nights, boys would creep in pairs from their dormitories down to the changing-room (where one window, due to some self-perpetuating oversight, could easily be opened) and out into the cool kitchen garden to eat peas fresh from the pods. The clandestine atmosphere of these escapades – the dark, the dew-damp grass under naked feet, the guilty taste of food on a green-stained tongue – heightened the metropolitan magic which in my view surrounded Henderson, who was often my partner on them. Once, however, we nearly had a quarrel. Something which he said had betrayed the fact that Henderson, in common with many of his contemporaries at that time (the mid-1930s), believed that babies were born out of their mothers' navels. I had already been given a rather sketchy version of 'the facts of life' and tried to convince him of his error, but with no success.

'Well, how *are* they born, then?' asked Henderson.

As I stumbled through an explanation, while we both stood shivering in the garden, his expression registered first bewilderment, then obstinacy, then scorn.

'You must be quite mad,' he said. 'I shouldn't tell anybody else what you've just told me if I were you or they might lock you away in a straitjacket and a padded cell and a jolly good job if they did too if you ask me.'

'I'm sure it's true,' I insisted, but with waning conviction.

'And I know that it isn't, so snubs. That's what navels are *for*, you *idiot*. Anyway, men and women aren't made in a different way like that.'

'But you can *see* they are! Women have *paps*, don't they?'

'Oh, oh, thank you very much indeed, now we know, don't we?' said Henderson, jumping up and down in the moonlight and wagging his head wildly, as if drunk on his own sarcasm. 'Of *course* women have paps, but what's *that* got to do with anything, you *idiot*? They've got *cocks* too, just like we have.'

'Well, they *haven't*, that's all, I'm very sorry, and if you think they have that just shows how much *you* know about it.'

'I know they have,' said Henderson more seriously. 'I'm absolutely positive.' He turned away, and seemed ready to end the conversation.

'You don't know,' I taunted him, 'so don't tell lies.'

'I do know.'

'How?'

'Well, my mother's got one.'

'I bet she hasn't. Bet you anything.'

'Yes she has. I've seen it.'

'I don't believe you,' I said, beginning to feel uncomfortable.

'I slept in her room once when Daddy – when my father was away, to keep her company. She came in from the bathroom with nothing on and walked over to the dressing-table. I think she thought I was asleep but I wasn't. I was looking at her.'

That silenced me. Was Mrs Henderson some kind of freak, then? Or could it be that her son was so reluctant to lose an argument that he had invented this extraordinary story about her? Or was it perhaps I who had been misinformed about the basic distinction between the sexes? In those days, at that age, it seemed that nothing to do with the subject was allowed to remain clear for long.

This was in fact one of the very few occasions on which Henderson and I talked about sex, but our association was none the less disapproved of by Mr Philpots, the dormitory master, who presumably suspected that we discussed it all the time. He thought we had a bad influence on each other, giggled too much, were in some unspecified way 'silly', and if he caught us together he would try to break us up, indignantly muttering something about a 'mothers' meeting'. He was an unattractive old man and his nickname, Old Pisspots, suited him only too well. His baggy tweed plus-fours stank of stale tobacco, sweat and excrement; even his white hair and moustache had yellow stains as if splashed by his own urine. While one of his shaking hands was visibly engaged in a game of 'pocket billiards', the other would jerk out unexpectedly to tweak the nape of a pupil's neck. Too decrepit to teach, he spent most of his time in his own small room on the dormitory floor, into which he would sometimes invite one of the younger boys for a chat. He had his favourites, and Henderson was prime among these. Often, just before lights out, Henderson would be summoned in his pyjamas to the master's stuffy little cell, then after about ten minutes return in the dark and slip smoothly back into bed. Later, when most of the boys were asleep, Mr Philpots would come shambling along the passage in slippers and a greasy flannel dressing-gown to visit each dormitory in turn. He would make for the bed where his current favourite lay, and for minutes on end would address the sleeping figure in a scarcely audible monotone, mumbling terms of endearment and vague reproaches before gliding on like a grey somnambulist through the silent school.

If Henderson was Old Pisspot's pet, I was his *bête noire*. He was able to make life hard for me in many ways, but there was nothing he could do to prevent me from being 'taken out' by Henderson's parents one Sunday tea-time when they visited the school. Henderson himself had made it clear, while suggesting this excursion, that it had been their idea rather than his that he should invite a friend; they were apparently beginning to worry that he might not have any at all, and his desire to reassure them on this point must have outweighed his considerable embarrassment at the prospect of our social confrontation.

We were both ready, in stiff grey shorts and smelling of Honey and Flowers, when the Ford V8 drove up to the front door. Mr Henderson was at the wheel: with rabbit teeth beneath a toothbrush moustache, he resembled a *Punch* cartoon of a henpecked husband. Henderson briskly entered the front seat beside him, while I clambered into the back, where Mrs Henderson was sitting with an expensive-looking rug over her lap. She absently adjusted it to cover my knees as well, and the Ford moved off. I prayed that I wouldn't be car-sick or want to go to the lavatory.

Mrs Henderson came as a shock: she was a beauty. With the same complexion and blue-black hair as her son, she had a large drooping mouth and long violet eyes. Everything about her seemed to flop: her wide-brimmed hat, her scarf, her blouse, her long skirt and her long wrists. She appeared to be lost in a satisfied sulk and during the drive, as far as I can remember, nothing was said.

On a prickly common near a golf course, a sedate-looking establishment called The Three Monkeys sold garden teas. Mrs Henderson spread her car rug on the lawn and, after putting on a huge pair of purple-tinted sunglasses with white frames, lay down as if to sleep. Henderson and his father went off to play clock golf on the other side of the building, leaving me alone with Henderson's mother. It must often have happened, on similar outings, that a well-meaning adult has desperately tried to break through the reserve of a buttoned-up child. In our case, the roles were reversed. Mrs Henderson seemed either paralysed by shyness or overcome by apathy, while I for some reason could not stop talking. The only form of converse which I understood was that of question and answer: it was the first time I had consciously attempted to put another person at ease.

'What a nice scent you've got on,' I said.

'Thanks.'

'What's it called?'

'*Arpège*.'

'What's your favourite tune?'

For some seconds she gave this an almost solemn consideration. 'I think at the moment my *very* most favourite is a thing called "Would You?"'

'Who's your favourite film star?'

Again, she seemed to gather together all her powers of concentration to achieve a completely truthful answer. 'Either Robert Montgomery or Richard Arlen, I can't for certain say which.'

'That's a nice blouse you're wearing.'

'Thanks.'

'What's it made of?'

'*Crêpe de chine*.'

What I liked about Mrs Henderson was that, although she seemed so terribly bored, she didn't seem especially bored by me. She just didn't bother to take any extra trouble about me – an attitude which can be subtly flattering to an impatient child.

The tea-party was soon over: we had to be back at school by half past five. It seemed to me to have been a comparative success, but for some weeks afterwards Henderson avoided me. He probably guessed that his mother was much in my thoughts, and found the idea disturbing. Then, one morning, he came and stood beside me in the lavatory. 'I've had enough of this place,' he said after a while. 'I'm running away.'

'When?'

'Tonight. It's quite easy. I've worked it all out. Why don't you come too?'

At that moment the urinal flushed of its own accord, making a hysterical hissing sound as if the mechanism were not completely under control. 'How will you get out?' I asked.

'The same way that we go to pick peas. Once we're gone there's nothing they can do to us. You can come home with me and ring up your people from there.'

'But how will you get to London?'

'Simple. If I don't get a lift all the way in a car there's an early train from Oxford station. Our flat isn't far from Paddington. I'll be home in time for breakfast. Eggs and bacon and Golden Shred.'

I let him give me detailed instructions about how and when and where we should meet.

That evening, after returning from his visit to Mr Philpot's room, Henderson did not get into bed but quietly put on his day clothes instead. Then he left the dormitory without a glance in my direction. I covered my head with the sheet and stared at the luminous dial of my Mickey Mouse wrist-watch. After five minutes I followed Henderson downstairs to the changing-room. He was waiting patiently by the window. When he saw me, he frowned. 'But you're not dressed,' he said.

'I'm not coming with you.'

'You're too frightened,' he stated. I did not deny the accusation, although I felt incoherently that the truth was somehow more complicated than this.

'Oh, well, never mind, I'm going just the same.' His features had settled in a stubborn look which I remembered from earlier arguments, and I did not attempt to make him change his mind.

Henderson raised the lower sash and eased his body through the aperture. I stood at the window and watched him make his escape, scampering across the moonlit playing fields, over a low stone wall and on to the open road. When he had disappeared from view I went cautiously back to bed. Mixed emotions – remorse, relief, intense excitement –

prevented me from sleeping and I was still awake hours later when Old Pisspots came shuffling down the passage. He stood for a while at the entrance to the room, his head trembling as he greedily swallowed his excess spittle, before moving as usual towards Henderson's empty bed. In the dim light its rumpled condition made it appear occupied to the besotted schoolmaster's rheumy eyes. He began to whisper. This time I could make out most of the words.

'Darling boy, darling imp, darling scamp, *what* a bad lad! Oh, you little rogue, what do you mean by sleeping like that, my darling, as if butter wouldn't melt in your mouth, you naughty, naughty boy? Oh, I'll wager somebody had a sore bottom, somebody had a tender behind, didn't he, darling? Couldn't sit down for a week, eh? Not after having your little sit-upon spanked for you, what? Never mind, little boy, there's nothing the matter with a good old-fashioned . . . and you did ask for it, you know, didn't you, darling? Such a cheeky little arab. What a sauce, eh? Well, if you still have an aching bum in the morning, don't come running to me, darling, wanting to kiss and make up, what? Oh, my darling . . .'

The dormitory windows whitened and he muttered on. I heard the desolate whistle and purposeful rumble of the milk train as it crossed a distant viaduct. Could Henderson conceivably be on it? It suddenly struck me that he had no money to buy a ticket. More likely, he had hitched a ride on some lorry and was now journeying along the Great West Road, past deserted factories and pallid petrol stations, towards his native London with its cavernous cinemas and subterranean nightclubs. Was he in panic-stricken flight or on an adventurous voyage of discovery? I only knew that Henderson was going back home to his mother, that aloof hermaphrodite and elegant sphinx, who carried beneath scented *crêpe de chine* pyjamas the threat of her phallic secret.

Obsessions

C'est ce que j'ai d'inhabile, d'incertain,
qui est bien moi-même.

Paul Valéry,
Extraits du Log-Book de Monsieur Teste

I still dream about the Manor, although I have not seen it for over thirty years and could not have entered it more than a dozen times in the days when I lived near by. In fact I have almost forgotten what it looked like, but can just recall the disturbing impression made on me by some hidden harmony in the relationship of its passages, staircases and rooms; and this subliminal memory sometimes surfaces through my sleep to form an incongruous though unsurprising background to people and problems that belong to later stages in my life.

More haunting than haunted, it was a placidly beautiful house, built in the reign of Charles II and set in a small park; on one side the grounds sloped to a valley where a trout stream ran through soggy watermeadows and on the other a softly wooded hill rose to the gusty downs. People who cared about furniture made pilgrimages in the hope of seeing inside it, but these were obdurately discouraged by the owner, Sir Jocelyn Bignall, who attached no aesthetic value to his inherited possessions although he would never have allowed the slightest displacement in their arrangement: the interior of the Manor had therefore remained more or less unaltered since the seventeenth century, preserved by the lazy philistinism and disinclination for change which characterised Sir Jocelyn and his ancestors. Over seventy when I knew him, he was like a clumsy caricature of the old-fashioned country squire, with pendulous purple cheeks matching the loud purple checks on his expensively tailored knickerbocker suits. He had the reputation in the village of being a very bad landlord, and had until lately been Master of the local Fox Hounds.

Sir Jocelyn was seldom seen at home because he got on his wife's nerves; she invariably addressed him in a hectoring, querulous tone and would sometimes openly dismiss him from the room if he happened to be found there when friends came to see her. A small, pretty old lady with bad-tempered features almost obliterated by powder, Lady Bignall modelled her appearance on the 'Marquise' look exemplified by Dame Marie Tempest and always wore a wig which, like a barrister's, was clearly not intended to deceive. An ancient Edwardian scandal, not yet quite forgotten in some pockets of the neighbourhood, surrounded the origins of their association with improbable romance. Lady Bignall (whose first name, by fateful coincidence, was also Jocelyn) had abandoned a former husband and 'bolted' with Sir Jocelyn to Boulogne. There had either been an unpleasantly protracted divorce, or else no divorce at all until the first husband died; in any event, the lovers had been forced to live openly together for some years at the Manor before becoming man and wife. It was rumoured that, had it not been for this equivocal episode in his past, Sir Jocelyn would have long ago been Lord-Lieutenant of the county.

The Bignalls were childless, but Lady Bignall had a daughter by her first marriage who often stayed at the Manor. Madge had married a soldier much older than herself; General Sir Archie Fuller was indeed nearly the same age as Sir Jocelyn. The Fullers had one son, named after his grandmother and therefore confusingly called Jocelyn too. Lady Bignall doted on him, but when he came to the Manor he spent most of his time fishing or shooting with old Sir Jocelyn while she sat impatiently indoors with her daughter.

Madge Fuller had a tall, slim body ideally suited to the clothes in fashion during the early 1930s, which she continued to wear long after they had gone out of date. Fur-trimmed collars seemed to raise her shoulders while her trunk was apparently lowered by skirts reaching below the calf, so that she gave an effect of elegant but painful attenuation, as if she had been stretched on a rack. On each occasion that I saw her she was wearing the same hat – or, at least, an identical copy of the original: a simple beret, part of which had been folded over on itself and fastened to the side of her head by a jewelled regimental brooch. Her manner was one of eager, almost avid welcome combined with exaggerated deprecation. Something aggrieved inside her drove her to disparage and apologise for every aspect of her own personality: she refused to allow that anything belonging to herself could be deserving of praise. This category included both her husband and, to a lesser extent, her son.

It may have been because he was now hers that she hated Sir Archie so fiercely; or perhaps she had disliked him on sight and her marriage (no doubt 'arranged' by the worldly and slightly *déclassée* Lady Bignall) had left her with a sense of disappointment which had developed into generalised resentment and eventually narrowed to a violent self-distrust. She treated him with even greater contempt than her mother showed for Sir Jocelyn, and persistently complained about his crass stupidity – even to people, like myself, who had never been given the chance to meet him.

This behaviour was, I believe, much criticised by her acquaintances, but Lady Fuller's loathing for Sir Archie was too strong to be denied expression by conventional opinion.

I went to the same public school as Jocelyn Fuller, but since he was four years older than I was we seldom came into contact and I only knew him there from a distance as an imposingly mature figure who excelled at games. One day I saw him trotting down a path towards me: I stood aside to let him pass, but he stopped and spoke. 'My mother's descending on the school next Sunday, and she'd love to see you. We're having tea at the Cockpit. Can you join us?'

In great confusion, I heard myself accepting the invitation, and as he turned away I immediately began to dread this engagement which I knew would be beyond my power to fulfil. As it happened, I had already obtained permission to go to London that Sunday for the afternoon, on the pretext of visiting a relation; but the real reason for my panic was more irrational. I was suffering from that mysterious self-consciousness which often attacks the adolescent, a malady as agonising and overwhelming as seasickness or stage fright.

My dilemma was acute: I could no more show up at the Cockpit than I could see a way of getting out of the obligation. Moral paralysis drove me to the extreme course of seeking my housemaster's advice. He was probably amused when my problem turned out to be social rather than sexual or spiritual, but he gave it serious attention. 'It's nothing to worry about. If you feel too shy to tell Fuller that you made a mistake, why don't you drop him a note? Just explain that you've already arranged to spend Sunday with your people.'

'But what shall I *call* him in the note?'

'What do you call him in the holidays?'

'Jocelyn, I suppose, if anything – but I really hardly know him at all.'

'I think it would be all right to call him Jocelyn in your letter.'

In the end I disregarded this suggestion and began the note with the formal address 'Dear Fuller'. After I had furtively left it at Jocelyn's house, choosing a time when I knew he would be on the playing fields, I felt delirious with relief. On Sunday I took a train to Paddington and went by myself to see Alice Faye in *Alexander's Ragtime Band*. A tune from the film took root in my brain where it lingered sweetly as a constant accompaniment and frequent alternative to thought. *Now it can be told . . .Told in all its glory . . . Now that we have met the world may know the . . . Sentimental story . . .*

Not long after this, when during the holidays I was asked to lunch at the Manor to meet Lady Fuller and Jocelyn, I felt no qualms about accepting: my hysteria had belonged to the unnatural and inhibiting atmosphere of boarding-school life. I walked the half mile from the village to the stone gates surmounted by subtly grotesque lions' heads, their prophetic grandeur if anything increased by their weather-beaten and dilapidated condition, up the long drive past unmown grass to the crystalline façade, unnerving in its symmetry. Lady Fuller came anxiously to meet me at the front door and led me to the Chinoiserie room where her mother was perkily waiting. Sir Jocelyn was away some-where, fulfilling his duties as a magistrate.

'It's such a treat for *my* Jocelyn', said Lady Fuller, 'to meet somebody of his own age for a change. You will be kind to him, won't you? He's not very intellectual, you know, and I'm afraid you may be too fearfully bored. But we'll try and make it up to you by giving you an edible meal!'

Jocelyn joined us, wearing white flannels; his friendly, candid face looked rather sweaty. 'Very sporty-boy!' said Lady Bignall with approval. 'Come on, let's all have a little drinksky-korsakoff.' Jocelyn poured us each a glass of sherry before we moved into the dining-room.

During lunch, Lady Fuller started a discussion on the dullness of country life. 'One's neighbours are apt to be so frightfully stuffy, unless one's unusually lucky. Sometimes I do rather hanker after London. A little house in Chelsea would be my dream – but then you see I adore being near water.'

'Mummy's a highbrow at heart,' said Jocelyn flirtatiously.

'I've no idea what Chelsea's like now,' said Lady Bignall, 'but in my day it used to be full of bounderinos.'

'One feels in such a backwater, stuck out in the wilds,' Lady Fuller continued. 'How one longs to know what's going on in the rest of the world! Oh, one reads the papers and listens to the six o'clock news, but it isn't quite the same. I do find things so terribly difficult to understand at the moment, don't you? The world situation is getting so complicated and I'm dying for somebody to *explain* it to me. Needless to say, when it comes to that sort of thing, Archie's no more good than a sick headache!'

'It would be fun to dash across to Monte or Juan for a spell and get a change of ideas,' said Lady Bignall. 'But *he* won't budge, so what's the use? And they tell me I wouldn't recognise the Riviera now – full of cads and Americans, I suppose, just like everywhere else.'

At the end of the meal, while her mother was pouring out coffee, Madge Fuller turned to me with an urgent expression on her face. 'I *do* hope you haven't succumbed to this ghastly custom I find now all over the place of going *back* into the drawing-room after luncheon and drinking your coffee there! I really cannot stand it: it seems to me to be such a mad idea! It quite takes away the whole point of having coffee at all if one has to move all the way from one room to another before one can get at it. I can't understand why everybody doesn't see what I mean about this — but apparently they don't. The most surprising people seem to be catching the habit. It's just the sort of thing that drives me absolutely *crackers*? she finished wildly, then paused, panting slightly, before adding on a brisker note: 'Now, why don't you two boys go off together somewhere for a good talk? Jocelyn is starved for conversation with people of his own generation, aren't you, darling? But you mustn't bore our guest, whatever you do: I sometimes think that being a bore is *the* unforgivable sin, do you know what I mean? Anything but that!'

I followed Jocelyn upstairs and into his bedroom. He wandered about for a bit with an abstracted air, as if he were alone, and then stood for a time at a window, looking out at the park. Embarrassed, I lowered myself into a chair. 'That's right,' he said, 'sit down, sit down, for goodness' sake.' He turned and gazed at me with blank gravity and then unexpectedly flung himself on the bed and stared with the same absent concentration at the ceiling. I could think of nothing to say: the silence was not unpleasant, but I perversely longed to break it.

Suddenly Jocelyn rolled round on the bed and lifted himself into a squatting position, supported by his knees and elbows with his face against the pillow and his bottom companionably in the air. 'Would you say that Flora Robson was a great actress?' he asked. 'She is very good,' I replied. He went on, his voice rather muffled: 'I saw her in that thing where she was meant to be Queen Elizabeth. Extraordinary woman, Queen Elizabeth, quite remarkable, a great queen, wouldn't you say? So was Queen Victoria in her way, I suppose, but I've always thought they must have been rather a stuffy pair, Prince Albert and her, do you know what I mean? She was a great queen but she must have been awfully stuffy and Victorian.'

'Do you think Flora Robson would be good as Queen Victoria?' I said at random. He raised his head from the pillow and turned it round to peer in my direction. 'I *wonder*,' he mused. 'I *wonder*. That's quite a thought. Quite a thought.' Then he leaped off the bed and ran his fingers through his hair, mildly massaging his scalp. 'Let's go down and see if Gan-Gan can rustle us up some tea. We *have* had a lovely talk. It's very nice staying here and all that but I do miss the company of people my own age. Elderly folk can be awfully stuffy, can't they? You must come over again soon.'

Later that year the war started, and I heard that Jocelyn had gone straight from school into the army. Lady Bignall boasted of his rapid promotion and military success: he was in something very dangerous and dashing, but so 'hush-hush' that it could only be described in the vaguest terms. She would sit in the Chinoiserie room beside the wireless and listen to the news. This was often bad, but Lady Bignall refused to be depressed. 'It all depends on the value you put on human life,' she said. 'I've been reading a lot of eastern philosophy lately and I've learnt that it's a great mistake to put too much value on human life. Anyway, you don't want to believe everything you hear on the wireless . . . Madge writes that she thanks heaven Archie's too old for a command: with him a Brass Hat we'd be *certain* to lose the war!'

As it turned out, I was one of the last people to see Sir Jocelyn alive. I spent a long, tedious afternoon acting as an amateurish beater on a shoot consisting of only two guns – Sir Jocelyn and his friend and contemporary, Admiral Bovill. (The Admiral and Lady Bignall did not get on: he thought her 'flighty' and she considered him 'much too churchy'.) We trudged over the countryside while the old men slap-happily blazed away, missing every bird, and I diverted myself by singing 'Now It Can Be Told', still my favourite song, in a tuneless undertone. We reached a river where, on the opposite bank, the dead body of an otter was pathetically exposed. The Admiral crept stealthily up to the water's edge and, after taking careful aim, fired in its direction. When we returned at dusk to the Manor, the otter's putrefying corpse (which I had to carry) was the only trophy of our chase. 'Glad you got that otter, Admiral,' said Sir Jocelyn. 'Adds a bit of variety to the bag!' That night, he died in his sleep. I laboured for days over my letter of condolence to his widow, which in the end proved too difficult to write and was never posted.

I left school as soon as I decently could and filled in time before the inevitable call-up by going to Oxford. The minimum academic qualification was needed for this: the university was only half full. My rooms there were large and gloomy, furnished darkly in carved oak with monumental dressers, creaking wardrobes and sinister sideboards. I was too depressed by the present, too fearful of the future, to do any work at all. At night a mouse would emerge from the shadows and play by my feet in the chilly grate. One evening, without my knowledge, a college servant set a trap for it; in the morning the cheese was gone with the trap still unsprung, and that night the mouse confidently returned. My days were spent in the cinema or changing library books at Elliston & Cavell's, where a branch of the Times Book Club, to which I subscribed, was then accommodated. I had developed a mania for the work of Mignon G. Eberhart, an American author of detective stories, and could read nothing else. Her books, like the films of Alice Faye, were so similar to each other that they might have seemed almost indistinguishable to an untrained eye, but subtle differences between them added piquancy to the expert's taste. Some of her earlier novels were difficult to find, and I would advertise for these in the trade papers. Just as the dreaded moment arrived when I had read them all, a new one was published by the Crime Club. I bought it at W. H. Smith's and, deciding that my future presence in Oxford was unnecessary, went back home about halfway through my first term.

There I found a letter awaiting me. It was from Madge Fuller, who explained that she had sent it to this address in the hope that it might be forwarded, as she was uncertain about which college I attended. She would be passing through Oxford in a few days' time, staying at the Mitre: would I care to dine with her there on Sunday evening? She ended in her old aggressively humble vein by writing that if I was much too busy swotting for Little Go, or just too bored by the prospect of spending an evening in her company, she would of course quite understand and I mustn't dream of coming. 'For goodness' sake don't bother to answer – a telephone message with the hall porter will do. I'll expect you if I see you!'

Once again, her well-intended offer of hospitality had placed me in a dilemma. The local myth of my status as an industrious student must at all costs be maintained before Lady Bignall, a fertile source of much disapproving gossip. At home I felt in hiding, on the run from some self-imposed standard of normal behaviour; my refuge was dangerously near to Lady Bignall, but this of course had been an unavoidable risk. Now Lady Fuller, impelled by her chronically tactless generosity, had innocently stumbled on my secret and flushed me out of my retreat. So I embarked on another of those desolate wartime Sunday travels: the bus from the village to the market town; the slow, crowded train to Didcot; the long, hungry wait at the junction; the brutally prolonged discomfort of the last lap. 'Well may they ask,' I thought, 'if this journey is really necessary.'

I walked downhill from Oxford station as light-headed and disorientated as a dreamer or a drunk.

Lady Fuller was waiting for me just inside the entrance to the Mitre. She immediately began apologising for her presumption in taking me away from my studies. 'You must be fearfully busy: I know how hard they make one work here. Now whatever happens, you mustn't let me *bore* you – when one's always surrounded by stupid people, one becomes such an idiot oneself! The least I can do in return is to offer you a decent meal, but I expect it will be *uneatable*, don't you?' She hurried me into the dining-room, where she sat for some time gazing at the menu with the air of someone meeting a challenge, as if it were at the same time intensely interesting and almost impossible to comprehend. She seemed to be in a state of nervous exaltation, and I thought that this could possibly be accounted for by the mere fact of her presence in Oxford, which she no doubt saw as the palpable embodiment of her cerebral ideal. Here she was, sitting in a seat of learning: I suddenly remembered that I was an undergraduate, and for the first time understood that this designation could carry symbolic overtones as potent as those of soldier, prostitute or priest.

After ordering the set dinner, she loosened her silver-fox, snapped open the clips of her crocodile handbag and cosily rummaged inside it for a gold cigarette case and lighter; then she began to pack the former with the contents of a bright red packet of Craven A. The regimental brooch sparkled in her bent-over beret: beneath it, her eyes fixed me with a kindly fanaticism. 'Now, you've got to tell me what the *young* are thinking about things, what they're reading, what they admire. You've no idea how I envy you being in touch with ideas. It must be so wonderfully exciting – I don't know when I last met anybody who had an idea in his *head*! How I wish I were brainy, like you (yes, you are, you know you are, you must be), because I do think, more and more, that in the end it's only brains that count. So do tell me, who are the really clever young men of your generation? I'm sure you must know them all.'

I tried to change the subject by asking after Jocelyn, who was now said to be the youngest major in the British Army and had recently been decorated, but she refused to be sidetracked and insisted on an answer. What did I tell her? I can't remember. Whatever it was must have struck her as bitterly inadequate, but she was too polite to show her disappointment. Perhaps my feeble, evasive replies only confirmed her modest belief that the intellectual life would always remain impenetrable to the uninitiated, a teasing riddle with a simple solution which lay just beyond the confines of her understanding. Anyhow, she seemed fairly satisfied. When the meal was eaten she leant towards me and said, with a jocular air of conspiracy: '*Shall we risk the coffee?*'

'I'd love some.'

'You're sure you have time? You're not dying to get back to your work? It will probably be simply filthy but we can always hope for the best.'

It was some time before the waiter responded to her signals; and then he told her the last thing she wanted to hear. 'Coffee is served in the lounge, madam.'

She caught my eye with a grimace signifying an only partly humorous despair. 'Rubbish! Surely I'm entitled to drink my cup of after-dinner coffee where I choose to? I'm staying at your hotel, you know, and this young man is my guest.' The elderly waiter repeated that he had to obey the rule, which was apparently quite inflexible.

Madge Fuller bullied him for a bit and then changed her tactic to one of seductive charm. She seemed to be trying to lure him into partnership with her on some voluptuously dangerous design as she pleaded with him, just this once, to break the establishment's repressive and unnecessary law. When this method failed too, she started to lose her self-control: indignation gave way to a rather frightening distress. She demanded an interview with the manager, and after a long delay was told that the manager could not be found. Beside herself with irritation, she repeated her protest like a litany: 'I will *not* drink coffee in the lounge! It's *so* much nicer at the table! It *ruins* the meal to have to move!' Alarmed and exhausted, the waiter began at last to back gingerly away from her, and then vanished altogether through the service door. She sat there implacably, as though on an unofficial strike for some doomed but high-principled cause.

'You do think I'm right, don't you? I mean, it only encourages them if one gives in. In *no other country* would one be prevented from drinking one's coffee at the dining table. It's typical of England, I'm afraid: no wonder it looks as if we're going to lose this ridiculous war! I do most *abjectly* apologise – it's too awful, you haven't had any coffee! But even if we *did* go into the lounge (which God forbid – what a ghastly word anyhow, *lounge*!) we'd be stuck there for hours because the service in hotels nowadays is practically non-existent, and I couldn't bear the guilt of feeling that I was keeping you away from your books. You've probably got exams coming up soon: now promise me you won't sit up all night preparing for them. I'm sure you've been working much too hard. You do look a little peaky – you'll only get brain-fag if you overdo it, you know.'

It could not have been more than eight o'clock when I left the Mitre – disconcertingly early, for my day was done. The town seemed empty and echoing, like a concrete swimming pool drained of water. I walked haltingly back to my rooms, postponing my return because I knew no novel by Mignon G. Eberhart (not even one already familiar) awaited me there. All bookshops and libraries were closed: I felt the throbbing onset of the addict's withdrawal pains. How would I get through the night? I made myself a cup of Nescafé and went wide awake to bed.

It was some years later, when the war was won and life had changed for the better, that I began to dream about the Manor.

The Half Brother

Jack 'did a Jack' and missed our father's funeral. He had taken his new girl to the Gargoyle Club the night before and had woken with such a monumental hangover that the train had left Paddington before he was out of bed. Explaining this to my mother on the telephone later in the day, he had boasted not only about the hangover but also about the new girl, who was just seventeen and had a marvellous figure – almost like a boy's. The joke was that he had been given twenty-four hours' compassionate leave *because* of the funeral. 'Father would have been amused,' he said.

'Oh darling, I'm almost glad you weren't there,' said my mother. 'It was a nightmare: you couldn't have borne it. Lady Bignall kept on saying: "What are your plans?" Wasn't that typical?'

'Typical,' said Jack. 'How Father would have laughed.'

'I can't stand it when people ask me about my plans . . . Oh, Jack, isn't it *awful*, feeling awful?'

'Awful,' said her stepson. On this subject he was indeed an acknowledged expert, and there existed a list of proscribed places (Villefranche, Sao Tome, Bordighera, Colwyn Bay) where Jack had experienced – with an intensity that elevated them into family legend – the dusty depths of *le cafard*.

In order to take Jack's call, my mother had been forced to re-enter my father's study because that was where the telephone was. During the last weeks of his illness my

29

father's bed had been moved downstairs to this seldom-used room: it was here that my mother had nursed him and here that he had died. The appearance of the bed in the study had been disturbing from the start, as confusedly ominous as a phrase out of context; now, stripped and desolate, it just looked pointless. One of its sides was set against a low bookcase which ran the length of the wall. This contained, among other 'uniform editions', the complete works of Turgenev, in fourteen tall grey volumes, translated by Isabel F. Hapgood. (My father had been military attaché at St Petersburg before the revolution, and *A Sportsman's Sketches* was his favourite book.) The top of the bookcase formed a bedside shelf, on which bottles of chalky medicine and boxes of little green pills were still scattered among the few art objects surviving from Stars, the vast Victorian Gothic pile near Salisbury Plain where my father had been born. These included Chinese porcelain bowls of *pot-pourri*, enamel icons by Alexander Fisher and a life-sized effigy of Horus, the ancient Egyptian god of the sky in the shape of a falcon, whose right eye was the Sun and whose left eye was the Moon. Fashioned out of dark rough stone, this squat and sinister statuette concealed beneath its flat tail a tiny trapdoor which opened on to a dusty cavity housing the brittle yellow bones, supposedly undisturbed since the second century BC, of the original bird.

Talking to Jack had upset my mother. The telephone was navy blue, shaped like a daffodil with a flimsy bracket protruding sideways from its upright stem: she had difficulty in replacing the receiver on this when their conversation was over. She was crying. 'Darling Jack,' she said. 'His voice sounded so like Yvo's. He's coming down as soon as he can . . .' She looked distractedly round the room and her gaze was arrested by sight of the falcon. 'Do you know, I'm sure that bird brings bad luck. I've always thought it was creepy but Yvo did love it so . . . It was next to his bed when he died: now I *know* it's unlucky. Oh, please, do help me to get rid of it!'

'You mean, throw it away?'

'Or sell it, or something. I know that Yvo always laughed at me for being superstitious, but I am sure that Jack would understand.'

Jack and I were half-brothers, although he was old enough to be my father. Jack's mother had died of influenza in 1919 and four years later the widower had surprised and relieved his son by a second marriage, this time to somebody much younger than himself: indeed, my mother was an exact contemporary of Jack's. My father retired from the War Office to a small house in Berkshire where my mother started a chicken farm and I was born. Jack had recently inherited Stars, left to him by a cousin in a will which overlooked my father in order to avoid unnecessary death duties; when the will was made it had seemed unlikely that my father would remarry and even more so that the cousin would die so young. Jack offered to give Stars to my father, who refused it: in return, Jack undertook to pay for my education. As things turned out, this promise was not kept.

Jack soon sold Stars (which became first a secretarial college and then a lunatic asylum before mysteriously burning down) and most of its contents; for a brief period he was a very rich young man. He had had a sad time at boarding school while my father was soldiering abroad, and a grim time as a subaltern during the First World War; now he was doggedly determined to have a *good* time at last. His money was spent on racing cars, aeroplanes, a famous wine cellar, a collection of 'modern' pictures and a series of difficult, exquisite girls. He enjoyed among his contemporaries a comfortable reputation for privileged Bohemianism, scandalising some by his licentious behaviour and distressing others by his 'arty' inclinations, but avoiding the kind of unpopularity that might threaten his status as a proud member of White's Club. When my father died, the Second World War was ending and Jack, nearly fifty, was broke.

On the day after the funeral, my mother returned to the subject of the falcon. By now she had succeeded in infecting me with her sense of urgency in the matter, which just stopped short of panic. So this is what I did. I packed Horus in a cardboard egg-box (before petrol rationing she used to sell eggs to Quaglino's, nipping up to London and back in the Baby Austin while my father anxiously awaited her return) and caught the carrier to Hungerford station. After an hour the uptrain sidled in: Kintbury, Newbury, That-cham, Aldermaston, Theale, Reading West . . . from Reading it was non-stop to London. My arms aching, I queued for another hour before a taxi took me to a shop in St James's called Spink's. There I asked to see an expert on Egyptian art. He was quite young, with white lashes. I unpacked the antique. He offered me a hundred pounds for it, which I happily accepted. Free of my sacred burden, I wandered round the capital: saw an old film called *Naples au Baiser du Feu* at Studio One, then gravitated down Oxford Street to Bumpus where I stole a novel by I. Compton-Burnett (I think it must have been *Elders and Betters*) before catching the six o'clock home. The whole transaction was accomplished during a halting adolescent reverie, and I never gave a thought to Jack. There, I was to discover, I had made a mistake.

He turned up one morning about a fortnight later, having commandeered an army jeep at Devizes, where he had been attending a course exclusively for majors. Throughout the 1930s, Jack's arrivals at our village had been god-like: emerging, goggled, from a long low Bentley with hyperthyroid headlights; or descending on to the local football pitch at the bottom of Spring's Hill in a skeletal flying machine, only too aptly named a Moth and disconcertingly reminiscent of the expensive toys from Hamleys with which he embarrassed my birthdays. This latest visitation, though inevitably less glamorous, was in a subtle way just as dramatic. Jack's tall gaunt trunk and unevenly articulated limbs managed to banish from his battledress any suggestion of a uniform; his peaked cap concealed his bald crown and dignified the wild, woolly white hair round his neck and ears. He climbed out of the jeep, stretched, belched, pissed against a cedar in the drive and proposed a walk to his favourite pub in a hamlet ten miles away.

Jack was a pub snob. He wouldn't be seen dead in a saloon bar, and many were the authentic 'publics' I'd sat in with him, surrounded by fascist farm-hands and their goitred mothers-in-law, dodging the dangerous darts as they sped from dainty thumb and forefinger to the pitted corky board, trying to master the rules of cribbage ('One for his nob') and staggering, beer-bloated, to the Gents – a midge-haunted half-wall of cement in a benighted backyard.

'But you've only just got here!' said my mother. 'There's plenty of drink in the house . . . I've talked to the Manor and you can fish there whenever you want.'

'Wonderful!' said Jack. 'I'll walk up as soon as we've had our lunch. All right, then, let's forget about the pub. I can stay till tomorrow morning: any exciting plans for tonight?'

'There's a film on in Hungerford with Hedy Lamarr,' I suggested.

'Or we might have some bridge, if I can get hold of the Admiral,' said my mother.

'Bridge!' Jack decided. 'Hedy Lamarr must be as old as Methuselah by now.'

He entered the house, accompanied as ever (or so I felt) by an invisible spirit of pure hedonism which quickened the atmosphere with its promise of an extended treat while setting an unnervingly high standard for any prospective participant. There seemed to exist a law (as far as one knew, unwritten) forbidding the world to subject Jack to one moment of boredom; to be in his company was to share in the privilege thus afforded, while running the risk of breaking the law oneself. He poured himself a large whisky and soda and, after some galvanic contortions, settled himself beside it on a sofa; my mother and I prepared ourselves contentedly for the fun his presence always guaranteed.

Jack's dissipated past revealed itself in his face and made him look almost twenty years older than his age, but in spite of this there was still something boyish about him, both in behaviour and appearance. His candid enthusiasm, his ungovernable touchiness, retained an adolescent innocence; the clumsy movements of his bony body suggested the physical uncertainty of a child rather than the stumblings of an elderly party. Behind the benevolent beam, or offended scowl, of a grizzled patriarch, the short nose, wide smile and cleft chin evoked the attractive lad, cheeky and vulnerable by turns, that he must once have been.

He had loved, but been shy of, my father, and their relationship had never fully emerged from a crippling cocoon of embarrassed reserve. With my mother he could be more comfortably – even cosily – affectionate, treating her as he might have done a sister, with genuine respect, artless trust and a touch of amused condescension. Their cordial intercourse had given birth to several family jokes, the ritual repetition of which bound them yet closer together. Both belonged to – had indeed invented – the Four O'Clock in the Morning Club, whose insomniac members were entitled to ring each other up at that lonely hour. These healing conversations might largely consist of warnings about an imminent New Moon, for they shared a fanatic belief in the danger of glimpsing such a phenomenon through intervening glass. (Spectacles, and on occasion windshields, they decided, 'didn't count'.) Their attitudes towards superstition were alike: serious to the point of solemnity, but moderated by an enjoyably guilty sense of the absurdity in abandoning rationality to this vertiginous extent. It was in fact the silliness of the traditional taboos (involving ladders, cats and salt) that attracted them, while in some complex fashion deepening their faith, as if they felt it fitting that so cruel and arbitrary a mystery as fate should provide clues to its intentions and means of forestalling them in banal or frivolous forms. A favourite family joke was about Jack saying one morning: 'Did you hear a terrible crash in the middle of the night? Well, that was me, touching wood!'

We were therefore astonished by the violence of Jack's reaction when my mother told him (in a thoughtless aside during her account of the recent horror of her husband's last illness and the present misery of her bereavement) about her sudden dread of Horus and impulsive decision to sell it. He started up in his seat, accidentally kicking over the tumbler which contained his whisky and soda: the glass shattered and the drink seeped into the threadbare Aubusson carpet, leaving a stain similar to those already made by the messes of Martha, my father's favourite dachshund. His face had gone stony with fury and his voice had acquired a barely intelligible parade-ground bark. 'No, it's not true! You can't have done! I don't believe it! Jesus Christ, this is just too bloody much! My dear girl, all I can say is, I only hope you realise exactly what you've . . . I mean, what in the name of? . . . of all the imperial *idiots*! . . . to do such a damn fool thing . . . why on earth didn't you consult me first? Would that have been too much to expect? That statuette was the *only* object of any *real* value among all the rubbish which my grandparents collected at Stars. What did you get for it? A measly hundred quid? Clearly you've been swindled . . . God *knows* what it's worth, but that's not my point, my point is that it's a fantastically beautiful thing in itself, a work of *art*, for Christ's sake! But I suppose that

35

means nothing to you – it can't do – well that's not your fault, I see that, but the thing that I *can't* get over is that you knew perfectly well that Father *adored* it. You had no *right* – neither of you did – to get rid of it like that without letting me know. Apart from anything else, I'd have treasured it as something to remember Father by – I haven't anything else of his. He was my father too, you know!'

My mother stared at Jack as if he had gone mad. Incapable of speech, she hurried unsteadily from the room and out of the front door. We could see her, through the window, wandering about the garden, as if distractedly seeking some means of escape. I wanted to join her but felt paralysed by shock. Jack's neck and cheeks were rust-red; he looked as if he were about to weep. When at last he spoke, his voice was husky but softer and the tone was no longer bullying but one of rough comradeship – man-to-man. 'Shit, I seem to have spilt my fucking drink! Pour me another one, will you, there's a good chap. Sorry about that outburst – but women can be such *cunts* sometimes, can't they? You'd better explain exactly where you took the sodding thing.'

I did so, and then he strode outside to apologise to my mother: from the porch I watched them embrace. He fished all afternoon and spent the evening listening to Mozart on the radiogram; he left before breakfast on the following day. A week later, he rang up from a call-box reversing the charge. I answered the telephone. Jack told me that he had been up to London and bought back the falcon from Spink's. 'But they really jewed me – charged me a hundred and ten for it. I make that a clear profit of ten per cent for them. But never mind, all's well that ends well! There go the pips . . . Goodbye!'

The private nursing home was near Sloane Square. I found Jack on the first floor in a large, high-ceilinged Edwardian room furnished only by a narrow bed, a small table with a Bible attached to it on a chain, an easy chair upholstered in a jazz pattern of oatmeal and nigger brown, an immense wardrobe of carved oak, and a chromium-fitted wash basin of aggressively clinical appearance. Wearing a voluminous jibbah, he was standing with his back to me looking out of the window at a white building of oriental design across the road. 'Wouldn't you say that was some sort of mosque?' he said. 'Well, it isn't. Apparently it's a Christian Scientist church!' He gave a hearty, social laugh and gazed round the room in an uncertain way, as though it were he and not I who had just entered it for the first time.

He had been incarcerated here for ten days, 'drying out'. A popular doctor of the day specialised in curing alcoholics by a series of injections intended to stimulate those cells of the brain where in his opinion a congenital debility had caused the original craving, combined with a brutal form of aversion therapy. On starting the treatment, a patient named his poison – whisky, gin, brandy, rum, champagne: Jack had opted for whisky. From then on, this was the only liquid available to him; if the gleaming new wash basin had functioned at all, whisky would have spouted from its taps; while regular and supervised intakes of an emetic called antabuse guaranteed that every sip of it would make him vomit. The doctor had achieved some spectacular successes by this method, and it looked as if it had worked with Jack. He had telephoned earlier in the week, asking for some clean clothes, his chequebook and some ready cash to be brought round to Wilbraham Place as they were letting him leave that morning and he had a lunch date at the Etoile with a promising girl.

I put the suitcase on his bed. 'Here are the things you wanted.'

'Thank you, darling,' he said absentmindedly.

Over the past three years, since demobilisation from the

Army, things had gone badly for Jack. His formerly flamboyant style cramped by money worries, he had found it hard to cash in on any one of his several remarkable gifts; unlike the 1920s, this second post-war period had so far shown few signs of favouring the dilettante. One of his love affairs had taken a fatally serious turn: he had become obsessed by a young woman and continued to be so long after she had grown tired of him and left him for somebody else. This setback had bred in him neurotic fears about loss of potency; groundless at first, they had perversely sapped his confidence to a point where they seemed to be justified. It had not taken long, in this discouraging atmosphere, for the epicurean wine-lover, honoured by the Wine and Food Society for his wide knowledge and discriminating palate, to degenerate into a drunk; but the degeneration was only partial, and Jack was a drunk determined to be cured.

To fetch the suitcase and some of its contents, I had travelled down on the previous day to his lovely, melancholy mill house by a Sussex marsh, scene of many fabulous orgies, treasure hunts and fancy-dress balls between the wars. Set in a damp, wooded hollow, its picturesque little rooms, once hung with nudes by Modigliani and Matisse, were echo-less though empty. I turned the pages of the Visitors' Book, where liverish guests had attempted to write witty coments on the food, the drink and the company after those famous weekend parties that had sounded so enviable to the uninvited. Many of these inscriptions contained private or topical references and no longer made sense to an outsider, but 'Widows are wonderful!' clearly celebrated Jack's Veuve Cliquot, and one of his literary friends had composed an ingenious anacreontic about a prizewinning hangover. As I walked away from the house, down the sloping croquet lawn to the silver pool, over the rickety bridge across the tranquil stream and up the steep lane of stubborn clay to the main road, I turned back for a last look. Was this because I sensed (as one often does) that something indoors was observing my departure? Then I noticed (what I had not registered before) a shapely shadow on the sill of an attic window: the once familiar outline of Horus the holy bird.

'How are you feeling?' I asked Jack now.

'Never better. In fact, I've got some very, very good news indeed. I didn't want to say anything about it before because I wanted to get this ghastly cure over and done with first. I've got a job! An extremely well-paid and – not to put too fine a point on it, as they say – really rather a grand and important job. That's why I took the cure – to make certain I'd be up to it.' Disarmingly pleased with himself, he struck an attitude. 'You are looking at the Middle East Correspondent of the *Sunday World*, no less! The paper with the biggest circulation in Fleet Street!'

Jack had had no previous experience of journalism, but had proved himself as a writer ten years earlier with a highly readable travel book, *Bulletin from Barbary*, about his adventures with nomadic tribesmen in North Africa. The *World*'s Foreign Editor, a White's Club acquaintance of Jack's, had remembered this while looking for a suitable expert to cover the Arab–Israeli war and had commissioned him to contribute a series of special articles at an unusually high rate of payment. Jack's sympathies were fiercely pro-Arab; in political arguments he would often point out that anti-Zionism and anti-semitism were two quite separate things, implying (but never quite confirming) that in his case they did not co-exist. The proud male dignity of the Berber warriors had made a strong appeal to his aesthetic sense; he found in the wearing of loose robes a comfortable liberation from buttons, braces, collar studs and sock suspenders; and there was nothing in the subjection of women at odds with his own erotic tastes.

'I start in a fortnight! Just time to fit in a crash course in

Arabic at the Berlitz school!' I began to congratulate him, but he cut me short. 'Which reminds me – I don't want to interfere – but isn't it about time for *you* to begin thinking about your future career? Everybody tells me that it's quite out of the question nowadays to keep oneself by writing – there's far too much competition and practically no demand. So you'd better put that idea right out of your head. If you don't feel cut out for the Diplomatic, or the Army, or the City, I couldn't understand more . . . neither did I . . . but I do believe that in modern socialist Britain it's essential to be *technically equipped* to earn your own living, to acquire some basic skill which is always going to be needed, whatever happens. Mightn't you perhaps take a *course* in something or other? I don't know what – glass-blowing, or something? Think about it, anyway. I know it's great fun sitting in the cinema all day but it doesn't really lead anywhere. Your mother's so sweet and I'm sure she'd be frightened of upsetting you so I thought I ought to speak to you instead . . . Look, I'm going to be late at the restaurant if we go on gassing like this, be an angel and pop downstairs and get them to order a cab for me, will you?'

A sacred place in Jack's life was reserved for his men friends. Furiously resented by his lovers, and humbly respected from a distance by his relations (who were seldom allowed to meet them), they represented a stabilising constant in his erratic emotional history. Most legendary of these – and in a sense the most mysterious – was Tony, a cheery little man who ran an art gallery in Mayfair. Tony had none of the obvious qualities (talent, wit, fame, wealth) which distinguished the other men friends and perhaps for this reason was ideally suited to fill the important role of confidential crony. It was from Tony that we heard the news of Jack's death. A sniper's bullet had hit him in the chest while he was incautiously standing without cover to take a photograph of a skirmish between Israeli troops and the Arab Legion: according to one rumour, he had been wearing Arab clothes at the time, but another eye witness reported that he had been dressed in khaki. Whatever the circumstances, this must have been that moment, which he had spent so much of his life dreading, when there just wasn't any wood around to touch. He had been working for the newspaper little more than a month; the Foreign Editor later forwarded a meagre parcel of personal belongings (a pocket diary, a cigarette lighter, an initialled handkerchief) but failed to recover his body; for reasons of diplomacy, the incident was played down in the Press.

My mother organised a memorial service for Jack at a Chelsea church. I sat next to his last girl, a streaky-haired beauty called Bobbie, who hadn't yet been properly taken in by the men friends and came as a shock to the longer-established mistresses. She cried miserably throughout the ceremony, incurring the disapproval of many in the congregation who seemed to feel that they had a greater right to grief but somehow lacked her facility in expressing it. Somebody gave an address about Jack, saluting him as an exemplar of the traditional British eccentric aristocrat with romantic leanings towards Islam: the names of Burton, Blunt and Lawrence were invoked. A theatrical clergyman read from Ecclesiastes: 'Also when they shall be afraid of that which is high, and fears shall be in the way, and the almond tree shall flourish, and the grasshopper shall be a burden, and desire shall fail: because man goeth to his long home . . .' The words awoke suppressed, unwelcome memories of my father's funeral and I suddenly understood why Jack had been unable to face coming to that.

After the service, several of the mourners paused blinking in the porch to point out that, moving though it had been, there was no doubt that Jack would have preferred his friends to remember him by a *party*. 'With bags and bags of booze,' said Tony. Catching sight of me, he squeezed my arm. 'Just the chap I want to see . . . Listen, so sorry, I should have told you sooner only there was a balls-up made by the solicitor. Dear old Jack asked me to be his executor, you know, and he's mentioned you in his will. It seems he added a codicil at the last moment, just before he went off to the Middle East — says something about knowing that you'll understand what he means by it. Anyway, he's left you a sort of statue thing — not cash, I'm afraid, old boy, worse luck! I've got it for you at the gallery. Queer-looking object — not my period, so I've no idea what it would fetch. A hawk . . .'

I thought: 'It must never come back in the house — never.' That afternoon I called round at Tony's gallery, where an exhibition of paintings by Derain was being hung. The falcon was waiting for me in an office at the back. I raced with it to Spink's: my demeanour must have appeared both frantic and furtive, almost as though I suspected that I was being followed. The albino expert on Egyptian art was still there; did I only imagine that his smile of recognition suggested that he had been expecting my return for the past three years? I placed the god before him. He offered me a hundred pounds for it, which I happily accepted.

When I left the shop I was overwhelmed by an un-familiar feeling of joy in which were mingled confidence, security and relief. It seemed to me certain that, by dispos-ing of the falcon this second time, I had somehow managed to ward off the evil eye for ever. A curse had been lifted, a demon exorcised. I had a confused sense of triumph in having struck an easy bargain: it was as if I had been granted some unearned immunity, had been rewarded for doing nothing at all by a plenary indulgence. My mother and I would be safe now, for the rest of our lives . . . But my mood of mysterious exaltation was accompanied by a nagging trivial desire to understand the exact nature of the commercial transaction that had just taken place. The triple sale of the statuette contained a puzzling element, like those simple mathematical problems, Brain Twisters or Brain Teasers, which are sometimes used in IQ tests. What, in the matter of the ownership of Horus, had really happened? Had anything been materially gained, and if so, by whom? I had nearly reached Paddington before I had succeeded in working out the answer.

My mother and I had got rid of the falcon and had made two hundred pounds. Spink & Son Ltd had recovered the falcon and were ninety pounds down. Jack had lost both the falcon and a hundred and ten pounds. The six o'clock train had left the station, bearing me back home, and was passing Waterer's Floral Mile before I remembered that he had also lost his life.

Ursula

Love worketh no ill to his neighbour;
therefore love is the fulfilling of the law.

1

It was not long after Jack's death that I appeared in print
for the first time. A friend of his, who had recently become
the literary editor of a highbrow weekly, agreed to try me
out as a novel-reviewer and published one short article over
my name. If I had hoped for some reaction to this debut
beyond my immediate circle, I was disappointed; but it
would not be true to say that there was none at all. A few
days later I was called to the telephone and addressed by an
unfamiliar voice in clipped, confident and cultured tones.

'Fay Hitchcock here – remember me? Probably not, but
I saw your stuff in the Staggers and the name rang a bell.
My, my, we *have* grown up to be a clever young man,
haven't we? Better watch out, though, if we get any sharper
perhaps we'll cut ourselves one of these days! No, but *sans
blague*, well done you, it was a remarkably able piece of
work on the whole . . . Look here, don't think me rude if I
make it snappy, but I'm cooped up in this grim and ghastly
bin – they call it a clinic but that's only window-dressing –
and I'm far from being my own mistress, I can assure you.
So listen, my real reason for calling is this: I thought you

just might know – *what the dickens has happened to Bunch Bunbury?* I think something fishy's going on, I really do. I mean, can't the woman answer her own bloody telephone? My dear, I've rung and rung . . .'

At this point, she was interrupted by an indistinct, yet audibly angry voice; there was the sound of an altercation succeeded by a scuffle, and then the line was disconnected. I was left with a troubled vision of poor Fay Hitchcock, having somehow managed to escape from the sinister vigilance of the *blouses blanches* to a telephone booth, being discovered there, roughly apprehended and hauled back to a padded cell. The vision was by no means clear as I had only seen her once, very briefly, just before the war. I had a confused memory of crisp grey curls, flashing grey eyes, a diamond brooch on a grey tailor-made suit, the depressing scent of 'Tweed'. Where had it been? Of course – in none other than Bunch Bunbury's flat, to which I had been taken by my half-sister Ursula, who had been an intimate friend of them both in the roaring twenties.

When I wrote about my half-brother Jack, I never mentioned the fact that he had a full sister. This was not because Ursula was less important in my life. It is true that I saw much less of her – in fact, for reasons which will become apparent, I only met her on rare occasions – yet I always felt that I knew her the better of the two. He had indeed been a formidable presence throughout my childhood and adolescence, but she was to remain for ever significant by her absence: a domestic legend, partly scandalous and partly cosy, with the charm of a mystery that, given time, it should be perfectly possible to solve.

At first, all I knew was that in the autumn of 1929, when I was five and she was in her early thirties, Ursula had boarded one of the great transatlantic liners and set sail for the United States. I accompanied my parents to Southampton to see her off, but my only memory of the occasion is asking the name of a tune which the ship's orchestra was playing over and over again, and being told that it was called 'I'm a Dreamer – Aren't We All?'. I think I must have expected Ursula to return after a short interval, but some time later I heard that instead of doing so she had decided to become an American citizen. I spent the next thirty-five years trying to imagine her life in New York.

In this attempt I was almost wholly unsuccessful. However, while still a child I found it easy to get some idea of what her life had been like up to the date of her departure, and to form a clear impression of her character and personality. My parents often spoke about her in my hearing. She was my father's adored only daughter, and he had observed her development since infancy with pride and amusement, preserving the recollection of significant occurrences during her girlhood in the ritualised – and subtly distorted – form of the family anecdote. She was also a close friend of my mother, who was only a few years older and had been her confidante during the early years of their maturity. My actual memory of Ursula grew increasingly vague throughout the decade that passed until I saw her again, and finally vanished altogether, having been replaced by a vicarious version of *their* memories – a vivid combination of second-hand knowledge and precocious intuition.

Photographs and paintings of Ursula as a little girl show a sturdy, stocky figure bundled into wide-collared Edwardian smocks and high button boots: brown hair, cut in a thick fringe and a shoulder-length bob, frames a round, beaming face. Her large grey eyes were her only beautiful feature, but the sweetness of her expression – suggesting an eagerness to please and the assumption of a similar generosity in other people – gave an effect of comeliness to her appearance as a whole.

From an early age she showed an extreme sensitivity to the sufferings (however slight and however brief) of other creatures, animal as well as human. That familiar nursery cry — 'It isn't *fair!*' — was often on her lips, but in Ursula's case it was uttered to draw attention, not to a grievance of her own, but to a suspected injustice visited on someone or something else. She was deeply upset by any manifestation of exclusion, of selectivity, of judgment — anything even faintly implying discrimination which (she had soon discovered) is likely to involve another person's feelings getting hurt; and, in so far as it lay within her power, she sought to prevent the expression of such tendencies in everybody with whom she came into contact. Her passionate commitment to total egalitarianism and unlimited tolerance inevitably landed her in the apparently contradictory position of exercising a certain moral authority; Ursula, whose affectionate nature made her popular with all her schoolfellows and won her many devoted 'best friends', was none the less seen by them as something of a bossy-boots.

Her family, too, while admiring her readiness to leap to the defence of any underdog, sometimes silently regretted that when Ursula brought a girl friend home with her she would almost invariably turn out to be unattractive or boring or maddening — and on occasion decidedly nasty; and that the slightest hint of even potential criticism of the guest would infuriate Ursula to a painful degree. Of course it was forbidden to laugh at these people, or indeed at any person whom she thought of as being disadvantaged, and this landed Ursula in yet another paradoxical situation, for she had a lively and spontaneous sense of the ridiculous and was often to be seen luxuriously incapacitated and lawlessly exalted by galvanic fits of the giggles. Unkindness made her ill; snobbery made her angry: once her eyes were seen to fill with tears and, when asked the reason, she explained that she had suddenly found herself thinking about little puppies being snubbed. After I was told of this incident many years later, I would lie awake at night worrying about Ursula

47

lying awake at night worrying about sick and ill-treated animals . . .

My father, a professional soldier, was often abroad, and Ursula spent much of her childhood staying with his parents at Stars – a large, inconvenient house which they had made famous for an atmosphere of enlightened and eclectic hospitality. Here idealistic High Tory politics were under-pinned by the Christian doctrine of all-embracing loving-kindness; reverence for art and beauty took the form of nostalgia for medieval romance and even contained a bracing element of Socialist principle (the interior of Stars had been designed by William Morris). One day, while Ursula and her grand-parents were being driven back to the house after a visit to Salisbury Cathedral, their landau was intercepted by a dirty, drunken tramp who, muttering abuse, tried with some violence to enter it. The coachman knocked him aside with his whip, and speeded up the horses; but before they had time to move off Ursula opened the carriage door, leant out and with a gesture of courteous invitation said to the tramp: 'You are heartily welcome!'

Ursula was spared a conventional 'coming out season' by the outbreak of war in 1914. She worked for its duration as a VAD, finding in nursing the natural outlet for those qualities of dedication and enthusiasm which – considered handicaps in a young lady by the artificial standards of peacetime fashionable society – would have seriously impeded her success as a debutante. She found that she was happy: the horrors of pain and mutilation and death were to some extent exorcised by the fact that she was allowed to participate in the effort to relieve or prevent them. Her work ended when the war did – and Ursula had nothing to distract her from a full appreciation of its tragic depredations. Her brother Jack had been spared – but most of the young men she had known, or expected to know, were dead. She was fighting against a delayed depression when the Spanish influenza epidemic killed her mother; this seemed too much to bear, and Ursula suffered a brief collapse.

She recovered to find herself in a world that appeared to have got stuck while passing through some necessary stage of transition: as if temporarily stunned by the recent past, everything and everyone around her seemed tentative, indeterminate, incomplete and almost blank. The few suitable young men who had not only survived the war but were also prepared to act as Ursula's dancing partners were an uninspiring lot. She and her girl friends would refer to them as if they were horses who must not be overtaxed on the hunting field. 'I can't possibly go to this party tonight, I haven't got an escort.' 'Why not take So-and-So? He's quite presentable and perfectly safe.' 'Oh no, I couldn't do that, I had him out last week.' Exhausted by always having to take the initiative in the social-sexual game, and discouraged by the insignificant results with which her enterprise was rewarded, Ursula solemnly announced to Jack that she had made an important discovery: 'I really do believe that *all* men are impotent!'

Ursula and my mother (also a VAD) had made friends during the war. Both at loose ends, they now joined forces in what they admitted to be a rather feeble attempt to give themselves an occupation and perhaps even make a little money: they set themselves up as teachers of ballroom dancing. Among their few clients was an elderly, but up-to-the-minute, aunt of Ursula's, and my mother was leading this aunt round the floor in a foxtrot when my father shyly entered the room, curious to see how his daughter was getting on in her new venture. Soon after that first meeting between my parents the dancing lessons petered out – but there were more meetings, developing into courtship, engagement and ultimately marriage. Ursula was delighted to get her recently bereaved father 'off her hands' and into those of a trusted friend, and exhilarated to feel herself suddenly free of all family ties. She moved into a Chelsea studio with a young woman known as Flash Rumbold, where they worked together as portrait photographers: Ursula was responsible for the artistic posing of their subjects, revealing for this a remarkable flair, while Flash coped with those technical problems of lighting, time exposure and so on which Ursula, congenitally clumsy in practical matters, found beyond her.

Her association with Flash introduced Ursula to the wilder fringes of the post-war social phenomenon known to the Press as the Bright Young People, and with a sense of release that surprised her by its intensity she flung herself into an ardent exploration of every offered excess. A passionate admiration for the current idol of the 'gallery girls', Tallulah Bankhead, shared by Flash Rumbold, Bunch Bunbury, Fay Hitchcock and others in their group, made drunkenness seem glamorous to Ursula, while Brenda Dean Paul by her persuasively poised example led her on to experiment with heroin and cocaine. It must have seemed to her family and friends that Ursula was risking a troubled middle age and possibly an early death by indulging so wholeheartedly in these profitless dissipations; then, as the roaring twenties whimpered to a close, the course of her life dramatically changed direction. She fell in love.

Throughout the decade a series of revues with all-black casts (*Shuffle Along*, *Runnin' Wild*, *The Chocolate Dandies*, *Dixie to Broadway*) had been so popular with American audiences that some of them were brought over to Europe, where they were equally successful. By the spring of 1929, the *Blackbirds* company had reached the Moulin Rouge in Paris and was causing a sensation which it would later repeat in England. Meanwhile, a similar but more modest entertainment had opened in a 'little' London theatre. *Keep It Dark!* was not exactly a smash hit, but it attracted a discriminating and appreciative public who had made it, for a short while, the fashionable thing to see. Ursula was taken to *Keep It Dark!* by Flash Rumbold. The best thing in the show was a number called 'Mean Man', performed by a strikingly beautiful woman who was billed in the programme as 'Miss Ruby Richards'. The composer of 'Mean Man' had intended it to be a torch song, but Ruby Richards had made a reputation as a distinguished tragic actress rather than a *chanteuse*, and so instead of singing the tune she declaimed the lyrics, transforming them into a dramatic monologue – to such overwhelming effect that her curtain calls were greeted by hysterical cries of 'Bravo!', 'Bis!' and 'Encore!' Ursula and Flash went backstage to congratulate her: at that first meeting, Ursula was so moved that she could scarcely speak, but she returned to the theatre every night until the end of the limited run, after which it became necessary for Ruby to go back home to New York. A few months later, Ursula followed her out there. Ever since then, Ursula had lived with Ruby in the same small Harlem flat.

Most of her friends considered this latest exploit of Ursula's to be so extraordinary that it almost transcended scandal. For a 'well-brought-up' Englishwoman to vanish for good, apparently acting on a sudden whim, into a remote Negro ghetto confusedly associated in the ignorant British mind with drugs, drink, crimes of violence and embarrassing excesses of childish religious fervour ('Lordy, Lordy, Halleluiah!'), appeared to many of them a baffling enormity which, since it had no precedent, could hardly even be gossiped about; while the less narrow-minded, though applauding the courage and characteristic lack of caution manifested by her pioneer spirit, feared that she had taken a final step into unexplored territory where it would be too dangerous for them to follow. Whether they thought of her as a social outcast who had wandered off for ever beyond the pale, or as an exiled heroine, a 'Queen over the water' who might some day return to her faithful people, for them all Ursula had been transmogrified into a 'lost lady' of legend.

2

When I was old enough to take a little of all this in, it struck me as a fascinatingly romantic story. I became obsessed by the need to understand it more clearly and felt perpetually teased by a sense of unsatisfied curiosity. Harlem! What on earth could it be like? To a schoolboy during the 1930s the name meant only one thing: jazz. This was puzzling, because I could make no connection between my memories of Ursula and that exciting, grown-up yet frowned-upon form of music. My mother was among the first English subscribers to the *New Yorker*, and I would spend hours studying the section at the beginning of the magazine devoted to night spots, supper clubs, jazz cellars and cabaret 'rooms', vainly trying to imagine the aunt-like figure of Ursula sitting in one of these (I had only a few Hollywood musicals to go by in my attempt to recreate the scene and the decor was maddeningly hazy) while Maxine Sullivan swung 'Loch Lomond' or Ethel Waters shouted the blues. There was always something basically improbable about these visions: Ursula remained Ursula and Harlem remained Harlem, and even though I knew that the two had somehow achieved a synthesis in the outside world, they were still thesis and antithesis to my private mind.

My mother shared to some extent my unbridled interest in the matter and blatant desire for further detail, while also participating in my father's indulgent and unquestioning acceptance of the whole eccentric episode as 'typical of darling Ursie'. I could tell that the more distant members of the family pitied him almost as if he had been the victim of some hideous outrage, but he deflected their patronising approaches to condolence by refusing to recognise any cause for it. He had inherited from his own mother and father their stern gospel of love: 'I do not mind what my children do, so long as they are happy.' (This gospel is not in effect quite so unrestrainedly libertarian as it seems, for it not only enjoins happiness on one as a duty but also carries with it the inhibiting implication that whatever one might do must automatically be right merely because one is a child of the speaker – and any act of defiance, experiment or destruction is thus rendered meaningless before it has been committed.)

Although Ursula and my parents hardly ever wrote to each other there was no real question of their having 'lost touch'; rather, their intimacy was felt to exist at a deeper level than the plane of formal social intercourse to which letters (other than love letters) belong, and indeed the few that did pass between them exuded an apologetic air of irrelevance. It was as if they sensed that a regular correspondence would have emphasised their separation more than it could have relieved it: instead they decided, as it were politely, to ignore it. Any important piece of news would be transmitted by cablegram, or in urgent cases by telephone: I remember the excitement of waiting for the insecure transatlantic connection and the sense of reassurance conveyed by Ursula's husky voice, faint but sturdily confidential, when it eventually reached us over the humming, crackling line. At Christmas she would send me flatteringly adult presents (*John Brown's Body* by Stephen Vincent Benét, *Will Shakespeare* by Clemence Dane) accompanied by notes as brief as they were affectionate. For concrete information about Ursula and her surroundings, we were almost totally dependent on Hope Barker and her annual visits to 'scout' for English books which might be suitable for publication by her husband's New York firm.

Ursula and Hope had been fellow pupils at a boarding

school for the daughters of Army officers, and had later worked together as VADs in the same hospital near Rouen: it was there that my mother had met them both, and the three high-spirited young women had become for a time inseparable. After the Armistice, their lives had taken different directions; but when Ursula first set foot on Manhattan to take up residence in Harlem, Hope had been for some years installed with her American husband in a duplex apartment on Beekman Place, and their former friendship was happily revived. Hope had taken no part in the *louche* life led by Ursula in London during the 1920s, and was herself irreproachably respectable; the conventional New York 'set' to which she belonged was far removed from the less privileged milieu so impulsively embraced by Ursula; and yet Hope was to remain Ursula's most loyal ally. She prided herself on the broadness and openness of her mind, and often said that the only thing that shocked her was the assumption by others that she had been shocked. With mock fury and conscious comedy, she would deliver herself of the cliché: 'I'm afraid it would take a great deal more than that to shock *me*!'

Yes, Hope Barker was a woman of the world: her manner proclaimed it as a salient fact. This manner had presumably been developed as a badge of superiority during periods of her life which had been spent among people to whom the phrase could not have applied (her contemporaries at the hunt balls and gymkhanas of her girlhood, the majority of her colleagues while nursing during the war), but even after her marriage to a successful publisher, when she moved in circles sophisticated enough to make the reminder unnecessary, it continued to be insisted upon. This was partly achieved by an air of immense, if slightly mysterious, authority; she gave the impression of being somehow special, a person of unusually wide experience whose words, pronounced with dramatic emphasis and charged with tolerant humour, carried peculiar weight. People meeting her for the first time found themselves after a while uneasily wondering why they had never heard about her before and sensing something shameful in their ignorance. Later, they would try to become better informed: was she perhaps a famous character actress? a distinguished novelist? a 'personality' of some kind or another? But Hope was none of these, nor did she wish to be; serenely secure in her comparative obscurity, she needed no vulgar testimonial of achievement to justify her superb self-confidence.

She would arrive to stay with my mother with some of the glamour of luxury shipboard travel still clinging to her, although she did not belong to a physically glamorous type. (One of her favourite stories was about her nephew who, asked to give a description of her appearance when she had somehow got lost going through Customs at Southampton, replied: 'My aunt could be said to possess the unique distinction of striking a happy medium between Claudette Colbert and Harpo Marx!') As soon as she had settled herself in the house, my mother and I would put her through an avid third degree: this produced some intriguing glimpses into Ursula's way of life, but (as when over-zealous interrogators find that their victim has fainted under torture) we were always ultimately frustrated in our thirst to possess a fuller picture.

'Do you see her often?'

'Not as often as I should like, alas. I don't think you people over here can fully comprehend the barbaric customs still in force in the so-called Land of the Free, but a ludicrous and abominable thing exists there called the *colour bar* – officially in the South, unofficially but none the less effectively in the North. It is just conceivable that if Ruby paid a call on me, the porter of the apartment building where I live might consider himself justified in requesting her to use the tradesmen's lift at the rear entrance. Ruby therefore quite rightly refuses to come and visit me, and darling Ursie naturally wouldn't dream of coming on her own, although Ruby has *begged* her to do so, literally on bended knee, time and time again . . . but you know how fiercely loyal Ursie is, and she also feels that she would be somehow giving countenance to the detestable system if she didn't take a stand. All of which needless to say I couldn't agree with more. So *I* go to *them* whenever I can – but I'm a busy woman and, as I say, it isn't *nearly* as often as I would wish.'

'Do they have a nice flat?'

'It depends what you mean by "nice". There's certainly nothing nasty about it. Quite simply furnished – apart from a few pieces which Ursie has clung on to from the old days at Stars, family pictures, some decent china, that kind of thing. It's too touching the way, ever since she's been living in Harlem, Ursie has become more and more of the county lady – which, God knows, she never used to be over here! Their apartment is probably the only place in the whole of the United States where one is offered Earl Grey tea, cucumber sandwiches and Gentleman's Relish!'

'What is Ruby *like*?'

'Simply delightful. A woman of enormous magnetism, great personal distinction, and knock-down charm!'

'Do describe her!'

'Describe Ruby?' Hope reflected. 'Not easy . . . You see, there's something very special about her that's almost impossible to put into words. To begin with, she has the most tremendous dignity. I mean, if she were to walk into the room at this moment, you'd say to yourself: *who* is that fascinating creature? It's not so much that she's pretty or elegant or what-have-you – but she just does happen to have been born with this extraordinary *presence*. And such warmth! I think she's probably the warmest person I've ever come across. Take it from me, Ruby Richards is a very remarkable human being indeed. Everybody I've met who knows her agrees that she's quite, quite wonderful. They're all bowled over. So would you be.'

'What does she *look* like?'

'Striking, I'd say – in the Spanish style. In fact, you'd swear she was Spanish if you knew nothing to the contrary. People often do take her for a Latin American or a Mediterranean. But of course she's much too proud to "pass as white". To be perfectly honest, it would have been better for her if she had, from the point of view of her career. She's a highly gifted actress, but she's always refused to play maids, or slaves, or any form of caricatured "coon", and those are almost the only parts offered to Negroes on the Broadway stage. So she's hardly ever *in* anything – which is a scandalous waste of talent. But all the same she's regarded with the highest respect by her fellow artists. I can vouch for that. Kit Cornell herself told me that Ruby's timing was impeccable. Impeccable!'

'What sort of life do they lead? Who do they see?'

'Well, Ruby has a fairly large circle of extremely interesting and worthwhile friends – actors, singers, writers, artists of all sorts, as well as people seriously dedicated to furthering the Negro cause. But I'm afraid she does find dear Ursie's total lack of discrimination just a fraction trying at times! You know how our angel has never been able to bear the *thought* of anybody being left out of things or made to feel the slightest bit inferior – and if she had her way, my dear, she'd fill the place with the sweepings of the Harlem streets: drug fiends, pimps, prostitutes of *both* sexes! It's too hard on poor Ruby, who has spent years struggling to establish a very highly regarded *salon* in order to scotch the purely sordid image of Harlem which prejudiced outsiders assume to be the norm.'

'How does Ursula go down with Ruby's friends?'

'Oh, I think they all adore her – though, as I say, some

of them feel desperately sorry for Ruby when Ursie's lovely unsnobbishness gets out of hand and she gives the unfortunate impression of liking *anybody* just so long as they're black! There are naturally just as many subtle shades of social distinction in Harlem as in any other community, and I think discovering this came as rather a shock to Ursie, who of course has always loathed that sort of thing and had hoped to get clean away from it. But on the whole I'm sure they do appreciate her throwing in her lot with them as the beautiful gesture it undoubtedly is. I think in the end she even won over Spencer, though it wasn't easy at first.'

'Who on earth is Spencer?'

'Ruby's husband,' Hope replied calmly.

'*What?*'

'Oh, yes. They were married practically in the cradle, I believe, and it's been what is politely referred to as a "union in name only" for years. I nearly,' said Hope wittily, 'called it a *marriage blanc* – but that wouldn't be quite the *mot juste*, would it? However – be that as it may, as they say – Ruby is utterly devoted to Spencer and won't *hear* of his being kicked out of the apartment. So he lives there with them. He's perfectly harmless – a charming good-for-nothing. Refuses to do a hand's turn, but it's hard not to like him. You know, the sort of person one talks about having a "soft spot" for.'

Gradually, some sort of blurred impression was emerging from Hope's brisk and bracing commentary: a small but otherwise featureless flat; Spencer hanging about in it all day long doing nothing; Ruby unable to find suitable employment as an actress but valiantly, and with her habitual dignity, persevering as a *salonnière*; Ursula an exotic, ungainly presence among them, accepted (with a touch of condescension) as an equal by their social circle in spite of the fact that she sometimes made a nuisance of herself – either by assuming the stuck-up airs of an English gentlewoman or by tactlessly insisting on opening their doors to the scum of the earth.

'Is she happy?'

'Blissfully. She worships Ruby, and asks nothing better from life than to be allowed to be near her. Also, she has found the perfect outlet for her crusading instincts and reforming zeal in the Negro cause – into which she has wholeheartedly thrown herself.'

It appeared, however, that even Ursula's selfless commitment to this had involved Ruby in some embarrassment. Hope told us about the case of the Scottsboro Boys, and tried to explain the split among their defenders between the moderate National Association for the Advancement of Colored People and the radical International Labor Defence. 'Ursie has been influenced by her old friend Nancy Cunard into unqualified support for the revolutionary ILD, which violently attacks the liberal NAACP and its magazine *Crisis* as bourgeois and reactionary – you know, the fashionable Communist jargon (not that Ursie is a Communist *herself*, I'm sure) – which is a *tiny* bit awkward as *Crisis* happens to be edited by the great Negro leader Dr Du Bois, who needless to say is one of Ruby's most valued – nay, *treasured* acquaintances! But Ruby takes it in her stride. "I rise above it," she says. At the moment Ursie is very busy helping a friend with research for some scholarly work in several volumes on the history of the American Negro. It's quite a humble job she's got, but an extremely demanding one, and she works at it like a – help! there I go again – not like a black, perish the thought – like a *horse*!'

It was this job that eventually brought Ursula back to us (her researches having led her to the British Museum and the Public Record Office), on a visit as transient as one of Persephone's, in the spring of 1939.

3

I missed her arrival as I was away at school but when I came home for the summer holidays I found her established in the house as harmoniously as if she had always lived there. She was to spend her weekends with us in the country and the rest of the time working in London, where she had various friends who could put her up. I think her appearance must have come as something of a surprise to me at first – perhaps even a shock – but in less than a day her physical presence had acquired a comfortable aura of familiarity, as if some homely and haphazard miracle had released a deeply buried folk memory and clumsily made it flesh.

Ursula, not much more than forty, looked years older. Her face had no more lines on it than was natural at her age but she made no attempt to conceal them apart from a vague sprinkling of powder. Her hair had become colourless and thin; when out of doors, she covered it with an extremely dowdy hat designed in the shape of a mushroom from scraps of grey felt and black satin. This hat (also sometimes sprinkled with face powder) appeared to have a squashy, almost squelchy consistency. Her manner was the reverse of effusive: dry, reserved, slightly governessy in tone, as if in dread of sentimental gush. It was clear that she was still very shy. She had a graceless, rather knock-kneed walk, which was none the less appealing in its suggestion of impetuous haste and eager welcome. Extremely short-sighted, she was constantly bumping into, knocking over or treading on things that had been placed in her path. This had made her devotedly dependent on a pair of spectacles with pale tortoise-shell frames – and not only as an aid to vision. If one was about to tell Ursula a piece of news which she expected to interest or entertain her, she would cry: 'Wait a moment

– *do* wait till I've found my glasses – you know I can't enjoy anything properly without them!' Then, spectacles on nose, she would turn to one a sweet, serious face in cosy complicity and confident anticipation of pleasure.

Ursula was worried about a book she had been sent. It was called '*Crinkum-Crankum* and other poems by Enid ffrench', and had been privately printed on a hand-worked press by a 'vanity' publishing firm in Eastbourne. Enid ffrench was a friend from the past: with shingled hair, a trim figure and a *gamine* face, she had been fairly well known playing supporting roles on the London stage during the 1920s, usually cast as a slangy Bright Young Thing in some starring vehicle for Lilian Braithwaite, Gladys Cooper or Fay Compton. (This I knew from drawings of her illustrating theatre reviews which I would sometimes come across in old bound volumes of *Punch*.) Then she had suddenly disappeared from view. Ursula had heard a rumour that she had become a nun, but apparently this was false. She had written an affectionate inscription on the flyleaf of *Crinkum-Crankum*, begging Ursula to tell her what she thought of the book ('I know you'll be truthful – you always were') and giving her present address in a Sussex nursing home.

'What on earth am I to put in my letter?' said Ursula. 'Normally the technique in this sort of tricky situation is to find *one thing* to praise in a friend's book and concentrate on that for several pages, but the fact is I can't discover a single line in these poems which I can honestly admire! It really is a poser. There's no point in faking it, either, the old girl's much too shrewd to be fooled by that. On the other hand I really *must* think of something kind to say to her. It looks as if she's been having a pretty thin time of it, poor darling.'

The poems in *Crinkum-Crankum* were indeed very bad, but none the less I found them fascinating. One in particular, called 'Gardening', had an opening line which haunted me

– and which I still remember: 'I hang my woollie on a branch.' There was something so feeble about this line that I became quite intoxicated by bewilderment at the thought that anybody (even if only the author) had presumed to call it 'poetry'. At the same time, the image of the woollie hanging on the branch did succeed in suggesting another, almost as vivid, of Enid ffrench's neat figure squatting near by, her shingled head shielded by a floppy sunhat and bent over the border she was weeding ... If it could do that, surely it must be 'poetry' after all? I said some of this to Ursula, who listened intently. 'Thank you, darling, you've saved my bacon!' She eventually sent off a long, loving letter to Enid ffrench, with an appreciation of her book so attentive to minor detail that the vagueness of the general verdict was effectively concealed, and finishing with a postscript: 'My young brother has been absorbed by "C-C" as well and asks me to tell you that he *particularly* revels in the one about your garden.'

One Friday evening, Ursula brought her former partner, Flash Rumbold, down to stay, warning us beforehand that she had recently dropped the nickname and wished to be known as Fleur. She was now an extremely successful photographer, with premises in Mayfair and a reputation for social portraiture rivalling those of Harlip and Yevonde. Fleur was tall and slender and ultra-feminine, with frizzy fair hair, round blue eyes and a round red mouth: her features appeared to have been nervously dabbed on her face just a little askew, as in a painting by Marie Laurencin. She wore expensive clothes made of soft materials in pastel shades – 'I'm model size, you see,' she would explain, lowering turquoise-tinted lids. In spite of a manner of speaking so affected as to induce symptoms of dissociation in her listeners, Fleur did exert a certain languid glamour: it soon became clear, however, that her egocentricity bordered on the monstrous.

After dinner on Sunday somebody — probably Fleur — suggested a seance. A round table with a slippery surface was produced; a wine glass was placed upside down in the centre and the cards of a 'Lexicon' pack arranged in a circle along the edge. My father did not take part — remembering all too clearly the sad vogue for spiritualism after the last war, when so many of his bereaved relations had been driven for consolation to mediums whom, in less stricken circumstances, they would have immediately recognised as blatantly fraudulent. Fleur, Ursula, my mother and myself sat at the table and each lightly rested a finger on the glass.

We asked questions about the crisis in Europe — would there be a war, and if so, when? — but the glass made no movement more decisive than a tremulous wobble. 'We're being too serious, I expect,' said Ursula. 'Perhaps we ought to start with a lighter topic.' For a while none of us could think of anything suitable to say. Then Ursula politely inquired whether Fleur would enjoy her projected holiday at Rapallo, about which we had already heard a good deal, and the glass hastened to spell out a definite yes. Further questions pertaining to Fleur and her affairs were received in the same positive spirit; but the glass appeared to be bored by any other subject, responding either with a stubborn refusal to budge or at best with a listless stagger towards letters which were impossible to form into any recognisable word.

It seemed to me obvious that Fleur was directing the glass herself, but this simple solution to the frustrating mystery did not occur to Ursula, who soon began to bully the 'control' which she assumed to be animating the wine glass. 'Go away!' she told it rudely. 'You're a nasty unclean spirit and we don't want you here. Go away at once and send a nice clean spirit in your place.' I noticed that Ursula was taking a much tougher tone with the wine glass than one could ever imagine her adopting towards a mortal being.

Finally the spirit surlily intimated that it was unable to cooperate until the doubter among us had been banished from the room. This could only refer to me. Terrified that I might be offended, Ursula insisted on calling the seance off, while Fleur gazed reproachfully at the mirror in her powder compact. I assured Ursula that I would be happy to sit in my father's study next door and read. 'It might be safer if he were on a different floor altogether,' said Fleur. 'I've always heard that hostile vibrations are more likely to carry horizontally than vertically.' In spite of the look of innocent distress on Ursula's face, I obediently said goodnight and went upstairs to bed.

The following morning I travelled up with Ursula by train to London, where I had an appointment with my dentist. Fleur, who had come by car, stayed behind before driving off a little later to visit friends in the West Country. Once alone with Ursula in the railway carriage, I could not resist telling her of my suspicions regarding the seance. 'Do you really think she was cheating?' she asked, surprised but only mildly so. Then she laughed. 'How *very* funny! I must say, the joke's on me – fancy my not spotting it! I'm sure you're right, but I think she deserves the benefit of the doubt and I'm going to try to keep this just between ourselves . . . though I must say it does make an awfully good story and I shall probably succumb to temptation.'

Ursula and I then talked for the first time about politics. She told me how exhilarated she had felt on leaving England for a society where the old class barriers no longer applied, and how swiftly she had been made aware of the yet graver injustice of racial prejudice; but she insisted that her experience as an immigrant had not been one of disillusion. Indeed, she spoke of America – and in particular of Franklin and Eleanor Roosevelt – with possessive patriotic pride. At the same time, she retained a vestigial allegiance to the old regime. She had bitterly resented the Abdication as an insult to American womanhood, and was still romantic about the Duke of Windsor: 'He will always be the true King of England as far as *I'm* concerned!' She described her present dilemma as a confirmed pacifist whose hatred of Nazism was so great that she sometimes found herself hoping for war. 'Do you know that horrible feeling of being just like a chameleon on a plaid? One hardly knows any longer *what* one thinks or what one wants to happen. I remember I first had it years ago when I decided the only thing to do was to become a vegetarian and then didn't go through with it as I still had to buy meat to give to my darling dogs and cats! But this of course is far grimmer. I can't *bear* the thought of the slaughter that another war would be bound to bring about . . . but then if the whole of Europe goes Fascist, *that* would be too hideous to contemplate as well!'

Ursula was staying at a flat in Wigmore Street belonging to her friend Bunch Bunbury, and on arrival at Paddington we took a taxi there. 'Do come in for a moment if you've got time before your appointment. I'm longing to show you off to more of my friends and I think you'll enjoy Bunch – she's got a first-class brain. There may,' she added tentatively, 'be somebody there called Fay Hitchcock who can be rather difficult, but she's very nice really. Just so long as she's not in a funny mood . . .' Ursula had a key to the flat, which admitted us into a long, dark passage with what appeared to me to be a great many doors leading off it, as in a hotel corridor. There was a strong scent of 'Tweed' and we seemed to be following it like police dogs to its source in a small drawing-room at the back, where we found Fay Hitchcock sitting morosely alone. After she had introduced us, Ursula asked: 'Where's Bunch?'

'Search me,' said Fay shortly, and then began to question me in a matey way about my life at school. 'Are you a wet bob or a dry bob, old boy?' On hearing that I was a dry bob she tried to get a discussion going about cricket, but this was a subject that bored me and soon my uninspired response started to irritate her. 'If you're not keen on games I suppose you must be artistic. What did you think of the Academy this year? Pretty good rubbish, wasn't it?' For a second I was tempted to bluff, but sensing that Fay would be hard to deceive I confessed that I had never been to Burlington House.

She turned in exasperation to Ursula. 'What the devil *does* this brother of yours take an interest in, for Pete's sake? God, how I hate indifference – especially in the young! Youth should be a time of passion, of bold adventure, of wholehearted commitment . . . If there is one thing I *cannot* stand, it is caution! There's nothing worse, in my humble opinion, than lukewarm lack of enthusiasm. I really don't care what people are enthusiastic about, just so long as they're enthusiastic about *something*! Better to feel strongly about anything than nothing at all! If you ask me, it's lack of enthusiasm which has got this world of ours into the stinking mess that it's in today!'

Fay was interrupted by the sound of the flat door opening; she stopped her tirade and furiously lit a cigarette. Bunch came into the room: a large, dark, brooding presence, she stood for a moment in dramatic silence, staring at the floor. I had time to notice that she wore a broad belt of shiny black patent leather and was carrying an outsize handbag of the same material: both belt and bag were studded by chips of coloured glass to form a pattern suggesting the night sky. Then she planked the bag down on a table, slightly displacing a framed photograph by Cecil Beaton of Ursula dressed in a French fisherman's striped jersey and a sailor's bell-bottom trousers.

'Well – you may congratulate me,' Bunch announced. 'I have just landed my first job. I think a little drinky-poo is called for, *non*?' She poured herself a whisky and soda, gesturing to the rest of us to help ourselves. After a long swig, she murmured: 'That's better. I needed that.'

Fay continued to sulk, but Ursula was generously excited by Bunch's news. I gathered from their questions and replies that the job was with a famous department store in Oxford Street and had something to do with the belt and the handbag, which she had designed herself. 'They want me to do more stuff for them in the same line, and if it goes down all right they might take me on as a buyer as well – for my sins! But at least it means the gas bill will be paid!'

After this the conversation became more enjoyable from my point of view, turning to films and the stage. Bunch was an expert on the French cinema, and told me that Arletty was a chum of hers 'in real life'. Fay declared that she was just about to join a theatre club which planned to produce works refused a licence by the British censor – 'Things like Lillian Hellman's *The Children's Hour*.' Ursula, who had seen this on Broadway, said that she thought it rather a silly play.

I left Ursula in the flat and walked to the dentist's in a state of moderate over-excitement; then I saw a film at the Curzon cinema which had been recommended by Bunch and took a train back home. That evening I noticed that my mother seemed preoccupied and a few days later she told me why. Before her departure, Fleur Rumbold had insisted on their having a private talk: apparently she was very concerned about Ursula. According to Fleur, a main reason for Ursula's visit to England had been to seek a cure for heroin addiction. She had been introduced to the drug in the wild old days at the Chelsea studio, and life in Harlem had offered irresistible opportunities to increase her dependence. Somebody had told her of a man in Harley Street with a wonderful new treatment and she had come over to consult him . . . 'I just thought her family ought to know,' Fleur had finished.

'I really shouldn't involve you in this,' my mother said now, 'but that awful woman upset me so much that I had to tell somebody. Whatever happens, Yvo must never get to hear of it: the worry would be so terribly dangerous for his health.' My father had suffered a severe heart attack the previous winter, and my mother was desperate to spare him anxiety.

But Ursula never underwent the cure; for the second time she was rescued from an impending ordeal by the outbreak of war. Her loyalties were painfully divided: she felt that she should stay in the land of her birth to share its danger, but she knew that she would return to her adopted country to be with Ruby. For a week or so she immersed herself in war work, helping at railway stations to deal with the problems of premature panic evacuation from London, and then she went back to New York. I was at school when she left, and unable to say goodbye. Another twenty years were to pass before I saw her again.

4

'She'll never come over,' Hope Barker reported decisively. 'Since her father's death, followed so tragically soon by Jack's, she has felt that England would be too full of sad associations. I honestly believe that she couldn't bear to see it again.'

This was in 1950. Hope's transatlantic trips had started up once more after a hiatus imposed by the war and prolonged by unexplained domestic complications. My mother and I had recently moved to a small house in Knightsbridge where she let rooms to young men from South American embassies while I worked fitfully as a freelance literary journalist. It almost seemed to us now that Hope didn't *want* Ursula to make a reappearance in our midst, as if such an event might undermine her authority as our sole source of news and weaken the impact of her artistically spaced revelations.

We already knew from Ursula herself that, as soon as America entered the war, she had enlisted as a private in the WACs. From Fleur we had heard that the stimulus of this challenge had enabled her to rid herself for ever of the heroin habit. Ursula had served with distinction as an Army photographer, ending up with the rank of sergeant. It so happened that she was the first WAC to set foot on Australian soil, and a blurred snapshot of her doing so was widely syndicated in the American Press. Another news photograph from that period had reached us: Ursula, beaming in khaki, stood between a nervous-looking young man in civilian clothes and an imposing lady, with a smile like Mrs Roosevelt's, dressed in a colonel's uniform. A caption explained that Ursula was introducing a distant cousin of hers, who was a member of the household of the Governor of New South Wales, to the Commanding Officer of the WACs in the South-West Pacific Area.

We now learned from Hope that, after demobilisation from the Army, Ursula had taken a post working for a government department in charge of the welfare of war veterans. 'She's absolutely wonderful about it, gets up at crack of dawn every single day of the week and struggles to the office by bus and the subway, which I can assure you is no picnic. The job isn't tremendously well paid but it carries certain privileges with it and she'll have quite a nice pension when she reaches retirement age – if she can only stick it out that long, which she is determined to do. I think she gets a big kick out of being the breadwinner – you know, very much the man of the family, coming home exhausted every evening to find Ruby waiting.'

In spite of this, Hope considered that it was really Ruby who looked after Ursula, rather than the other way round.

'I wish I had a dollar,' she said impressively, 'for every time that Ruby has poured out to me her desperate worry that there would be nobody to take care of Ursula should anything happen to *her*. "The truth of the matter is, Hope," I remember her saying, "that I *dare* not be the first to go! I can't stand the thought of what would become of my darling. I've just got to keep on living – whether I like it or not – because, quite simply, I'm too scared to die!"'

'But why should she die?'

'Oh, she's what is known as "getting on", you know. Ruby is at least ten years older than Ursula, though she looks years younger. She's not going to live for ever.'

'And what exactly is she afraid will happen to Ursula when she does die?'

Hope explained that, although it was true that Ursula had with considerable heroism given up drugs completely, her past indulgence had left her in superficially good health while damaging her brain to a degree where even the slightest sip of alcohol would make her as intoxicated as if she had been on a bender. 'Ruby has to be constantly on the lookout that not one drop passes her lips. I mean, if there's sherry in the trifle . . . *fatal*, my dear! And of course Ursula wouldn't take that sort of supervision from anybody else but Ruby, who knows how to be both tactful and firm. "For *my* sake, sweetheart," she says: and Ursula pulls herself together at once.'

'How does it affect her when she does get drunk? Is she violent, or what?'

'No, no, nothing like that. She just gets – well, *silly*. It's agony for Ruby to have to sit by while Ursie lets herself down by behaving – I can't offhand think of another word – in a thoroughly *silly* way.'

But on her next visit, Hope brought better news: Ruby had at last been offered – and had accepted – a role in a play that was almost worthy of her talent. It was a turgid poetic melodrama called *Twenty-Eight Young Men Bathe by the Shore*, set in Acapulco and dealing with murder, incest, homosexuality and witchcraft. Ruby played a Mexican peasant woman who crosses the stage at a crucial moment in the plot and utters a weird prophetic warning, something between a blessing and a curse. 'It's the *tiniest* part, but my God, does she make the most of it!' said Hope. 'She called me before opening night and said "Don't sneeze, darling, or you'll miss me altogether!" but she needn't have worried. The way she delivers that single line sends shivers down one's spine – *electrifying! Young Men* is *the* smash hit on Broadway at the moment – what they call over there "the hottest ticket in town" – and the critics to a man have given it rave reviews. Quite a few of them mentioned Ruby. It's most gratifying that after all this time she's getting something approaching her due. Ursie of course is as proud as Punch.'

I felt that I would have given anything to see Ruby in that play. Throughout the 1940s and the 1950s, America was the place above all others where I longed to be. My favourite films, my favourite singers, many of my favourite writers came from there. In spite of repeated warnings not to do so, I persisted in the pardonable error of identifying America with Hollywood and New York. The idea that so close a relation as Ursula actually lived in one of these glamorous cities was constantly thrilling and increasingly tantalising as, year after year, I failed to find an adequate excuse to justify the expense of the journey. I naïvely wrote to ask her if she had ever met Lena Horne, and she replied: 'No, sorry, I don't know your pin-up girl, but Ruby knows Hazel Scott's husband, if that's any good! The Rev. Adam Clayton Powell Jr – a truly remarkable person and the first Negro Congressman in New York . . . Sadie sends wishes, says she appreciated your gracious hospitality but complains that she thought it rather ungallant of you to refuse to escort her round the night-spots! What went wrong?!'

Sadie was one of the stream of people sent over by Ursula with letters of introduction to my mother. It must be said that these visitors nearly always turned out a cruel disappointment. Instead of Lena Horne or Adam Clayton Powell, we got . . . well, for example, Sadie. The remarkable thing about her was that she was a judge, though we found this difficult to believe. A well-preserved white woman in her fifties, she arrived at our house early one afternoon and announced that she was coming back later to cook dinner for us. She gave us a list of ingredients she would need, of which the main one was wild rice — at that time almost impossible to obtain in London. She also said that she expected me to 'squire' her round all the fashionable night-clubs ('and maybe a few honky-tonks as well!'), making it clear that the bills would be taken care of by herself. Sadie then left, to shop around for a sexy, slinky evening dress.

My mother set out on a frantic, unsuccessful search for wild rice, while I made a panic-stricken attempt to discover if any nightclub might be persuaded to admit two non-members. Sadie returned as promised, triumphantly smoothing the sexy, slinky dress over her hips, and almost immediately got aggressively drunk. The dinner was never cooked, and Sadie was clearly in no fit state to go dancing — although she did not see it that way herself. I finally took her in a taxi back to her hotel, which she was only persuaded to enter after an embarrassing scene, the details of which I soon afterwards contrived to forget. Ever since this incident, I find that the phrase 'sober as a judge' can reawaken a throbbing consciousness of my humiliating social ineptitude.

Shortly after Sadie's visit I got a job in publishing, and for a delusive moment in the mid-1950s it looked as if this might provide a pretext for visiting the United States: incontinently, I wrote to Ursula announcing my imminent arrival, but the whole plan had collapsed before I received her reply. 'I am so excited and delighted,' she wrote, 'to think that I am going to see you again after such a long, long time. It seems to me that last time I saw you you were a public schoolboy but rather a grand and grown-up one and now you are a distinguished man. "Well I never," as our Nannies used to say. As you see from above address, we now live in Brooklyn — what a pity that you never saw the old Harlem place! I wish you could stay with us, we have a lovely room for you with paintings of Jack and Father from Stars, but unfortunately it would not be convenient for you for business appointments. It is now a complete slum since the City took it over but the house is still nice and representative of what houses used to be like before the "City Fathers" determined that we should all live in little box-like apartments. I think we will have to move to the suburbs. You being the head of the family I will probably bore you considerably asking your advice on this. Are you a good businessman? At the moment I am very overworked which is why I did not answer your letter by return. The house is full of puppies but Ruby who wants to add a note will tell you all the home news as I must get off to work.'

Ruby's note read: 'Cheers! I never for a moment doubted that one day you would get to NY. Naturally you will be very busy, yet I hope we will see a lot of you. On the other hand, there is so much to see, such a variety of things you will want to do, in this unique conglomerate city, that I would not want you to miss a bit of it. Meanwhile, do remember what a warm welcome will always await you.'

'Ursie was heartbroken that you couldn't make it after all,' said Hope when I saw her next. My mother asked her if she knew what had prompted the move to Brooklyn.

'A number of factors, the principal one I believe being

the death of Spencer, which severed Ruby's last real link with Harlem. For some time both she and Ursie had been pining for a home where the atmosphere would be a little more *gemütlich*.'

Mention of Ruby's husband – for us a figure as shadowy as a minor character in a novel one has never read – reminded my mother of an even vaguer masculine image from an imperfectly realised episode in the whispered past. 'Wasn't there once, ages ago, some talk of *Ursula* being married – or, at any rate, engaged? I seem to remember Yvo getting letters about it, and saying it sounded like a good thing, and then suddenly telling me that nothing had come of it and it would be better if the subject was never mentioned again.'

Hope looked grave. 'That, my darling, was typical of your saintly husband. He was determined to shield you from any unpleasantness – and he clearly succeeded in doing so.' I remembered how determined my mother had been to shield my father from knowledge of Ursula's drug addiction – and how she too had apparently succeeded in her aim.

'What *are* you talking about, Hope darling?'

Hope's instinct for drama stood her now in better stead than (so far as we were concerned) it ever had or ever would. She managed to guy its expression without diminishing its effect. 'My lips, as they say, have been sealed hitherto – but so many bridges have gone under the water since then (to coin a cliché!) that I see no reason why you shouldn't hear about it now, so here goes. *Well* . . . a year or so after Ursula's arrival in New York, she became involved with this deeply deplorable creature. He went by the name of Morton Van Schlemmer the Third, no less. A roaring pansy – but not at all of the *simpatico* type.'

Hope lowered her voice and inclined her head towards my mother's ear: '*Public lavatories*.' She gave an ironic laugh. 'I remember darling, *darling* Ursie saying to me: "I

74

respect him, you see, because he reminds me of Father"! My dear, anything *less* like . . . ! But never mind. He claimed to come of good old Dutch stock and did have some money of his own but had lost it all trying to set up a Nigger Heaven which collapsed, I gather, through sheer inefficiency and sloppy management. Anyway, their engagement was announced, and then almost immediately something took place (I never quite knew what) which opened her eyes and she came to her senses and broke it off. My dear, *would* you believe it, the swine kicked up the most frightful song and dance and threatened to take her to court for breach of promise! That, at least, was the *official* version. But behind the scenes, what he was really up to was far, far worse – nothing short of blackmail! Unless you pay up, he said – or words to that effect – I intend to inform the Yellow Press that the first cousin once removed of a former British Ambassador to the United States of America is practising the Lesbian perversion with a noted actress as black as the ace of spades! Oh, it jolly nearly caused the most godal*mighty* scandal – it was touch and go! I can't tell you exactly what happened for the simple reason that I don't know – but I do know that Ursie's father was too wonderful and staunch and somehow or other strings were pulled and the situation was saved. But it *could* have been ugly. Very, very ugly indeed.'

As often with Hope's bombshells, there was something a little inconclusive and not entirely convincing about this one; in spite of the impression she produced of substantiating her story with graphic detail, I remained uncertain about what exactly had happened in it. My mother was also bemused.

'All that is fascinating,' she said, 'and yet it doesn't quite ring true to me. It's not that I'm surprised that Yvo didn't tell me about it. Apart from wanting to spare me anxiety, he had a horror of gossip and simply never repeated anything unpleasant about other people. I believe he had once confided something to my predecessor – Ursula's mother – and she passed it on to her sister, and a whole lot of mischief was made as a result. He always said one could never trust a woman with a secret – Shakespeare says the same thing somewhere, doesn't he? And I suppose he was right: I might easily have mentioned something about Ursula and this man, without thinking, to somebody else. But what I *can't* believe is that he would have been able to keep it from me if he had been seriously worried about her at that time. On the other hand, do you think it could have been that which brought on his illness? It was around then that he started having trouble with his heart . . .'

'Would it have worried him?' I asked.

'Oh, unbearably – Ursula being unhappy, I mean, not the scandal, he wouldn't have minded that at all. He refused to admit that homosexuality even existed, you know: if I ever said that a friend of mine was queer, he would tease me about having a nasty mind. He would just have thought that his daughter was being persecuted by some motive-lessly malevolent fiend, like Iago, and he would have suffered deeply for her sake. Poor angel, his loyalty to his loved ones did sometimes lead him to back the wrong horse – not in this case, of course, but I was thinking of a *cause célèbre* during the First War, before I entered the family. Do you remember it, Hope? Mrs Warburton-Wells.'

'Do I!' said Hope. 'I could pass an examination on it.'

Mrs Warburton-Wells was in fact the elder sister of my father's first wife – the one who had received, and betrayed, the fatal confidence. A 'professional beauty' and favourite of King Edward VII, she was famous for her boisterous high spirits and daring practical jokes. When she descended a staircase it was never on foot, but either sliding down the banisters or seated on a tray; once, when leaving Sandring-ham after a shooting party, instead of leaning out of the carriage and waving a last goodbye with her graceful arm, she had stuck an equally graceful leg out of the window and waved that.

'The Warburton-Wells affair was extremely unsavoury but wildly enjoyable,' said Hope. 'She was getting rather long in the tooth but still had plenty of pep so when the war broke out she turned her house into a convalescent home for wounded soldiers, both officers and men. She designed a most becoming uniform for herself and took some phoney title – Matron-in-Chief or Hospital Commandant or something – but really all she did was carry on with the patients. OK, bully for her, you might say – except that one of them wasn't having any, a young private who had just got engaged to be married. She was so livid with rage when he turned her down that she cooked up some story and tried to have the wretched boy court-martialled for cowardice, if you please! All the top brass were her ex-lovers so they backed her up to the hilt. If he'd been found guilty he'd have been shot at dawn – for not going to bed with Mrs Warburton-Wells! A bit much, don't you agree? But he managed to bring an action for slander against her first, which thank God he won, so justice was done in the end.'

'Well,' said my mother, 'all I know is that darling Yvo went willingly into the witness box to give evidence for her *defence*. He just could not believe that his own sister-in-law would be such a monster as to ruin the poor soldier merely because her sexual vanity had been hurt. As a rule he was absolutely right about everything – it was a mixture of sweet natural innocence and blind family loyalty that made him lose his judgment on this occasion.'

'There's a lot of him in Ursula,' said Hope.

After this, Hope's business trips to London ceased, and we felt ourselves further removed from Ursula than ever. My mother did, however, receive a letter from Ruby, giving a different Brooklyn address. 'Above, our new abode, where we have been in residence for the past month,' she wrote.

'Another letter was started, in which I told of my unhappiness at having to give up our very nice house and my complete dissatisfaction with this cramped, inconvenient and unsightly apartment – Ursula's valiant battle with the City Fathers having ended in defeat. But it did not seem fair to pass on to you my personal misery, so I destroyed it. And now, though in less detail and fewer words, I have managed to duplicate my original imposition. Forgive me! Ursula has planned a letter to you for some time, but she is quite worn out when she gets home in the evenings and her weekends are spent in recuperation. This from me is merely a "push" in the right direction . . .' There was a terse postscript from Ursula: 'Be a saint and give the new address to all my friends. Have misplaced my address book in the move. No doubt will find it in a few years' time.'

But, in the end, Hope's prophecy that Ursula would never return to England proved to be false. Early in 1959, Ursula wrote to my mother that, in celebration of her recent retirement from the Veterans' Bureau with a pension and a 'handshake', she had decided to come over for three weeks in the spring – this time accompanied by Ruby, who was said to be eagerly looking forward to making the acquaintance of Ursula's family at last.

I had just started working on a glossy magazine, which paid slightly more than the publishing job had done, and we could now afford to dispense with the South American lodgers – so there was enough room in our house to accommodate Ursula and Ruby during their visit. My mother proposed giving a cocktail party in their honour, and asked them to send a list of the guests they wished her to invite. This reached us only ten days before they were due to arrive themselves; my mother happened to be abroad at the time, and so I had the task of ascertaining the whereabouts, if any, of their friends on the list (some of them once-celebrated names that had dropped out of common currency over the past thirty years) and running them to earth.

It was easy enough to trace Fleur. Having married, comparatively late in life and with a certain amount of publicity, she was now called Lady Carter-Banks and was listed under that name in the London telephone directory. But no sooner had I made this discovery, than another letter arrived from Ursula: Fleur, after all, was on no account to be invited because Ruby did not care to meet her and, should there be the slightest danger of Lady Carter-Banks appearing at the party, Ruby herself would refuse to attend it. 'Sorry if this has landed you in the soup,' Ursula wrote. 'If you'd be an angel and wire me Fleur's address I'll write to her and try to explain. I'll promise to come and see her on my own while I'm over there – I *think* Ruby can be persuaded to agree to that (*touch wood*!)'

Finding Bunch also presented no difficulty: she was even more famous than Fleur and, like her, had acquired a title, being now known as Dame Beryl Bunbury. She ran (among other concerns) a chain of shops selling cheap, chic fashion accessories which were successfully exported all over the world, and she had been awarded the DBE in recognition of her services to the national economy. When I rang her up she was extremely friendly – 'What *glorious* news!' – and she solved my remaining problems in tracking down the other people on the guest list, promptly providing the present address of such legendary black entertainers as Turner Layton and Elisabeth Welch.

'How thrilling,' I said. 'I used to love their records. Tell me, am I right in thinking that Ruby was never a singer herself?'

'Quite right. She can't sing a note.'

I explained that my insatiable curiosity about Ruby had led me to search for references to her in every possible source, and one of the few I had managed to find (in some obscure theatrical memoir of the 1920s) had described her singing a negro spiritual at a musical *soirée*. This had been puzzling me for ages.

'Oh, that wasn't her,' said Bunch. That would have been the other Ruby Richards.'

'The *other* Ruby Richards?'

'Yes. Wasn't it awful? There was another woman with exactly the same name – also black, and also on the stage. Ruby minded dreadfully about it: it couldn't have been more maddening. Both of them absolutely refused to change their names, so it all went on being frightfully confusing. You're not the first person to fall into that trap, by a long chalk. Anyone else I can help you with for the party?'

'What about Enid ffrench?'

'Oh dear, *too* sad – she died last year.'

'And Fay Hitchcock?'

Bunch hesitated before replying, and then chuckled. 'No, love, I'm afraid la Hitchcock *won't* be able to make it. It's all a bit embarrassing, but the truth is that she's landed herself in jug and is likely to stay there for quite some time.'

'Whatever for?'

'Assault. If she'd been a chap they'd have called it Grievous Bodily Harm.'

It seemed that Fay, after recovering from 'that whopping great nervous breakdown she had not long after the war', had found employment as a Gym and Geography mistress in an expensive boarding school for girls; unfortunately, during an argument with one of her favourite pupils, she had lost her temper to the point of punching the child on the jaw. There had been a muted scandal (reminiscent of *The Children's Hour*, the banned play that Fay had wanted to see twenty years ago) as a result of which the school had been forced to close down.

5

I had been speculating about Ruby with so obsessive an intensity for so many years – at least a quarter of a century – that I was prepared for our first meeting to contain an element of unreality; when I was finally confronted by her visible presence, it failed to make any impression on me at all. I had come home early from the office, to find her sitting at the dining-room table having tea with Ursula and my mother; I joined them, but after spending several hours in her company I would have been incapable of describing her appearance beyond the vaguest outline. However, I can fill in this dazzled blank and reconstruct what I must have seen from evidence provided by two photographs which I still possess.

One, taken on board the *Queen Elizabeth* during the voyage that had brought them over, shows four elderly ladies grouped cheerfully round a table in a room like a hotel lounge. At a first glance, they might be taken for Daughters of the American Revolution out on a decorous spree. Two of them – plump, matronly figures – appear to be sisters; a third, sitting bolt upright, slightly scowling and stiffly brandishing a cigarette, is Ursula – frozen by camera-shyness into an unnaturally formal pose. The fourth is a delicate little thing, with shining smooth silver hair and a radiant smile, elegantly clothed in a simple but expensive-looking black dress, clearly the star of the occasion: Ruby, who was then approaching her middle seventies. On the back of the picture, in Ruby's handwriting, are the words: The night I won 30 dollars at Bingo.

The second photograph was taken, without their knowledge, after they had landed. Ruby and Ursula are queuing at a desk before going through Immigration and Customs.

Both are in profile. Concealed impatience has made Ursula's serious expression almost grim; her short hair has been pushed behind her ears and a wispy bit of veiling has been crookedly tied round her pudding-basin hat. Clearly tired, she stands in a slumped position with her elbow on the desk. Behind her, Ruby's head is uplifted to give her a mildly martyred look. Her smart tweed coat contrasts with Ursula's shabby fur; she wears a beret set far back over her silky *coiffure* and a spotted veil covers the upper part of her face, enhancing the attraction of her raised eyebrows, tiny tilted nose and shapely pouting mouth.

At tea, on that first day of their visit, Ursula looked much happier than she did in the photographs. 'I can't believe that we're all four actually together at last, sitting here in this sweet little house!' she said. 'I'm longing to explore the neighbourhood, which of course is full of memories for me. Ruby, I'm afraid you're in for a conducted tour! How well I remember, on Sunday mornings, playing tennis with Father in Cadogan Square, then strolling up Sloane Street very pleased with myself for having taken all that exercise to meet my friends for lunch at the Hyde Park Hotel, which was a favourite haunt of ours. The barman there was famous for mixing the best White Lady in London.'

As part of my duties on the glossy magazine was to review plays I had been given two seats for a matinee of *Othello* at Stratford-upon-Avon, starring Paul Robeson. I asked Ruby if she would like to come with me, as I knew Robeson was an old friend of hers. Ursula looked at her expectantly, her eyes bright with pleasure. Ruby accepted formally and gravely, but did not immediately appear to be overjoyed by the invitation. Some ten minutes later, however, when the conversation had passed on to other subjects, she slowly and deliberately cut off a sliver of cake from a larger piece that she had been about to eat. Balancing the morsel on her knife, she solemnly transferred it from her plate to mine. I looked at it in perplexity. 'That,' she explained archly, 'is for *you*. To thank you for taking me to see Paul on Saturday.' She gazed at me fixedly for a while, and then turned to Ursula, who was anxiously watching this little drama. 'He's my buddy,' she said.

It was hoped that the Stratford outing would consolidate this promising *rapport* between Ruby and myself, and establish an even closer relationship. To some extent it did so. I had hired a chauffeur-driven car for the day and booked a table for lunch at a highly recommended hotel: this was to be an occasion. As it ceremoniously unfolded, two separate aspects of Ruby's personality were revealed to me. One was a frail, unassuming old lady, easily tired and anxious to please. The other was a self-conscious siren, who set a high price on the value of her company and (once this was understood) took pains to elevate any shared experience into the special category of a treat. Like the hero of a romantic American film, I seemed to be forever clutching the back of her chair as she serenely lowered herself into it; leaving the car by one door, rushing round behind it and opening the other to facilitate her exit; helping her in and out of her coat, holding her handbag and lighting her cigarette. It was as if the slight hint of a Southern drawl in her voice had confused me into attempting a slapdash caricature of old-world antebellum courtesy. Ruby kindly ignored the farcical element in this behaviour, and rewarded me by dignifying our adventure with an atmosphere of complicity, heightening the simple pleasures it afforded by subtly suggesting that we were a couple of kids playing hooky from authority – a gang of two.

We talked mainly about plays, films and books, but during lunch Ruby volunteered a few details of her family history. Her grandmother had been a slave on a Mississippi estate. At the age of fifteen she had been raped by a white man, the plantation owner's son. She died giving birth to his daughter. This child was smuggled to the North during the Civil War, grew up to be a beauty, and went on the stage. She married a gifted musician, who came from a prominent middle-class Negro family with lawyers, doctors and teachers among its members. They had eight children, one of whom was Ruby.

We just had time to peep at Anne Hathaway's cottage and Shakespeare's birthplace before the matinée began. Ruby was most complimentary about the design of the Memorial Theatre, declaring that it was far superior to any she had seen in the States. She also praised the production – 'A *much* higher standard than you could find back home.' For me, both of these were of interest only as a background to Paul Robeson's performance, which had been disliked by most of the critics but which I found overwhelming. Some of the most beautiful lines ever written were spoken by one of the most beautiful voices ever heard. His impressive stature and physical strength made the gradual exposure of Othello's weakness seem to threaten an unthinkable cosmic disorder; when he crashed to the ground in a sudden fit, one recognised a primitive dread of some arbitrary last collapse; when he said: 'Chaos is come again', the rumble of the syllables sounded like a warning echo of the primordial void.

After the play, Ruby took me backstage to congratulate the star. We found him still standing in the wings, quite alone and at some distance from anybody else, naked to the waist, pouring with sweat and rubbing himself down with a towel – more like an athlete than a leading man. We approached him timidly. When he saw Ruby, he gave a roar of surprise and delight. I remained a few paces apart, to observe a long, intimate and animated conversation between the handsome giant and the fragile, dainty woman. The scene moved and deeply satisfied me, because it realised almost exactly one of the fantasies I had entertained so persistently since childhood about the exciting and exalted world which Ursula had entered when she went off to live with Ruby.

At a quarter to six on the day of the party, Ursula, Ruby, my mother and I were posted about the drawing-room in attitudes made artificial by apprehension: even the room looked quite unlike its usual self although no palpable alteration had been made to it. We could hear the ominous movements of the butler hired from Searcey's as he polished glasses and positioned bottles at a bar he had created in the dining-room across the narrow hall. Ursula was handsomely arrayed in a green and gold caftan; Ruby wore a pretty little cocktail dress which showed off her still beautiful breasts and legs. The knowledge that Ursula was longing for a drink, and that she had promised Ruby not to have one, raised the nervous tension of the waiting period beyond the norm: it was a long three quarters of an hour before the doorbell rang. But from that moment on, there were no more worries. Everybody on the original list turned up (except for Fay, Enid and Fleur), all eager to welcome the guests of honour, to tell them (and be told in return) how little they had changed after so long an absence and how deeply they had been missed.

It was Bunch more than anyone who made the party go. An air of authority, which I had sensed in her at our first meeting in the Wigmore Street flat when there had been little apparent justification for it, had matured and mellowed with her worldly success and now infused her rather gruff manner with a potent charm. She was extremely excited by the *Nouvelle Vague* and told us all about the brilliant young film directors in France, introducing into the occasion a heady feeling of being behind the scenes and in the know at the very latest thing, and thus saving it from too strong a dependence on nostalgic reminiscence. But she was equally adroit at evoking a pleasant past. 'Darling!' she called across to Ursula. 'Remember Punkadillo?'

Ursula was delighted. 'Can I ever forget him?'

'When I first knew Ursula, back in the twenties,' Bunch explained, 'she had this pet jerboa. A tiny little thing with enormous eyes, which moved in huge leaps like a kangaroo. I shall never forget the sensation she caused when she took it with her to tea at the Ritz.'

'Oh, no, I'm sure I never did that,' said Ursula. 'But I did once smuggle him into the cinema with me. I thought nobody had noticed — but a few days later I read in the paper that the movie-house was going to close as someone had reported seeing a rat in it! Fancy you remembering Punkie!'

Bunch took me aside and lowered her voice. 'Tell me, dear, before I put my foot in it — is Spencer still in the picture, do you happen to know?'

'No, I believe he died a few years ago.'

'Oh dear, poor soul. I wasn't certain whether to ask for news of him or not: the last I heard, he had become rather a trial.'

'Did you know him?'

'Yes, a bit, in the old days. He was awfully sweet, but *the* most tremendous lecher. I remember getting a terrible ticking off from Ursula because I wouldn't go to bed with him. She was simply livid. Accused me of every kind of racial prejudice, which I *did* think a little unfair . . .' Seeing that Ruby was approaching us, she turned towards her and continued smoothly: 'I was just boasting about how long you and I have been friends. Bet you don't remember where and when we first met! It was at a party for the cast of *Four Saints in Three Acts* in New York in 1934! Freddie Ashton had invited me, and you and Ursula came with Carl Van Vechten.'

'And to this day,' said Ruby, 'I can hear Ursula's cry of rapture when she saw you there. "*Bunch!*" She was in the seventh heaven.'

'But rather cross with me for being in New York without letting her know. I'd planned to surprise her, you see.'

'They did a revival of *Four Saints* a few years ago . . .' Ruby began.

'I caught it when it came to Paris! Leontyne Price sang too divinely for any words. I can't tell you how moving it was to see Alice B. Toklas sitting in the audience . . . so proud of Gertrude, and missing her so terribly.'

'I know, I know . . . Carl keeps in close touch with Alice and sometimes reads us her letters. She sounds a perfect honey. She always calls Carl her Papa Woojums and he calls her his Mama Woojums – and Miss Stein of course was their Baby Woojums! I think that's so cunning, don't you?'

'Too sweet,' said Bunch rather drily. 'I must say, this *is* a joyful reunion – a real gathering of the clans, *non*? Now let's have a proper look and see who's here.' She dipped into one of the big, bold handbags that had become her trademark (and were sometimes just referred to as 'Beryl Bunbury bags'), extracted a glittering pair of harlequin spectacles, pushed them on to her nose and surveyed the room. '*So* many old chums . . . I can't get over it. But I see no sign of Flash – or Fleur – or whatever she calls herself now. Couldn't she come?'

'If you are referring,' said Ruby with saccharine sarcasm, 'to *Lady* Carter-Banks, I regret to say that Her *Lady*ship has been informed that her presence here would not be welcomed. And now, dear hearts, if you will excuse me, I see that a very special friend of mine has just arrived and is looking rather lost . . .' She drifted off.

'Ouch!' said Bunch, making a rueful grimace. 'I seem to have put my big foot in it after all. The *way* she emphasised that title! Have you ever heard anything so sinister?'

'Do you know why she hates Fleur so much?'

'A bit of the green-eyed monster, but there's more to it than that. I believe it dates back to the very first time Ursula and Ruby met. Flash was there too, and perhaps she felt her nose had been put out of joint or something, anyway I understand that she said something tactless and patronising about black people, you know what a silly ass she can be when she gets on her high horse. I assumed it had been made up long ago, but apparently not.'

As often with successful parties, the festivity ended as abruptly as it began. Suddenly at nine o'clock there seemed to be a panic rush for the exit, leaving the room empty except for Ursula, Ruby, my mother, myself and Bunch, who announced that she was taking us all out to dinner at the Brompton Grill. It was a gently convivial meal, until Bunch made the innocent mistake of asking Ruby's opinion of Marlon Brando. 'I think he's such a marvellous actor. Weren't you in a play with him once, before he became famous? Do tell us what he's like.'

Ruby smiled fondly. 'Ah . . . my Marlon. How I love that boy! He has had the worst possible press, but in fact he is the kindest, most sensitive human being you could hope to find. He is just too good to be true – and vice versa. It seems impossible for him to avoid – how shall I phrase it? – female complications, put it that way. But none of us is perfect.'

Ursula looked stern. 'I hardly know him, but what I do know I can't say I care for. A very conceited young man indeed.'

Ruby continued: 'It so happened that, some years after I first met Marlon, I had to undergo a brief period of hospitalisation. In the intervening time, he had become a great star – but that did not prevent him from coming to visit me in the public ward. No, sirree! And you should have seen those young nurses when this celebrated Adonis came marching in – they were all swooning away like bobby-soxers! Oh, I got *very* special treatment after that, believe you me!'

'Why on earth shouldn't he come and see you?' said Ursula pugnaciously. 'I should hope he would. And I think it's shocking that the nursing staff made a pet of you as a result. When I was a VAD favouritism was strictly forbidden, and quite right too. What about all the other poor patients who didn't have the luck to know Marlon Brando?'

Ruby pretended not to hear. 'Oh, he's such a darling person! As you know, he is . . . what shall I say . . . extremely easy on the eye – and in the acting department he is a very, very great artist indeed. But also – and here I *do* know what I'm talking about – he is the loveliest and loyalest of friends.'

'Ruby's quite potty on this subject,' Ursula muttered. 'I wish she'd get off it.'

'And on top of all that,' Ruby pursued, 'he is an extremely amusing companion. I remember, when he first became a buddy of mine, he had just been on tour in some vehicle for Tallulah which closed on the road . . .'

'I *hate* this story,' said Ursula, quite loudly. Ruby slightly turned her head and shoulders away from her, to concentrate on Bunch. 'And he was so comical about it!' she went on. 'It seems that in the old days Miss Bankhead had always taken it for granted that the juvenile lead would . . .'

'I refuse to listen to this!' Ursula interrupted, putting her hands over her ears.

'As you choose, my precious . . . the juvenile lead would – er – enter into a romantic relationship with her. It was kind of an old theatrical tradition, you see. But I'm afraid she was barking up the wrong tree with my Marlon! Oh my, oh my! His imitation of Miss B. trying to seduce him had us all in a roar! If only you'd heard him, Bunch, you'd have died laughing. I'm not the brilliant mimic he is so I can't do justice to her husky voice and deep, deep Southern accent, but apparently one night she . . .'

'Stop it!' Ursula shouted. 'If you go on with this dirty libel on Tallulah, I warn you, I shall go straight home! All right, so maybe she *did* make a pass at him, but what's so hysterically funny about that? He should have thought himself damned lucky, in my opinion. You seem to forget that Tallulah is an old and dear friend of mine and, whatever her faults, she is in her own way a very fine and brave and beautiful person. I can't *stand* hearing her talked about in this degrading way – and what is more I *won't* stand it! And don't try to make out I'm tipsy, because I stayed on the wagon all day!'

Ruby leaned forward and clasped Ursula's hand. 'I *know* you did, darling heart, and all honour to you! Of *course* I won't continue with the anecdote if it upsets you. This has been such a heavenly evening, it would be a wicked shame to spoil it now. So – a ban on Marlon and Tallulah from now on!' She earnestly pressed Ursula's hand and slowly withdrew her own. Then, turning to Bunch, she added in an undertone: 'I'll tell you the rest some other time, if it interests you. It was silly of me to forget how *crazily* jealous she always becomes at the mere mention of that boy.'

Ursula, fortunately, did not hear this. With glistening eyes, she was herself whispering to me: 'I'm so sorry to make a scene. People say it clears the air but I'm afraid it does the reverse. I just couldn't help it, though. I'm positive she was trying to provoke me on purpose, and the only reason I can think of is that she wanted to punish me for going to see poor old Flash while *she* was off gallivanting with you at the theatre.'

6

A year after their return to America we heard that Ursula and Ruby had moved house once again. Their new apartment – still in Brooklyn – was in a large tower block. It was small, but skilfully designed for maximum comfort and equipped with every possible labour-saving device. They loved it. We could glimpse a corner of it in a coloured photograph they sent us, which showed them both, happily smiling, sitting side by side on a sofa. They were wearing the clothes they had worn at my mother's cocktail party; a portrait in oils of my father as a young subaltern in the 16th Lancers, painted in the 1880s, hung on the wall behind them. On the back was written: 'Christmas, 1960. Ain't she beautiful? Love Ursula' and beneath that: 'Ain't *she* beautiful! Love Ruby'.

There followed a presumably contented silence of four years, and then suddenly I received a letter from Ruby. 'I have taken the liberty,' she wrote, 'of giving your name and address to a friend of mine who will be in London shortly, and of asking him to present my greetings to you. I did so because I am sure it would be a mutually agreeable acquaintance. I mentioned the possibility of your being out of the city so he is quite prepared to miss you. However I will appreciate the courtesy of your permitting him to call on you, if it will be convenient. He is about your age, a charming person who shares with you an interest in things theatrical. He was assistant stage manager on *Twenty-Eight Young Men Bathe by the Shore*, a fact that we small fry in the company resented because, knowing him to be a very rich young man, we felt that someone less affluent should have the job. *Young Men* was not far into its phenomenal success before we learned to love him. He is now producing on his own, mainly in the off-Broadway field, and I daresay his visit to London has something to do with theatre. Naturally he will be busy for he is certainly not a dilettante and may not have the leisure to contact you. But if he does you will know who he is and why I want you two to know each other. I hope all is well with you very dear folks, who have a place in my heart and in my prayers. Fondly, Ruby. P.S. I nearly forgot! *Beau Maclean* is the name of the gentleman in question.'

Beau Maclean must have been as busy during his London trip as Ruby predicted – or possibly it was cancelled at the last moment; at all events, I heard nothing from him. But any disappointment that this minor anti-climax might have caused me was soon overwhelmed by excitement in the knowledge that, after waiting so long, I was actually on the point of going to America myself. I had recently left the glossy magazine for a job on the colour supplement of a Sunday newspaper, and one of my first foreign assignments, early in 1965, was to interview a famous actress who was filming on location in Mexico. I would have to fly out direct to Mexico City, but on the way back I could arrange to break the journey for a night or two in New York.

So my first experience of that city came after a bewildering fortnight spent in the hysterical atmosphere of big-budget multinational movie-making, where journalists were simultaneously courted and kept at bay, against the inhospitable background of the fierce Mexican landscape; by contrast New York, with its cosy skyscrapers and friendly freeways, seemed reassuringly familiar. As the plane touched down, I had a sense of return rather than arrival; riding in a yellow cab from the airport to the Gramercy Park Hotel, I felt the placid anticipation of a traveller who is nearing home. By the time I had checked in and unpacked, it was early evening: I rang Ursula and Ruby (it was the latter who answered) to tell them I was on my way.

But things did not at first go smoothly. On the previous night a taxi driver had been murdered in Brooklyn and now I found that driver after driver refused to take me there. Realising that I was going to be late, I started to panic. At last one man, albeit repressively, allowed me to enter his cab. I had written the address on a piece of paper, which I gave him. He glanced at it, then told me that he had no idea where it was but would put me down somewhere in the neighbourhood. Unlike the New York cabbies in Hollywood films, who incessantly and wittily converse over their shoulders with their fares, this one didn't speak a word throughout the journey. As we crossed the Brooklyn Bridge (which did look as hallucinatory as it does in films) I fancied that the back of his head might have belonged to Charon, silently ferrying an apprehensive passenger over the Styx.

He stopped the car, apparently in obedience to some arbitrary decision, after about half an hour's drive on the Brooklyn side, speechlessly accepted the money I gave him, then shot off. Conscious of having been dumped, I stood on the kerb, at a loss. My surroundings appeared to be entirely without character; I might have been in any town in any country; there seemed to be no passers-by. Brooklyn, I knew, was immense: would I ever find my way? I walked on a few paces, until I came to a crossroads, where instinct made me turn to the left. I was looking down another long, equally featureless street, at the far end of which a solitary female figure could be seen in the dusk, standing erect and peering in every direction like an anxious sentry, clearly on the lookout for an awaited stranger. The figure waved: it was Ursula. As impervious to surprise as a dreamer, I walked to meet her with the complacent lack of haste that follows a reprieve.

Relief at my arrival increased her natural reserve and she was almost as taciturn as the taxi driver while she hurried me into the building. We emerged from the elevator on the eighteenth floor and walked down a corridor towards the distant figure of Ruby framed in the open door of their apartment, her arms extended in greeting. 'Welcome, welcome!' she cried, as soon as we came within earshot. When I got nearer, I saw that she was holding a glass containing whisky, soda and ice already mixed. She presented this to me before we embraced. 'I did not want you to have to wait *one extra second* before tasting your very first drink in our Home Sweet Home!'

She led me through a minute hallway into a small, bright, crowded room, filled with plants and cut flowers. The furniture was new and plain while the pictures and ornaments were antique and elaborate. Ruby settled me into a comfortable armchair. 'Now you just relax and enjoy a cosy chat with your beloved sister while I fix something for our supper. She's been so blissfully excited ever since she knew you were coming! And just this once, as a special treat to mark the occasion, she's going to have a highball too!'

Ruby ceremoniously handed Ursula a drink and then moved gracefully behind a waist-high partition which divided the kitchen from the living area. Ursula gazed after her, almost as if she had never seen her before, and murmured: 'She walks in beauty . . .'

'What nonsense!' said Ruby. 'Don't forget, I'll be eighty next birthday!'

'You weren't supposed to hear,' said Ursula. Turning her attention to me, she saw that I was studying a painting on the wall. It was a portrait of my father's mother in old age. 'Isn't that lovely of darling Grumps? You never knew her, did you? What you missed! How you would have adored her! I've always said, I've been lucky enough in my life to know two saints. One was Grumps – and the other is over there in the kitchen at this moment, cooking her own very special chili con carne! Wait one moment and I'll show you something that will interest you . . .' She fetched a volume from a low bookshelf in the hallway and placed it in my hands. 'My most treasured possession. Grumps's Bible.'

Bound in white vellum, the Bible had been transformed by my grandmother into a combination of personal diary, family history and commonplace-book. Flowers and grasses had been pressed between its pages and also tiny loose photographs, faded to the same pale brown; favourite passages had been underlined, or copied out in the margins and on the flyleaves; the births, marriages and deaths of children, grandchildren and even some great-grandchildren had been recorded in her ample Victorian hand – and between the years 1914 and 1918 the deaths in battle of more distant relations and of the sons of friends had been added to the Roll of Honour. Beside a drawing of two attenuated angels in the manner of Burne-Jones she had written: 'The more of those whom we love that God takes unto Himself, the greater the Communion of Saints with all our Beloveds. Easter Sunday, April 20th, 1919'. One photograph larger than the others had been pasted on to the inside of the back cover. This showed Ursula, wearing school uniform and a straw boater, seated on a bench in a town square between her grandparents, a distinguished white-haired couple dressed in formal black, while a greyhound and a dachshund, vague as apparitions formed by ectoplasm, wandered out of focus away from the camera's scrutiny. Beneath it were the words 'June 1910 – the day we went to London – our last season – sweet of darling Ursie but Fly and Welcome refused to sit still!!!' On the opposite page two quotations had been transcribed, one from the Old Testament and one from the New: 'He that covereth a transgression seeketh love; but he that repeateth a matter separateth very friends (Proverbs, 17:9)' and 'Love worketh no ill to his neighbour; therefore love is the fulfilling of the law (Romans, 13:10)'.

'Come and get it!' Ruby called out gaily, untying the apron she had put on to protect her elegant white trouser suit. We joined her at a card-table covered by a lace cloth on which three places had been invitingly laid.

Before starting the meal Ruby paused for a while in a significant manner, as if about to say grace. 'I just want you to know,' she said at last, 'how proud I am to offer hospitality to a member of my darling's family. I don't think anything could truly mar the happiness of the years we have spent together – but I confess that I have had my one little private cause for sadness. And that is the nagging sense of guilt that – through my fault, however unwittingly – she has been separated for so long from her own flesh and blood and the land of her first allegiance. Your presence here this evening eases that feeling of – no, not remorse, let us say of *regret* – just a little bit.'

I was wondering what on earth to reply to this when Ursula came to my rescue. 'Don't, darling, please,' she said to Ruby. 'We've *been* through this so often before. I knew exactly what I was doing all along and there is nothing for anyone to regret. Well, I don't know about you guys, but I'm ravenous,' she went on cheerfully. 'Gosh, this looks good – do let's start. To tell you the truth,' she said to me while we ate, 'we're both a bit shaken by the death of Malcolm X. I expect you read about his assassination last week. The police are trying to make out that he was killed by the Black Muslims.'

'His own people,' said Ruby bitterly. 'In the bad old days, when an atrocity was committed against a member of my race, it was so easy to feel indignation against the whites. Now, it isn't so simple. I find that peculiarly distressing.'

'I *hate* extremism and violence as much as anyone,' said Ursula. 'Everything in me longs for moderation and peace. But when years and years of moderation and peaceful protest produce so little result, one can at least understand *why* you get a frightening fanatic like Elijah Muhammad.'

'Maybe,' said Ruby. 'But I also understand that such people do immeasurable – perhaps even fatal – harm to the cause that they claim to espouse.'

'Anyway, I'm by no means convinced that it happened the way they said it did,' said Ursula. 'I shouldn't be surprised if the FBI wasn't behind the whole thing.'

'Oh, let's not talk politics tonight – it's so boring for our guest,' said Ruby. Before I could remonstrate, she addressed me directly. 'We've planned a great treat for you after supper. You're going to meet a really lovely person, our very dearest friend in all the world. We're taking you to see Bobby Smith.'

'Not *the* Bobby Smith? The pianist?'

'Yes, *the* Bobby Smith!' said Ursula triumphantly. 'There – I told you he'd know all about him.'

'I only know that he ran a wonderful nightclub called Bobby's Place which I used to read about and longed to visit,' I said.

'Very few English people have heard of him because he's never been out of the States,' said Ruby. 'But I'd say that throughout the thirties Bobby's Place was just about the most glamorous joint uptown. Everybody went there but it never got ruined. Bobby's taste, and the sheer charm of his personality, managed to keep it exclusive.'

'I think you're rather giving the wrong impression by calling it "exclusive",' said Ursula. 'I'm sure Bobby never wanted to keep anybody out.'

'Of course not – he's the most unsnobbish person that ever lived – but we must face the fact, darling, that the basic idea of any club is to limit its clientele to a certain type of member,' said Ruby. 'It was the people who patronised it, as much as the music and entertainment they went to enjoy, that gave it such a pleasant atmosphere.'

'Anyway, it's been closed now for about twenty-five years,' said Ursula. 'But he still lives in a beautiful apartment only a few doors away from where Ruby was living when I first came over here and where I myself spent so many happy and exciting years. I know you'll love Bobby: he's a pussy-cat. The car's on the blink, so I can't drive you – just as well, no doubt, as I intend to have another highball when I get to Bobby's. We'll have to take a cab.'

Luckily, taxi drivers did not seem nervous of *leaving* Brooklyn – not even to go to Harlem, where there had been recent riots in the wake of Malcolm X's murder. Sitting in a cab between Ursula and Ruby, I crossed the magical bridge again; once on the other side, we all three became infected by the party spirit and started to sing Rodgers and Hart's 'Manhattan' in loud tuneless voices.

The party spirit accompanied us into Bobby's flat, where it rose to an almost Bacchanalian pitch. The place seemed purpose-built for revelry – fantastic as a pleasure-dome, ephemeral as a painted backcloth or circus tent. The walls were black, the curtains were gold, the furniture was upholstered in plum velvet, the bar was decorated by silver stars on a ground of midnight blue. The general effect was of a ballet design by Bakst crossed with the dream night-nursery of a precocious little girl.

Bobby, a black man in his sixties, looked as young and lean and supple as he had in his heyday when his nickname had been 'Snakehips Smith'. The powerful attraction which he exerted was generated by a combination of elegant refinement and affectionate spontaneity. After embracing us all and calling us 'Pussy-cat', he set out to show us a good time. He sat down at a white grand piano and played and sang: smart show tunes with saucy lyrics by Cole Porter, tragic love songs which had become identified with the mythic martyrdom of Billie Holiday, traditional spirituals which had been given a new resonance by Martin Luther King. He performed without appearing to seek applause but with the modest generosity of a host putting a new LP on the record player for the amusement of his guests. Then he entertained us with anecdotes about Bobby's Place in its palmy days and the fascinating people – gangsters, boxers, film stars, kings – who had come there.

'Hey – I've an idea,' said Ruby. 'Ursula hasn't seen her long-lost brother for ages and he's only in town for one night. They must have so much to talk over. So why don't Bobby and I go into the room next door and give them a little precious time alone together? Because we've got plenty to talk about as well, haven't we, Pussy-cat?'

As it happened, Ursula and I didn't have a lot to say to each other; but there was nothing awkward about the silence that soon fell between us. We were like two constant companions who have no need to converse, enjoying a night out in a favourite haunt – perhaps at Bobby's Place, which I could imagine having reopened its ghostly doors after a quarter of a century to provide a congenial setting for our quiet celebration. It seemed to me that I had at last learned the answer to a question I had been asking ever since, at the age of five, I had heard a band on a boat play 'I'm a Dreamer – Aren't We All?' and I felt a sense of calm fulfilment.

Ursula's face wore a contented expression although there were tears in her eyes. 'I'm so glad you've met Bobby,' she said after a while. 'His existence takes a great load off my mind. My one big worry for years and years has been who would take care of Ruby when I kicked the bucket. My pension dies with me, of course, and so does the tiny income I still get from what was left of our family fortune. I've saved and saved all my working life and I'm glad to say there's a nice little sum in escrow – absolutely and *sacredly* untouchable by me while I live – that she'll inherit. But the important thing is that, so long as Bobby is around, I know she'll be lovingly looked after and won't be lonely.'

After another comfortable silence, she began to talk about the past, before I was born. 'It was wonderful in a way, I suppose. And one was always surrounded by love. Yet I was never as happy as perhaps I should have been. It was all that goddam privilege that stuck in my throat. I don't mean that it was abused by my parents and grand-parents – though, heaven knows, there were some perfectly ghastly specimens among their family and friends, callous and selfish and worldly people like – well, I'd better not name names. Your darling mother would know who I mean – though she's always been so sweet and has such vitality that she managed to get on with them all without minding too much. I'm afraid I wasn't very good at that. But even with the wonderful ones, like Grumps – well, I suppose I really felt that *nobody* could be *quite* wonderful enough to justify that amount of privilege. Because all privilege must be won at the expense of other people's deprivation. And what could justify that? When I told Ruby, at dinner, that I've never regretted anything, I meant it. But of course she is right in thinking that I have sometimes been terribly homesick. Not for the place (though I do still miss riding on the Wiltshire downs!) but for the people: for Grumps and Jack and . . .' A sob forced her to pause.

'We've never really spoken about . . .' (she couldn't say the word 'Father') 'have we? It's agony, how I miss him. When he died . . . I've felt so terrifyingly bereft ever since. And in a way before that, too. Did I make him suffer a very great deal? I never quite knew. He said not. The last time I saw him, he said . . . he told me that . . . that all he wanted . . .' She was now crying so much that she could not continue. She looked at me through her tears – in supplication, in panic, in trust, in torment – trying to tell me something.

I knew what it was, or thought I did. Something about the dreadful simplicity of true goodness, the infuriating innocence which can accept, and perhaps rightly dismiss as irrelevant, those minor vices (pathetic snobbery, insecure egotism, scared conventionality) which madden the more complicated and drive them to desperate measures. Something also about that legacy of absolute love which is intended to shield one through life like a magic cloak but instead leaves one indecently disarmed and vulnerable to the most trivial adversary. I sat with Ursula in this exotic room, surrounded by signed photographs of Mabel Mercer, Bricktop and Florence Mills, while she wept for the old Edwardian days at Stars — not because she wanted them back again, but because of her nightmarish suspicion that she had never really left them.

The tears stopped, but she went on helplessly looking at me. Then she said: 'I'm afraid I've allowed myself to get a little drunk. Ruby would want me to go home.' Both of us somewhat dishevelled, we stumbled hand in hand into the next room where Bobby and Ruby were waiting. Sleek, sophisticated and composed, they turned to greet us in loving sympathy.

7

Two and a half years later, just before her seventieth birthday, Ursula died of cancer of the bone. In reply to my letter of condolence, Ruby wrote: 'I could never make up to Ursula for all she has meant to me. Everywhere I turn or look — everything I touch — are reminders of what we shared and enjoyed together bringing back memories of her magnificent character. I only wish you could have known her during her years in this country when, though totally inexperienced and unprepared for the rat race, she carved out a comfortably successful career and was respected and admired by all who were fortunate enough to come into contact with her. One day I shall send you letters from her superiors in office to confirm this. When Mrs Roosevelt passed, Adlai Stevenson said of her: "She would rather light a candle than curse the darkness." The same is true of our darling and the glow from all the candles she has lit in her lifetime will never die.'

Ruby herself lived to be ninety. In her will, she left me Grumps's Bible.

The Ground Hostess

> Still when, to where thou wert, I came
> Some lovely glorious nothing I did see.

> John Donne, 'Air and Angels'

The telephone rang. It had to be Hurricane Harriet.

'Hi,' she said.

'Hi. Listen, I can't talk now . . .'

'You sound funny. Is something the matter? Look, why don't I come over right . . .'

'No,' I said in a panic, and I hung up on her. The telephone rang again at once. This time it was Jeremy – who else? 'Hi,' he said.

'Hi. Sorry, but this isn't an awfully good moment . . .'

'Oh, my dear, how awful. Are you all right? You sound a bit odd. If anything's the matter I could always whiz straight round . . .'

'Nothing's the matter. I'll ring you later. 'Bye for now.' And I hung up on Jeremy too. But I still couldn't concentrate.

Something had to be done.

I always knew she'd die some day and I always dreaded it and now it's happened. So what? So where does one go from here? Nowhere, Stay put. If they'd only let one. If they'd only . . .

No, that isn't the right beginning. Start again. From scratch. But where's scratch? Ah, if one only knew *that* . . .

*

For the first few weeks the letters of condolence flopped through the box in a steady spate. Variously combining conventional expressions of sympathy with licensed emotional indulgence, they gave a total effect of slightly smug hysteria. Some of them read like reasoned reviews – of a life, not a book or a play: all, naturally, 'raves'. It was almost an agony to open each one, and yet they *were* vaguely comforting, and comforting in their vagueness: at least they made some comment on my obsession, for although grief may sometimes imagine that it wishes its privacy respected, in fact it senses insult when it is ignored. Replying brought a tiny, masturbatory release; the least welcome were those with a well-meaning postscript: 'On no account, *whatever* you do, must you *dream* of answering this – you must be inundated!' Then the flood degenerated into a tardy trickle – startled, apologetic or impertinently reproachful: 'Why did nobody tell me sooner?' Some of these struck a subtly hectoring note: 'Please be *sure* to let me know if there is to be a memorial service!'

So there was one. The arrangements for this were supposed to 'take my mind off' by giving me something to do: they gave me something to do, but their essential irrelevance to the obsession only fixed it more securely in the forefront of my mind. When it was over, the trickle continued for a little while (with excuses for not having been able to attend and with congratulations – reviews again – on the success of the occasion) and then suddenly the whole thing stopped altogether. But the obsession, if anything, increased. The service, though religious in form, had been too social in spirit to work the intended trick of exorcism. A blank remained to be filled. Bereavement began.

A memoir. That might be the answer. Several of the letters, taking a cautious peep on the bright side, had suggested that *now*, with all the time in the world, I might be able at last to get down to some serious writing. A memoir of the mother I had lost. Of course it would be very difficult to do, perhaps even impossible, and nobody must know of my plan: secrecy would be an insurance against failure. But the harder my self-imposed task proved to be, the nearer it might come to filling that blank. Don't tell a soul. Just *do* it.

Soon, then, every evening after work at the office, my formerly reluctant steps from the Underground station to the empty flat would be impelled by a sense of purpose. As for the weekends, they would seem a luxurious orgy of stillness, like a cool clearing in the jungle towards which I had been hacking my way all week. The lonely evenings, the uncharted wastes of Saturday and Sunday, were to be filled by literary endeavour. The sadness of my solitude could thus itself be turned to advantage – for the activity of writing is known to be an essentially isolated struggle, and the necessary conditions for its practice are not available to all.

I had forgotten about my friends.

There is a form of loneliness so complete that it transcends any need for human companionship; it is an end in itself, a pure state of possibly fruitful suffering. This is not, however, readily acknowledged by outsiders. My friends were kind; they wanted to help; and help took the fairly regular form of ringing me up to suggest a meeting. I have always felt vulnerable when answering the telephone, as if I were naked; indeed, sometimes I *was* naked when it rang. Cravenly, I fell in with any sociable plan that was proffered. This made it difficult to get on with the memoir.

What am I saying? It made it *impossible* to *start* the memoir. And the recurring dream began – not a nightmare (it was quite pleasant) but none the less disturbing. In the dream she was still alive, still there: everything I remembered about the death had been the result of some sort of silly mistake. The grim cremation, the exalted memorial service, had been elementary errors, quite easy to explain away should anybody ask me about them. The notice in the 'deaths' column of the *Daily Telegraph* was potentially embarrassing – but nobody seemed to have seen it anyhow, so perhaps it didn't matter. In my dream I felt a mixture of slight anxiety that I could have made such a mysterious muddle and deep, calm, fulfilled relief. When I woke, I felt a mixture of mild assuagement that I hadn't, after all, made such a fool of myself and acute disillusionment followed by renewed sorrow.

I told my doctor that I couldn't sleep and he prescribed some pills which prevented me from dreaming, but I was still balanced enough to know that the Mogadons were a remedy rather than a cure and that only the finished memoir could reconcile me to my spiritually amputated condition and put an end to the period of mourning. What little time I managed to reserve for myself was wasted in embarking on aimless walks and making pointless lists (of Margaret Millar's novels, or Danielle Darrieux's films) although there were still things I couldn't do (play Lisa Delia Casa singing *Beim Schlafengehen* on the gramophone) and places I couldn't visit (the house in St Luke's Road with a bronze plaque in memory of W. H. Hudson) because they either reminded me of her and therefore of death or of death and therefore of her. I kept on telling myself: 'I mustn't be rushed.' Somehow or other, the friends had to be warned off, kept at bay. I desired the hitherto unattainable – to be left alone: what Henry James once described as 'uncontested possession of the long, sweet, stupid day': that peace to which no living creature has a natural right.

Yes, for a time I was decidedly neurotic on the subject of my friends. I even imagined a kinship with Dorothy Edwards, who wrote two remarkable books in the late 1920s, was taken up by Bloomsbury and then killed herself, giving as her reason (or so I had been told) that she had too many friends and didn't like them. But soon I realised that most of my acquaintances had no wish to intrude on my precious privacy and were on the contrary only too happy to leave me to my own devices. The merest hint (that I was tentatively engaged on some unexplained 'work' and needed time to myself) was sufficient, as it turned out, to silence the telephone. I must admit to having felt a slight, illogical pang of resentment at finding myself so blandly abandoned, and the pang might have developed into a palpable hurt if the silence had been total. But it wasn't. Two of my friends — perhaps, as these things are reckoned, the two 'greatest' — refused to accept the new regime. Hints, in their case, were not enough; they demanded details and assumed that I would welcome their inhibiting desire for participation. Harriet was interested in herself and Jeremy was interested in me, both to the point of monomania: I don't know which was the more exhausting. For her, I was an audience — convulsed with laughter or purged by pity and terror; for him, I was the show itself. Such intense relationships are stimulating when life is going smoothly, but they can take a lot out of you if you aren't feeling quite up to the mark.

Harriet was involved in a protracted and painful divorce from her third husband, a rich man who had craftily gone to an aggressive young woman solicitor while Harriet was stuck with the stuffy old family firm, so that it looked as if she would emerge from the case with very little of his money. Her latest novel had just been published and was receiving patronisingly dismissive reviews; in it this husband was clearly identifiable as one of the less attractive characters. Meanwhile, she was herself bringing an action for libel against a journalist who had printed something disrespectful about her in a gossip column. One of her daughters was undergoing a cure for heroin addiction and her son had recently been sacked from Stowe just before sitting his A levels. She lived with a mild young man who was beginning mildly to bore her and she was blatantly on the lookout for a more exciting lover. She would come to me for advice with a solemn yet perfunctory insistence, as though consulting the I Ching, and would sometimes volunteer some disconcerting advice of her own. Small, blonde and assertive, she had the unsettling charm of a ferocious nature tempered by a cosy disposition.

Jeremy might be described as a professional fan. All his energies had been channelled into enthusiasms outside himself which he expressed in a manner bordering on the manic. In his moral make-up, the extrovert element had been overdeveloped like some hyperactive gland; his lack of ego was so spectacular that it paradoxically drew attention to itself. Self-deprecation ran riot in Jeremy, turned inside out and emerged as aggression; violent in his humility, he was a reverse image of that old Warner Brothers cliché, the sensitive gangster. He had read every recent book (often before it came out), seen every current opera, ballet, play or fringe revue; he was as exhaustive as the information columns in *Time Out* or *What's On* and his many friends, puzzled as to how he found time to cover so wide a field, sometimes caught themselves wondering whether he might not employ a team of researchers . . . But there was nothing split, let alone multiple, about his personality; having cast himself as an ideal audience, he had the serene integrity of a collective noun. Tall, dark and very thin, he was insistently generous and relentlessly lively; his interest appeared never to wane. Both he and Harriet had a power to stimulate which made them irresistible; but they also shared (after lack of resistance in their interlocutors had assumed a pathological tinge) the power to deplete.

A typical evening: I entered the flat, put on my dressing-gown, poured myself a drink and opened a tin for the cat. These routine actions, briskly performed, were followed by an uncertain pause. What next? Perhaps there was something on the television. After a long wait a juddering green and mauve herring-bone pattern galvanised itself into an advertisement cartoon about a bouncing blob called Tommy the Thermostat . . . I averted my gaze, which happened to fall on the writing-table. If at that moment I had caught sight of my bed I would probably have climbed into it instead, but as it was – why not sit at the table and work? It suddenly seemed possible. So I prised open the typewriter, twiddled in a stiff quarto sheet, and started. Not the memoir – not yet – but something less ambitious, a kind of warm-up, just to get back into the habit of thinking in words. This story, let's say: how did it begin? 'The telephone rang. It had to be Hurricane Harriet.' And then the telephone rang . . .

'What's the *matter* with them all?' she demanded. 'Are they all demented, or what? Would somebody kindly explain to me, please? Because it's way beyond *me*. I give up . . . The reviewers, I'm talking about, who else? Some of my very best work went into that book and they're treating it like a Mills & Boon potboiler, it just doesn't make sense. I don't expect them to give me the Nobel Prize, for Christ's sake – I do know my own limitations, only too well, alas! – but isn't it rather peculiar that not *one* of them so far has spotted the perfectly obvious point that the whole thing is meant to be an allegory of Good and Evil? I promise I'm not going potty or anything like that, but I do sometimes wonder whether there might not be some sort of conspiracy at work here. Doesn't it strike you as a *leetle* bit odd that they all seem to say exactly the same thing? As if they'd been primed: the word has gone out – get Harriet! And don't you think that it just conceivably might *not* be a coincidence that every single one of them is a MAN? Listen to this snide bastard in the *Listener*, and I quote: "if the word 'compassionate' did not already exist I'm afraid it would have to be invented to describe *Bleeding*. The authoress, who is clearly in love with her heroine, is so busy saying 'yes' to life that she neglects to provide more than the barest minimum of characterisation, narrative structure or plot", unquote. Did you notice that "authoress"? Well, there's a giveaway, for a start. I mean, this is 1979 we're living in, right? No wonder this bigoted ignoramus can't understand that my emphasis on the theme of menstruation is merely a reworking of the Little Red Riding Hood myth in a post-modernist mode! What never ceases to amaze me is the way they all make the same stupid mistake and complain that I haven't written a totally different novel to the one that I set out to write. Why just one of them can't quite simply sit down and review the book in front of him, which has been sent to him for that purpose and for which no doubt he is getting handsomely paid . . . oh, who cares anyway? To hell with the lot of them. Hasten, Jason, bring the basin – they make me *sick*!'

And there she left me, *planté* by the telephone, gazing across at the writing-table a few feet away, but now so incapacitated by the strain of trying to match her mood of indignation that to cross this space had become a physical impossibility. Closing my eyes, I made a concentrated effort to banish Harriet's words from my mind . . . and as this began to succeed I comforted myself with the notion that perhaps her interruption had not after all been entirely negative in its effect. The story was clearly a mistake, not so much a rehearsal for the memoir as an alternative to confronting the challenge it presented. A memoir (surely this hardly needed to be said?) involved a conscious and sustained act of remembering, but my injured sensibilities were still instinctively united in a defensive flight away from grief towards forgetting. Instead of shrinking from memory, I must plunge into its depths: the shock of total recall might be brutal enough to numb the pain that would inevitably follow. It was dread of this pain which had brought about, as an inconvenient side effect, the mental paralysis from which I was suffering. I started to steer my thoughts, gingerly at first, in the desired direction, and was feeling that some progress might have been made when the telephone rang once more.

'You mustn't be cross,' Jeremy announced, 'but I've done something which I really believe may help to bust your writer's block! No, listen a moment, don't say anything now – I warn you I'm going to be very Aries about this and you may not like it but I don't care! There's somebody I admire *enormously* – I'm not going to tell you his name just yet, but you must take my word for it that he's simply *brilliant*. Sensitive and subtle and tremendously point-seeing and really one of *us* – a very rare and remarkable and special person, actually. He's a publisher, but not a ghastly one at all. I know it sounds poncey and I do loathe the word, but the only way to describe his quality is to say that he's an *artist*. Well, I've told him about you . . . What do you mean, *what* about you? Naturally I've told him that it's a tremendous secret but that you're working on something at the moment which *I happen to know* is going to be extremely remarkable and quite extraordinary and he'd be crazy if he didn't sign you up at once with an enormous advance. I also suggested that he ought to be rather firm with you about a deadline, because he's such a civilised creature – so unlike you-know-who, the *dreaded* – that he might have wanted not to seem too beady and tough and the whole thing might fizzle out which I think would be a *tragedy*. I won't say any more. Forget about the whole thing if you can't face it. I'd love to go on talking for hours but, alas, I've got to fly . . . I'm meeting someone at the NFT – the William Wellman retrospective – it's terribly late and *I've* got the tickets . . .'

Such interruptions as these continued to be a daily occurrence throughout a period of several weeks, during which I was indeed able to think about the memoir at regular intervals but only as a finished object, while remaining quite incapable of guessing at its possible contents. My reveries were taken up with visualising the dust jacket, seeking a title with the correct amount of characters in it to balance my name in harmonious typographical proportion, toying with the ideas of an allusive dedication (but to whom?) or an introductory quotation from my favourite poem by John Donne, rehearsing the terms of restrained self-promotion in which to couch the perfect blurb. I was relieved to find that reflections of this nature still achieved a satisfactory standard of consecutive coherence as far as they went, but depressed to discover that they always stopped short of any concrete anecdote, telling phrase or evocative incident which might have formed the basis for an opening paragraph of the actual text. When it reached that point, my mind seemed automatically to shift from one gear to another – or, rather, to stick in some vague and motionless condition in between. However, there was one occasion when it seemed that the vital transition might be made – when, like a curly cloud glimpsed in the far distance of a parched desert landscape, an episode came back to me out of the past that seemed to offer itself as a candidate for re-creation, even already accompanied by a few words that might serve as a start in the delicate task of describing it . . . but the words were scattered and the memory shrivelled at the sound of the telephone bell.

Harriet began the conversation with a statement: 'I'm interrupting your dinner.' Her tone was intended to suggest contrition but the words none the less emerged as an accusation. 'No, of course you're not,' I stuttered in self-defence. 'That's all right then,' she said. 'It's just that you sounded as if you had your mouth full . . . Well, I've written a thriller and I may be quite mad but of course I think it's really rather brilliant. You've just *got* to read it as soon as possible and tell me *exactly* what you think. Be as brutal as you like. And I very much want you to tell me if all the Agatha Christie bits of it work or not because I'm not very good at clues and red herrings and things like that . . .'

'I'm terribly sorry but I've got to ring off. That was the front doorbell and it may be something important so I'd better answer it,' I said. This emergency – often fallaciously invoked in the past to provide an excuse for abruptly ending a draining talk on the telephone which threatened to go on until some definite plan for a meeting had been arranged – was for once an actuality. I was prepared for Harriet (seldom fooled) to counter it by a callous 'Let it ring: I haven't finished' but instead she replied with satisfaction: 'I know what it is – that'll be the mini-cab I sent the manuscript round in. They *have* been quick! Do hurry down and open the door . . . Oh darling I told the man he'd be paid your end, you don't mind, do you?'

But it wasn't the mini-cab at the door: it was Jeremy, nearly obliterated by a vast fur coat which had recently been bequeathed to him by an aunt. This tubular sheath of yellowish curls, punctuated by pale patches of baldness, stretched from a collar concealing his ears to the hem of its skirt round his ankles. From a pocket in its folds, somewhere near his heart, he produced some typewritten pages of lined foolscap fastened together by a small gold safety-pin. As if hypnotised, I accepted them from his hand, feeling like the last, doomed player in a game of Old Maid. 'Won't stay,' he whispered. 'Can't come in. This is for you. To read, if you can face it. It's *tremendously* important to me what you think of it. I won't say more – only that somebody's whole future as a creative artist depends on your opinion. One more thing, and then I'll leave you in peace: if you *love* it, ring me tonight. And if you *hate* it – lie. Because that's something I just wouldn't be able to take. Bless you. Take care.' He blew me a middle- and forefinger kiss; then, his body bent in a purposeful stride and occasionally stumbling over the coat, he hurried off down the street just as Hurricane Harriet's minicab drew up at the kerb where he had been standing.

Yes, something had to be done.

And then I had an idea.

It first came to me one pale summer evening about two months after the memorial service. I was wandering down Westbourne Grove, headed for home past the local landmarks with their intense but limited associations: John Nodes, Funerals; austere, exotic Baba Bhelpoori: the convent, mysterious in its quiet seclusion, of the Bon Secours Nursing Sisters; the block of mansion flats where (as Jeremy once told me – it was the kind of thing he knew) Irene Handl lived; Elliott the shoe shop on the corner with that maddening squiggle under the tiny, crooked, elevated golden 'o'. As I approached my own front door I heard the sound, both plaintive as a mew and contented as a purr, of a telephone ringing not so very far away and (assuming it to be my own) walked straight on without pausing or turning my head, as if it were necessary to mislead some phantom follower by pretending that the house had nothing to do with me. If I had entered the flat, and my telephone *had* been ringing, I should have answered it – although (as I often reminded myself) there was no necessity to do so as neither Jeremy nor Harriet could possibly know that I was in. It was in order to forestall this weakness that I had refrained from going indoors, suddenly realising that there was no necessity to do that either.

On the other hand, I had to be somewhere . . . I turned into Micky's Fish Bar, sat at a table and began to read the label on what looked like a bottle of vinegar. 'Sheik nonbrewed condiment', it said. 'Unexcelled for its purity and keeping properties. Ingredients: acetic acid and caramel . . .' I ordered a vanilla ice from the Italian waiter and I thought: 'What am I doing in this pointless place, as if I had no home of my own to go to? Why am I behaving like someone in flight? How is it that I have come to feel so pathetically at the mercy of these two benevolent and affectionate creatures? Why do I allow them to hound me? I could just tell them to leave me alone. But that would hurt them. Is that what I'm afraid of, then – hurting people? Evidently. Is there *no* reason I might give for not wanting to see so much of them that would spare their feelings and also have some effect? Well, there is *one* excuse for neglecting one's friends (other than work, which seems to have failed in this case) which is always accepted with equanimity and even respect. A love affair! Exactly. Both Jeremy and Harriet would only be happily reconciled to scarcely seeing me at all if they believed that the time I spent out of their company was sacrificed to the demands of some over-riding sexual and romantic passion. It's true that I am not involved at the moment in any such relationship, but that's no snag, for surely nothing could be simpler than to pretend that I am. If I don't find a lover, I shall just have to invent one.'

As things turned out, it became necessary to invent two.

After arriving at my decision, I was nervously undecided about what means to choose of putting it into effect; Harriet's first call, however, could be said to have played straight into my hands. She had herself just embarked on a flirtation with a successful author of science fiction and was anxious to take it a stage further, but was finding it difficult to deceive her resident boy friend. Would I provide her with an alibi? 'Of course he won't check up, but just in case he should, remember – I was with you all tomorrow evening.' I said I would be delighted to oblige, and muttered something fairly incoherent about being in the same sort of situation myself. She sounded rather surprised. 'Oh, really? Somehow or other I didn't think of you as going in for scenes.' But she did not on that occasion ask any questions: her own adventure was naturally monopolising her attention. Relieved at having so effortlessly broken the ice, I felt confident of coping with Jeremy's next approach.

This took an unexpected form. 'I'm making my will,' he announced, 'and I can't tell you what fun it is. Have you made yours recently? You must . . . Anyway, I'm putting you down as one of my literary executors and I'm going to leave you a tiny something as well though I haven't yet quite made up my mind what it will be. Would you prefer a little cash, or some personal belonging of mine, like a book? Think about it and let me know – there's no hurry. I know you'll make a marvellous literary executor. I hope you don't mind my asking – if you find the idea too much of a bore, just say so – but I think you'll have quite an interesting time going through all my letters and so ·on deciding what ought to be done with them. And by the way, if you *do* feel like bringing your own will up to date, I would simply love to return the compliment and be *your* literary executor. There's always such a muddle when some-body dies, and it might be a relief to know that a friend you can absolutely trust would come flying round at once and destroy anything you didn't want kept. I think you can rely on me to understand your wishes and respect them.' In momentary confusion, I was about to ask how he would be able to dash round and inspect my private papers when he was already dead himself, but instead I explained that I was rather preoccupied at that moment with an affair of the heart, and found it hard to concentrate on anything else. This was greeted by a very long pause. At length Jeremy said: 'Wow! Well, all I can say, my dear, is congratters! I think that's a simply fantastic piece of news. The moment you feel like telling me more about it I shall be all ears. And needless to say, should you ever want any advice . . . But I'll take the hint and leave you in peace for the time being.' He hung up, and that was that.

Subsequent, less guarded conversations made one thing

clear: Jeremy and Harriet had formed startlingly opposite views about the nature of my sexual partner. As I had never made any kind of pass at either of them, Harriet had convinced herself that I was gay while Jeremy had vaguely assumed that I must be straight. When they began to inquire a little further about the course of my romance, she automatically used the masculine pronoun and he the feminine. Somehow unable to maintain a total silence on the subject, I found myself gradually divulging small items of information about my imaginary lover, subtly attuned to fit in with the preconceptions of my two listeners. Thus the lover split into twin images, male and female, Apollo and Venus, Yin and Yang, and from a series of hints and denials while talking on the telephone two separate personalities were brought into being: that of Linda and that of Tone.

Tone, of course, was short for Tony, who originally acquired his name as a result of Harriet mis-hearing a remark of mine quite unconnected with the subject. The Electric Cinema was showing a Pasolini season and I must have volunteered something like 'I'm going to *Accatone* tonight', which she interpreted as 'I'm going back to Tony tonight', assuming that I had quarrelled with my friend but had decided on a reconciliation. Emboldened by this break-through, Harriet soon after it risked a leading question: 'What does Tony *do*?' My mind at that moment was almost blank; I happened to be staring at a newspaper headline containing the fashionable acronym 'Quango' which (as I wasn't wearing my reading spectacles) I misread as 'Qantas'; I answered, before I had properly taken thought, 'He works as an airline steward.' He was thus established as an Australian, and the diminutive 'Tone' seemed naturally to follow.

Linda's primary characteristics were more slow in taking shape because Jeremy, though just as inquisitive as Harriet, chose less direct methods of satisfying his curiosity. It was not long, however, before a few tentative facts emerged: she was an actress, though not yet well known; she had been named after Linda Darnell, her mother's favourite film star; she adored cats, but was allergic to their fur. She was involved with various liberal causes, and sometimes asked me to accompany her on protest marches. (Tone, on the other hand, while claiming to be totally non-political, would often express opinions that were uncomfortably close to Fascism.) When I first met her Linda had been a passionate admirer of the works of Tolkien but (possibly under my influence) was now beginning to grow out of them.

Such feeble scraps of elementary data were about all that Jeremy and Harriet managed to glean from me, but the knowledge that at any time I might be called upon to produce fuller details of personal description kept my imagination perpetually on the alert, and I gradually amassed substantial dossiers on both Linda and Tone, to be held in readiness at the back of my brain in case of sudden need. My ruse, though succeeding in one sense more completely than I had anticipated, must therefore be said to have failed in its ultimate purpose – to win more time for myself in which to work on the memoir: I had gained the time, but only to fritter it away in maddening, monotonous, obsessive speculation about these two irrelevant inventions. The reserves of energy which, liberated from the exorbitant demands of friendship, should have flowed into the mainstream of literary creation, found themselves disastrously diverted into a sterile tributary, from the imprisoning banks of which there was no apparent release.

But it wasn't until last Tuesday that things began to get downright funny. I'd come home from work and was sitting on the sofa surrounded by comfortable stubby pencils and sturdy yellow pads but hadn't yet made any notes. Guiltily, I thought I'd have a look at the *Guardian* crossword, but when I folded the paper at the right page I found it had already been filled in by somebody else. This seemed decidedly spooky; until, after a minute, I remembered that, of *course*, I had done the whole puzzle myself while having my morning coffee. That shook me, rather. Was I completely losing my memory? Or just not taking things in? Then the telephone rang. I knew it couldn't be Jeremy, because he believed that I always spent Tuesdays with Linda (he had a catch-phrase: 'Tuesday night is lover night') and I had instructed him never to disturb me on that evening. So it could only be Hurricane Harriet. I didn't lift the receiver immediately, but a dogged quality in the ring told me that she wasn't going to give up easily (why is it that some people ring on and on as if they knew you were there while others hang up almost at once so that you couldn't answer even if you wanted to?) and eventually I succumbed.

'Hi. Listen. I hope I'm not interrupting anything but I've just *got* to tell you something, that's all. You'll be simply fascinated. You'll never guess what it is, never in a million years. Are you ready? Well, here goes – I've met Tone!'

Needless to say, I was much more surprised by this announcement than she could have possibly expected, but I tried to betray no greater degree of amazement than might strike her as normal. 'Are you sure?' I asked cautiously.

'*Almost* sure – no, I *am* sure, I'm quite sure, I'm quite certain it was him. For God's sake don't worry, I was terribly discreet and never mentioned your name or anything like that. So he's absolutely no idea that I know you or have ever heard about him.'

'Well, I'm glad of that. But when did you meet him? And where?'

'Last night. I'd been invited to drinks by a girl I used to know years ago and of course had no intention of going but then at about six o'clock I suddenly got fed up with thinking I'd got agoraphobia and decided the thing to do was get *out* of the house by hook or by crook so I rang up an Austin Princess and took it to Hampstead and told it to wait outside for twenty minutes while I went to this creepy party. Of course the whole thing turned out to be a total failure and the party was a *complete* nightmare, but never mind, I was introduced to this young man who when he opened his mouth sounded like that Barry Humphries character, you know, the Cultural Attaché to the Court of St James's, so I knew he was Australian for a start, and when I asked him what he did he said he was a Qantas airline steward, and when I asked his name he said it was Tony Something or other, now isn't that too extraordinary for words? . . . Actually, darling, you never told me how wildly attractive he is.'

'Perhaps I didn't like to boast,' I heard myself coyly saying.

'You sound awfully self-conscious, and I must say I *quite* see why. I suppose I'm being frightfully embarrassing – I *am* sorry – but I can't help it.'

'I'm not in the least embarrassed. It's just that I'm not yet quite convinced. There must be *hundreds* of Qantas airline stewards. Well, maybe not hundreds – but lots, anyhow,' I finished lamely.

'But how many of them are called Tony?' Harriet persisted. 'I tell you, that *was* him I spoke to yesterday. I just know it, and that's all there is to it. But I'll never breathe another word about it as long as I live if you'd really rather I didn't.'

'It might be better – just for the time being – if we *didn't* discuss it any more,' I said. 'There's a sort of reason for keeping it all a secret which I can't quite explain – that's all part of why it has to *be* a secret, if you see what I mean.'

'I don't see what you mean at all, love. Not in this day and age, I don't, with everybody leaping out of the closet left right and centre like so many *kangaroos*. To tell you the truth, I think it's a little bit snobbish of you to be ashamed of Tone. I thought he was *sweet*.'

'I'm not in the least ashamed of Tone,' I defended myself at random. 'In fact, it would be much nearer the point to say that *he's* ashamed of *me*. But that's all part of this tiresome business which I really mustn't talk about at this stage.'

'Is it because he's married, or something?'

'I *told* you, I don't wish to talk about it,' I said with exasperated dignity – and then spoilt the effect by asking: 'Why, did he mention being married?'

'No, of course not. We hardly spoke two words to each other, if you must know. Oh well, I'm sorry if I've been tactless. I just thought you'd be interested, that's all. It's no skin off *my* nose whether you ever utter his name again. It's nothing on earth to do with *me*.'

'I was fascinated by what you said. Thank you for telling me.'

'OK, darling. See you later.' Hurricane rang off.

This ludicrous conversation, innocent enough when you analyse it, left me with a feeling of irritation which quite prevented me from doing any work that night, and even made it impossible for me to concentrate on a book or television. On the following evening I still felt vaguely upset by it, and began to wonder whether there was any point in what I was trying to write, or indeed in anyone writing anything at all – a dangerous frame of mind. So I was almost relieved when the telephone rang, and not too depressed to hear Jeremy's voice on the other end of the line.

'Is this a bad moment?' he asked.

'Not a bit.'

'I know it's not lover night, but you're sure you're not watching telly or just having a lovely meditation or anything?'

'No, this is fine.'

'Well, are you sitting down? Have you got a drink in your hand? You're going to need it. Because I've got great news! Great, great news . . . And I'm not going to spoil it by telling you what it is straight away. You've got to guess. God, I am enjoying this! Now, guess, who do you think I met today? I'll give you a clue — no, I won't. I'll give you three questions and then you've got to guess. Only three. Go on. Fire away.'

'Man or woman?'

'Woman.'

'Where did you meet her?'

'Lunchtime theatre — the Soho Poly. I was in the audience and so was she.'

'Linda?'

'Right! Brilliant! Well? I knew you'd be riveted.'

'How do you know it was Linda? I mean, *my* Linda?'

'I sort of felt it in my bones. The boy I was with introduced us — Linda Something, he said, I can't remember her last name. And when I asked her what she did she said she was on the stage, mainly fringe things, lunchtime and so on. I thought she was *fantastically* nice and sympathetic, I really fell madly in love with her in a way and I couldn't understand more what you see in her . . . but I'm being insensitive, aren't I? I'll shut up in a minute, I promise. But I just had to tell you because it was all so odd. I can't get over it, actually, I mean if one put it in a story nobody would believe it, my bumping into her like that when I'm the *only* person who knows about you and her . . . That's all I wanted to say. I'll ring off now. *Lots* of love. You don't mind, do you? See you very soon. 'Bye,' he ended in a soft gasp.

Poor Jeremy had meant no harm, but this exchange left me with a sense of outrage. The pompous phrase 'invasion of privacy' entered my mind and lingered there, somehow comforting in its overtone of righteous indignation. The whole situation seemed to be getting out of hand! All right, so I had lied — but there was no malice in my falsehood; rather it had been nearer (or so I hoped) to that exercise of the imagination necessary for art. Now I understood what my punishment was: to be believed. My powers of invention were called into question; I had been taken literally; irresponsible fantasy was reduced to inconvenient fact. I felt angry, as though I had been caught out in something shameful, and sad, as though I had suffered yet another deprivation, and frightened, as though I had lost my way in hitherto familiar terrain. 'Wait till tomorrow,' I told myself. 'You'll have forgotten about it by then.'

Thursday evening: I still couldn't work. There are two kinds of writer's block. With one, you know what you want to say but find it impossible to choose between the alternative ways of expressing your thought: there seem to be too many words at your disposal. With the other, your mind goes hollow and the very word 'idea' becomes a meaningless concept, while your vocabulary shrinks to a few stale tokens. I had the second kind of block.

I switched on the television. Before the picture came into focus, I could hear a voice say good-humouredly: 'You've about as much charm as a dyspeptic alligator' and the dutiful laugh of a studio audience. Then the screen showed a group of people playing a word game called 'Blankety Blank'. Terry Wogan continued his pretence of insulting a guest celebrity. 'Haven't I spoken to you before about not answering back?' he was saying when my telephone rang. I stretched out my toe to extinguish the programme while I stretched out my hand to lift the receiver. Would it be Jeremy this time, or was it the turn of Hurricane Harriet? Indifference prevented me from saying 'hullo' and during the second or so of silence that ensued I suddenly guessed who it was at the other end of the line. When the caller spoke – 'Hi. Are you there?' – the marked accent convinced me that my intuition had been correct. You could say that I recognised the voice, although in fact I was hearing it for the first time. 'Yes, I'm here,' I replied.

'Sorry to call you up out of the blue like this, but I thought maybe it was time for us two to get together.'

'Yes, I think it is. High time.'

'Sure you don't mind?' said Tone. 'I mean, is it really all right, me calling?'

'No, I'm very glad that you did.'

'Then what about meeting up for a jar one evening? How does that strike you?'

'I think it's a very good idea. When do you suggest?'

'How are you fixed tomorrow, say around six?'

'That would be perfect. Where shall we meet?'

'Think you can find your way to Chiswick?'

'Of course.'

'There's a pub down there, just around the corner from the Qantas Regional Headquarters Admin Building, where me and some of the guys do some of our drinking some of the time. They get a nice crowd there. Nothing flash, but a friendly atmosphere. I use it quite a lot because it's handy for the orifice – I *beg* your pardon, I will read that again – handy for the office. It's called "The Ground Hostess". Think you can find it?'

'I'll manage.'

'Don't be late, will you, there's a good bloke?'

'I'm never late.'

'See you tomorrow, then.'

'Right.'

I think that was all we said. After I had hung up I immediately opened my engagement book and wrote down '6.00 p.m. The Ground Hostess' on the page for Friday: this act made the recent telephone conversation seem more real. Then I tried to imagine telling another person about what had just happened. They – he – she – whoever it was that I confided in – would almost certainly suggest that somebody had been playing a practical joke on me. This explanation of the mystery struck me as unlikely. Harriet could never have disguised her voice to sound like the man who had rung me up. It is true that Jeremy just conceivably might have done so – but then he knew nothing at all about the existence of Tone. Not that 'existence' was exactly the *mot juste* . . . or was it? I was reminded of a short story by Anatole France, which made a deep impression on me when I read it a long time ago. It's about a woman who invents a fictitious character called Putois as an excuse for getting out of any boring social engagement, and this figment of her imagination gradually assumes a life of its own. I think the story may have been at the back of my mind when I first embarked on the stratagem of Linda and Tone. Anyway, as far as I can remember it ends with the woman being told that Monsieur Putois had called to see her while she was out . . . I decided that the best thing to do for the time being was to think about nothing: blankety blank. Then the telephone rang again. I picked up the receiver and said at once: 'Is that you, Linda?'

She sounded slightly taken aback. Like Tone, she began by apologising: was I quite sure that I didn't mind her ringing up like this, 'out of the blue'? I agreed with her that it was high time we got to know each other. In my conversation with Tone, the initiative had remained with him throughout; but with Linda, I was able to take it out of her hands from the start. I told her that I would be having a drink at 'The Ground Hostess' at six o'clock on the following day, and invited her to join me there. She didn't know the pub, but thought she could find it without much difficulty. Yes, she'd love to come, she said. Something hesitant in her voice made me think that she needed reassurance, and with a rather ridiculous approach to old-world courtesy I told her how much I looked forward to making her acquaintance.

'And I'm *dying* to make *yours*.'

'See you tomorrow, then.'

'Right.'

After this, I left the telephone receiver off the hook. I swallowed my last two Mogadons and passed a long night of dreamless sleep. Looking back on it now, I'm not quite sure how I spent the early part of the next day. At one stage I must have rung the office with some excuse for staying at home: I was much too excited to go to work. And then I know that I searched everywhere for my copy of Kafka containing his 'Reflections on Sin, Pain, Hope and the True Way' because I needed to remind myself of the last page, and that I finally found it on the edge of a shelf about lunch time. 'You do not need to leave your room. Remain sitting at your table and listen. Do not even listen, simply wait. Do not even wait, be quite still and solitary. The world will freely offer itself to you to be unmasked, it has no choice, it will roll in ecstasy at your feet.'

Yes, that's what I wanted to read again. I even typed it out on my Hermes Baby in the hope of ramming its message home. But it wasn't any good. I still had to get to Chiswick to keep the appointments I had made. Then I needed my *A to Z London Street Atlas* and that took a bit of finding too – though not so long as the Kafka. I worked out a route, and set off in plenty of time. At the Notting Hill tube, where I usually boarded a train on the Central line to carry me east to work, I took one instead on the District line travelling west. This subtle adjustment of a daily routine had about it something aberrant, as in a dream where perverse and disturbing events occur among natural and familiar surroundings.

Incurably afraid of being late, I reached the meeting-place at twenty past five, and had to wait outside for ten fretful minutes. I felt something of the desperate impatience of an alcoholic as I counted the seconds till opening time. Ignoring my surroundings in the street, I stared at the locked, chained and bolted door: the world of my imagination had shrunk to whatever lay beyond it. When at last I heard and saw signs of its being opened, I felt that this predictable event had only been brought about by the intensity of my concentration.

For some reason I waited a further, unnecessary moment or two before entering the pub. The pale youth who had admitted me had now gone behind the bar and was talking in an undertone to his colleague, a middle-aged woman with dyed red hair. Neither of them took any notice of me. The room, which was otherwise empty, struck me as abnormally large. The bar occupied the centre, and the surrounding space had presumably once been divided into partitions – saloon, public, private, snuggery and so on. The removal of these had left behind an impression of desolate immensity. The walls were papered in a timid design, pale brown on cream, faintly reminiscent of the jazz patterns admired in the 1920s, and this fussy motif was repeated on the plastic seats of the banquettes. What little colour the decor contained (paintings of Spanish dancers on the walls; dark green tin ashtrays on the tables; the domesticated rainbow effect, like an old-fashioned chemist's shop-window, of the bottles behind the bar) seemed to be suddenly sucked away when the barmaid switched on the overhead strip lighting. At the same moment, the youth tuned in to a radio. Frank Sinatra and his daughter were singing an old number: 'And then I go and spoil it all by saying something stupid like – I love you.'

I bought a Bloody Mary and took it over to a corner. A limp evening paper had been left behind by one of the morning customers. As it was a *Racing Standard*, most of it was already out of date, but I glanced at Katina (never at her best on a Friday, when she had to provide a comprehensive forecast for the weekend and Monday) and read the whole of Bridge with Rixi. I had just started Classics on Cassette by Christopher Grier when I was overwhelmed by a feeling of restlessness and began to wander round the room. I still had nearly half an hour in which to explore 'The Ground Hostess'.

There was more to see than I had realised at first. A blank television screen hung from the ceiling, tilted forward at a tipsy angle. The lavatory doors were identified by twin ideograms, one tubular and one triangular, suggestive of trousers and skirt. A wide, shining jukebox: this I was tempted to play, but its music would have conflicted with the barman's radio and I lacked the courage to risk anything approaching provocation. A form of football for two players, featuring a quivering dot of electric light, like Tinker Bell in *Peter Pan*, and accompanied by a thin, non-stop, whining noise. A more than usually complicated fruit machine, offering an extreme variety of winning permutations and bewildering instructions: 'Reel may be nudged in chosen direction by selecting nudge up or nudge down when nudge panels flash. Nudges available as lit. During a game numbers on win line light letters of word NUDGE. Players may hold numbers to complete word and achieve Nudge Feature.' This, however, was out of order. A game called Master Mind, which tests your IQ and rates the results in categories ranging from Average to Genius. It asked me who wrote *Paradise Lost* – John Milton, John Osborne, Shakespeare or Margaret Mitchell? I pressed the button for Milton, but the machine firmly indicated that my answer was incorrect. I think it must have been out of order too.

Then I visited the Gents, although I had no desire to piss. There were some puzzling graffiti: 'I thought pubic hair was a friend of Bugs Bunny until I discovered Smirnoff'; 'My girl's so dumb she thinks Hertz Van Rental is a

Dutch footballer'; 'Who is Milton Keynes? An economist. No, that's Maynard Keynes. No, that's Milton Friedman. Both wrong – he's a sadistic poet.' This place seemed to have an obsession with Milton: did he (I found myself bemusedly almost wondering) have any connection with Chiswick? Pulling myself together, I went back to the remains of my drink and the *Racing Standard*, in which I located the TV Guide on an unfamiliar page with a new photograph of Celia Brayfield. A young couple came into the pub, walking very close to each other. It was only when I noticed that they were holding white sticks that I understood that they were blind. They stood together happily for a while (I heard the man say: 'She's Steering Wheel – you know, the Motoring Correspondent for *Hullabaloo*') and then he deliberately approached the bar and negotiated the purchase of two drinks. He returned to the girl and they sat, just touching, in companionable silence.

The red-haired woman behind the bar was more audible now. 'Do you the world of good,' she was saying. Take you out of yourself. You don't want to sit on your bum for the rest of your life feeling sorry for yourself, now, do you? Oh, if I was you, I wouldn't think twice. You wouldn't see me for dust. Leap at the chance, that's what I'd do. I know what I'm talking about. I've been there, haven't I? Oh, when it comes to that, I wrote the book . . .'

'That's all very well,' said the pale-faced youth. 'It's easy to talk like that. But I don't know, I'm sure . . . Dashing around like a fart in a bubble-bath – where does it get you? You only have to come home in the end, when all's said and done.'

I had become so engrossed in this dialogue that I had forgotten my purpose in coming to the pub. I felt panic. Where was I? Who was I? I looked at my watch, as if the answer to these questions lay there. It was six o'clock. I raised the newspaper to cover the lower part of my face, and over its top I gazed at the entrance to the street. The door opened, and Tone came in.

He was shorter than I had expected; indeed, his figure could almost be described as stocky. His hair was concealed by a furry Russian hat, his eyes by large rimless glasses and his mouth by a soft brown moustache of the kind once known as 'Zapata'. He wore a navy blue jacket with a double vent and bright brass buttons; a fawn polo-neck pullover of thin wool which wrinkled so tightly over his chest that his nipples were visible in outline beneath it; conventional blue jeans; and lace-up canvas kicker boots of vivid orange and chalky white. Over one arm he carried a neatly folded raincoat, also navy blue, and under the other he held a smart black briefcase. He looked round the room in a manner both cautious and arrogant, but seemed to find nothing in it to arrest his attention; then he crossed to the bar with a jaunty strut that betrayed to me his lack of social confidence. After carefully placing his briefcase and raincoat on one stool he hoisted himself on to another, leaned his elbows on the counter, cupped his face with his hands and stared fixedly in front of him. When the barmaid moved into his line of vision, he spoke. 'Lager and lime, please, dear, if it's not too much trouble.' After paying for the drink he resumed this semi-crouching posture, from which it was difficult to tell if his mood was meditative, sulky or shy. Every so often he shot out his wrist and consulted an expensive-looking digital watch. There was something faintly sinister about him, like a character in a book by Frederick Forsyth, and at the same time something so sharply poignant that I ached with pity at the memory of his shallow vulnerability and shivered at my intimate knowledge of his deserved discomforts.

Anyway, it was quite clear that he hadn't taken *me* in. I began to wonder what on earth I was doing, sitting here in this really rather depressing place. I was about to get up and go over to talk to him (though I had not yet rehearsed any opening remark) when the door opened once again. How typical of Linda, I thought, to time her arrival exactly ten minutes after the agreed hour. Women are always self-conscious about entering pubs alone, so she could not have risked being the first to get there; at the same time, she had enough consideration for others not to be annoyingly late.

She wore jeans, plimsolls and a child's Snoopy T-shirt. She was pale and slight, her fragile figure scarcely able to support the weight of her immense leather shoulder-bag, which was heavily tasselled and embroidered with a design of vaguely peasant origin. Her dark hair was cropped short, giving an effect of careless austerity which only emphasised the beauty of her violet eyes, straight thin nose and short upper lip, helplessly lifted over tiny china teeth. She was clearly nervous, for she hovered on the threshold of the room as if she still might escape back into the street; it looked as if she could not bring herself to shut the door behind her. 'Make up your mind, darling, if you don't mind,' the barmaid called out. That's one hell of a draught you're creating by just standing there.' 'Sorry,' said Linda, and she let the door bang to, imprisoning herself in the pub. She gazed searchingly at the sightless couple, as though appealing for some kind of help which of course they were unable to provide, and then carefully examined the rest of the room. I had once more defensively lifted the newspaper but above it my eyes met hers for a moment, and I can only say, in the words of the cliché, that she seemed to 'look straight through me'. For a while she studied Tone's back view with no expression on her face, and then deliberately walked to a part of the bar some distance from his seat but where he would be able to see her if he ever raised his eyes from his drink, into which he was now intently staring. She ordered a Tio Pepe, and after it was bought consumed it with delicate sips, evenly spaced, as if performing a ritual.

She gave an impression of innocent refinement and seemed lost in some private reverie – 'miles away', as they say – but I knew that in fact she was acutely conscious of everything that took place around her and I ached with pity at the memory of her proud little gaucheries and shivered at my intimate knowledge of her touchingly hard-earned triumphs.

Tone finished his lager and lime with a deep draught, smacked his lips, made an appreciative noise and ordered a large Scotch. While it was being fetched he added: 'And kindly be so good as to give the young lady opposite another glass of whatever she's having.' Linda began to protest, but Tone raised his hands and insistently pushed their palms in her direction several times. 'My pleasure, my pleasure,' he repeated. Linda soon gave in, and when she was halfway through her second sherry Tone gathered his belongings and ceremoniously carried them over to a stool next to hers. He offered her a Marlboro, and while she was fumbling in her cavernous shoulder-bag for a box of matches he efficiently clicked a pale blue Crickette lighter to which she submissively dipped her head.

There were now three groups in 'The Ground Hostess' carrying on conversations too low for me to overhear: the blind pair, the two behind the bar, and Linda and Tone. But I didn't need to know what they were saying – I had heard it all before. 'Oh, when it comes to that, I wrote the book . . .' After a few more minutes Tone was handing Linda down off her stool and escorting her to the door. He turned and with uneasy affability said ''Night, all' to the room at large; then they left the pub together. There's no doubt that they made a very attractive couple, and as I watched them vanish I couldn't help feeling a twinge of pride at the thought that if it hadn't been for me they might never have met.

THE OTHER GARDEN

FOR DAVID AND JUDY

Faut-il partir? rester? Si tu peux rester, reste;
Pars, s'il le faut.

Charles Baudelaire,
Le Voyage

1

'How soon will lunch be ready?' my father would ask. Assuming that hunger had made him impatient, my mother would answer with eager apology, 'Oh, any minute now – it must be nearly one.' But she had misinterpreted him. He had really wanted to know if he still had time for a further look at the other garden before sitting down to the meal. In dismay, she would watch him put on an old grey trilby hat, choose a stick, pass purposefully through the front entrance, then walk serenely down the short drive and vanish into the open road. Almost immediately opposite, a painted white wooden door in a red brick wall admitted him to this beloved extension of his property, subtly but certainly separate from the house and its bland surrounding lawns. Once in the other garden he was safely out of earshot – but a few minutes later I would be sent in search of him with a summons to return, the serving of our food having been innocently hastened by his ambiguous question when what he had hoped for was delay.

He had designed the other garden himself. It was in the formal tradition, of an artificially geometric kind already unfashionable in the mid-1930s and later to become more so: an almost perfect square enclosing yews clipped into animal shapes, low box hedges, crescent and oval flower beds, circles and triangles of mown grass embellished by stone bird-baths and straight symmetrical paths converging on a central sundial. Four ornamental benches stood at the corners of the intricate pattern thus composed; the vegetable garden and tool-sheds were screened from this purely decorative expanse by tall rows of sweet peas and raspberry canes. The whole lay on a slope above the main street of the village, so that facing south one could look past the roofs of the houses down to the river beyond, and across the damp green water-meadows in the valley up to the steeper hill on the other side. This commanding position gave a slightly vertiginous feeling, as if the ground had suddenly tilted to topple one, and also an exciting consciousness of being unusually exposed: people, after all, might be looking back from the village at the denizens of the garden.

The view to the north was reassuring: there, unexpectedly close, were the stable buildings and thick trees only partly hiding the place where we lived just over the invisible road. To be in the other garden, therefore, could to the senses of a small child combine the exotic with the familiar, the adventurous with the secure. As in the half-remembered excursions of my babyhood, passively mobile in an ample pram, or in the imagined experience of travelling in cosy railway sleeping cars and the cabins of luxury liners, I felt in the other garden that I had gone on a perceptible (if spatially infinitesimal) journey without forfeiting the protection and comfort of home. My father, who hated holidays and was bored by 'abroad', may have recovered a vestige of the same infantile satisfaction when he habitually surrendered to *wanderlust* in the early afternoon with no risk of missing his lunch.

At the lower end of the other garden, the wall was pierced by a wrought-iron gate. This opened on to a flight of steps, with ramshackle greenhouses on either side, ending in a footpath which led at right angles to a narrow street known as Love's Lane. Beneath the path, behind a brief fringe of turf, stood Love's Cottage – thought to be the oldest surviving dwelling-place in the village. Top-heavily thatched and emphatically half-timbered, with low beams, an enormous open fireplace and an outside Elsan, it was picturesque and primitive enough to satisfy the most romantic taste for 'period' discomfort. This taste had not been shared by its last occupant, an elderly bachelor who had worked as a gardener for the previous owners before retiring to one of the new council houses going up along the Swindon road.

My parents had left Love's Cottage empty for some years, and then they offered to lend it throughout the spring and summer months to an old friend of my father's family, an impoverished widow who had once been famous as 'the beautiful Mrs Bassett'. Of Mr Bassett, little was known and less remembered: people sometimes asked incurious questions about him and received frank answers which they immediately forgot. Since the 1890s Dodo Bassett had been the *maîtresse en titre* of a distinguished general, whose wife steadfastly refused to give him a divorce, and a mild scandal had been caused during the First World War by the conspicuous presence of Dodo among his entourage during his visits to the Front. The General had recently died when Dodo began to spend from May to September of every year at Love's Cottage.

She must have been sixty, but her beauty still blazed; buttercup hair; long eyes that seemed as soft as purple pansies; generously curving lips that never quite ceased to smile. These features were often partly hidden by the wide brim of a picture hat, which she wore at a slant to cover one side of her face and around which an admirer had to peer in order to enjoy an uninterrupted view. She had lost her figure decades ago, but it didn't really matter; that mysterious deep bosom, with no visible cleft, which vaguely and not ungracefully merged into a comfortable stomach and rolling hips, only added to her womanly glamour. Dodo indeed was womanliness incarnate, in the sense that her

Edwardian contemporaries had given to the word: sweet and warm as a bower, apparently slightly scatter-brained yet assumed to be essentially wise.

I was nearly thirteen when I first knew her. Intrigued by her worldliness and reassured by her conventionality, I responded to her gently ruthless pursuit of pleasure with recognition, surprise and delight. Sometimes I would find her sitting on a deck-chair in the other garden, calmly rereading her signed copy of *Under Five Reigns* by Lady Dorothy Nevill. Often she would arrive to visit my parents, panting slightly after the short climb, bringing with her a scrap of harmless gossip for their entertainment. She had the hedonist's magic power of dignifying the most tentative sortie with the excitement of an outing and of transforming the tamest indulgence into a special treat.

We both spent much of our time scheming to find a way of getting into Marlborough, which although only a distance of ten miles from our village was not easily accessible as Dodo had never ridden a bicycle or learnt to drive a car. If we failed to wangle a free lift we would make the journey together by bus. Once in the town, Dodo would head for W. H. Smith's in the hope of finding the latest issue of one of her favourite magazines: *Vogue*, *Harper's Bazaar*, the *Tatler*, the *Sketch*, the *Bystander* or the *Sporting and Dramatic News*. We would then cross the broad High Street to settle in at the Polly Tea Rooms for scones and jam and Devonshire cream. The feeling of sickness which this feast invariably produced in me, soon to be augmented by a headache as I tried to read the glossy pages of Dodo's magazine on the jolting homeward bus, seemed so intrinsic a part of the pleasure jaunt that it scarcely counted as pain.

Occasionally, after tea, Dodo and I would stay on in Marlborough to attend the 'six o'clock house' at the cinema a few steps away from the Polly. One of the first films that we saw there was *Dodsworth*, starring Ruth Chatterton,

Walter Huston and Mary Astor. I knew that she knew that it was a type of movie considered 'unsuitable' for me, but this was an impediment to enjoyment that she superbly ignored. Dodo was in fact particularly anxious to see it because one of the minor parts was played by David Niven, at that time still in his twenties and not yet widely known. Although Dodo had never actually met David Niven, she had been an acquaintance of his mother's and took a keen interest in his career, on which she was remarkably well informed. She told me that he had distinguished himself by passing brilliantly out of Sandhurst but that later he had impulsively left the army to seek his fortune in Hollywood. During his scenes in *Dodsworth* she leant forward to watch him intently, and appeared to be pleased by what she saw. I felt that (as at Sandhurst) he had satisfied some exacting standard set by an expert judge, and that Dodo had awarded him full marks not only for acting ability and for good looks but also for some other quality which I could not define but of which she was an acknowledged connoisseur.

The following year, we went again to the cinema in Marlborough. 'It's an English thing called *The Vagabond Heart*,' Dodo explained beforehand at the Polly, 'and I don't expect it will be much of a film. But I hear that the son of a friend of mine has a tiny part in it and I'm curious to see how he's turned out.'

'Do you mean David Niven?'

'No, no, this is another one. Sybil Demarest's boy. I knew her pretty well at one time – we often used to run across each other at Biarritz – but that was years ago and we've quite lost touch. She had this *very* handsome son called Sandy. He was only a little boy when I saw him last, but I often come across his photograph in magazines. He made quite a name for himself as an amateur jockey – I'm not sure he didn't win the Grand National one year. But poor old Charlie Demarest came a cropper in the Crash, like so many others, and I suppose Sandy needed to make some money, so he went on the stage. Purely on the strength of his looks – I'm told that he can't act for toffee. He doesn't really belong with the theatrical crowd, you see, more in the horsey set.'

The opening credits to *The Vagabond Heart* did not include Sandy Demarest. Dodo seemed puzzled. 'Perhaps he uses another name when he acts,' she said. 'Yes, I expect that's it.' She was proved right about the film not being up to much, but our attention was held throughout by the possibility of Sybil Demarest's good-looking son putting in a sudden, brief appearance. Whenever a male figure not easily identifiable as one of the leading players entered the aimlessly episodic story, Dodo would say, 'There he is! . . . No, I don't think it can be . . . No, that wasn't him after all. How odd.' At the end of the movie, we stayed in our seats to watch while a list of the entire cast was shown on the screen. The very last character mentioned was 'Man in night club . . . Alexander Demarest.'

'Oh dear, what a pity, we must have missed him,' said Dodo resignedly. 'I don't remember a scene in a night club, do you? Well, I know I'll never be able to sit through that silly film again, so there we are.'

But only a week or so after this disappointment, Dodo came to have tea with my parents in a state of unusual animation. 'Such an extraordinary coincidence! I thought I'd go for a stroll along by the river – you know, that part that's so lovely, down near the Manor gates – and I was standing on the bridge looking at the water in a sort of day-dream, when I heard a voice just beside me say, "That's never the Bassett Hound!" I nearly jumped out of my skin – nobody's called me that for ages! And who do you think was standing there? Sybil Demarest – quite a ghost from the past, as far as I was concerned, and I must have seemed the same to her. I assumed at first that she was staying at the Manor, but no. "Hadn't you heard?" she said. "Charlie's taken Watermead." That's the sweet little house tucked away right down on the river, about a mile from the village. One can't reach it by road, only by a path through the fields . . . Anyway, I walked back with her as far as Watermead and then came straight on here. I said I was longing to hear all her news, and she did tell me a bit about what has happened to her since I saw her last – so I'm afraid I'm still quite full of it!'

Nothing much, as it turned out, *had* happened to Sandy's mother during that interval, and to judge from Dodo's account the Demarests were an unremarkable couple. However, one aspect of their circumstances did constitute a departure – if rather a tepid one – from the conventional norm: although living together as husband and wife, they were in fact divorced. 'Sybil was a beauty, you see, could have married almost anyone, and we were all a bit surprised when she settled for Charlie. He'd made a fortune on the Stock Exchange and he simply worshipped the ground she trod on, so when after a time she got fed up he agreed to a separation, and eventually gave her a divorce, but still went on being incredibly generous. People did think it a bit hard on him, I seem to remember, but one heard that he didn't mind anything so long as they stayed on friendly terms. Then, out of the blue, he *lost* all his money – or most of it, people never lose it *quite* all, do they? He just couldn't afford to go on supporting her *and* himself in the way they'd grown used to, and as she hadn't remarried they thought the most sensible thing to do was to get back together again. For part of the time, at least: they still have separate flats in London – quite tiny, she tells me – but spend their summers together down here. Rather a romantic story, in a funny sort of way, isn't it? Sybil says she shudders to *think* what the stuffy county neighbours would say if they knew that technically she and Charlie were living in sin! They're both coming to tea with me at the Cottage on Wednesday. Can I bring them up here afterwards for a moment? I'd love you all to meet.'

Sybil Demarest materialised on Wednesday afternoon wearing a smart suit of heather-coloured tweed and a green felt pork-pie hat with a pheasant's feather stuck in the brim. She was a few years younger than Dodo and her beauty was of a less showy type: round pale blue eyes, delicate features and a small, prissy mouth. Her fair hair, faintly greying, was parted in the middle, gently waved and loosely knotted at her neck. Unlike Dodo, she gave the impression of intending to 'grow old gracefully'. Her husband was more than a little deaf, which may have partly explained the worried and irritable look that seldom left his aquiline, rather haggard countenance. His body was spare, compact and beginning to be slightly bent; he had an impatient, clipped way of talking and seemed to be continually on the watch for some anticipated offence against propriety – some breach, however minor, of the rules which he believed should govern correct social behaviour.

The conversation started with a tentative analysis of current affairs. 'What price the Nazis, eh?' Mr Demarest asked.

'The only one that I've got any time for,' said his wife, 'is Field-Marshal Goering. I hope this doesn't sound too fearfully snobbish, but I'm told on good authority that he's what we used to call a gentleman by birth. Which is more than can be said for Herr Hitler.' Sybil had a low, musical voice and spoke in measured, stately tones.

Charlie nodded. 'Don't know whether I'd agree about his being a gent, but he's certainly a damned fine sportsman. Man at my club I sometimes play cards with tells me he's never come across a better shot. Best of a bad bunch, if you ask me.'

'But I don't care much for his looks, do you?' said Dodo.

'I always think a good figure is every bit as important in a man as in a woman.'

'Dear lady, we are not discussing a beauty competition,' said Charlie. 'We are contemplating the possibility of war.'

'Oh no!' cried Dodo. 'I don't think I could stand another one!'

'Personally,' said Sybil, 'I think all this talk about a war is quite unnecessary, rather irresponsible and, what is more, extremely dangerous. People panic so easily — just like sheep. But if it should be decreed in Heaven — or in Hell, or wherever — that there is to be one, well then, so be it, say I. Mind you, I speak as someone who has already been through two wars. I see no reason why I should consider myself incapable of surviving a third.'

'Oh do let's change the subject!' said Dodo. 'How is dear Sandy? I saw that he won another race not long ago, before the flat season started. He *has* done well for himself, hasn't he?'

The faces of both the Demarests altered at the sound of the name. Charlie's frown of angry concern smoothed and his mouth twisted into a reluctant, reminiscent smile; Sybil's self-consciously noble expression softened to one of doting indulgence.

'He'll be down here soon, I've no doubt,' said Mr Demarest. 'Can't keep away from the river for long. Though I say so myself, that boy of mine is no mean dry fly fisherman. I thought *I* knew how to use a rod until he grew up and started to show his poor old father what was what.'

'Oh yes, he spends every *second* he can spare at Watermead,' said Sybil. 'But at the moment he's frantically busy filming and I don't know when he'll be able to get away.'

Dodo was tactfully silent about *The Vagabond Heart*. 'I saw him in that very amusing play with Gertrude Lawrence . . . didn't I?' she ventured.

'Indeed, yes,' said Sybil. 'Darling Gertie is a very close

friend of Sandy's and tries to get a part for him in all her shows.'

'*What* an attractive girl!' said Dodo. 'I'd love to know her secret. She's got no looks, strictly speaking, but *such* charm, and that's half the battle, isn't it?'

Charlie grunted. 'She turns herself out well – I'll give her that.'

Sybil Demarest looked grave. 'Do you know the thing about Gertie that I admire most? It may surprise you, but I'll tell you just the same.' She paused. 'That woman is the *cleanest* creature it has ever been my good fortune to meet. Yes . . . I would be perfectly happy to eat a poached egg off any part of Gertrude Lawrence's body!' She paused again, to savour the effect of her words; but, finding our response to them inadequate, felt that she had to continue. 'And on top of that, she's got what I can only call a hell of a lot of guts! She hasn't a nerve in her anatomy! Jeepers *creepers*, how I envy her!'

'I *would* love to meet your son,' said my mother. 'Do bring him to see us when he's next here.'

'How extremely kind of you,' said Sybil coldly. 'I shall certainly give him your message but I'm afraid I'm not able to offer you very much hope. His days here are so deeply precious to him that any time *not* spent in the open air what I call flogging the water counts as time wasted for Sandy.'

This speech was succeeded by a silence which gave everybody full opportunity to take in its insulting implications. After a few seconds Sybil's face showed that she had taken them in herself; she appeared to hesitate on the brink of making some kind of apology; but, realizing that this would only confirm and compound her bad manners, she rose instead to leave.

'I can see we're never going to be allowed to get so much as a *peep* at Sandy!' said Dodo indignantly after the Demarests had gone. 'How *silly* of Sybil to try to keep him tied to her apron strings like that! It's always a mistake – I've known so many cases. What was that thing – *The Silver Cord* – such an unpleasant play, but damnably clever . . . It's such hard lines on *him*, that's what gets my goat.'

By now Dodo's desire to lay eyes on Sandy Demarest had spread not only to my mother but also the rest of us. His link (however tenuous) with stage and screen made him an object of interest to me; and even my father, having heard Sandy's horsemanship highly praised as well as repeated rumours of the young man's unusual good looks, declared himself curious to see this modern Adonis in the flesh. My mother defiantly resolved to find some method of getting past Sybil Demarest's guard and scraping an acquaintance with her son. Then, one day, Dodo reported that, while standing on the same bridge that had witnessed her reunion with Sybil, she had caught sight of a tall male figure in waders fishing in a distant reach of the river. 'I'm quite sure it wasn't old Charlie – this was a much younger man. Bet you anything it was Sandy! And I happen to know that Sybil's away in Newmarket, visiting an old flame of hers who trains up there and who, as a matter of fact, used to be quite a flirt of *mine*.'

'Right!' said my mother. 'What's to prevent me from ringing up Mr Demarest straight away and inviting him to a very small and informal and last-minute cocktail party this evening and asking him to bring whoever else is staying in the house? If I take him by surprise, it might just work.' She walked determinedly to the telephone, and could soon be heard talking slowly and very loudly to the deaf Charlie. After a short conversation, she hung up.

'What did he say?' Dodo eagerly demanded.

'It's really rather funny – but the joke's on us. He can't manage tonight, but he'd simply love to look in around tea-time tomorrow. Sandy's leaving first thing in the morning so would it be all right if he brought his daughter Kay with him? Of course I said "yes". Did you know there was a daughter too?'

'First I've heard of her,' said Dodo.

So Charlie Demarest paid us a second pointless call. As before, he gruffly volunteered a series of civil banalities in a manner which suggested that any response to them would be unwelcome (because inaudible) and might easily cause him to lose his temper. This inhibited the smooth flow of social intercourse, creating a 'sticky' situation in no way lubricated by his daughter who, beyond a few muttered pleasantries, hardly spoke at all.

Kay Demarest was then in her early thirties. She wore no make-up, which gave her a prematurely weatherbeaten appearance; her reddish hair hung to her shoulders in a long untidy bob; she was extremely thin. Her evident shyness gave her a hunted look, the gauche grace of a deer who senses danger but is uncertain of the exact quarter from which it threatens. She had her mother's large, sad aquamarine eyes in her father's narrow, ascetic face; also like her father was the way in which her apprehensive expression (a less fierce, more vulnerable version of his) could on rare occasions of confidence or amusement relax into a crooked, rueful smile of considerable charm. She had on a tartan shirt, brown corduroy bell-bottom slacks and high-heeled shoes which seemed to hurt her (perhaps because she wore neither stockings nor socks); she carried a big, battered handbag (made of some expensive skin such as alligator or crocodile but now split and wrinkled like a stretch of parched and pallid desert) to which she clung as though for reassurance, while with an air of secretive concentration she chain-smoked throughout the visit.

To me there was a mystery almost as fascinating as Greta Garbo's in Kay's offhand behaviour, laconic speech and deliberately shabby clothes, but she was also the reverse of intimidating and I found in her an attractive combination of the cosy and the strange. When she shook hands with me to say goodbye, she unexpectedly added a few hesitant words to the formal valediction. To tell you the truth, I was scared stiff of this tea party. I nearly funked it, but Daddy made me come. I thought you'd all be simply terrifying, but you're not. You've been sweet. I like the atmosphere here – I feel I can be myself.' She had been speaking with head averted, but now she turned to face me and I saw those enormous eyes, of a blue both pale and piercing, in the lean, bony face. 'Thank you.'

2

That autumn, I was as usual a few days late going back to the public school where I had already spent three bewildered, anxious terms. My dread of the holiday's end invariably lent me sufficient will power during its last hours to send my temperature the necessary degrees above normal to qualify as an official invalid – but I could never keep it up for long enough to win more than a tantalisingly brief remission. Hopes of a further reprieve were temporarily raised by the Munich crisis, in which I perceived a promising possibility that the school might be bombed, or in some other way put out of action by war. One of my few friends there was a boy called Billy Phipps, who was a year older than myself and whose worldly experience impressed me though I was often offended by the implacable snobbery of the conclusions he had drawn from it. He thought that to be *petit bourgeois* was so disgraceful as to be almost obscene, and while he loved to analyse this dreaded state and its various tell-tale manifestations he could hardly bring himself to mention them by name and had therefore constructed a set of euphemistic codes by which to refer to them. 'MC' for 'middle class' was comparatively easy to decipher, but 'K' (facetiously standing for 'common') and 'NQOCD' ('not quite our class darling') were impenetrable to the uninitiated – and the cryptic acronym 'MIF' retained some of its mystery even after one had been told that it was an abbreviation of 'milk in first'.

There were several grounds on which I was resentfully obliged to acknowledge myself inferior to Billy Phipps, and the fact that these tended to be social rather than moral or intellectual did not make the admission less humiliating. For example, his wide circle of acquaintance made me feel as if I and my parents knew hardly anyone at all, passing our lives uneasily in a pathetic and slightly sinister void. In an attempt to imply that our isolation might not be total, I mentioned to Billy that the Demarests had recently become our neighbours and was pleased to find that this piece of news not only caught his attention but was even greeted with wary approval. His aunt was a successful breeder of race horses and a well-known figure at the smarter meetings, so Billy was familiar with the subtleties of that world and considered himself an authority on its totems and taboos.

'How did you get on with Sandy?' he asked. 'My aunt says he can be very good company when he feels like it.'

I told him that I had not yet met Sandy but that I knew his sister slightly. Like Dodo, Billy Phipps had never heard of Kay, suggesting by his manner of saying so that he suspected me of having invented or imagined her. After the Christmas holidays, however, he condescendingly confirmed her existence. 'I asked my aunt about your friends the Demarests,' he said, 'and you're perfectly right, Sandy does have a sister. But I gather she's rather *mal vu* on the race course. Doesn't go down at all well, I'm afraid.'

With some vague notion that Kay might have been 'warned off the turf, like the hero of *The Calendar* by Edgar Wallace, I asked him what he meant.

'She's supposed to sleep with jockeys,' Billy explained. 'Mind you, my aunt says that there may not be a word of truth in it – but once a girl gets that sort of reputation, she's done.'

'What else did your aunt say about the Demarests?'

'Parents *très ordinaires* – Stockbroker Surrey, if you

know what I mean, though there is a theory that the father comes from an old Huguenot family and I believe the mother has some quite respectable Norfolk connections . . . As for Sandy, opinion seems to be divided. My aunt says of course he's much too pretty for his own good but he can be *so* amusing that one forgives him a lot. At first you think he must be either a roaring pansy or a poodle-faking gigolo – you know, the type of chap one's Nanny might describe as "Good-looking – *and* knows it!" – but my aunt says no, that's not fair, *other men like him*, and my aunt says that's always an infallible sign in a fellow that there's nothing really the matter with him.'

I repeated a part of this to my parents and to Dodo, but something made me suppress the malicious remarks about Kay.

The following summer, I saw her again. I had set out early one afternoon on an aimless walk: through the other garden, past Dodo's cottage and down Love's Lane to the main street of the village. Kay was standing at the bottom of the lane, a bulky square black box on the pavement beside her. When I reached the street I recognised the box as a portable wind-up gramophone.

'I say,' said Kay, 'you wouldn't do me the most tremendous favour, would you, and help me with this thing? I was so afraid it was bust for good, and then my friend Reg at the garage was terribly sweet and saved my life by repairing it for nothing, but I'd quite forgotten it was so damned heavy and I'm not sure I can lug it all the way back home by myself.'

Of course I said I would be delighted to carry her gramophone, and we started off together down the street. 'We'll take it in turns,' she said. 'I absolutely insist on that because it's quite a long way, so promise to call out as soon as you begin to feel exhausted . . . Listen, would it drive you mad if I popped for a moment into the paper shop?

There's something rather important I've got to collect there.' She emerged from the shop with the latest issue of a weekly film magazine. 'Sorry to be such an awful bore, but can you bear to wait just one more second while I find out if they've printed a letter I sent them?'

With urgent concentration, Kay leafed through the magazine, but failed to find what she wanted. 'To tell you the truth,' she said, as we continued on our journey, 'I'm beginning to get a bit fed up with George of *Picturegoer*. I'm beginning to wonder if he isn't really rather a swindle. You know, he boasts that he can answer *any* question – within reason, of course – that a reader puts to him. He guarantees to publish your request plus his answer within a month of receiving it. That is, unless you want to keep the whole thing private, in which case you enclose a stamped addressed envelope . . . Well, it must be more than six weeks now since I sent in a perfectly straightforward query – which has been greeted with dead silence! I seem to have totally stumped him. Too pathetic!'

'What did you ask him?'

'The date of Tyrone Power's birthday. As simple as that.'

'Why do you want to know his age?'

'I don't – I want to know his astrological sign. So that I can cast his horoscope. I saw him in a thing called *Rose of Washington Square* and thought he was the most attractive man I've ever seen, that's why. It's a good picture, too. If it's ever showing anywhere near you, for God's sake, take my advice and go. I can thoroughly recommend it. I should be very surprised indeed if it disappointed you.'

We had now come to the end of the village and instead of continuing along the main thoroughfare, which would have taken us past the Manor gates in the direction of Marlborough, we turned left down a minor road and crossed a bridge over the river. Just as the ground was steepening, at the bottom of Larch Hill, Kay led me over a stile and into a field on the right. The path to Watermead took us through further fields and meadows which became increasingly soggy underfoot. Some gates could be opened but others had to be climbed over, under or through. The house was hidden from the path by tall bushes; an almost invisible gap in one of these admitted us on to a sloping croquet lawn. The building was low, of two storeys, and gave the impression of leaning solicitously over the river – a tiny tributary of which flowed beneath the rooms at the back. Life at Watermead, I was later to learn, unfolded to a constant accompaniment of varying liquid sounds – trickling, roaring, bubbling, lapping – which suggested to the spirit an endless alternation of refreshment and erosion.

'You've simply got to come inside and recover,' said Kay. 'The very least I can do in return for your kindness is to offer you a cup of tea! Don't worry, it's quite safe, the coast's clear. Mummy's with her boyfriend in Newmarket, thank God – long may she remain there, though I suppose I shouldn't say so – and Daddy won't be back for hours, so we shan't have to make polite conversation.'

I said that I didn't want any tea but would love to listen to something on her gramophone.

'Would you really? I used to have rather a good collection of records but most of them either got broken or are scattered around the country – I've moved about a lot in the past few years, you see. But I've clung on to a few precious favourites. They're up in my bedroom. Make yourself comfortable in here while I go and fetch them.'

She showed me into a long, dim sitting-room furnished with Knole sofas, chintz-covered armchairs and rickety round occasional tables fretted to a vaguely Oriental design. The walls were hung with glass cases containing stuffed trout, each one captioned by details of its weight and date of death, between a series of small casement windows with mullioned panes; the floor was uneven, and perceptibly lower at the farther end. Two framed photographs stood on the mantelpiece, one of Sybil Demarest *en profil perdu* and the other of Queen Marie of Romania, the sitter's face almost obliterated by her signature; next to these I noticed the glossy calendar sent out to their clients by Ladbroke the bookmakers, with a flattering caricature of some racing celebrity for every month. The room satisfied an undemanding standard of impersonal comfort, neither repelling nor absorbing the visitor, and I felt as if I had been left on an empty stage in a scene set to represent the lounge of a typically English country hotel. The continual murmur of moving water around and below me seemed as illusory as a theatrical 'special effect' while I waited — both audience and actor — for the play to begin.

Kay returned with an armful of records and we both crouched by the gramophone while she wound it up. Just the sight of the labels was enough to put me in a party mood — smart Parlophone in deep blue and white, festive Vocalion in bright red and gold, sober Brunswick in understated black. It was apparent that the tunes preferred by Kay were torch songs: she played me Connee Boswell singing 'Say It Isn't So', Ruth Etting singing 'Lost — a Heart as Good as New', Alice Faye singing 'There's a Lull in My Life', Helen Morgan singing 'Why Was I Born?'. But the despairing lyrics and sensuous, sedated *tempi* did not strike me then as depressing. They seemed rather to convey, in an inviting form, the essence of a distant, adult world of melodrama — a world from which Kay, for reasons as yet mysterious, had decided for a while to retire. I had fantasies, as we listened to the luridly defeatist music, of Kay having been forced to 'hide out' like a gangster's moll at Watermead, for there was certainly something furtive and temporary about her manner of inhabiting this inhospitable house.

'Why did you say that you thought we'd be frightening, when we first met last summer?' I asked her before I left.

'Oh – nothing personal. It's just that I'd understood that your parents were friends of *my* parents, and for as long as I can remember the sort of people that Daddy and Mummy approve of have invariably made me feel hopelessly inadequate, to the point where I just sit there tongue-tied like an idiot. But I soon realized that your family aren't like that at all . . . Talking of which, Mummy will be back in a day or two and it looks as if this lovely sunny spell we're having might last a bit longer. I wonder if you'd do me another great favour and give your mother a message from me? Would she be angelic and let me borrow just a corner of your garden to sun-bathe in? I wouldn't be any trouble – no one need know I'm there. It's just that I adore the sun, but seeing me lie about all day half-naked gets on Mummy's nerves. She's bound to complain to Daddy sooner or later, and then all hell will break loose and my life here won't be worth living.'

'Of course I'll ask her and I'm sure she'll be delighted for you to use the garden whenever you like . . . But, when you have a row with your parents as you've just described, doesn't your brother take your side?'

'Sandy? Oh, poor lamb, I wouldn't want to involve *him* in one of those ghastly scenes. It would only make him miserable. Besides, he's hardly ever here.'

So, while the fine weather lasted, Kay would turn up regularly around noon, wearing shorts and a shirt and carrying a car rug which she would spread on a patch of lawn at a tactful distance from the house. After removing her shirt, she would tie her headscarf round her bosom – thus freeing her untidy mane of copper-coloured hair. Surrounded by bottles of sun-tan oil, packets of cigarettes and books of matches, a recent number of *Picturegoer* and a paper bag containing sandwiches and a chocolate bar, with a battery wireless hissing and mumbling near her head, she would lie almost motionless with eyes closed in ecstasy until the evening chill. When she turned on her front, she would untie the scarf, and if she shifted her position once again her small breasts would be briefly revealed, pale round vulnerable patches in the dark brown of her body.

There was something paradoxically unhealthy about the intensity of Kay's sun-worship. Her skin acquired an unpleasantly leathery texture as its tan deepened; the effort of so dedicated a surrender to passive immobility seemed to be draining her of all vitality. Occasionally, she would join my family indoors for a drink at the end of the day; more often, she would creep or stagger back home, like an early morning reveller sated but befuddled after a night of dissipation. She soon struck up a friendship with my mother, who was nearly as intrigued by her as I was; but my father, although he hid the feeling, did not really like her. Her lack of the more conventional social graces made him uncomfortable; he found her air of self-absorption an irritant and a bore. It was therefore lucky that Kay instinctively refrained from choosing a site for her sun-bathing activities in the other garden.

In the end, the meeting with Sandy which had been so eagerly desired the previous summer came about quite naturally through the mediation of Kay. She telephoned my mother one August afternoon. 'I've got my brother here on a flying visit and he says he's heard so much about you all that he simply must know you. Do you think we could possibly come round straight away?' I ran with the news down to Dodo's cottage, and she followed me back to the house. But the excitement of the year before was lacking; the period of waiting had been too long for it to survive, and I think we may even have felt that there had been something slightly silly about the fuss over Sandy that we had been ready to make then. So his eventual appearance – though not exactly a disappointment – was inevitably an anti-climax.

My mother and Dodo and I were sitting on the front lawn just outside the house (my father had absented himself to the other garden) when Kay turned in at the drive accompanied by a tall dark-haired man in his late twenties. She walked towards us with the tarty gait that she affected when she was happy, swinging her hips and shoulders and taking slow, deliberate steps. 'I'll never be able to introduce you properly – he's been making me laugh too much!' she said, collapsing on to the grass beside me. 'But anyway, this is Sandy!'

Billy Phipps's aunt had been inaccurate when she described Sandy as 'pretty': his good looks were rather of the gentle but decidedly masculine type exemplified by Gary Cooper, which often appear to be a burden to their owner and are worn with an air of apologetic diffidence. In Sandy's case, one felt that he would have liked to ignore them but that circumstances had somehow made this impossible. His lanky body moved with hesitant caution instead of the ease expected of an athlete, and the geometrically regular features in his long, grave face were troubled by an apprehensive expression at odds with the confident charm of his social manner. There was something stagily synthetic about this manner, as if it had been assumed in order to allay suspicion of narcissistic conceit without going to the tedious extreme of crude virility; perhaps as a result of the strain involved in adhering to this middle course, the total effect of his personality contained a surprising suggestion of asexuality. As some young men are said to have 'outgrown their strength', so Sandy seemed to have been subtly emasculated by his own beauty.

'Yes, the dear girl had a frightful attack of the giggles just outside the Post Office and I'm sorry to say made rather an exhibition of herself,' he explained. 'I even feared for a moment that she was going to "do herself a mischief". God knows what it was that she found so funny – I merely told her a very old and rather asinine joke. Quite unrepeatable, I'm afraid,' he added firmly.

'It was the way you told it . . . But we were laughing before then.'

'You mean, the Football Club game? They'll think us *quite* mad if we tell them about that . . . You must forgive us, you see, but my sister and I suffer from an extremely infantile sense of humour. The Football Club game is really very simple – literally anyone can play it! You just imagine the club as a married couple of title, being announced by a butler at some very grand party. Sir Aston and Lady Villa, for example – can't you just see them? Kay's favourite is Sir Woolwich and Lady Arsenal.' Sandy assumed an accent like Noel Coward's to add, 'What did you think of the Arsenals? . . . Loved him, hated her!'

Within a few minutes of his arrival, he had us all merrily competing at the Football Club game. Its possibilities, however, were soon exhausted – and there followed a pause in which, though it remained unuttered, we seemed to hear the sweet, silly cry of the spoiled child: 'What shall we play next?' Dodo had brought with her a capacious sewing bag, patterned with green and yellow storks on a black background, which contained no sewing but was filled instead with cosmetic accessories; this bag had now companionably subsided in a colourful spread at her feet. Spotting a copy of the *Tatler* obtruding from its open clasp, Sandy squatted beside her deck-chair. 'May I?' he asked, smiling up at her as he extracted the magazine. Opening it at the page devoted to photographs of recent marriages, he informed her in a conspiratorial half-whisper of the rules of another 'game'. One had to guess from the wedding pictures (beaming brides wreathed in orange blossom, sheepish grooms in tails or braided uniforms) at the quality of each couple's love life. 'This pair, three or four times a night, I'd say, at least to start with, wouldn't you? But these with the Guard of

Honour – oh dear, once a month at *most*!' Dodo was flattered and amused by his attention, but she was also offended and annoyed. She gave a repressive shake of her head and, glancing at me, muttered, '*Pas devant* . . .' Almost snatching the *Tatler* from his hands, she replaced it in her bag – withdrawing from its depths a copy of *Gone with the Wind*.

'Isn't it disgraceful?' she said. 'I've been reading this religiously ever since it came out *donkey's* years ago and I still haven't finished it! Mind you, I'm loving every word of it – but I just can't seem to get to the end!'

Sandy made a mock-penitent grimace in rueful acknowledgement of misbehaviour, and smoothly adapted to the change of topic by giving us an inside account of the circumstances surrounding the casting of Scarlett O'Hara in the film version of Dodo's book. This led on to other enjoyable theatrical anecdotes. When Sandy referred to 'Larry and Viv' or 'Noel and Gertie' he did not seem to be dropping names in the vulgar cause of self-promotion; such allusions to the famous were camouflaged, as it were, by more frequent mentions of less easily identifiable diminutives – Betty and Bobby and Boots and Babs – belonging to actors and actresses as obscure as himself. Nearly all his stories centred on some onstage disaster which had befallen him or one of his friends. Sandy's underpants had dropped to his ankles and tripped him up while he was carrying a spear in *Julius Caesar* when the Duke and Duchess of Gloucester were in the audience; Babs, after years as an understudy, had finally landed the lead in *Hedda* at Scunthorpe rep, only to 'corpse' on the line about vine leaves in Ejlert Lövborg's hair; poor Bobby suffered so severely from stage fright that on a famous occasion he had let off a fart in the middle of the Messenger scene in *Antony and Cleopatra*. While he spoke, Kay listened in silence, neither watching him directly nor laughing at his jokes, but with an expression on her face of the deepest content.

'How is your dear mother?' Dodo asked. 'I don't seem to have seen her around much lately.'

'The Head Woman?' said Sandy. 'She Who Must Be Obeyed? It's quite all right, she knows the rude names I call her. As a matter of fact, I think she rather likes them . . . She's staying with friends in Scotland. Left last night. Coming back in a month.'

'Which will be a signal for *me* to make a move,' Kay murmured so that only I could hear. 'I can just about cope with Daddy on his own, but I'm afraid the two of them together rather get me down.'

'Where will you go?'

'Not sure yet,' she replied evasively. 'Brighton, possibly. I'll find somewhere.'

During this muted exchange, Dodo had started to reminisce about the old days, when she and Sybil had first been friends. 'One episode I remember in particular – so killingly funny, it was, we always laugh about it when we meet – I *don't* think she'd mind my telling you. There was some new fad that was supposed to be frightfully good for one, and very rejuvenating and all that, called the Garlic Cure. One just ate nothing but garlic for days on end – it cleaned out the system, or something. Anyway, I had a little place in the Cotswolds then, and I said to Sybil, why don't you come down and stay with me and we'll give it a try together? *Too* boring on one's own, you see. So there we were, my dear, perfectly happy, having eaten *not one thing* that wasn't garlic for an entire weekend and no doubt smelling to high heaven (we didn't notice it ourselves, because one doesn't) when to our *horror* one afternoon we looked out of the window and saw two horsemen come riding up to the front door! It was two rather special beaux of ours – the Merton twins, Jumbo and Boy – who were in the neighbourhood and thought they'd give us a nice surprise by calling unexpectedly! Well, of course, there was no *question* of letting them in! We just stood at the window shrieking, "Go *away*! Go *away*!" In the end they did, but they must have thought us completely bats!'

Throughout Dodo's story Sandy stood beside her chair, bending a little towards her in order to hear every word, his brown eyes blank and his upper lip slightly raised in a politely appreciative smirk, frozen in preparation for the long-delayed release into loud laughter which only the end of the anecdote would permit. When this happened, Kay spoke again, still in a low voice as though addressing herself as much as me. 'How spooky . . . I was watching Sandy while she was talking and I suddenly had a sort of vision. I suddenly saw *exactly* how he'll look when he's very, very old. So now I know what he'll be like then . . .'

Dodo then rose, and said she must return to her cottage; Sandy and Kay offered to escort her there, on their way back to Watermead; the little party broke up. While Sandy was bidding my mother goodbye, he suddenly leant forward and gave her an impulsive kiss. 'That's to thank you for being so sweet and kind to our darling Kay!' he said.

A week or so later, war was declared. On the following day, I met Kay coming out of the paper shop in the village. She called out to me, 'Guess what! At *last*! George of *Picture-goer* has answered my question! I can't think what took him so long, but better late than never. Power was born on May 5th, which makes him a Taurus. I had a feeling he might be.'

'Isn't the news awful?' I said.

Kay seemed to flinch. 'The war, you mean?' she muttered, clearly at a loss as to how to react to my remark. I wondered for a moment if I had ignorantly flouted some tacit code of wartime behaviour which forbade any direct reference to the war itself. Then, with a mixture of her father's curt authority and her mother's complacent inanity, but redeemed for me by a touch of the gruff bravado that I had come to recognise as peculiarly hers, she announced, 'I give it a month!'

3

I can't remember exactly how soon it was after the outbreak
of war that work began on the building of a large military
aerodrome along the top of Larch Hill – above the village
and just out of sight from it – but it must have taken some
considerable time because I'm sure that it wasn't finished
until the spring of 1941. By then I had left school and was
hanging about at home waiting to go up to Oxford for a
year or two of further study before the inevitable Army
call-up. In the meantime, I had joined the Home Guard. One
of my weirdest duties was to spend a night on this aerodrome – recently completed but not yet operational – with
only one other Home Guard private, presumably in order to
defend it from the possible threat of attack. My companion
was Harry Vokins, a boy of my own age (nearly seventeen) who lived above the village paper shop. Neither of us
understood whether the Government property we had been
ordered to protect was thought to be in danger from German
forces or merely vulnerable to mischievous local vandalism
– and, if the former, whether enemy approach should be
expected by land or from the air. Obediently but uncertainly, dressed in our baggy, prickly uniforms and armed
with bayonets and rifles, we climbed the hill at eight o'clock
in the evening to start our twelve hours' vigil.

As a small child, my fantasies of flight had centred on
this hill and its peak had symbolized the limit of my infantile
horizon. One winter, when the house was full of guests

for Christmas, I had been moved upstairs from my night nursery on the first floor to an attic bedroom, and from its unfamiliar window (low in the room but high in the outside wall) the summit of Larch Hill had seemed almost within leaping distance – much nearer than the church and the village street and the river in the valley between us. But the fantasies always stopped short at the hilltop, ending with a gentle landing on the crest and never indulging in curiosity about what, if anything, lay beyond. And later on, as I grew older, the impression persisted that nothing in fact did lie beyond the hill, even though I often climbed its grassy slope on foot or was driven up and over it on the minor road which led away from the village to the south. This was because, once Larch Hill had been ascended, it no longer seemed to have been a hill at all; the ground imperceptibly steadied itself before settling into a flat viewless field, so lacking in drama that it could not even be described as a plain.

But now it lacked drama no longer: a silent desert of crescent-shaped hangars, brutalist huts and endless runways, of tarmac, concrete and corrugated iron, the aerodrome awaited Harry Vokins and myself on the top of the hill like an immense ghost town, spooky in a peculiarly modern – even a futuristic – way. It was of course only empty because it had not yet begun its useful life, but in the grey dusk it seemed as though it had already been abandoned by some new form of existence too sinister to survive.

We found an open hut with some camp-beds in it, and made this our headquarters. Harry had brought with him a Thermos full of tea, a chocolate cup-cake, a child's comic and a torch to read it by. I had already eaten and had forgotten to bring a book. We had been advised to share our watch by dividing it into four sections of three hours each, with one of us acting as sentry while the other slept.

Harry picked the first and third periods, which meant I was to be on duty from eleven o'clock until two in the morning, and again from five o'clock until we knocked off at eight. He deposited his belongings on one of the camp-beds, then wandered out of the hut, dragging his gun behind him. I lay down on another bed but was unable to sleep. Soon I also drifted outside, where it was still faintly light. I walked around the aerodrome for nearly an hour before I came upon Harry squatting on his haunches outside a vast hollow hangar. I stood beside him and together we looked down at the blacked-out houses in the moonlit village. Neither of us spoke, until Harry amiably volunteered, 'My Gran reckons I'm stouter.'

Harry's grandmother, old Mrs Vokins, ran the paper shop; his mother, Miss Vokins, was weak in the head but a harmless and popular figure in the village; he had never known a father. Miss Vokins, who always wore black, was tall and very thin, with an impediment in her speech and a goitre; Harry resembled her in height and extreme emaciation, but he was not as simple-minded as she was although he was decidedly backward for his age. It was rumoured that he liked to expose himself to little girls in country lanes, but nothing of this kind had ever been proved against him and he was certainly incapable of inflicting physical hurt on any living creature.

Harry's gaze now shifted away from the village, following the dim glitter of the river to the left and stopping where the clump of bushes screening Watermead was darkly visible on its bank. 'But *her*,' he said, nodding his head in that direction, 'she don't agree with that, and all. No, she won't have it at any price. She reckons I'm still so skinny you could thread me through the eye of a needle, know what I mean? My Gran said she had to laugh. Oh, she's a caution like, that Kay.'

'Oh, you mean Kay Demarest. She's a friend of mine too.'

'I run errands for her, like,' Harry explained.

'So do I, sometimes.'

'She's a real lady,' he said, rather repressively. He rose to his feet and stretched. 'Nearly time for my kip,' he muttered, and then went off on his own. Although I had left my rifle in the hut, I decided that there was no point in following Harry back there before two o'clock, when it would be time to wake him for his second watch, so I stayed where I was and thought about Kay.

It interested but did not surprise me that Harry should turn out to be a friend of hers: so too were his rather similar contemporaries, Reg at the garage and Tom, the freckle-faced, sandy-haired boy at the Post Office whom she had nicknamed 'Spencer Tracy'. The only adult male friends whose names I had heard her mention were Roy Halma, a fortune-teller in Hove whom she regularly consulted by letter and sometimes visited in person, and Roy Halma's boy friend Ernest, a waiter at the Old Ship Hotel in Brighton. She also corresponded with another clairvoyant to whom she just alluded as 'my sand man'. Kay would send him some trivial object which she had carried about in her handbag for a while. Clutching this in one hand, with the other the sand man would gently agitate a soup plate on which he had sprinkled a quantity of sacred grains gathered centuries ago from the Sahara Desert; within the patterns they formed, he claimed he could discern the salient aspects of Kay's immediate future.

She did have several women friends, but I had not yet succeeded in clearly establishing their names or identifying their separate personalities, because when she referred to any one of them she would do so by the inclusive term 'my girl friend'. Such a reference usually took the form of indirect quotation, giving vehement expression to some mildly eccentric but fiercely held prejudice. 'My girl friend refuses point blank to wear anything but silk next to her skin.' 'My girl friend can't stand Michaelmas daisies. Won't have 'em in the house. She's just got a thing about them – they make her quite ill.' 'My girl friend won't live north of the park. She's funny that way. Knightsbridge, Kensington, Chelsea – that's fine by her. But if somebody said to her, why don't you move to Bayswater, I'm very much afraid they'd get a flea in their ear.'

Kay was equally uncommunicative about her former lovers, who also remained anonymous and whose characteristics were only hinted at. I could tell, however, that there had been a number – a married man, a man's man, a ladies' man, a gentleman jockey, an irresistible womaniser, a hopeless case, a bad lot, a good shot, a lovable shit. Some of these attributes may have coincided in the same person – but of this and other details I was never quite sure. The vagueness about facts did not irritate me, because the emotional atmosphere surrounding them was so potently evoked by Kay. Something – a snatch of song, a name glimpsed in a newspaper, a view from a window, the whistle of a train – would stir her memory; her face would assume that rueful, reminiscent, secretive expression which I had come to know well; she would mutter some barely intelligible phrase suggesting affectionate regret; and I felt that she had conveyed to me the very essence of her past relationship with a shadowy masculine image about whom I needed to know nothing more definite than that Kay had been reminded of him at that moment.

Like me, but for different reasons, Kay was now living in a kind of limbo, and our intimacy had greatly increased over the past few months, accelerated by propinquity and a shared, somewhat shameful although involuntary, *désœuvrement*. The war, which was causing so much misery elsewhere by separating lovers and fragmenting family life, had done the Demarests a subtler disservice: it had thrust them into undesired proximity. Fear of the Blitz had forced Sybil and Charlie to relinquish their London flats and to make Watermead their permanent and only home. Kay, too, after several sporadic and unexplained absences during the early days of the war, had reluctantly come to roost there, as it seemed for the duration. She did not want to live at Watermead and her parents did not want her to do so, but none the less there she appeared to be stuck, as if she had been officially evacuated from some danger area and billeted, against the will of all concerned, on her own family.

'I'm only there on sufferance – they make that *crystal* clear,' she had told me on one of our walks. 'What I can't stand is the way they insist on treating me as if I were still a child – they seem to forget I'll be thirty-five next birthday! They make me feel like an unclaimed parcel that has been returned to sender – in a rather battered condition! Or as if I had been let out of some prison or loony bin or other on parole, or bound over on a promise of good behaviour, or whatever the expression is. You may well ask why I put up with it. But the simple truth is, I just don't have anywhere else to go.'

So Kay, at a time when the presence of political refugees from Europe had become a familiar feature of English life, wandered round the village in search of temporary shelter as if she too had been driven into exile from the purely domestic hell of Watermead. Toting her rations in a shoulder-bag, with a once-smart scarf thrown over her head and tied beneath her chin like a peasant's shawl, she would beg to be allowed to eat her evening meal – and sometimes stay the night – at the Post Office, the garage, the paper shop or at my parents' house. 'There's such a ghastly atmosphere at home today that I just couldn't face dinner there, I'd really rather die. If I can only keep out of their way till tomorrow I'll be perfectly safe, because we're expecting Sandy back then on forty-eight hours' leave so they'll be on their best behaviour.' Sandy had enlisted in the RAF as soon as war broke out (to the distress of Charlie, who would have preferred him to have joined an old cavalry regiment) and had become a hero of the Battle of Britain.

There were people in the village who wondered why Kay did not escape from her predicament of dependence by entering one of the Women's Services or working in a munitions factory. I knew her well enough by now to understand that such obvious solutions to her problem were out of the question, although it was difficult to explain to strangers exactly why this should be the case. The self-consciousness which made her so socially maladroit in civilian life would almost certainly, in circumstances involving regimental discipline or the rigour of an assembly line, have found expression in a physical clumsiness that would have limited her usefulness and might even have constituted a potential danger. She was not, however, totally unemployable, having held down several jobs before the war, though never for very long; selling hats in a Mayfair shop called Odile, for example, and appearing as an extra in films ('One got paid double if one turned up in a presentable evening dress'). Shortly after drifting back to Watermead, she had succeeded in getting herself taken on as a part-time assistant to Mr Tripp, who managed the NAAFI canteen recently installed at the British Legion Hall in the village High Street; but this work was very poorly paid.

As Kay received no unearned income, she was always hard up. Her life was conditioned, and her movements restricted, by the nagging memory of innumerable small debts — many of them so minor that they had long ago been uncomplainingly written off by her creditors. But Kay's conventional upbringing, combined with her spontaneously generous nature, had made her essentially scrupulous over money matters, and the knowledge that she owed anything to anybody caused her genuine distress. She was equally punctilious about fulfilling the obligations imposed by formal 'good manners': if one gave Kay lunch, and then met her in the village before she had posted her letter of thanks, she would either try to avoid one altogether or would anticipate any greeting by a remorseful cry of 'I owe you a letter!' She was even more furtive if confronted unexpectedly by an acquaintance who had once lent her sixpence to tip a porter, or placed a modest bet for her on a losing horse in a long-past race because she had feared no bookie would give her credit.

Kay suffered from a congenital lack of energy, and after taking books out of W. H. Smith's lending libraries in Swindon or Marlborough she would succumb to a mysterious, destructive lassitude which prevented her from returning them until long after the dates written on the little tickets dangling reproachfully from their spines. Conscious of having incurred a debt which mounted terrifyingly with every day that went by, and unable to compute with even approximate accuracy the sum of the fines to which she might eventually be liable, she would postpone their settlement yet further. When at last Kay feared that some river of no return had been fatally crossed, she judged it too much of a risk to be seen passing W. H. Smith's shop windows in either town, and to escape notice, recognition and exposure she would condemn herself to inconvenient detours, dodging down side alleys or hiding behind traffic in the main streets except on safe Sundays and early-closing afternoons. Most of the borrowed books did in the end find their way back to the libraries (sometimes conveyed there by me) but one of her favourites – *Without My Cloak* by Kate O'Brien – still remained in her possession. Kay's sense of guilt at having in effect stolen *Without My Cloak* had become so overwhelming that she now refused to visit Marlborough or Swindon at all unless she was covered up in some sort of wrap as a token disguise – in fact (I made myself laugh at the thought as I waited for the hours to pass in my lonely dark hilltop watch) in those places she was *never* without her cloak!

At two o'clock in the morning I re-entered the hut. Harry was sleeping so deeply that his face no longer resembled a sentient countenance and the prominent Adam's apple in his long white neck, more than usually exposed by his supine position, seemed to be the most expressive feature in his body. I thought it might be difficult to wake him, but after a tentative touch on the shoulder his eyes opened at once and he submissively rose from his bed. I lay down on mine but still could not sleep although my thoughts were becoming as painfully pictorial and uncontrollably inconsequent as dreams. They circled round a scene that had recently taken place at Watermead and which had been described to me in hallucinatory detail by Kay.

Father, mother and daughter were assembled in the sitting-room to listen to the BBC evening news. This programme was invariably preceded by a performance of the national anthem. On the night in question, as its opening chords were struck, an event took place at the Demarests' hearth that had never happened there before: apparently in hypnotised obedience to a sudden over-mastering impulse, Sybil had slowly and gracefully risen to her feet and had continued to stand stiffly to attention on the Axminster carpet, her blue eyes staring steadily ahead of her at the Ladbroke calendar on the mantelpiece in a solemn gaze which implied a combination of personal humility and patriotic pride.

Kay glanced up at her in bewilderment and then tactfully looked away. 'I thought Mummy was making a complete ass of herself by getting up on her hind legs like that but it's her own drawing-room and how she behaves in it is no business of anybody else's. Though I did find it devilishly embarrassing. To tell you the truth, I nearly went through the floor!'

A second or so later, Charlie noticed the alteration in his wife's posture, and he too eyed her in startled irritation for a moment before taking in the significance of her action. 'He's deaf as a post, you know, so he probably didn't even realise it was "God Save the King" they were playing. But when the penny finally dropped, of course *he* had to get in on the act as well!' Clumsily and apologetically, he clambered out of his armchair and stood frozen in a military stance even more rigid than his wife's, but with a look of fury on his face that contrasted comically with her expression of noble serenity.

Kay soon saw that Charlie's anger was directed at herself, and understood that he was silently accusing her of disloyalty to her country and irreverence to her God by continuing to remain seated in this exalted atmosphere. He made her feel, in fact, that she was doing nothing so innocent as merely sitting down, but that she was provocatively lolling, impertinently lounging, almost indecently sprawling. Part of her longed to get up ('Anything for a quiet life'), however ridiculous she would have considered such a surrender to the hypocritical hysteria that seemed to have seized her parents; but a greater part was gripped by the same moral paralysis and morbid passivity that prevented her from returning her library books on time, and she found to her horror that she was quite unable to move.

The spectacle of her stubborn stillness – which he interpreted as a wilful refusal to surmount a sickly, self-indulgent languor – drove Charlie to a climax of exasperation where he lost all control. Grunting inaudible curses, he abandoned the pretence of respect due to the anthem which was still playing on the radio and precipitately stumbled to a point just behind Kay's armchair. He then began to push vigorously against its back in a frenzied attempt to overturn it, with the intention of tipping her on to the carpet. But the solid weight of the chair frustrated this plan, and all he managed to do was to shove it forward a few inches, still bearing the inert figure of his daughter, who was now seriously frightened.

The music stopped and Sybil, who had pointedly ignored Charlie's slapstick antics by preserving a sentry-like immobility during the whole episode, felt free to relax at last; raising her dress a little over her hips so as not to 'seat out' her skirt, she gravely lowered herself back into her chair. Charlie returned to his and the three of them proceeded to listen to the news, cosily grouped round the wireless like so many other anxious families throughout the beleaguered country, the only evidence of anything untoward having occurred being the sound of Charlie's panting and the fact that Kay's chair had been shifted slightly askew from its accustomed position.

The vivacity with which Kay recounted such secret family dramas made her an amusing companion on a walk, or indoors by the gramophone, gossiping while she painted her nails a new colour after we had read our daily horoscopes (and those of absent friends) or competed in a private game which consisted of naming as many of Carole Lombard's films as we could remember. But I knew that the hostility she inspired in her parents hurt her like a constantly throbbing wound, and as I lay in the hut on the desolate aerodrome I longed to help her to escape from their petty persecution and give the wound a chance to heal.

The sun rose during my second watch. The gardens behind the houses on the southern side of the High Street, which enviably bordered on the river, became visible in detail as the light gained strength. From some of these I had been allowed to bathe as a child. An early ray caught the glass conservatory at the back of the doctor's surgery, transforming it into a brilliant translucent globe which seemed on the point of floating free from the building to which it was attached. Some elemental quality about its bulbous shape and crystalline consistency must have corresponded to an obscure stimulus in my pre-conscious memory, for the sight had the same unsettling effect on me – an acute aesthetic nostalgia – as that of the pointed white tents, glimpsed from a distance through the window of a moving car, which used to materialise on Salisbury Plain during peacetime army manoeuvres.

Above the High Street, I could see the churchyard where my father had been buried at the beginning of the year, and just beyond it the other garden, which did not yet show any palpable signs of decay as a result of his inability to tend it. And above the other garden, my home. For some reason, the curtains of my bedroom window had been drawn the night before: I confusedly imagined that behind them I must be still asleep in bed. My long vigil had left me shrouded in a fierce fatigue, an insubstantial but poisonous vapour which seemed to spread back into my past and seep ahead into my future, staining not only my body and mind but also my entire existence. Through it, I was dimly aware that rest and relief were near. Soon I would stagger down the hill with Harry Vokins and, after parting with him at the paper shop, would walk up through the churchyard in a dream, my steps growing heavier and heavier as they approached the house. This would appear oddly unfamiliar, as the impression made by a place seen for the first time differs subtly from the way in which it is later known and remembered. Once back upstairs in my own bed – and for as long as I remained there – I would be safe: safe from the war with its teasing threat of further death and its yet more fearsome challenge to an intenser form of life than any I had known.

4

When I reached Oxford I discovered Billy Phipps already in residence at the same college. It soon became clear that our former friendship had lost its point although at first we made half-hearted attempts to keep it going. He invited me to come out beagling with him and announced that he had put me up for membership of the Gridiron, one of several clubs to which he belonged. I ignored the first suggestion and, since I heard no more of the second, could only assume that I had been embarrassingly blackballed by Billy's fellow members.

His wizened worldliness no longer struck me as a respectable form of sophistication, although this quality still seemed desirable in my eyes – partly because I didn't understand its precise meaning and so could never be sure if I had correctly diagnosed its presence or not. I was persuaded that it was less likely to be found among the undergraduates at the depleted University of those war years than in the busy town, which then housed the personnel of various Government Ministries evacuated from London. The friends I finally made were mainly art students at the Slade School, which had also moved from bomb-threatened Bloomsbury to premises in Oxford. The most gifted of these, the most flamboyant and the most delightful, was Denis Bellamy, whom I got to know during my second term.

Being with Denis was like finding oneself in the cast of an 'intimate revue' or a lavish Hollywood musical, unprepared for the performance but secure because the star would carry one. He spoke with the dizzily inventive timing of a comedian and moved with the lazy discipline of a dancer. One might be walking with him from his rooms in Walton Street to the Randolph bar, discussing Géricault's studies of the insane or Blake's engravings, when he would suddenly break into a rumba in the middle of Beaumont Street, singing in imitation of Hermione Gingold: 'And when I'm *out* with *Jack* I really *find* the *black-out* very pleasant . . . 'cos his moustache is phospho*res*cent!' – his voice rising to a wild shriek on the last word; or else impulsively dash up the steps of the Ashmolean and then descend them at a stately pace with his body turned a little to one side, his arms extended in a graceful pose and a condescending smile of ecstatic self-admiration on his lips, pretending to be Hedy Lamarr or Lana Turner in the 'You Stepped Out of a Dream' number from *Ziegfeld Girl*, while he crooned an improvised parody of the lyric: '*You* stepped out of a *drain* . . . where did you *get* that hat? . . . You look quite *insane* . . .'

He was tall and thin, with thick chestnut hair, high cheekbones and large eyes and mouth; although he dressed conventionally, some inner lack of inhibition must have shown through the grey flannel trousers and tweed jackets because people often stared at him with disapproval in the street and – by the rigid standards governing masculine comportment at the time – he was considered somewhat outrageous. But Denis was without any exhibitionist desire to shock and his charm was entirely unaffected. He conformed naturally to some aspects of the current 'camp' culture but his wit was never bitchy and his character had no trace of competitive envy. Somewhere in his make-up was a down-to-earth, no-nonsense North Country landlady who would give sound practical advice when consulted and had no time to waste on any form of pretentiousness. In love he was ardent and artless, either romantically faithful while an important affair lasted or dangerously promiscuous after it had come to grief. As a friend he was loyal and generous: when one of his paintings was included in a mixed show at the Leicester Galleries in London and subsequently sold, he gave all the proceeds to a girl student at the Slade who needed money for an abortion. He had been tubercular for years but quixotically refused to seek treatment for the disease or to follow the careful régime that might prevent it from getting worse.

I did not see as much of Denis as I would have wished during that spring and summer – he was not only in great demand from other friends but also absorbed both in his work at the Slade, where he was a brilliantly promising pupil, and in the cliff-hanging serial of his erotic adventures – but I found that even a short time in his company would cheer me up to such an extent that I did not grudge his absences. In between our meetings, I mooched about Oxford, haunted by the hit song – 'Blues in the Night' – which floated ceaselessly through open windows in the town and from distant river-boats. The music uncannily epitomised a tempting mood of solitary sadness, unfocused longing and vague expectation into which it was all too easy to sink.

Shortly after his twenty-first birthday party (which started with drinks at the Playhouse bar, moved on to the George for dinner and ended with an all-night dance at a don's house in Holywell) Denis had a serious haemorrhage. This frightened him into taking the advice which his friends had been proffering for so long: he went into hospital at last. He wrote me a letter from a sanatorium in Cornwall. 'There's a funny idea going around that consumption is romantic – you know, Mimi or *La Dame aux Camélias* daintily coughing blood into a lace hankie and Katherine Mansfield drawing her *chaise-longue* a little bit closer to the window every day. Well, my dear, don't you believe a word of it! TB couldn't be more squalid if it tried – take it from Mother, she knows! They're going to collapse one of my lungs, which I'm told is "unpleasant" but not the worst. What I'm terrified of is having to have some of my ribs removed, but with luck that won't be necessary. I've got a mania for Elizabeth Bowen and am reading all her books. I'm dying to know what she's like. There's a very arty lady here with her hair done in "earphones" – exactly like Gingold in that sketch where she gives a lecture on "mew-sick". Well, the doctor told her the other day that she hasn't much longer to live. It's rather got me down because she's really awfully sweet ... Among all the patients there's only one who's rather attractive, but he's almost cured and is probably leaving next month. Another myth about this illness is that it makes everybody madly randy. God, I hope I get out of here soon!'

After Denis's departure, the sense of unreality which I had felt at Oxford from the start grew more oppressive. It was June 1942, and I was nearing the end of my third term. The beauty of the place in summer only seemed to enhance its latent melancholy. I saw little point in working for a good degree when the future (my own, the world's) was so uncertain. In retreat from a looming depression, I tried to get back home as often as I could. There was no great distance between the University and my village, but a comfortable and reliable method of covering it was frustratingly hard to find. The two places were only indirectly linked by an inconvenient network of stopping trains with ill-timed connections and rare rural buses; petrol rationing had ensured a scarcity of private motorists; hitchhiking on lorries was a chancy business.

Kay Demarest, however, had worked out a scheme by which I might travel in security and for nothing. She was one of those people who enjoyed inventing ingenious ways round minor difficulties, whether these were imposed by the war or not; for example, rather than risk posting an expensive parcel to London, she would find out whether a friend of a friend might know somebody who was going there anyway, and would sometimes succeed in persuading a complete stranger to act as her courier. The more complicated the plan, the greater would be her gratification at its execution. She now suggested that I should be given a lift in the car which delivered cake to the NAAFI where she worked; she had discovered that it began its rounds at Oxford. After lengthy preparations, she wrote to tell me that it was all fixed: I could 'come with the cake'.

Kay arranged a rendezvous for me and my transport at seven o'clock one Saturday morning outside the entrance to the Cadena Café in the Cornmarket. I had been waiting there for half an hour before a small van drew up driven by a woman dressed rather like a Land Girl: she told me to hop into the seat beside her. Behind us, a pile of cardboard cartons and tin boxes rattled when we moved. These contained various kinds of cake: small hard rock scones, fat Swiss rolls, truncated segments of dark Dundee and pale Madeira in transparent wrappings and samples of fancier brands such as marzipan layer and lemon curd sandwich confined in coffin-shaped cases.

The journey turned out to be the longest and most boring that I had ever undertaken. The van slowly traversed a meandering cross-country route linking hamlet to village to market town, in each of which one or more leisurely deliveries were made at British Restaurants or NAAFI and Church Army canteens housed in municipal buildings or newly erected Nissen huts, as well as at several commercial cafés and one isolated farm house in the middle of open fields. The driver never spoke, and neither did I: perhaps we both didn't like to be the first to do so. It was nearly seven in the evening when, stiff and weary and hungry, I was deposited at our destination in the High Street of my own village – only a distance of about thirty miles as a crow might have flown from the spot where we started out.

This sluggish pilgrimage reminded me of my night on Home Guard duty the previous year and, as then, I spent some of the time thinking about Kay, whom I expected to find waiting to greet me when it was over. My mother had recently passed on to me some dramatic news concerning the Demarests. A month or so earlier, Sandy's plane had been shot down over occupied France and he had been reported missing, believed killed. But only a few days later, his family were officially informed that he had been captured alive and unhurt by German forces, and was now a prisoner of war. Knowing Kay's instinctive preference for undemonstrative behaviour, I decided not to mention this subject unless she did.

She didn't; but the relief she must still have been feeling after hearing of Sandy's reprieve was shown in the elation of her welcome. 'How wonderful! You made it!' she exclaimed, while the driver was helping the canteen manager to unload his order from the back of her van. 'You actually came with the cake! I'm so glad it worked out all right – you must often do it again. Listen, Mr Tripp has given me the evening off, so now that you're here let's go on a pub crawl. I need cheering up. This morning I heard some rather touching news. My friend Roy Halma wrote to tell me that poor Ernest has died. He's frightfully cut up about it . . . But you must be starving. Here, have a slice of this coffee gâteau before we set out. It's on the house!'

Owing to the scarcity of spirits, cigarettes and even matches, a pub crawl in those days took on something of the glamour of a quest. There were seven to choose from in the village, ranging from the stately Lion in the centre of the High Street, which was also a small hotel, to a minute, nameless back-room in a Beatrix Potter cottage standing by itself at the far end of a lonely lane. Word would get round that one or other of these had received a consignment of Gordon's or Player's Weights – but when one got there, more often than not, it was to find that the gin had run out already and rum was on offer instead, while the cigarettes were only being sold singly or in pairs, carelessly handed over the bar in a sodden, stained condition and smelling of stale beer.

Kay and I fetched up in the back-room of the cottage, rather drunk on several pints of bitter and a few glasses of sweet, sticky rum. We each had one Weight left, but nothing with which to light them.

'Leave it to me,' said Kay. She boldly surveyed the small, almost empty room. A GI was standing on his own at the bar. 'Just watch this,' she murmured, and with her 'tarty' walk she approached and (there is no other word) accosted him.

'Got a match, soldier?' she asked, flourishing her damp, discoloured gasper as stylishly as if it had been a Balkan Sobranie in an ivory holder. The GI produced a lighter and as she ducked her head to the flame he said, 'Did anyone ever tell you that you look like Jean Harlow?'

Kay lifted her head and fixed her eyes on his in an expressionless stare while she slowly dragged on her cigarette and, after an alarmingly long pause, exhaled the smoke through her nose. 'What's it to you if they have? Mind your own business!' she said rudely, and then rather grudgingly added, 'Oh – and thanks for the fire.' She sauntered back to her former place, where she lit my cigarette from hers.

She was obviously very pleased with this exchange. 'Funny he should say that,' she mused. 'Nobody's ever told me that before, as it happens. People used to say I looked like Joan Crawford. But that was ages ago, when she first started. Speaking for myself, I shouldn't have thought I was the Harlow type at all – can't see the faintest resemblance, frankly. I can *just* see Crawford, but for the life of me I can't see Harlow.'

There was in fact no physical resemblance between Kay and either of these actresses, but it struck me then that her manner with men in a potentially sexual context must have been strongly influenced by that of Joan Crawford on the screen. This manner would swing between two extremes. At one, the woman in the film who suspected some guy of 'getting fresh' with her would be bad-tempered, impatient, quite unnecessarily snubbing and sometimes almost unforgivably insulting. Watching some of Joan Crawford's performances, I had been reminded of the way a bitch on heat behaves to a dog who is sniffing her hindquarters – venomously snapping at him and leaping away as if in furious outrage, but somehow still remaining on hand. At the other extreme, reached with apparently arbitrary abruptness and with no intervening gradations of mood, she would melt into a state of exalted tenderness and submissiveness so totally overwhelming as to produce a stifling effect of menace . . . Kay's favourite films – *Man's Castle* and *Strange Cargo* – were romantic melodramas, and she often affected an air of sentimental toughness which made me think of Joan Crawford and other movie stars who played hard-working, hard-done-by women ready and able to humiliate the harmless men they despise but also – and not always convincingly – capable of suicidal sacrifice for the cruel men they love. It was the sentimental toughness of numerous popular songs between the wars, celebrating the sordid lives of tired taxi-dancers, heartbroken tarts and ill-used one-man-girls which managed to distil a heady drop of bittersweet poetry from trite and depressing themes.

Shortly before closing time, I had to go to the pub's primitive Gents. While I was pissing against a wall in the yard, I became aware of the GI doing the same beside me. 'Is she on the make?' he suddenly asked.

I was embarrassed and pretended not to understand him.

'The dame you're with – is she on the make?' he patiently repeated. I could think of nothing better to reply than, 'I don't know.'

The three of us left the pub together. The GI was called Howard Spangler – a quiet, courteous young man, short and thickset with a large, low bottom. I left them outside the Lion, taking the path home through the churchyard while they walked slowly on down the High Street. The GI was whistling the tune of 'Stardust' and Kay was singing the words.

When I next saw Kay, she told me that she had fallen in love with Howard Spangler and was having an affair with him.

'Did you go to bed with him that night after the pub?' I asked.

'Well, not exactly – but as near as makes no matter! I went to field with him, if you really want to know!'

Kay's graphic answer brought home to me for the first time the inadequacy of the current euphemism for love-making which I had used as a matter of course, and initi-ated another of our private jokes. On a later occasion, Kay announced that she had 'gone to floor' with Howard Spangler – the floor being that of the NAAFI canteen. 'And damned hard it was, too!'

The joke, however, was a wry one, underlining the fact that Kay had no place of her own where she could meet her lover in comfort. (To present him to her parents was out of the question: an earlier wartime romance of Kay's, with a captain in an infantry regiment stationed near Swindon, had fizzled out because Charlie had banned him from Water-mead on the grounds that 'he couldn't speak the King's English'.) At first, the pride and fun in 'having an Ameri-can' raised Kay's spirits to a point where she could laugh about this handicap, and even find in it a welcome element of melodrama to dignify the rather prosaic relationship that had developed between Howard and herself. But, almost from the beginning, she feared that it could not last. Other GIs who had taken up with women in the village were enjoying fringe benefits in addition to simple sexual satisfaction: home cooking, cosy domestic interiors, a friendly social atmosphere, and it was mainly for these that they paid happily with gifts of chewing gum, peanut butter and Lucky Strikes. Apart from her own body, and a provocative line in movie-script repartee, poor Kay had only the fields and the NAAFI floor to offer Howard, and she doubted that this would be enough to hold him for long.

My mother assured Kay that she and Howard could meet at our house whenever they liked, but this did not solve her problem: army officers had been billeted on us, occupying more than half the available space, and the part retained for our own use was too exiguous to accommodate a lovers' tryst. Kay did, however, arrange for Howard to pick her up at our place on one of their dates. She was anxious to introduce him to my mother – hoping thus to sketch in, as it were, some sort of respectable background for herself.

Kay turned up hours before Howard was due to arrive, wearing her familiar uniform of headscarf, slacks and shoulder-bag – the latter unusually heavy, as in addition to its regular load of knitting, cigarettes and magazines it also contained various cosmetic preparations (mascara, nail polish, Odorono) as well as a change of costume. Clothes of course were rationed then, and women used to buy, borrow or swap each other's garments. Kay had been lent a skirt by Mrs Tripp, the wife of her boss at the NAAFI, and my mother gave her one of her own blouses to go with it. Kay had also brought with her a bottle of some liquid application with which to stain her naked legs and produce the illusion that she was wearing nylon stockings. Howard was expected to call for her at seven; he had promised to escort her to a dance at the Village Hall, in aid of the local Women's Institute, and had been invited to 'look in' for a drink with us first.

But he didn't show up at seven. By nine o'clock, Kay conceded that he was unlikely to do so that evening. She had been looking forward so intensely to the outing that we expected her disappointment to be devastating. Kay surprised us by appearing neither hurt nor angry but, if anything, rather relieved. 'Well, at least I can relax now in something comfortable!' she said, as she changed back into her everyday attire and wiped the make-up off her face. 'I do think he might have let us know – but it's probably not his fault. One does tend to forget that these people are fighting a war.'

'What a shame,' said my mother. 'I would so much like to have met him.'

'I think you'd have got on with him if you had. Mind you, he's no oil painting, that I grant. And he's not exactly what one's parents would call a gentleman – ghastly expression – but we're none of us snobs here, are we? Oh, to hell with him. I'm going to celebrate by making myself look as ugly as possible! To which no doubt you might say: *that* wouldn't be hard!'

For years Kay had suffered from a dread of looking her best when there was nobody to admire the effect she made, of being 'all dressed up with nowhere to go'. She was the opposite of those legendary imperialists who insisted on changing for dinner in the jungle. The wasted effort involved in such disciplined behaviour did not just strike her as comically pointless – its crazy conventionality contained for her a peculiar element of horror. The experience of being stood up by Howard Spangler promoted this characteristic of hers from a mild neurosis to a morbid obsession.

Kay never again applied make-up to her face and body

or put on a pretty garment: she seemed to take a grim delight in 'letting her looks go' altogether. This extreme reaction was probably prompted by a romantic pride, with perhaps a touch of conceit. Kay longed for a lover, longed for a husband, longed for children – but she was only interested in the kind of man who would 'take her as she was', independent of any artificial aids to beauty or simulated allure. Did she see herself as a sleeping Brünhilde, preserved by a ring of fire from any but the most heroic suitor? I think her attitude was less arrogant – she merely wanted to spare herself the hideous humiliation of trying to attract, and failing.

So instead she gave the false impression of trying to repel. Kay stalked the streets and lanes, still (as it seemed to me) an arresting and pleasing figure, but so gaunt in outline, so bereft of the accepted manifestations of feminine charm, that she almost seemed a creature for whom definition by age or sex would have hardly any meaning. Some of her back teeth had recently had to be drawn and she resolutely and perversely refused to have them replaced by false ones, thus giving her face an unnecessarily sunken, even a skeletal appearance. Kay's stated reason for this deliberate neglect was an understandable reluctance to incur large dentist's bills, but I think she was really motivated by the irrational valour of the stoic for whom self-mutilation may be a secret challenge to the inevitability of decay, a device to negate its terrors by hastening its approach.

Howard was soon scared off: shortly after the broken date he vanished from her life. I once overheard her discussed by two other American soldiers outside the Lion – they said she looked like the witch in *Snow White*. There was nothing witch-like (either black or white) in the Kay I knew and loved; rather, she seemed to me the hapless victim of a mysterious spell binding her to the callous custody of her parents.

No doubt because her waking life was so unsatisfactory, Kay paid close attention to her dreams. Some passing reference of mine, during one of our long walks by the river, would cause her to exclaim, 'You've broken my dream!' – and she would then describe it to me in detail. Often her very first remark, when we met by arrangement at the paper shop before the walk, would be, 'I dreamed about you last night.' The news that I had featured in Kay's dreams was flattering, even exciting, but also rather disturbing, and my instinct on hearing it would be to apologise for any crass, boorish or unseemly behaviour of which I might have been unconsciously guilty: it was hard not to feel that the responsibility for my speech and actions in her dream was mine instead of hers. But it always turned out that I had played a harmless, and usually a subsidiary, role: the star part, more often than not, belonged to Sandy. Night after night, Kay would dream that she was with him somewhere in Europe; blissfully happy, she would be sitting by a trout stream while in companionable silence he squatted on the bank beside her intently choosing a fly from his colourful collection of purples and browns, or stood tall in the water laying his line across the ripples with a kind of hesitant courtesy, as though diffidently but gracefully executing a respectful bow. Screened by trees on the opposite shore, she could dimly see the prison camp from which he had either escaped, or been let out on forty-eight hours' leave: in obedience to the scrambled logic of dreams, it looked exactly like Watermead.

5

Later that summer, I was invited to a tea party by Dodo at Love's Cottage, where she now lived all the year round; Charlie and Sybil were to be the other guests. I arrived early to find Dodo chortling to herself over *What I Left Unsaid*, a book of memoirs by an old friend of hers, Daisy, Princess of Pless. 'Oh, dear, she *could* be such a silly ass! Just listen to this − it's the first sentence of her chapter on King Edward's Coronation: "London was upside down − and so was Daisy!" That *might* have been phrased a tiny bit more elegantly, don't you agree? As one of the reviewers remarked − it would have been better if she *had* left it unsaid!'

I asked her if the Demarests had had any news of Sandy and she told me that letters from him had indeed reached Watermead, that he was in good health and spirits, well enough treated by his captors and complaining only of boredom. 'It is such a pity,' Dodo went on, 'that Kay and her parents can't get on a bit better: it would worry Sandy so terribly if he knew. I must say, brother and sister aren't at all alike − she's a striking girl in many ways but she certainly doesn't have Sandy's looks. I believe that there *was* some gossip − but I'm sure it was nonsense − that after Kay turned out to be a girl Sybil changed the bowling.'

'You mean, that Charlie isn't Sandy's real father?'

'But I don't believe it for one instant. One could understand a woman doing that when the family were longing for a son and there'd only been rows of daughters, but in this case it really would have been a little soon – and it's not as if an old title were involved, or a big place somewhere, or anything like that. Help! – here they come, I can see them through the window. Wouldn't it be awful if they knew what we'd just been saying about them?'

Sybil entered the cottage carrying several copies of a new novel by John Steinbeck called *The Moon Is Down*: she pressed one of these on me and one on Dodo. 'I simply insist on you both reading this book at the very earliest opportunity you get. I came across it quite by chance – a friend lent it to me, as a matter of fact – and it impressed me so deeply that as soon as I had finished it I wrote off at once to Hatchards and ordered two dozen copies. I make a point of giving it to everyone I meet – well, everyone, that is, whom I consider capable of appreciating it. I won't say anything about what it's about, for fear of spoiling your pleasure, but if you're anything like me you won't be able to put it down. Charlie will tell you that it's very rare for me to go off the deep end about a thing like this, won't you, Charlie?'

'Certainly,' said Charlie. 'The last time she had a craze was for that weird musical play, *The Immortal Hour*. I think she went forty times!'

'Oh, wasn't it divine?' said Dodo. 'That heavenly song – "How beautiful they are, the lordly ones, who dwell in the hills, the hollow hills . . ." Oh dear, my voice has quite gone, but I think that's roughly how it went. I always thought "the lordly ones" was rather a ridiculous phrase, to tell you the truth, but it's such a pretty melody. How sweet of you to give me this book, darling, it looks lovely.'

'I found it most inspiring. I should perhaps warn you that it's not for the squeamish – but for Heaven's sake don't run away with the idea that it's in any way offensive! I only mean that it doesn't come under the heading of what is now called "escapist" entertainment. On the other hand, there is absolutely nothing defeatist about it. If there's one thing that makes me see red, it's defeatism. Oh dear, there are moments when I do so desperately wish I'd been born a man! Don't you?'

Dodo had quietly left the room to fetch a milk jug from the kitchen, so Sybil found that she had addressed these last words to Charlie and myself.

'Oh – but of course you *are* men! Needless to say, I never for one second intended to imply anything to the contrary and did not expect to be taken *au pied de la lettre*. No, the point I was trying to make is that, *being* men, you couldn't possibly either of you hope to enter into a woman's feelings about certain subjects.' She raised her voice. 'Dodo, dear! I was just saying how much I wished I were a man. Don't you?'

'Do you mean, do I wish you were a man, or do I wish I was?' said Dodo, rejoining us. 'On the whole, I think I'm all right as I am. I mean, one has the vote. I know one ought to be frightfully grateful to the suffragettes for fighting our battles for us, but I'm afraid I did think them an awful nuisance at the time.'

Charlie muttered something about race meetings having to be cancelled.

'No, dear,' said Sybil, 'you don't quite understand me . . . It's just that I sometimes find myself envying the male sex its God-given right to quite simply go out there and take a jolly good swipe at the enemy. Not that I'm the slightest bit bloodthirsty by nature. I'm quite prepared to carry on doing my bit by just carrying on – which is what we poor women are always being asked to do – but I do on occasion feel an overwhelming urge to *get cracking*! Don't you?'

'I sometimes think if I'm told one more time to carry on,' said Dodo naughtily, 'I *shall*!'

'I do believe,' Sybil continued, 'that when the history books come to be written it will emerge that the great unsung heroine of these terrible times we're living through will be none other than that much maligned creature, the British Housewife! I'm thinking, in fact, of writing a letter to the *Daily Telegraph* to propose that some promising young sculptor – or perhaps a *sculptress* would be a better choice – should be officially commissioned to design a statue in her honour, and that the result should be prominently erected in some public place. I don't know about you, but I for one am getting sick and tired of looking at monuments portraying middle-aged men on horseback!'

'Where's the money going to come from?' asked Charlie. 'Out of the taxpayer's pocket, you can bet your boots, as per usual.'

'I'm terribly sorry, but I had rather imagined – naively, no doubt – that the artist and stonemasons concerned on such a project might be willing to work for nothing. However, if sufficient funds are not forthcoming,' Sybil went on, 'perhaps it might be humbly suggested to His Majesty King George VI that a brand new medal might be struck, to be awarded at the appropriate times of the year to a selection of especially deserving women who would stand as representatives of each and every British Housewife in the land. But, very likely, reasons will be found to prove this scheme impractical, too – I confess to being an incorrigible idealist! Though I can't help thinking it would do a power of good as regards the not unnegligible matter of boosting the nation's morale.'

'You mentioned the King,' said Dodo. 'Well, personally, I think it would give a boost to the nation's morale if the female members of the Royal Family had a tiny bit more dress sense! You never saw such an un-clothes-conscious bunch! Queen Elizabeth's fur-trimmed coats are becoming almost as tiresome as old Queen Mary's *toques*!' (Dodo pronounced the last word with a French accent, and I did not immediately recognise it.) 'The only one with any claim to *chic* was dear Queen Alexandra. Her taste was always flawless.'

'But I shall never forgive her – never,' said Sybil, 'for going into colours so soon after King Edward's death. I think in that respect she showed far from flawless taste. In fact, I think she showed deplorable lack of respect and quite indecent haste! I can't remember precisely how long she waited, but it seemed that in no time at all she was appearing before the public – not in *demi-deuil*, nothing like that – but in the brightest hues of the rainbow! I'm afraid it set a very poor example to the rest of us.'

'Oh, I think those long periods of public mourning were such a dreary hypocritical Victorian custom!' said Dodo. 'I was only too thankful to see them begin to go out of fashion after what I always call *our* war – and if they're completely done away with after this one, then that would be *one* good thing to come out of it, at least.'

'I feel very differently,' said Sybil, 'but it's a tricky question and we really *shouldn't* quarrel over it so shall we just agree to differ? To change the subject, I must say I do think you're not *quite* fair to the Royals. You're forgetting the Duchess of Kent.'

'Oh yes, so I am. She's too lovely, isn't she? *And* she dresses divinely. How silly of me – she completely slipped my mind.'

'Princess Marina,' said Sybil, 'not only dresses divinely, as you say, but with what I can only describe as that elusive thing called "style". To illustrate my point one need look no further than her sister-in-law, Wallis Warfield Simpson. (I'm sorry, but I flatly refuse to refer to her by her courtesy title!) Wallis Warfield Simpson proves that it is perfectly possible to spend a great deal of money on smart clothes and still look rather common. You see, it all boils down to breeding in the end, like so much else. Take good looks, for example. So many of these pretty little faces that people make such a fuss about nowadays — these pin-up girls and blonde bombshells and so on and so forth — won't last *five minutes* over the age of, say, twenty-five.'

'What the French call *la beauté du diable*,' said Dodo.

'But Princess Marina has bone structure. That's what counts. She happens to be still a young woman but her age is neither here nor there. With bone structure like that one could easily be a raving beauty at the age of ninety.'

'It's absolutely true,' said Dodo wistfully. 'I never had it myself, so I know! Without bone structure, one's too fearfully *journalière* — looking one's very best on a good evening and then, for no known reason, like the back of a bus the next day!'

'I agree with Sybil,' said Charlie. 'There's a darn sight too much emphasis placed on youth nowadays by people old enough to know better. It's all a lot of rot — you're as old as you feel, always have been.'

'But that's just the trouble!' said Dodo. 'I feel a hundred! If I'd *only* had the courage — not to mention the cash — to get a face-lift when the time was ripe, I'm quite sure it would have done me the world of good. But I didn't quite dare and now, alas, I've left it too late.'

Charlie chuckled. 'That reminds me of rather a nice story a friend of mine tells. You probably know it — the one about the ageing film star who went and had her face lifted. Only trouble was — it fell again when she got the bill!'

The tepid laughter which greeted Charlie's joke was broken into by Sybil.

'But, Dodo *darling*,' she protested, 'you will persist in the fallacy that good looks are everything! It's just too silly of you for words! I'm quite cross with you — you ought to know better! Now you just listen to me. If a young woman who felt that she was hanging fire came to me for advice, I would tell her exactly what my own mother told me when I first came out. "Never, never be a bore! It is the unpardonable sin!" Men don't give a damn about any-thing else but they *cannot* stand being bored! When you're put next to somebody at a dinner party, for Heaven's sake, *say* something. It scarcely matters what – the first thing that enters your head will be better than nothing – just so long as you don't sit there in dead silence like a stuffed dummy while *he*, poor fellow, has to rack his brains in search of some polite way of opening the conversation. You may be looking as pretty as a picture – it makes no earthly differ-ence. "Never, never," my mother would say, "under-rate the value of small talk. It is vital to be well-informed – though don't, whatever you do, let him think that you're too brainy, because that can be fatal as well. But somehow or other find the time to read *all* the morning papers from cover to cover, so that you have some idea of what is going on in the rest of the world and need not be at a loss for a suitable topic. You'll find that men will put up with a lot, but they will run a *mile* from a woman who bores them, even if she is as lovely to look upon as Helen of Troy." And that advice of my mother's has stood me in very good stead. Not, let me hasten to add, that I am in the slightest bit intolerant of bores *myself*. In fact, I really don't believe that I would recognise a bore if I came face to face with one. You see, I'm lucky – I am never bored! I'm desperately sorry for my friends when they complain of boredom, but the truth is that I don't know what the heck they're talking about! There always – in whatever situation I happen to find myself – seems to be something to occupy my mind – to interest or amuse me. Sad, yes – deeply moved – frustrated – angry – hurt – all these on occasion I may be. But bored – never. I don't know the meaning of the word!'

Sybil triumphantly surveyed her audience. Charlie and I were staring at our shoes, and Dodo had fallen asleep.

After tea, as I walked through the other garden back to the house, I recalled what Kay had said when she heard that

I was going to see her parents again. 'Remember, they're on their best behaviour when you meet them socially. They can be perfectly charming if they care to try. But they're hell to live with. And she's far the worst. He's all right on his own, so long as one keeps out of his way. But she seems to set out deliberately in search of some fault she can find with me. And if she fails to find it, she'll invent one. I don't know why she hates me so much. I'm not aware of having done her any harm. She always gets her own way with Daddy and Sandy – I'm no threat to her there. An ex-boyfriend of mine who's a bit of a highbrow – you know the type, lives in Bloomsbury and writes books – he said it was Freudian. Said she was in love with Sandy and jealous of me because I was younger than her. But I think that's too far-fetched. It's true that, when I first grew up, one of her admirers seemed to fancy me and there was the most God-almighty dust-up. But nothing of that kind has happened since. No, I think she's just never liked me, from the moment I was born. Perhaps she had a particularly bad delivery, or something. I suppose it's not really her fault. It must be awful to have a child and just not like it. Almost as bad as being the child.'

There seemed to be no way of freeing Kay from her parents (and, for that matter, ridding them of her), although my mother and I tried again and again to think of one. However, early the following year, an opportunity presented itself for her at least to achieve a comparative independence by earning more money than her present tiny salary. A team of smartly uniformed American Red Cross workers had arrived in the neighbourhood and were busy establishing a canteen at the aerodrome. This was to be an elaborate and glamorous affair, as superior to the High Street NAAFI as the Ritz Hotel to an ABC, and the organisers had advertised for auxiliary helpers among the local ladies. It was rumoured that there were a great many vacancies and that the jobs would be extremely well paid. Kay applied for an interview, and was told to appear at eleven sharp one morning outside the Lion, where a jeep would be ready to drive her and a few other applicants to the Red Cross headquarters on the hill.

Shortly after eleven on the day of the interview I saw the forlorn figure of Kay turn into the drive of our house and struggle through the piercing cold and squally wind of a February sleet-storm to the front door. She almost collapsed when I let her in. She had been a few minutes late for the appointment and the jeep had left without her; she couldn't possibly walk up the hill in this weather; she had missed her chance of the job.

'It's so humiliating – something like this always happens – what *is* it about me? First one thing cropped up to detain me, then another, it seemed I just *couldn't* make a start . . . And when I finally did get off, I had to run all the way so I arrived sweating and breathless and exhausted and feeling quite mad . . . Why couldn't the bloody car have waited a few seconds longer? I was *so* nearly on time . . . But it's obviously hopeless, I'll never be able to manage to get through life like other people do, I can't seem to cope with even the simplest challenge, it's no good my trying any longer, whatever I do is doomed to go wrong . . .'

Kay stopped speaking and broke down in agonised tears. It was the first time I had seen her lose control in this way and I was completely unnerved by the experience. I felt confronted by something unspeakably piteous, as if forced to witness a scene of physical torture or hearing from a soul in hell, and yet Kay's words struck me as in no way out of the ordinary. The bleak message they conveyed gave a straightforward, balanced account of how the world can appear to people invisibly handicapped by a certain kind of temperament, and Kay's was an extreme example in which I recognised some elements of my own.

Once her crying fit was over, Kay acknowledged that her despair had been out of all proportion to its immediate cause; after several telephone calls, it was arranged for her to be included in a second batch of candidates later in the week. She felt that the interview had gone reasonably well, and when asked to undergo a routine medical examination she interpreted this development as a hopeful sign. But an X-ray of her chest revealed a dark patch on her left lung; further tests confirmed tuberculosis as the cause. Employment with the Red Cross was out of the question: she was urgently advised to see a specialist. After consultation with the Demarests' family doctor, she was sent off to the same Cornish sanatorium where Denis Bellamy had spent the last eight months.

I immediately wrote to Denis to tell him about Kay, and soon after her arrival there she wrote herself. '. . . I adore your friend Denis and feel he's already saved my life in this ghastly dump. He came bursting into my room on my first evening here, looking too extraordinary in a bright green silk night shirt, and said, "Now, dear, you've got to tell me all about the Bright Young Things in the Twenties!" I said, "That's going a bit far back, I'm afraid, but I'll tell you all about the Thirties with pleasure." He says he wants to paint me. There was an awful "atmosphere" before I left Watermead – Daddy livid because this place is so expensive, and Mummy saying, "It's all a lot of fuss about nothing if you ask me, nobody's ever been chesty on *my* side of the family, the best thing to do would be to hide the thermometer from Kay, she looks a very healthy invalid in my humble opinion!" Typical! Denis sends tons of love and so do I. Kay.'

6

'Two letters for you — lucky man!' said Sister, holding them behind her back. 'I'll hand them over in a tick — but first I want to take a look at how you're getting on with my belt. My word, you *are* a slow coach! Better buck up about it, you know — I can't wait for ever!'

Sister's belt was a strip of leather on which I was clumsily stitching a childish pattern of bunny-rabbits, daisies, sunflowers and lambs in wools of varying pastel shades. I had already completed one belt of almost identical design for Sister, which she was wearing while she spoke, and I thought it rather odd of her to be so impatient for a second. The pointless labour on which I was employed was known in the convalescent home as occupational therapy. Sister had started me off with knitting, but I had made such a hash of this that I was soon encouraged to turn to crochet work, thought by her to be simpler: trimming leather belts had been the third and last resort.

The military convalescent home was situated in one wing of a large country house in East Anglia and the vast dormitory in which I lay had once been the ballroom. It was now bare of everything except for sixteen army beds arranged in two parallel rows: as in a barracks, the tops and bottoms of the beds were alternately reversed, so that the head of each occupant was on a level with the feet of his neighbours on either side. It was a sunny autumn afternoon, and I was the only patient indoors; through three sets of french windows in the opposite wall I could see most of the others, dressed in the bright blue suits and scarlet ties of the walking wounded, as they hobbled about the parkland surrounding the house. Their injuries had all been sustained not in battle but on the football field or (as in my case) in the gym.

I had arrived ten days before in an ambulance. My papers had somehow got lost on the way, but I was able to explain to Sister that I had been sent there to recuperate from a broken ankle after treatment in the orthopaedic ward of a hospital in Norwich. They had since turned up, but nothing in them explained the fact that, although the ankle was satisfactorily healing within its plaster cast, I was still so weak in myself that I could barely manage to make my own bed without collapsing. When I remarked on this, Sister muttered something about 'shock' in an unconvinced voice, and urged me to put my trust in occupational therapy.

The main buildings of the house were still inhabited by its owner, a widow to whom Sister referred as 'Lady Connie' and whose surname I had never happened to hear. The convalescent home was Lady Connie's war work. She had created a rank for herself ('Honorary Commandant') and had designed a personal uniform to wear when she considered herself on duty. This consisted of a navy blue skirt and tunic (the latter embellished by gold braid epaulettes), black stockings, stout brogues, a short red cape and a funny little hat pulled down over her ears with a low peaked brim. The uniform, especially the hat, gave a rather fierce aspect to Lady Connie's appearance, but this was misleading: she was extremely shy. For most of the time she remained concealed from us in her private quarters, but occasionally she would feel that she ought to make some sort of social contact with the invalid soldiers in her care. Announced in advance by Sister, she would come marching into her former ballroom and pause for a moment beside each of our beds – suggesting a cross between some rabid NCO conducting kit-inspection and the Princess Royal politely reviewing a troop of Girl Guides. But Lady Connie would be so paralysed by embarrassment that the whole ceremony would unfold in a sad, self-conscious silence.

The food in the convalescent home was very bad; I had lost my appetite so did not suffer from this as much as the other residents, who constantly but unavailingly complained. At breakfast the porridge was grey and glutinous and the black beetles imbedded in it as conspicuous and plentiful as the slugs in our lunchtime vegetables. One evening, an ENSA concert party invaded the ward and awkwardly entertained us while we sat on our beds – two ladies in Pierrette costumes, one a soprano specialising in Ivor Novello, Victor Herbert, Rudolph Friml and Sigmund Romberg, the other a *diseuse* whose digressive monologue was entitled 'Just Nattering'. We were an inattentive audience. Unknown to the performers, a scandalous event had taken place during the supper preceding the show. The main course, intended as a special treat, had been steak and kidney pie. When it was opened, something was revealed inside it that was clearly neither meat nor pastry. This object was difficult to identify by its size, shape, colour or consistency, and nobody volunteered to test it by taste. Could it perhaps be some monstrous mushroom? Amid some excitement, it was eventually recognised as a dirty dressing, which had presumably been removed from a patient's wound earlier in the day or week and mysteriously diverted from its proper destination down the incinerator to end up instead in the cooking pot.

When the concert party had left, our indignation about the dirty dressing in the steak and kidney pie erupted in open rebellion. We refused to turn in for the night until we had lodged an official protest. Sister (herself a little shaken by the incident) at last agreed to convey the substance of our grievance to Lady Connie, 'first thing in the morning'. She later reported back that Lady Connie had been appalled by the episode, and had sworn to make up for it in some way by providing us with an extra luxury. Reparation was made at the following evening meal, and took the form of a classic mayonnaise, scrupulously prepared from the finest ingredients by Lady Connie's own hands, as a substitute for the customary bottle of Heinz's Salad Cream.

Now, Sister's eye was suddenly caught by the squat figure of Lady Connie in her Commandant's uniform stumping past the french windows outside. 'I'd better see what she wants,' Sister said, and hurriedly left the room, tossing the two letters on to my bed.

One was from Denis. '. . . Kay sends lots of love,' he wrote. 'The doctor says she's making good progress and he may let her go home before Christmas. But if she does she'll have to take very great care of herself and won't be able to work or anything. She's worried about how her parents will react to this — thinks they would prefer her to stay where she is, but would also love to get out of paying the sanatorium fees if they can do so without it looking too bad. I must say, they do sound a nightmare couple. I shall miss Kay if she does leave (it looks as if I'm stuck here for another year at least). She's so wonderfully restful. She'll creep into my room while I'm sketching or reading or just day-dreaming and she'll sit there for hours knitting something she's making for Sandy — she *says* it's meant to be a Balaclava Helmet but it looks to me suspiciously like a Pixie Hood! — and even when we hardly exchange two words she's somehow very consoling company. Or I go to *her* room and try to make her laugh while she's washing her hair. The other day I did it up for her in a Victory Roll but it collapsed after five minutes. Only there is something tragic about her, isn't there? I've never known anybody with so little confidence. I suppose the trouble is that she's madly in love with Sandy. From what she says he sounds very glamorous. Do write and tell me what he's like – I long to know. Bet you dollars to doughnuts he's really queer as a coot (you can't fool Mother, dear!), but when I said so to Kay she got rather heated and swore it wasn't true. My guess is he's the pseudo-hearty kind who pretend to be normal and stalk about the place being terribly, terribly manly. *Mee-ow*! I sound just like Ros Russell in *The Women*, don't I? I can't think why I said that about Sandy – it just popped out! I've always sworn I would never turn into one of those dreary old queens who try to make out that everybody else is queer too – no, dear, that sort of behaviour is definitely *not* my *tasse de thé* – so I take it all back!'

The other letter was from my mother. '. . . Darling, I do think it's worrying that you go on having such a high temperature when you've only broken your ankle! Do please get the doctor there – if there is one – to examine you properly. If only I was well enough I'd come up myself. The woman who owns the house you're in turns out to be an old friend of Dodo's. Apparently she used to be called Connie Phipps and Dodo says she's "a sweetie". Listen, darling, *please* make yourself known to her and mention Dodo's name and draw her attention to the fact that you *shouldn't* be having this fever when all you've done is hurt your foot and ask her to get a second medical opinion!'

Reading the letters had brought on a fit of dizziness, and I lay back on my pillow to rest. Could Lady Connie possibly be the racing aunt whose social judgments had been so frequently quoted by her namesake Billy Phipps? Before I dozed off, I decided that – even if it should turn out that my friendship with her nephew and hers with Dodo did in fact establish a double link between Lady Connie and myself – her own shyness, to say nothing of mine, made it quite out of the question for me ever to 'make myself known' to her . . .

I had been called up about three months earlier, in the summer of 1943, as a private in the Infantry. After a few weeks of preliminary training near London, the batch of recruits in which I found myself had been moved to Norwich for a slightly more intensive course. My companions in the draft were either youths of my own age (just nineteen) or mature men twenty years older, and there was considerable rivalry, amounting on occasion to hostility, between the two groups. Although still under forty, the seniors seemed to the rest of us revoltingly decrepit, with their false teeth, thinning hair and pot bellies; while we were resented by them as spoilt, insolent youngsters for whom the discomforts of communal life must be comparatively easy to bear, who should therefore volunteer to relieve our elders and betters of some of their more arduous duties, and whose failure to do so showed a deplorable lack of respect.

Two of my fellow-conscripts had worked in civilian life as apprentice cinema projectionists; their professional expertise happily coincided with my amateur obsession and I was able to talk about film stars with them in the same compulsive detail as I might have done with Denis or Kay. On free evenings the three of us would spruce ourselves up and descend the hill from Britannia Barracks to the town centre. After a cup of tea and a slice of cake at a NAAFI or Church Army canteen, we would sit together through a double feature. Once I deserted the others and paid a solitary visit to the live theatre: but the entertainment on offer happened to be a CEMA tour of the Ballets Jooss in a renowned piece of expressionist mime called *The Green Table* and I was punished for my pretentious defection by extreme boredom. On other occasions when I felt a need to be alone I would go off by myself and sit in the railway station. This was one of the most depressing spots in the city, but when one is confined by circumstances in a place where one has no wish to be the nearest station can seem an exotic symbol of release or escape. In the gloom of the dirty waiting-room and the squalor of the dingy buffet I could imagine myself a little nearer to the metropolitan glamour of London and, beyond that, the security of home.

After the course of training at Britannia Barracks was over, I was due to appear before a Selection Board with the idea of trying for a commission − but I had made up my mind that, nearer the time, I would somehow get out of going. I disliked everything about the life of a private soldier except for the total lack of responsibility that went with it and which helped one to endure the rest by allowing one to live almost entirely in the present − an advantage denied, of course, to officers and NCOs. There was nothing pleasant about the grumbling, obedient, boring existence I was leading, but it seemed to me that the removal of all options except the most limited and immediate had also to some extent removed the element of anxiety. With nothing to look forward to, one might at least have the negative consolation of also having nothing to dread. When I found that I was dreading the Selection Board, it struck me that I should exercise the last option I was likely to be offered by choosing to remain in the ranks.

But of course there is always *something* left to dread, and for us at Britannia Barracks it was a forced march lasting two days which was scheduled to take place shortly before the end of our training period. This climactic test was persistently evoked by our NCOs as an ultimate terror with which to cow us into submission or exhort us to greater effort. The daytime ordeal (during which we were to be heavily clothed and weighed down with rifle, pack and gas mask) would be much tougher physical exercise than any we had so far undertaken, but this in itself was apparently nothing to the psychological torment of the night in between, spent on the floor of a rat-infested barn in some distant farm. 'The rats run over your face while you're trying to sleep!' we repeated to each other with the pleasurable excitement – and also the genuine fear – of children discussing a forbidden horror movie. In the event, the dread turned out to have been unnecessary – at least as far as I was concerned. I was so tired when we reached the barn that I fell asleep at once and remained unconscious until woken in the morning. I never knew whether or not rats ran over my face and would not have cared if they had.

There was also something left for me to look forward to. I had successfully applied for a weekend's leave on compassionate grounds to visit my mother in a London nursing home where she was recovering from a hysterectomy. In order to turn the event into an extra special treat, she had booked me a room for one night at the Savoy Hotel. A comfortable bed with sheets and pillows, a private bath, breakfast brought to one's room: such luxuries had become almost past imagining . . . On the Saturday after the march, I took a train to Liverpool Street Station. Arriving at midday, I bought the latest Agatha Christie from the bookstall, planning to read it in bed that night and add a perfect touch to the anticipated hedonistic paradise. I sat with my mother till evening; the operation had left her frighteningly weak and in uncharacteristically low spirits. When I checked into the Savoy, I was in a daze of worry and fatigue – too exhausted to enjoy the ritual bath, to take in the softness of the bed or to read more than a page of *The Moving Finger* before passing out in a heavy slumber from which I emerged ten hours later even further depleted of energy. The longed-for night of sensual ease and extravagant self-indulgence had proved in fact to be indistinguishable from the notoriously squalid endurance test of the doss-down in the barn.

I spent Sunday at the nursing home and then had to bear one of those long, tedious, desolate wartime journeys on the crowded train back to Norwich. Tightly packed against other travellers in the dim corridor, swaying in rhythm with them when the train was moving, rudely jolted and then dejectedly drooping with them when it suddenly stopped for no reason between stations and stayed stubbornly still for hours, I felt delirious with discomfort. As I finally plodded up the hill that led back to the Barracks, I knew for sure that I was ill. The next morning I reported sick, but the medical officer suspected me of 'swinging the lead' and refused to examine me. This comedy was repeated every morning for three more days.

The end of the course was approaching, and I had still said nothing about my reluctance to go before the War Office Selection Board. Then, during PT, I was confronted once more by a challenge which I had never found easy: to climb a vertical rope about twice my own height, to crawl upside down like a monkey the length of a second rope hung horizontally across the gym, and eventually to slide down a third rope on the other side. I had got half-way along the horizontal rope when, as in many a nightmare, I was convinced that I was going to fall. Fear of this possibility had induced a panic which made the accident a certainty; at the same time, I longed for the fall as a terrified dreamer longs to wake. So I fell. I was taken to hospital where my fractured ankle was set and my lower leg put in plaster of Paris, and a few days later I was forwarded like a parcel to Lady Connie's convalescent home on the Norfolk Broads . . .

Beyond the french windows of her ballroom I could see Lady Connie pacing the garden in conversation with Sister.

After a while Sister returned to my bedside. She looked rather put out, I thought. She told me that I was to be transported later that day back to the hospital from which I had come. Lady Connie had received a letter from a friend of hers advising this course. 'All most hush-hush,' said Sister. 'I've never approved of people going behind other people's backs, but I don't suppose that any of it's *your* fault. I've phoned the hospital and there's a bed there ready for you – not in Orthopaedic, mind, where you were before. No, this time they're putting you in the General Ward. Going up in the world, aren't we? Never mind, they're just going to run a few tests on you, nothing to get in a flap about. And I notice that you *still* haven't finished that belt, you bad lad!'

The tests revealed a pleural effusion of tubercular origin, and a large quantity of fluid was drained from my chest. If the pleurisy had been diagnosed sooner it would have been a minor malady, but the delay had nearly killed me. One thing was clear: my army career was over. The merest suspicion of TB in those days was enough to guarantee an immediate discharge from His Majesty's Forces as it was thought to be highly infectious. I lingered on where I was for a time, and was then brutally transferred to the TB ward of another military hospital. This was a gloomy Gothic building near St Albans which had been a lunatic asylum before the war. Once again, my papers had been mislaid in transit and so my stay there was much longer than necessary. It was a grim experience, which I later managed to blot out almost completely from my memory. But I can still see the rows of thin naked torsos punctured by needle marks and surgical scars and hear the harrowing noises made by a patient having a haemorrhage – a common occurrence, which usually happened at night and often proved fatal. I tried not to think too often about Denis and Kay.

The calf of my leg had shrivelled within its plaster and

itched maddeningly: the cast should have been taken off by now but among the horrors of the TB ward this was too trivial a complaint to mention. At last my papers were found and I was officially 'invalided out'. I moved to a private nursing home in London where my foot was released from its shackle and I began to take in the wonderful fact that I was already back in Civvy Street.

The classic treatment for TB had been to send the sufferer to a sanatorium, preferably in Switzerland, but the war had of course put an end to travel outside Britain and a fashionable lung specialist had initiated a remedy by which he claimed the illness could be cured, or at least held in check, in the patient's own home. It was simply a question of plenty of rest, lots of milk and graduated exercise. For the first week one went every day for a very short walk, but the extent of the exercise was gradually lengthened week by week until by the end of a year one was tramping for miles over the countryside. One went to bed at ten in the evening and got up at ten in the morning. Extra milk was made available to be consumed throughout the day. This was the régime prescribed to me for an indefinite period.

So by Christmas of the same year as my call-up I was back home again in the village where my mother (who had saved my life by getting Dodo to write to Lady Connie about my condition) was slowly recuperating from her operation; where our house and the whole village were filled with the officers and men of an American parachute regiment stationed in the vicinity of the aerodrome on the top of Larch Hill; and where Kay too had recently returned under strict orders that she must lead the life of an invalid and be protected as carefully as possible from all unnecessary exertion and any kind of stress.

The following year of 1944 – so crucial to the course of the war, so eventful for the rest of the world – was therefore passed by me in an atmosphere of remedially arrested development, of unnatural stasis sweetly prolonged. The late rise; the morning walk; the early lunch at the British Restaurant established in the Church Hall a few paces from our house; the afternoon lie-down; the stroll to the Post Office to see if anything had come by the afternoon post (only the morning post was delivered since Tom, the postmistress's nephew and friend of Kay, had joined the navy); the evening walk; the early night: such an existence confirmed in me a taste for boredom and inaction which, like a drug habit formed in youth, I was never to succeed in conquering. And in this existence Kay (whose circumstances, in many ways so different, yet essentially continued to parallel mine) was my companion, my confederate, my spiritual cell mate.

7

'Would you believe it?' said Kay one day. 'Mummy's got an American! Wonders will never cease . . . Quite a feat, at her age. I take off my hat to her.'

'Do you mean Colonel What's-it?' I asked. I knew that Sybil had established some social connection with the commanding officer of the parachute regiment (she claimed that a cousin of hers had known his mother in Boston) and on this pretext had been trying to get him to come to tea at Watermead.

'No, this is a GI, a kid of about twenty. She behaves as if he was a proper boyfriend but I don't think he *can* be – except that with these Americans anything seems possible. She met him at the Red Cross canteen up on the hill – she goes there to help out sometimes, on a voluntary basis. This boy came up to her and said he had never seen such lovely grey hair on anyone – quite an original line to shoot, don't you think? She was tickled pink and he hasn't left her alone since, and vice versa. Apparently he works as an army cook. It sounds to me as if he must be a pansy but I may be quite wrong, perhaps they spend hours together making passionate love. In which case all I can say is good luck to her – more power to her elbow, to coin a phrase. Though it does have its funny side. If it was *me* who was going out with a GI she'd be saying, "Typical of Kay, she's always been man-mad, my dear – anything in trousers!"'

'Is Charlie jealous?'

'I'm pretty sure he hasn't taken it in yet. Anyway, the whole thing has certainly sweetened the atmosphere at home as far as I'm concerned. Butter wouldn't melt in Mummy's mouth nowadays. She's all over Daddy (out of guilt, I suppose), which makes him a lot easier to get on with – and she's even quite civil to me. So thank God for the army cook!'

We were taking an evening walk along the downs to the north of the village and the sun was beginning to set. Kay was sensitive to natural beauty but her dread of sounding 'arty' usually inhibited her from voicing her feelings in this respect. Now she stopped moving and stood staring at the sky. I heard her say under her breath, 'Makes you understand what Turner and those people were driving at . . .' Suddenly a wolf-like figure detached itself from some nearby farm buildings and ran towards us, then halted in a pose reminiscent of *The Monarch of the Glen*. It was an Alsatian dog. Kay gasped. 'What a handsome creature!' she exclaimed. The dog trotted up to us and cautiously licked Kay's extended hand – then became more effusively affectionate, leaping up excitedly to lick her face. He accompanied us for a mile or so farther, and when we had turned back and were passing the farm a second time he made it clear that he did not intend to be left behind there.

'I wonder if this is where he lives?' said Kay. There seemed to be nobody much about, but after a search we came upon a youth inspecting a broken tractor.

'Does this dog belong to you?'

'Oh no, 'e don't belong to me.'

'Who does he belong to, do you know?'

'I don't know. Nobody don't know.'

'Then what's he doing here?'

'My dad's minding 'im for a spell.'

'What's his name?'

''Avoc. Everybody knows 'Avoc but nobody don't know where 'e come from.'

'Well, you'd better hold on to him a bit while we walk away,' said Kay, 'because I think he wants to follow me home and though I'd love to take him back with me I'm afraid it's not possible just at the moment. But, look, would it be all right if I came back tomorrow morning and took him out for a real walk then?'

The boy nodded. For a long time as we continued on our way back to the village we could hear the dog whining sadly as he struggled to shake off the boy's restraining grasp.

Kay kept her word and returned the next day: Havoc greeted her as if she had always belonged to him. After a week or so of worrying about his welfare and contriving to spend as much time with him as she could, it was plain that he had become the centre of Kay's life. There was no question of his being allowed to enter Watermead, but in spite of this handicap she managed to assume responsibility for his feeding, his exercise and his general care and was soon his acknowledged owner. As he had never known a permanent abode, he adapted easily to the rota of temporary lodgings which she organised for him – sometimes at the farm, sometimes with me, or with her friends at the garage and the paper shop and the Post Office, or with Mr and Mrs Tripp. We were part-time guardians who were only requested to watch over him at night: by day, he was inseparable from Kay.

He was not a pure-bred Alsatian and his appearance was somewhat battered – one of his ears looked as if another dog had taken a large bite out of it. But he was astonishingly beautiful. His colouring seemed to change as one looked at him: in some lights his markings appeared to be charcoal on cream, in others walnut on honey, and his coat contained further, fugitive, transitional tints – apricot, amber, mustard. It irritated Kay that he was already called Havoc: she thought it a silly name. How he had come by it was a mystery; it was in some ways so apt, and proved so difficult to supplant, that one might almost have fancied he had given it to himself. Kay announced that, whatever anyone believed, it was *not* his name, and that she had rechristened him Mustang. But nobody except for Kay (and sometimes, tentatively, myself) ever remembered to call him Mustang; when Kay referred to him thus, people did not understand what she was talking about, and neither did Havoc. Eventually she was forced to capitulate to the power of oral tradition and admit that 'Havoc' had stuck so firmly that it would be simpler if she authorised it as his rightful name and reverted to its use when addressing or discussing him.

Kay defied doctor's orders and resumed her part-time job at the NAAFI: the small salary helped pay for Havoc's food and to settle the occasional vet's bill. Havoc would sit quietly in the canteen while she was on duty and the customers did not complain of his presence. 'I'm not telling the family that I'm back at the NAAFI,' Kay said.

'Might they object to your working so soon after being ill?' I asked.

'Good Heavens no, they wouldn't give a damn about that. What I'm afraid of is that if they knew I was earning again they'd expect me to contribute towards their household expenses.'

The pleasant atmosphere at Watermead brought about by Sybil's romance with the army cook soon soured, presumably because the affair had for some reason or another come to an end. Kay hoped that her own almost continual absence from the house would give her parents the minimum cause for complaint, but they had heard about her relationship with Havoc and resented the idea of the animal almost as much as they would have disliked his actual presence. 'Sybil and Charlie say that this dog is the last

215

straw,' Dodo reported. 'But as they forbid it to come anywhere near the place, I don't really see what they're kicking up such a fuss about.'

Charlie imposed a curfew, insisting that Kay should get home every night in time for supper at eight o'clock, giving as his reason a paternal solicitude for her health. But her health could only suffer as a result, for if she was late by as little as three minutes she would find the front door locked implacably against her and she would have to walk through the damp meadows back to the village in search of a bed. Each evening, having fixed up Havoc's shelter for the night and exhausted by the demands of her intricate nomadic existence, Kay would have to make a nerve-racking decision: whether to hurry back to Watermead and risk just missing the deadline, or whether to defy Charlie's injunction altogether and stay until morning at whichever friend's house she happened to be. If she took the latter course, there would be a row; if she took the former course and miscalculated the time, there would be a row; if she took the former course and succeeded in gaining admittance to the Demarests' dining-room, there would not exactly be a row but the experience of sitting in silence through the ritual consumption of powdered egg omelette followed by either macaroni cheese or savoury rice – ignored, disapproved of and mysteriously disgraced – was in its way as painful.

Havoc was on the whole a biddable, friendly and good-tempered dog, but traumatic incidents in his buried past had left their mark on his character and he was capable of reacting to certain people and events in an unpredictable, neurotic way. He had been known to snap at strangers, perhaps even to bite them. I believe that his association with Kay, though it vastly improved the quality of his life, did some subtle harm to his reputation. Invariably seen hovering on the outskirts of the village in the company of this supposedly witch-like figure, Havoc began to be thought of in sinister terms by observers as (not quite literally) her demonic familiar. He became branded as a public danger; any unexplained deaths of chickens and other farm animals were automatically – and nearly always unfairly – blamed on him; householders felt themselves justified in throwing stones at him if he approached their property; farmers were heard to threaten that they would not hesitate to shoot him on sight. This hint of impending persecution added an acute anxiety to the other difficulties confronting Kay in her already harrassed life. When I was not in their company they often appeared to my imagination as hunted outcasts, Hagar and Ishmael abandoned and wandering in a psychic wilderness of their own creation; but when I went with them on our long – and ever longer – walks I regained my sense of proportion and recognised them as just my friend Kay (whose romantic nature and eccentric mannerisms were underpinned by conventional ethics and philistine tastes) out exercising her good-looking high-spirited dog.

Kay and I often talked about Denis on these walks. She was deeply attached to him, but this feeling was only expressed in a characteristically understated way. At the mention of his name her lips would twist in her reluctant, secret half-smile and she would say drily, 'I've a lot of time for Denis. He makes me laugh.' During the summer he wrote to us with the good news that after more than two years in the sanatorium he was at last on the point of leaving it and was looking for somewhere to stay in London. He sent me a birthday present – a King Penguin book called *Children as Artists* which was attracting attention at the time. The short, serious text was generously illustrated by paintings and drawings with such captions as '*Mummy*, by Shirley, age 4, pupil at an evacuated Nursery School'. On the flyleaf Denis had written, in the hectic, spiky capitals of an infant's script, with numerous erasures and ink blots: *FROM BINKY*

STUART (EALING STUDIOS) TO AUNTIE AYMEE WIF LUVE. I thought this very funny although the full point of the joke went over my head and had to be explained to me later: launched in the 1930s as Britain's answer to Shirley Temple, Binkie Stuart had been a child star who failed to fulfil her early promise and was in fact so profoundly obscure that neither Kay nor I had ever heard of her.

Throughout that sleepy year of my TB cure at home (for even on our most strenuous walks I often felt as if I had not fully woken and that the physical activity was only part of a dream) the conflict between Kay and her parents continued to provide me with an alternative object of interest and focus of concern to the real war raging in the outside world: the miniature is easier to contemplate than the immense. The almost nightly succession of rows and near-rows that took place at Watermead established a combustible but apparently static situation, like a magazine story endlessly strung out in serial instalments, which echoed aspects of the greater struggle. Of each, one knew that it could not go on for ever while helplessly suspecting that it might, defeat being too dreadful to imagine and peaceful victory too wonderful. In Kay's case, the crisis was reached on the very last day of 1944.

'I thought it would be tactful to spend New Year's Eve in the bosom of the family,' she explained, 'so I settled Havoc in for the night with Reg at the garage and got back to the house in time for supper. Well, there we were sitting as usual in dead silence having just finished the meal when imagine my horror on hearing his bark outside the dining-room window and then the sound of him scrabbling with his paws at the front door! I shall never understand what happened, he *knows* he's not supposed to set foot in Watermead and he's always been as good as gold about it. Reg swears that nothing occurred at the garage to upset him and says he can't think how Havoc gave him the slip. Anyway, there he was. Daddy had heard nothing, of course, and I thought the only thing to do was somehow to slip out of the house and try to persuade Havoc to go off on his own, or if the worst came to the worst take him back to the village myself. So I mumbled an apology, hoping they'd think I wanted to go to the lavatory, left the room and got out into the garden. Needless to say, Mummy hadn't missed a trick, and lost no time at all in putting Daddy in the picture.

'My dear, he went completely off his head. He rushed to the store-room where the fishing rods and Sandy's cricket things are kept and grabbed hold of an air-gun (which I had no idea was in the house) then tore upstairs to the first floor, flung open the window on the landing (breaking every blackout regulation, incidentally) and aiming it at Havoc he started to fire away as if he were in a butts shooting clay pigeons! He could easily have hit me by mistake but I was much too scared for Havoc to bother about that. As it happened, he missed us both. Havoc galloped off terrified into the darkness. I was too frightened to go back in the house so I followed him, worried sick that I'd never find him: but there he was, only two fields away, waiting for me quietly, as if everything was perfectly normal. So I took him back to the garage and then went on to the Tripps, who very sweetly let me spend the night on their sofa.'

It was now the morning of New Year's Day; Kay had arrived early at our house to tell us the news. 'One thing is certain – I've got to get Havoc out of here! I know it sounds absurd, but the truth often does – the fact is, this place has got too hot to hold us! I am quite literally convinced that if I don't rescue that dog his life will be in grave and imminent danger. So we're off to London – quite frankly, I'd rather face the V2 rockets than Daddy when he's in the kind of murderous mood that overcame him last night. He'd got such a filthy temper that something like this is bound to happen again – and next time he might not miss.' Kay stood with hands on hips and head defiantly erect, like Joan Crawford as Julie in *Strange Cargo* about to be deported from one island penal colony to another. 'God knows how we'll get up to town or where we'll live when we do. But we'll manage somehow. I've been in tighter corners than this and something has always turned up.'

8

So Kay and Havoc left the village for ever in January 1945. Mr Tripp drove them up to London in a small delivery van, similar to the one that had brought me and the cake from Oxford nearly three years before. Kay sat in the front seat and Havoc crouched at the back, guarding the two small suitcases that contained her entire possessions: his long face could be seen frowning anxiously through the rear window as the van moved off. Kay's last words to me had been, 'I'll be all right – I can always go to Lady Le Neve's for a bit.' A week or so later she wrote to me, giving me her address, and soon after that I travelled up by train to visit her.

Lady Le Neve was an old acquaintance of Kay's who had been left a widow with a large house in Cadogan Square where she continued to live alone, occasionally letting or lending rooms to friends (and friends of friends) in an amiably slapdash way. She opened the door to me herself – an untidily dressed woman in late middle age with a vague manner and a slight Irish brogue. The house was rambling, dark and dusty, with stained glass windows and inglenooks in unexpected and inconvenient places. She told me that Kay was lodged on the top floor; when I was half-way up the wide, shallow staircase (there was a capacious Edwardian lift but it hadn't worked in an age) I was able to locate her whereabouts more precisely by the sound of Havoc's barks. As I drew nearer I could hear Kay's voice gruffly reassuring him and as soon as she opened the door he sprang forward to welcome me.

Although its position suggested that it had once formed part of the servants' quarters, the room gave an impression of space and comparative grandeur; perhaps it had originally been intended for use as a nursery. It was sparsely furnished with big solid pieces. Havoc's occupancy (indicated by basket, feeding bowls, etc.) was more evident than that of Kay, whose few clothes and accessories had been swallowed up in a heavy mahogany wardrobe. I noticed the usual film magazines on her bedside table with one battered library book – *Me* by Naomi Jacob, an old favourite – and on the mantelpiece an engraved invitation card from Doris, Lady Orr-Lewis, requesting the pleasure of Kay's company at a tea party *cum* committee meeting at which arrangements for a charity dance were to be discussed. The date of the tea party was already in the past. I guessed that this invitation had been sent at the suggestion of Lady Le Neve and that Kay had answered it in the negative, but that (as its survival on the mantelpiece implied) she found some faint cheer in contemplating its existence.

Kay was thinner than ever and looked tired but not unhappy. It struck me that, like a private in the ranks, she had become so preoccupied with the struggle to surmount each small, immediate obstacle in her journey through the day that she had no time left for conscious discontent. 'I'm terribly sorry but I'm going to have to rush you off the moment you've arrived,' she said, briskly clipping a lead on to Havoc's collar. 'I must fetch his food – if we leave it too late they'll have run out.' We set off on foot with Havoc to a shop near Victoria Station which sold horse meat. When we got there we found that a long, motionless queue had already formed outside it; we stood at the end of the line, feeling rather hopeless, but were soon illogically relieved to see that yet more people had joined it behind us. I gathered from Kay's conversation while we waited for the shop to open that Lady Le Neve was allowing her to stay at Cadogan Square rent free while she looked for a suitable part-time job, and that even if Kay did find work she would charge her very little. 'Oh yes, she's a dear – and what's more she's nobody's fool, although she doesn't always let you know it. Thank God, she was brought up with animals in Ireland so she understands about Havoc and has no objection to his being in the house. The place may not be Buckingham Palace, but it's perfectly civilised and it's what's known as a "good address" which of course means nothing but sounds well in interviews and things while I'm hunting around for gainful employment.'

The horse meat eventually purchased, we went back to Lady Le Neve's and descended to a cavernous basement kitchen where Kay put it on to boil. A strong, sweet, unpleasant smell emerged from the saucepan and slowly rose to the top of the house, where it would still be discernible hours later. After Havoc had eaten, he curled up on Kay's bed to sleep and I took her to lunch at the Unity Restaurant in the King's Road. It seemed to me that she could hardly wait to finish her meal for fear of being late home and keeping Havoc from his walk. He was indeed awake and ready for us when we returned. We set off once more, this time for Hyde Park, where Kay produced Havoc's much-chewed stick from her shoulder-bag while he bounded and yelped with delight. The afternoon passed happily with the stick being thrown by Kay or myself and with Havoc tearing after it, ferociously worrying it for a time with bared snarling teeth and convulsive shakes of the head, only to trot peaceably back to us and lay it gently at our feet. As soon as he had done this, however, the fever of the chase was automatically rekindled, and he again flung himself about in wild sidelong prances, surrounding us in dizzy circles as he anticipated the excitement of yet another throw.

That evening, leaving Havoc shut up in Kay's room, we went to have a drink with Denis, who was living in a basement flat in Pimlico. 'It's all very *Fanny by Gaslight*,' he said as he admitted us, looking plumper, pinker and somehow more matronly than he had at Oxford. 'Come in, my dears – I want you to meet a friend of mine. This is Veronica Lake!' he announced impressively, indicating a weedy, anaemic youth in pale grey flannel trousers and an Aertex shirt.

Denis laughed at our looks of surprise. 'That's only her camp name on the Dilly – you should just see her when she's all got up in drag!'

'The Fabulous V – There'll Never Be Another,' said Veronica Lake self-consciously.

'The Fabulous One is maiding for me at the moment,' said Denis. 'You know, I've discovered something about myself since I came out of hospital. And what I've discovered is that I just *have* to be waited on. So there we are.'

'I know what you mean in a way,' said Kay. 'But I've always found it rather embarrassing having people fetching and carrying for me. It used to be such agony in the old days staying with friends in country houses when one was expected to tip the housemaid and had no idea what to give her. There seemed to be no way of finding out without making an idiot of oneself. So one always ended up either leaving much too little, which made one seem frightfully stingy, or much too much, which made one look like a vulgar *nouveau riche*. And I simply *hated* being unpacked for – one was haunted by the fear that one's knickers were full of holes or something, and dreaded meeting the housemaid's pitying gaze!'

'You wouldn't believe how pernickety Denis can be,' said Veronica Lake. 'Works me off me feet! Everything has to be just so – or else Madam throws a tantrum.'

Denis put on one of his funny voices and mouthed to us

in an elaborately staged aside, 'Our Mavis is getting ever so independent these days!'

'Talk about bossy-boots,' Veronica Lake went on. 'It's like being back in the Merchant Navy, picking up after that one!'

'Well – I like that!' said Denis in mock outrage. 'Just look who's talking! *She's* the bossy-boots, let me tell you! I call her Mrs Danvers. Stalking about the flat with a face of thunder and her *châtelaine* clanking against her private parts . . . why, I hardly dare ask her permission to put on the kettle for a cup of tea. Talking of which, let's all have a drink . . .' And, assuming his Hermione Gingold voice, Denis sang as he served us, 'While you're working overtime – I'll be drinking gin and lime – I'd adore that – Would you like it too?'

'I've got lots of fascinating scandal to tell you,' he went on while we drank. 'I picked up a Yank the other day who worked in a big actors' agency in Hollywood before he was drafted, and he told me all the dirt about the sex life of the stars. I bet you'll never guess what Joan Crawford's favourite kink is. *Well*, my dear,' – Denis paused portentously – 'this person says that what she really likes best is peeing on people! An actor friend of his had an affair with her and was simply terrified when she suddenly stood up on the bed and loomed above him with her legs apart. When it dawned on him what she was going to do he said, "Wait just one moment, please," and dashed off to the bathroom to fetch one of those waterproof shower-caps!'

This story shocked and saddened Kay. She tried to smile at it but she could not control a slight flinching movement, and the expression on her face was grave as she mumbled, 'Rather takes away from the glamour, what?' I had often thought that there was an unusual purity in her way of being a film fan and in her attitude towards the famous. She loved to read about them but had no desire to meet them and it offended her to hear ill of them. Her interest in their doings was respectful and protective, as free from hysterical hero-worship as it was from envy and spite. It was a sober hobby, absorbing but impersonal.

When the gin and lime juice had run out, Denis suggested that we should all go on to a queer drinking club in Chelsea called the Rochester. As the four of us were crossing Sloane Square, an ugly tramp-like old man, who was selling papers on a corner, thrust his face into Denis's and, with a lewd grimace, shouted, ''Ullo, darlin', 'ow's yer bum off for spunk?' Kay and I were considerably taken aback by this insult, and even Veronica Lake clicked her tongue in disapproval like an affronted dowager, but Denis himself was obviously delighted. He gave the smelly old paper-seller a playful tap on the shoulder and drawled, with affectionate reproach, 'Bold number!' before continuing on his way with a beaming smile which seemed to embrace us, the tramp and every passer-by on the King's Road in a loose fraternity of complicit amusement.

The Rochester was designed to echo the pompously masculine atmosphere of more conventional clubs in and around St James's but it only succeeded in achieving a clumsy parody. Sporting prints, reproductions of Rowlandson and Gillray cartoons and caricatures by 'Spy' were hung too close together on fake Regency striped wallpaper; those members who were not in khaki wore cavalry twill trousers, fancy waistcoats and tweed hacking jackets with leather elbows and aggressive vents; there was a depressing smell of expensive hair oil, male sweat and sewage (it transpired that the lavatory cistern was out of order). Veronica Lake seemed somewhat awed by these pseudo-hearty surroundings; Denis clearly thought them a great joke.

'It doesn't *look* very promising,' he conceded, 'but what I always say is, you never can tell. I've got a funny feeling that this is going to be one of those wild nights when one meets the person who changes one's life for ever. One wouldn't *expect* to find him at the Rochester (I know what you're going to say, dear) but odder things have happened.'

'I don't want to be a spoilsport,' said Kay, 'but I'm worried that you're not taking nearly enough care of your health. Too many wild nights can't be good for you – and I'm not at all sure that living in a basement flat is a sensible idea for someone with your chest.'

'Oh, it's only for a short time,' said Denis. 'I've met a very kind and generous person who likes my painting and he says the same as you do. The wonderful thing is that he's awfully rich and as soon as the war is over – or even sooner, if it becomes possible – he's going to send me to one of those very grand and expensive sanatoriums in Switzerland for a proper cure. So until then I'm determined to burn the candle at both ends like Edna St Vincent Millay.' Denis then gave a piercing imitation of Joan Cross as Violetta singing 'Sempre Libera' from *La Traviata*.

Well before closing time, Kay began to worry that Havoc might be needing her; we left Denis and Veronica Lake in the Rochester and made our way, rather tipsily, back to her room. I had missed the last train and Kay invited me to sleep on her floor. After taking Havoc for one final run round Cadogan Square, we settled in for the night. Havoc spurned his basket and slept on Kay's bed with his body stretched across the lower end so that she was unable to move her legs. I wrapped myself in Havoc's rug and curled up comfortably on the carpet. The next morning, we all three walked through Hyde Park to Kensington Gardens where I said goodbye to them near the Peter Pan statue and went off on my own to Paddington Station. Kay called out cheerfully after me, 'Oh, and if you should chance to run into Mummy or Daddy, remember to give them my hate!'

As it happened, I *did* run into Sybil Demarest in the High

Street quite soon after my return. It was a rainy day and she was wearing a voluminous oilskin coat and a heavy sou'wester. She was also carrying an umbrella which the wind had evidently blown inside out and from which naked spokes were dangerously protruding. 'If there is one thing I cannot abide,' she said, 'it is shoddy workmanship. What is more, I refuse point-blank to put up with it. I bought this umbrella in good faith – and it wasn't cheap, I must say – but that is by the by. I have never objected to paying out good money for good service. But in this case I'm very sorry to say that I consider I have been cheated. The woman who sold me this umbrella is quite simply a criminal, neither more nor less. And I have no intention of letting it rest at that. All through my life, I have been governed by one golden rule – and I'm perfectly prepared to tell you or anyone else who happens to be interested what it is. *Always go to the top*. Don't waste time footling around with underlings or middlemen – there's no earthly point and life's too short. Find out who's the boss and go *straight* to him – or to her, as the case may be. And that is what I plan to do in this affair. So very shortly somebody who shall be nameless is in for a nasty shock and will be looking round for another job.'

'I was in London the other day and spent a nice evening with Kay,' I heard myself saying. Sybil's ice-blue eyes surveyed me from within the frame of her sou'wester with no change of expression. She did not so much ignore my remark as behave as if I had not spoken at all but had farted instead – had been responsible for a series of sounds which decent society could only pretend had never been made. 'I wish you a very good morning,' she said, quite kindly, and smoothly continued on her measured, purposeful mission to the umbrella shop.

A day or two later, the name of Demarest hit the newspaper headlines. Sandy, after several abortive attempts and months of ingenious preparation, had with three other prisoners of war succeeded in escaping from a camp in Germany by digging a tunnel under the noses of the guards. They had walked for miles through enemy territory, in the greatest danger of discovery, before reaching the sanctuary of liberated Europe. They were national heroes and would probably soon be decorated. We heard from Dodo that on his return to England Sandy had paid a short visit to Watermead, where his parents were in ecstasies of triumphant pride; he was then posted to an RAF station in the Midlands to assist in the training of new recruits.

My mother wrote a polite note of congratulation to Sybil and received a polite reply. I was able to congratulate Charlie in person when, during a walk by the river, I came across him crouched on the bank, gazing into the water with apparent disapproval. He spoke so animatedly about Sandy's adventures and achievements that I found myself warming towards him. Either misled by this feeling, or prompted by an imp of defiance, I once again blurted out the information that I had seen Kay recently and spent a pleasant time with her. Charlie looked very grumpy indeed. 'I'm extremely sorry,' he muttered, 'but to be perfectly frank with you I haven't the faintest idea what you're talking about.' This was a formula he often used when his deafness had prevented him from following a conversation, but in this case I think he had heard what I said.

The next news of Kay was in early spring when she rang me up one evening in great distress. 'Thank God you're in! I felt I just *had* to talk to somebody who would understand and Lady Le Neve very sweetly said I could use her phone. I'm going nearly mad with worry – I've lost Havoc! Nothing like this has ever happened before and I'm desperately anxious about him. I've done everything I can think of – I've got in touch with the Battersea Dogs' Home and the RSPCA, and I've told the police who promise they'll do everything possible to find him. Actually it was a bit embarrassing because the awful truth is that I quite forgot to take out a dog licence for him – or rather I kept on meaning to but just never got round to it – and I was scared stiff the police would ask to see it, or somehow know that I didn't have one, but the subject never came up, I can't tell you how relieved I was. I swear to God that if he does come back the very first thing I'll do is buy him a licence!'

'How did it happen?'

'We were in the Park as usual this morning, quite near Bayswater Road, when some bloody car in the street made a funny noise which startled him and he went racing off in a panic before I could stop him and vanished behind some trees in the distance and I haven't seen hide nor hair of him since. I searched the Park for hours and hours but could find no trace of him at all. I can't think why he should suddenly take it into his head to run away like this – it's so unlike him. He *is* a nervous dog in some ways, I admit, but he's not normally frightened of anything so long as he's with me. And where on earth is he hiding? I'm quite sure nobody's stolen him – he would never let a stranger get near enough. The whole thing's a mystery – and damnably upsetting into the bargain!'

'Would you like me to come up tomorrow and help you look for him?'

'Oh, what a lovely idea. I knew you'd understand why I'm in such a state. But quite honestly, I'm not sure it wouldn't be better if you stayed where you are for a bit. You know how uncanny these animals can be and I think it's quite probable that he'll find his way across country, trying to get back to the places he associates with me. So if he should by any chance turn up in the village it would be a great load off my mind to know that you were there to take care of him and that you'd get in touch with me at once. The thought of his coming face to face with Daddy is too ghastly to contemplate! I'll give you Lady Le Neve's number – she says you can ring her up about this at any time.'

I said that I would definitely telephone in the morning to find out how the hunt for Havoc was progressing, whether I myself had anything to report or not.

'Oh, would you? How wonderful. I'd better ring off now, in case the police or anybody else has been trying to get through while we've been talking. I'm going to sit up by the telephone all night praying that somebody will call to say they've found him – or better still that I'll suddenly hear his bark in the Square outside.'

The next morning I rang Lady Le Neve's number again and again but each time failed to get a reply. At last, early in the afternoon, the telephone was answered, rather breathlessly, by Lady Le Neve herself. She told me what had happened since I had spoken to Kay on the previous evening.

For a time, Kay had been true to her word and had patiently sat near the telephone waiting for it to ring. She was prepared for one of three possibilities: Havoc might appear at Cadogan Square, or he might instinctively undertake the long and difficult journey back to the neighbourhood of Watermead, or he might have been involved in some accident (run over by a car, shot by a frightened citizen or angry farmer, trapped in a strange building) in which case she could hope to be notified in due course by the police. But after a dismal, restless hour or so, while the telephone remained callously silent, a fourth alternative occurred to her: Havoc might return to the spot where he had left her. She was immediately convinced that this was the most likely development and, cursing herself for not having thought of it sooner, she frantically put on a coat and hurried back to Hyde Park, confidently expecting to find Havoc waiting for her at the place where he had last been seen. But there was no sign of him there.

Night fell, and Kay remained where she was: she felt more optimistic, less passively forlorn, in the open air with moonlight glinting on the barrage balloons than she had when settling in for her housebound lamplit vigil. She sat on a park bench and after a while she drifted into a trance-like half-sleep from which she was awakened, shivering, by the dawn. When she got back to Cadogan Square her teeth were chattering; she had clearly caught a chill which Lady Le Neve was afraid might turn into pneumonia. And she was spitting blood again.

'I got my own doctor to come round at once,' said Lady Le Neve, 'and he popped her straight into St George's Hospital where she's having the very best attention. I've just come from there – I took her round a few things she needed. So there's nothing for you to worry about – she'll be just fine now. I managed to reach her brother (he took a bit of finding) because I thought somebody in the family ought to know, and he's with her at this very moment, so she's as happy as a sandboy – bless her, poor soul.'

I thought I understood exactly how Kay had felt when she decided that some form of action (however apparently pointless) was preferable to an indefinite period of submissive waiting and, although she had instructed me to stay put in case Havoc should miraculously materialise at my front door, I determined to disobey her by travelling up to London as soon as I could in the hope of being some support to her there.

By the time I reached Paddington that evening, it was too late for Kay to receive visitors. I spent the night on a sofa in the sitting-room of Denis's flat. He was concerned about Kay, but had worries of his own. The Fabulous V had recently been arrested for soliciting in the Piccadilly

Underground Gents and was out on bail awaiting trial. 'You can't imagine the drama – it's been a *cauchemar*!' said Denis. 'The irony is that she wasn't doing a thing, just having a perfectly innocent and rather pathetic pee. Luckily I got hold of this brilliant woman solicitor. She's a great big bulldike, dear, and she specialises in rescuing queens who get nicked in loos. The police are terrified of her. She comes tearing round and shouts at them and they let you off at once. Unfortunately the Fabulous One had completely lost her head and had already owned up to all kinds of dreadful and totally imaginary crimes before the solicitor arrived.'

'They got me in such a tizz that I didn't know what I was saying!' Veronica Lake complained. 'They've a way of putting words into one's mouth, if you know what I mean. And then they locked me up in a tiny cell and left me there all night. If I rang the bell once I rang it a hundred times, but nobody paid the slightest attention. I think it's a disgrace, and I intend to say so when my case comes to court.'

'You'll do nothing of the kind, girl,' said Denis. 'What on earth did you expect? You were banged up in a police station, not staying in the Royal Suite at Claridge's!'

'I had to have some refreshment, didn't I?' said Veronica Lake indignantly.

I hurried to St George's Hospital as early as possible the following morning. After a long wait I was admitted to a crowded ward. I moved uncertainly from bed to bed until I recognised Kay. She was lying very still and she was smiling. Something about her – at the same time peaceful and intense – reminded me of her concentrated sunbathing sessions on the lawn at home.

'Sandy's been angelic,' she said. 'He's taking care of everything. I shan't have to stay in here for very long, the doctor says, but Sandy thinks that when I leave I ought to go back to Cornwall for a while and have a thorough rest, so he's making all the arrangements. Listen, I don't know *what* to do about Havoc. One thing I know for sure – if he's alive, he'll try to find me. I've asked Lady Le Neve to keep a lookout for him, but I still think he's more likely to make his way back to the village and if he does I think 'he'll try your place first. So when you see him, or if you have any other news of him, good or bad, will you promise to send me a telegram to the sanatorium at once?'

I promised. And when I got back to the village I waited for him. But he didn't come and I never saw him again.

9

My twenty-first birthday was spent alone at home. It fell on a Sunday in the summer of 1945, half-way through that ambiguous period of fourteen weeks which separated VE Day from VJ Day – a trancelike hiatus of anticipated relief poised between war and peace. Those rooms in our house which for nearly six years had been occupied by British or American military personnel were now empty, and badly in need of repair: their silence seemed to impose itself on the atmosphere as a positive force. My mother had put the place up for sale and was now staying with a friend in London, trying to secure the lease of a small house in Knightsbridge which had been damaged by the blast of a nearby bomb and might therefore be obtainable at a low rent without a premium. Soon I would be leaving the village for good. I was fiddling about with the radio, hoping to find some jazz on the American Forces Network, when I saw a jeep drive up to the front door. Assuming that it belonged to a prospective buyer sent by the estate agent with an order to view, I hastened outside to admit the visitor. But the man who stepped down from the jeep was Sandy Demarest.

He was wearing the uniform of the RAF, in which he had reached the rank of group captain. Sandy was only thirty-five but his wartime experience had aged him. His face was as handsome as ever but had become almost haggard, the lined skin stretched thinly over the gaunt bones. His fine dark eyes still burned, but their glance had grown remote. One felt that he had survived his various ordeals (suicidal missions, humiliating captivity, daredevil escapes) unmaimed though not unhurt. Perhaps heroism must of necessity desensitise in one way or another: in Sandy's case, a stylised manner originally assumed as protective armour had hardened yet further under adversity to a point where it paradoxically rendered him endearingly defenceless.

'I cannot begin to describe to you the depths of corruption to which I was forced to sink – the whopping lies I had to tell and the shameless bribes I had to offer – in order to get hold of this jeep!' he said, after I had ushered him indoors. 'I have no right to it at all, really – not nearly grand enough! But thank God I did. I've just been down to see our darling girl in Cornwall. Frankly, I couldn't have faced the journey by train. And as I had to pass by your gates on my way back to London I thought I'd just pop in on the off-chance of finding you at home. Kay particularly wanted me to see you and give you her love in person. As a matter of fact, she entrusted me with a special message for you, under strict instructions to deliver it without fail when next we met. So here goes. It doesn't seem to me to make any sense at all, but no doubt you'll understand what she's driving at. She said, "Ask him if he remembers the time when he came with the cake." I do hope it doesn't mean anything too rude!'

'How is she?'

'In great heart. Yes, in great heart. Of course, she's been having a very thin time of it for a while now, poor love . . . One thing, they're allowing her to smoke again, so she's thoroughly enjoying that. You remember what a chimney she used to be? She nearly went mad when they told her she had to give it up.'

'But that must mean they think the TB's almost cured?'

'No, old boy, I'm afraid not. In fact, it means quite the opposite . . . Look, I've got to get back on the road at once, but before I do could I borrow your telephone for just one local call? I might as well ring home now that I'm so near. Of course, they've no idea where I've been . . .'

He spoke for some time on the telephone to both his mother and his father while I tried to avoid confronting the significance of what he had implied – that Kay's doctor no longer thought it was worthwhile forbidding her to smoke. When he had hung up, he explained, 'I didn't say where I was – better to let them think I was calling from London – it seemed easier that way. Once the old girl cottoned on to the fact that I'm in the neighbourhood she'd want to know what I was doing here and if I told her the truth about Cornwall – I mean, that I'd visited Kay on the sly – it would only upset her and then the fat would be well and truly in the fire. So should you run into either of them in the street, don't say anything about having seen me, there's a good man.'

'But surely they *couldn't* mind your wanting to be with Kay when she's been so terribly ill?'

I regretted my outburst when I saw the expression on Sandy's face. It was one of deep and dangerous exhaustion.

'There'd be a row, you see, and I just – could – not – stand it,' he said, smiling gently and spacing the words to give them an emphasis of quiet desperation. 'I've been through quite enough already over the past few days. Please forgive me, but I can't bear to talk about it. Darling Kay . . . it was harrowing . . . we neither of us said so, but we both knew it was goodbye . . . Listen, *I* must say goodbye this very minute, I really must. I've got this important meeting tonight in London with a movie producer and it would never do to keep him waiting. I'm going to be demobbed at any moment and I've just got to find myself a job. This chap might have a part for me in his next film. It's one of those beastly war epics, something to do with the Battle of Britain . . . so wish me luck!'

Although he was now talking almost jauntily, Sandy still looked stricken. When we parted he squeezed my shoulder hard and then gave it a little pat.

It was only after he had driven off that I took in fully what he had been trying to tell me. He was clearly convinced that very soon Kay was going to die. She was presumably too ill to see anyone outside her immediate family and therefore, as far as I was concerned, she might as well have been already dead. I began to realise that I would never see her again. Feeling trapped by grief, I instinctively left the house, as though it were possible to leave the grief behind there, but it only grew heavier the farther and faster I tried to walk away from it. I retraced my steps and sought refuge in the other garden, where I stood very still, bemusedly hoping that the grief might lessen if I made no move to attract its attention.

Little was left here of my father's orderly creation. The vegetable garden had been expanded to dominate most of the available space, and the small area that remained for ornamental plantation had become overgrown by weeds, beneath which traces of the original arrangement of ovals, crescents, triangles and circles could only faintly be perceived. The undipped yews had long ago lost their animal shapes and the bird-baths, benches and sundial had been sold to an antique dealer in the High Street. The church bells were ringing as relentlessly as they had on VE Day, but on this occasion they were celebrating nothing more momentous than the imminence of Sunday evening service.

The bells made me think of the war that was nearly over and of the people who had died in it. It struck me as ironic that the same disease which was bringing Kay's life to a premature end in her fortieth year had very probably preserved mine. If I had not been invalided out of the army while I was still in training I would certainly have taken part in the Normandy landings of 1944 and might well have been killed then or later, as my friends at Britannia Barracks had been and so many others of my contemporaries – Billy Phipps and Harry Vokins among them.

Throughout the war I had somehow managed to keep full awareness of its import on the edge of my consciousness, so that while I imagined I felt concern about the slaughter involved, I had not really been affected by it at a deep personal level. Why then was I touched so keenly by the approaching death of Kay? Was I so mean a spirit that I could only react to human tragedy if it occasioned a loss in my immediate circle? Or was it because I vaguely felt that if I had tried harder I might have done something to save her? Reviewing my relationship with Kay, I found no valid cause for remorse: if I had been guilty of sins of omission they had only been of a normally venial kind. Yet it was inescapably true that the sense of bereavement which now overwhelmed me with such frightening force was accompanied by an equally crushing sense of defeat, with its attendant emotions of anger and shame.

Seeking some comfort in righteous indignation by externalising the responsibility and exaggerating the blame, I tried to see Kay's story in over-simplified terms of melodrama. She had to all intents and purposes been destroyed by her parents, and Sandy had morally colluded in the metaphorical murder, unmanned by the mysterious terror which that silly old bore Sybil Demarest seemed able to inspire in her family . . . But I had to acknowledge that according to this interpretation my complicity in the alleged crime was at least as great as his, because in his absence I had witnessed every stage of its development and had still been incapable of preventing it.

I preferred to believe that nothing and nobody *could*

have prevented it, that Kay was an inevitable casualty of one of those mock battles of which the outcome is predictable from the start because the winners have the ruthless will to victory and the losers are stubbornly committed to failure. For a moment she appeared to me as a martyr whose wasted life could be taken to symbolise an unholy triumph of corrupt compromise over artless purity. Then I seemed to hear Kay's cosy, laconic voice and to see her high-shouldered figure moving with the deliberate, deceptively confident steps of her 'tarty' walk, and I rejected as sentimental and patronising the notion that she was a natural victim, fated from birth to frustration and despair. All the same, as a tribute to her memory, I romantically swore a loyal oath in the other garden that until my own death I would eschew ambition for worldly success and avoid the wielders of influence and power, choosing my friends among the innocently uncompetitive. It is not a vow that I have always been able to keep.

OUT OF THE WAR

Preface

These stories were written between the ages of seventeen and twenty, from 1942 to 1945, while I was hanging about waiting to be called up and while I was convalescing after I had been invalided out of the army. I believe I made tentative efforts to get them published, but cannot recall any details beyond the fact that all were unsuccessful: my collection of rejection slips has not survived. Indeed, I thought that I had destroyed the manuscripts as well until I came upon them not long ago, while I was preparing to move house, hidden at the back of a drawer. Enough time had elapsed for me to be able to read them, if not with complete detachment, at least with a minimum of self-consciousness. They seemed to have been written by someone else – and, in a sense, I suppose they were.

Lately, I have been trying to remember things which for thirty years I had been trying to forget. The war was a tragic time for most people, exciting perhaps for some: for me, an adolescent when it began and a delayed adolescent when it ended, it was a period of stagnation. Uncertainty and inaction are negative ills of which one cannot bear to be reminded until a long time later, when even the depressing contours of frustration may be softened by nostalgia. Many people pass their adolescence in an emotional void, waiting for something – anything – to happen, and wondering with increasing desperation if it ever will. In wartime, everyone not directly involved with the fighting found themselves in a similar state of suspension. I now see that this condition gave my stories a unifying theme, although I was unaware of it when I wrote them. Their desolate cinema-cafés, dirty milk-bars and dimly-lit station-buffets evoke for me not only my own frame of mind at that time, but a mood which was then more widely shared than I had realised. For this reason, I am less embarrassed by them than I had expected to be.

The rejection slips had almost convinced me that I would never make a writer − the one thing I wanted to be. None the less, the story called 'Davenant Road' was published in 1946 in the *New Savoy*, a periodical whose first and last issue was edited by Mara Meulen and myself. Raymond Mortimer of the *New Statesman* and Alan Pryce-Jones of the *Times Literary Supplement* liked it enough to give me work as a reviewer. My own life seemed to start up again, together with the post-war world: the stories had belonged to an interim. From then on, I confined myself to various forms of journalism. When I rediscovered them in 1972, I showed them to Karl Miller, who had recently asked me if I had ever tried to write fiction. He published 'Punctuality' in the *Listener*: an encouraging gesture which has led to the belated appearance of this book.

I remember that 'Saturday' was the earliest story to be written, and 'Sunday' the second. The hospital described in 'Out of the War' (the only straightforwardly autobiographical piece in the collection) was the first of several in which my brief career as a soldier was passed. Enforced passivity sometimes stimulates invention, and it was here that I started 'Davenant Road', followed by the other stories about lonely girls whose socially limited predicaments I imagined as a metaphor for my own physically restricted situation. I am sure that they all eventually joined the Women's Services (Edna the ATS, Agatha the WAAF and Iris the WRNS) and I hope they had a good war.

Francis Wyndham,
Boxing Day, 1973

Out of The War

It was about six o'clock in the evening when I was brought into the orthopaedic ward. The two girls in the ATS who had taken it in turns to drive the ambulance carried me in on a stretcher, which they laid down on the floor, so that the room seemed very big to me, and the ceiling very high. The girls did not know what to do next, and whispered together uneasily. At length one went to fetch my papers, which had been left in the ambulance, and the other disappeared in search of a nurse.

The walls of the ward were white; so were the bed-spreads and the patients' faces and their huge bandaged limbs suspended a few inches from the beds. As it was evening, all these things seemed grey, and there appeared to be a light grey mist filling the room. Nobody spoke or moved while I lay on the floor. The ten patients sat still, propped up by many pillows, and some had the black earphones which hung behind each bed clamped to their ears. These had an abstracted air, but the wireless pro-gramme, inaudible to me, seemed not to prevent them from reading their magazines, and, turning a page of *Picture Post* or *Everybody's*, one would lift his head for a moment to attend to the broadcast buzzing at his ears; then, no longer seeking meaning in the noise, transfer his mind to the printed page lying on the white counterpane.

Not far from me a man stood upright. His body from the waist to the neck was encased in smooth plaster of paris, and one of his arms was supported at an angle, shoulder-level. He had the look of an enamel model in a draper's window or a cardboard advertisement propped upright in a cinema foyer. When he blinked, or turned his head, the effect was therefore rather sinister.

A wardmaid came into the room. I knew that she was a wardmaid because of the dinginess of her dress; her halo-like cap was on askew at the back of her head. She bent over me a kind, intelligent face; then she looked at the man who was standing, and, moving her lips with care, she uttered a strange babbling noise, a string of vowel sounds slightly distorted by a gurgle in her throat, as though there were a bubble there, continually bursting and re-forming. I learnt for certain later, what I guessed then, that many of the wardmaids at the hospital were patients who were deaf and dumb.

The ambulance driver came back with a tall nurse (from where I lay she looked a giantess) who approached the wardmaid and shouted into her ear, 'You'll find Sister in her office, Elsie.' Elsie went away and the nurse and the drivers helped me into bed (for the other driver had returned, munching a biscuit bought at a Church Army mobile canteen which stood at the hospital entrance). I was to know that this nurse was called Nurse Bennett. She had a long freckled face, and crinkly reddish hair. Always smiling and humming to herself, she was brisk, efficient and good-humoured.

One of the drivers, a fat, dark girl, said 'Cheerio, laddie,' and went away with her friend. I knew that they were bound for a restaurant opposite, where they would drink some tea, as they had arranged this on the way to the hospital, and I wished that I could go with them.

The ward was divided by a partition built across it which had an open space in the middle for the aisle to run through. I was next to the partition, which was as high as the bed; above it there was a curtain which, when drawn, separated one set of six beds from the other – each division consisting of three beds against the two opposite walls. Nurse Bennett had drawn this curtain, cutting me off from one half of the room, with some idea that I might prefer the semi-privacy it afforded while the stretcher was lifted to the level of the bed and while I rolled off it, on to the rubber ring which had been placed beneath the sheet.

'All right, old chap?' she asked.

'Yes, thank you.'

'Good man.'

She strode away, leaving the curtain still drawn. I lay back on the pillows and the feeling of sickness caused by the jolting ambulance drive began to pass away. I was conscious of a muttering noise just above my head; this came from my earphones, which stuttered away distantly and maddeningly, only to assume volume and coherence when actually over my ears.

A red-haired man, evidently a soldier, looked up from his magazine.

'She sang that well,' he said appreciatively, and I gathered that an invisible crooner had that moment finished her song.

It was then that the curtain beside me began to twitch. I understood that the man in the bed beyond it was trying to draw it. I saw a hairy hand with a ring on one finger jerking it back nervously, but the hand could only draw the curtain half-way and its owner remained invisible to me. I drew the curtain all the way back. In the bed next to mine a dark-haired man of about fifty was smiling at me. Both his legs were supported by a kind of pulley so that they should not touch the bed.

'I don't like to have the curtain drawn like that,' he said. 'I can't see what's going on. But they're always drawing it. It cuts me off from half the room and I like to see what's going on.'

Almost at once he told me his story, the reason for his presence in the hospital. He told it in an unemotional voice, not at all the sort of voice usually used to describe catastrophes, and while doing so he continued to smile his nervous smile, baring uneven teeth in a haggard face.

He was a postman in the town, a widower with an only son, a boy of fifteen. They had been walking together one evening, returning home from a public house, when an army lorry which was passing had swerved into the side of the road and run them over. This was some months ago. His legs and arms had been badly injured, but he was now doing surprisingly well, and although it had at first been predicted that he would be crippled for life, it seemed likely that he would make a complete recovery. His son had lain in the bed on the other side of mine. The doctors had operated on the boy, taking off both his legs, without asking his father's consent. Shortly after that the boy had died. The postman repeated, 'It was very wrong of them not to ask my permission. I was very poorly then and perhaps they didn't want to worry me, but they should have told me they were going to take off his legs.'

It seemed that the shock of the discovery of this operation had been so great that it still outweighed in the postman's mind that of his son's subsequent death.

I offered him a packet of cigarettes, of which I had a store, because it appeared that he had no money at all in the world, and depended entirely on his friends who came to see him every visitor's day. He refused them, and seemed rather embarrassed. A few minutes later he in his turn offered me a biscuit, saying, 'My neighbour brought me these yesterday. She's very good to me.' I refused, and he seemed satisfied; I understood that it worried him to borrow from someone whom he would think it necessary somehow to pay back.

He repeated his story to me the next morning, and after that every morning and evening. Whenever my curtain had been drawn to screen me while I washed, used the bedpan, or was visited by a doctor, I could sense his uneasiness on the other side of it. The nurses never remembered to draw it back. When whatever private activity I had been engaged on was over, there would be a short time of suspense; then the hand would start its ineffectual twitching. The curtain drawn, he would smile apologetically.

'I hate to be cut off like that. I like to see what's going on.'

Shortly after my arrival in the ward, another stretcher was brought in, and the patient deposited on the bed next to mine, which had till then been empty. At first it seemed that the newcomer was a young man, probably a soldier; but when the time for the evening wash came, and he took off his pyjama jacket and sat up in bed, the thinness of his arms and the whiteness of his chest showed that he could not be more than fourteen. This pleased the postman.

'It's funny,' he said. 'There always seems to be a lad in that bed. That was the bed my boy was in, and after him there was another lad of fifteen. He was a nice boy, he left before you came. Now there's another laddie.'

He leant forward and smiled at the boy, and would have liked to have spoken to him, only my presence between them made this difficult. He did shout a remark, but the boy did not know it was meant for him, although several of the other patients looked up.

I soon found that the only nurse who made any impression on the ward was Nurse Bennett, the tall one with red hair. She was always addressed as Nurse Bennett, while the others were merely known as 'nurse'. She was very friendly with the patients, who loved to tease her. One day the red-haired soldier called her as she passed his bed.

'Nurse Bennett.'

'Yes, Ginger?'

'I want to ask you something.'

'Well, buck up about it, because I'm busy.'

'It says in the Bible that Adam and Eve were the first people on the earth, doesn't it?'

'Yes,' said Nurse Bennett guardedly.

'And they had two sons, Cain and Abel, didn't they?'

'Yes.'

'Cain killed Abel, is that right?'

'Yes, Ginger.'

'Then Cain went off somewhere and got married. Who,' Ginger asked triumphantly, 'did he marry?'

Nurse Bennett pulled a face. 'You've got me there, I'm afraid, Ginge. But I think I can explain. You see, we're not supposed to take the Bible too literally. It describes things how they probably did happen, but it can't know for certain, and all it says isn't strictly true. But it is true, though not always absolutely true. Do you see?'

'I see, Nurse Bennett,' said Ginger, grinning and winking at the other patients.

'Now I want to ask *you* something,' said the nurse. 'Adam and Eve and pinch me . . .' but she was interrupted by Ginger who pinched her arm. She gave a little shriek, then walked off smiling; her voice could be heard shouting orders to a nurse in the passage.

The red-haired soldier would often tell Nurse Bennett coarse jokes, to see how she would react. She never laughed at these, but continued to smile indulgently, only saying, 'I think you're revolting,' or, 'I'm surprised at you, Ginge. You wouldn't talk like that to your mother, now would you?' Ginger would say of her when she was out of the room, 'She's a caution, that Nurse Bennett. She's got red hair like me, we're a pair. We get along all right.'

There was one subject about which the ward liked to tease Nurse Bennett, which offended her and made her cross. She was the captain of a hockey team made up by the nurses at the hospital. She took this very seriously. Before a match, there would be an atmosphere of restrained excitement in the ward. Nurses, while washing patients, would talk about the game to each other over their bodies. 'My dear, I haven't played for *years*. Not since school . . .' After the match, Ginger would say to Nurse Bennett, 'Who won?'

'They did.' The opposite team was that of the Technical College in the town.

'How many goals did you score, then?'

'I didn't score any. I nearly got one just before half time, though.'

'How many goals did your side get?'

'None,' she answered angrily. 'They beat us 6–0 if you really want to know.'

'Don't you ever win a match then?'

'Only when we play South Gate.' (This was a girls' school near the town.) 'That's because they've got about three teams, and they send their C team along to play us. Even then it's a struggle. Still, it's all good fun.'

'And what do they call you in the field? Slasher Bennett?'

Someone suggested, 'Tiger Bennett?'

'Or just "The Dumb Blonde"?'

Nurse Bennett went red with anger.

'Oh come on, be sports,' she said. 'I can take a joke, but you go on too much about it. Anyway, I can always get my own back, can't I?'

'What would you do, Tiger?'

'Well, next time you want the bottle, I can keep you waiting for it, can't I?'

'Oh, you wicked old cuss!'

Nurse Bennett walked out of the ward, taking long strides and muttering to herself.

In the evening, Nurse Bennett read prayers in the ward. The only light still lit was a green-shaded lamp on the table where the night-nurse was to sit all through the night. Nurse Bennett read well, and the atmosphere in the ward was suitably devotional, because the patients liked the prayers, and repeated the 'Amens' clearly and reverently. But before Nurse Bennett, walking stealthily on creaking shoes, head bent and hands folded over the prayer-book, had left the room, this atmosphere would immediately be dissipated by an exaggerated belch from Ginger's bed, and a giggle from the postman.

'That's them beans we had for supper, eh, Ginge? They repeat something terrible.'

In a bed in one corner of the room there lay a very old man, who was in hospital owing to a poisoned hand. The postman, who always referred to him as 'that bloody old man', told me about him on my first night in the ward.

'He's a nuisance, because you see he's silly in the head. He thinks he's still at home. He's always taking off his bandages, and he gives the nurses a lot of trouble. He gets out of bed because he thinks he has to get in the coal.'

This was embarrassing, because the hospital was short of pyjama trousers, and few of the patients, among them the old man, wore any. He would choose a moment when there were no nurses in the ward to get out of bed, and would then make for the door which led to the women's ward, and which he believed to be the coal-shed in his own backyard. The old man usually fell down on the floor before reaching the door, and then all the patients would shout, 'Nurse! Nurse! Dad's on the move again.' Nurse Bennett would then appear and, smiling cheerfully, and saying, 'Come on, Pop. That's all right, you'll be OK,' would lift him up and carry him in her arms back to his bed.

One day there was a new nurse on duty, a young, small girl who seemed struck dumb and almost paralysed by shyness. Nurse Bennett had explained her duties to her kindly and at great length. The new nurse, biting her lip, breathing heavily and staring at the watch which she pulled up from her bosom, clasped my pulse with an iron grip. She took the thermometer from my mouth and brought it into the middle of the room, frowning at it worriedly. Then, her breast heaving, she marked the results of these investigations on my temperature chart with care, terrified that her fountain pen would make a blot. While this was happening, the old man had been slowly climbing out of bed. I called her attention to it. She stared at him, blushing and frightened by the sight of his thin hairy legs and shaking movements, and seemed unable to move.

Sister passed the door at that moment, and said to her angrily, 'One of your patients is getting out of bed, nurse. Please will you see to it.'

She approached the old man with diffidence, and could be heard muttering something to him.

Ginger called out, 'Pack it in, Pop. You've 'ad it!'

This seemed to frighten the new nurse even more. Fortunately Nurse Bennett came in then, and lifted the old man's legs with her strong arms back into the bed.

From the moment, after prayers had been read and the night staff had arrived, when there was silence and semi-darkness in the ward, until half past five in the following morning when the impatient night-nurse began to take the morning temperatures half an hour before she was supposed to, the old man in the corner talked to himself, loudly and without pausing, whether in his sleep or not it was difficult to determine. His words were impossible to make out; this endless, meaningless conversation continued all night, and made sleep possible only for those patients who had grown accustomed to the noise. The others could sleep for a few minutes now and again, and then the old man's voice mingled with their dreams to disturb them.

I had only one night disturbed in this way. On my second evening in the ward, a doctor, tired of the complaints of the other patients, gave the old man a morphia injection, to keep him quiet for the night. The injection did have this effect; but on the following morning, there was still no sign from the old man's bed, and he lay in this condition, quite still, for three days and nights. The others in the ward missed the diversion which his continual journeys across the room had afforded; they glanced uneasily at his silent bed, and did not mention him. The nurses whispered together. 'It appears he has heart; Doctor didn't know.'

On the third day, when we had grown accustomed to the old man's silence, an orderly hid his bed behind three of the green screens which slid along the floor on castors and were always used when it was necessary to isolate a patient for some reason. This was one of the two visitors' days in the week. At two o'clock I could see pass the window a procession of friends and relations, all carrying parcels containing eatables. Some of these penetrated into the ward and clustered round the different beds for two hours. Conversation was at first lively, but at three o'clock it began to flag, and it was usually with a feeling of relief that the visitors rose from their chairs at four, hearing a nurse march up and down the passage ringing a handbell to announce that their time was up. The postman had more visitors than anyone else in the ward, but they came singly and in shifts, and did not stay the full two hours. They were mostly men connected with the post office where he had worked; sometimes his neighbour came with a bag of biscuits, sometimes a sister-in-law with a packet of Woodbines; once a solicitor had arrived, with some papers for the postman to sign, as he had been trying since his accident to get some compensation money, but had so far been unsuccessful.

This afternoon the visitors watched the screens being wheeled round the old man's bed, and everybody knew, without saying anything about it, that he had died under the morphia. The day which had been looked forward to by everyone was therefore spoiled; patients and visitors were depressed by the knowledge that the nurses were washing a corpse behind the screens, and many of them were unhappy that the old man whom they had thought such a bore was dead, as they would miss him. Later on, a woman dressed in green arrived, and disappeared behind the screens. These were then stretched end to end, from the corner to the doorway, and we could hear a stretcher being wheeled behind them. Then they were folded up, and leant against the wall, revealing an empty bed, newly made, the sheet turned down ready for the next patient. The woman in green, who might have been the old man's sister, wife or landlady, sat down in a chair by the fire. She was crying. Nurse Bennett brought her a cup of tea.

'Now, dear, you must drink this.'

The woman shook her head.

'No, you must, it will give you strength.'

Nurse Bennett's voice comforted the woman, and she began to sip the tea.

'I'm going to fetch Sister to speak to you now. You stay there, dear.'

But when the nurse had gone, the woman laid the teacup carefully down on the floor, rose and left the room. Sister came in and, finding her gone, sent a nurse to fetch her. She could not be found in the hospital. She must have walked blindly through the confusing passages, by instinct finding the entrance, and then hurried home through the town to her house in one of its suburbs.

These events were the only things that disturbed the monotony of the hospital routine during the week I spent there. The time was passed staring at the white walls, waiting for the next meal to be wheeled in by Elsie. I was to be taken by ambulance to a Convalescent Home five miles away. My life in the hospital had been lived in a void; in fact, I had hardly lived a life of my own at all, and felt as though I consisted only of eyes and ears to record the few things that happened around me. I had been carried as it were blindfold into the ward, and would be carried in the same condition out of it; I did not know my way about the hospital, or even what it looked like from outside; and if I had been put down at the entrance, and walked out into the town which I hardly knew, I should not have known where to go, and would have lost my way. For a week I had just been part of this white room, like a chair or table in it.

On my last morning there, when I felt as though I had already left the place, an orderly was told to give me a blanket bath, so that I should arrive clean enough to make a good impression on the Convalescent Home. Usually, the blanket baths were done by nurses, and then they were very slapdash affairs. Blankets were modestly heaped on one's shivering body, and only one's arms and legs were washed in tepid water by reluctant feminine hands. The orderly, however, did it thoroughly, and washed every part of me vigorously and conscientiously, even taking the water away to be changed half-way through. He wore a linen mask over his mouth and nose. He had a bad cold, and sniffed and breathed with difficulty behind the mask. When he had finished, he wheeled away the screen, but left the curtain by my bed still drawn. I had only now to wait for the ambulance, and I longed for it to arrive.

As on my first day there, the postman's hand began to draw the curtain back. I would have liked to have spent my last hours in the ward with the curtains drawn, so that I could almost imagine myself alone, and I felt irritated and did not help him to draw it. When he had done so, I waited for the usual explanation.

'I hate to have that thing drawn. It cuts me off from what's going on.' Then he added, 'They used to draw it when my boy lay in that bed by you, so that I shouldn't see him. My hands were bad then so I couldn't pull it back. I reckon it was silly of them to do that, because even if I couldn't see him, I could still hear him call out, couldn't I?'

Matchlight

The smoke of Woodbines floated up from the plush one and ninepennies to evaporate in the baroque ceiling of the cinema, clouding on its way the flickering beam of light which like a tape connected the small square projection window with the large square screen. A draught stretched down the aisle from the foyer. There were coughs and sighs and the sound of Mars Bars being opened in the cinema. An usherette sat on a stool with a torch on her lap and gazed at the film which was ending.

Although the house was packed, the seats on either side of that occupied by Edna were empty. Edna could not help regarding this as a slight on herself; nobody wanted to sit next to her. Her body had been braced defensively during the programme, her eyes never straying from the screen, for she had never before been to the cinema alone, and did not want to be thought common. If someone had sat by her, she would not have felt so conspicuous, nor dreaded the moment when the yellow lights lit up along the golden walls and she had to stand to attention during the anthem, conscious of the hostile stare of the audience.

Edna considered leaving the cinema before this moment arrived, but decided to stay and see the end of the film. A fair actress sang the sad song which had run through the story in a deep, contented voice, her hair like custard and her cheeks, neck and shoulders like white cushions. On the final note her lover took her in his arms; they kissed slowly and carefully while her slim china hands clasped him in simulated ecstasy. The End appeared on the screen, but one could still see the lovers dimly, and Edna wished she could stop them from fading quite away, for her loneliness, dispelled during the film, must return with accumulated force on their final disappearance.

The crowd pushed out of the theatre into the dark and soon vanished, each particle of it bound for some room in the spreading town, leaving Edna standing alone and hesitant outside the closed cinema. She did not want to go home yet. The stars provided a faint light, illuminating form and outline but leaving feature and detail to the imagination. The only sounds were those of footsteps far away and once the rumble and whistle of a train. Edna began to walk slowly down the street, singing just audibly the song she had heard in the film, so that a man who passed her turned round to watch her in surprise. It seemed to her that in every doorway in the street a silent couple stood still, pressed so near to each other that they might have been one person. She passed a public house which had just closed, and could see through a window a bar empty but for the proprietor who was collecting dirty glasses.

She came to a bridge over the river which crossed the town, and stopped to look down at the water. The river was like a length of dark blue material on a draper's counter, but the starlight gave it a disturbing radiance. For some time Edna stood there alone, her thoughts confused as though just before sleep. The film she had seen, and her idea that each member of the audience but herself was purposeful and happy that night, made her dread returning to her house, where her mother would have gone to bed having left a jug of cocoa in the kitchen for Edna to warm up on the oven. Her mother believed that she had gone to the cinema with another girl from the office where she worked. Beneath her dark blue coat Edna was wearing a grey satin blouse and a brown woollen suit – her best clothes; it seemed a shame that nobody would know this. How could she take them off, alone in her bedroom, with the knowledge that no one had noticed, and remarked on how nice she looked? She felt pleasantly removed from her daytime life, and somehow superior to every part of it.

When she heard a limping footstep approach she felt obscurely that an unformulated wish had been granted, and her hands gripped the railing of the bridge. She forced herself not to turn round. The steps slackened behind her, passed her, and then stopped. She had expected them to stop, but now she felt frightened. The steps approached her again, and a voice said, 'A penny for your thoughts.' It was almost a whisper, but seemed very loud to Edna.

She turned towards a tall figure, and could just distinguish a long rectangular face, which in the dark seemed to be made of grey leather, beneath a hat with a sharp wide brim. She guessed from the hat, and a note in the voice, that this was an Australian soldier. He carried his shoulders high, and his hands in his overcoat pockets.

'Just day-dreaming,' she said unnaturally. 'Or night-dreaming rather.' She laughed quickly, and turned again to stare at the water.

'Feeling lonesome?'

'Perhaps.'

'Me too.'

'Haven't you friends in the town?' she asked, in the voice she used to address people who came to tea with her mother.

'Christ, no. How should I know anyone in a place like this?'

'You needn't use bad language,' she said, although she had liked the way he said 'Christ'.

'Pardon,' he said, and she was both glad and sorry to discern a note of respect in his voice, which had not been there before.

'On leave?' she asked jerkily, still not turning towards him.

'Forty-eight, and nowhere to sleep.'

'I'm very sorry, I'm sure.'

'You're not very talkative,' he said after a silence.

'I'm not in the habit of talking to strangers.'

'I suppose you want me to push off?'

'No.' Edna faced the stranger, and although her brain was excited her body felt tired and relaxed.

'What I thought was,' he said carefully, 'if you're on your own, and what with me being on my own too, we might spend the evening together.'

'What do you take me for?'

He thought a bit, and then said, 'A bit of all right.'

She thought, 'He can't see me really, that's the blackout,' but she could not help being pleased. She said, 'That's as maybe.'

'Come to think of it, I have got a mate in town. He'd give us a drink.'

'I don't drink.'

'It would be somewhere where we could talk. I like you, and you might get to like me.' He leant towards her so that his coat touched her. 'What about it?'

'I don't mind.' She could hear him breathe deeply, relieved. 'That's it,' he said. 'Hold on half a mo while I light up. Do you want a smoke?'

'I don't smoke either.'

'That's what I like to hear.'

She was happy now. She liked this man – or what she could guess of him, for she could see nothing of him but a lean black shape, with a grey insertion which was his face. The darkness made her feel very near to him, as though

260

already in his arms. They stood isolated on the bridge, above the blue water, with the black forms of houses, factories, churches and gasometers stretching away on either side. She felt all at once confident; her sense of lassitude, shame and fear had passed away.

When he bent his arm to place a cigarette in his mouth she heard a small cracking noise, a sort of squeak; it might have been a shot in the distance but she knew it came from him and wondered what he had in his pocket to cause it. 'Now I shall see his face,' she thought; and then she was blinded for a second by the light of his match. What she did see, in the moment it took for him to hold the flame to his cigarette and suck in the smoke, was a deep purple scar down one side of his thin face. When the match had been tossed over the bridge into the river she remembered also a dark patch over one eye. He had held the match between his thumb and forefinger, and she had seen, but had not registered the fact until it was again dark, that there were no other fingers on his hand – the top of his palm was a flat surface. Now she realised that the squeak she had heard – and heard now once more – was made by the bending of a wooden arm. In an instant she recalled the limp – and the reconstruction was complete. He was not young, perhaps forty years old. He must have been very badly wounded.

'I can't come with you,' she said in a louder voice. 'I'm not that sort of girl.'

She turned round and hurried away. She did not know where she went in the dark; once she bumped against another person walking fast, and once she almost ran into a lamp post. She felt feverish with terror, tears were in her eyes, and she imagined all the time that he was following her, and calling after her. When at last she stopped in a dark side street she could hear nothing but her own loud breathing.

What had he done when she left him? She imagined him

still standing there, stunned by her sudden cruelty, deeply hurt, and angry with himself for betraying his deformity too soon. Or had he done so on purpose, to test her and avert a later, even ruder repulsion on her part? She had obeyed an instinct when she ran away, but now she felt the pull of another, contrary one. She could hear his voice in her mind ('That's what I like to hear'); he seemed to be shouting it in her ear while she stood in the street shivering. His voice was kind, and pathetically confident. She felt that she knew all about him; the sort of man he had been before his injuries, and the sort of man he was now. She was embarrassed, and ashamed of her behaviour. She longed to comfort the Australian, to hold his head in her lap and stroke his hair; to prove that she was too fine a girl to be repelled by what he could not help.

She walked slowly back towards the bridge, but was soon lost. Before she panicked, a policeman saw her and asked if he could help.

'Where is the bridge by St Mary's?' she asked urgently.

When he had told her she hurried away, almost running, following his directions. She prayed that the man would be waiting for her where she had left him. She was out of breath when at length she reached the bridge. She walked up and down it, straining her eyes, but there was no one there.

'Where are you?' she asked aloud.

For an hour Edna wandered through the town, gazing into the face of every shadowy figure she passed, walking in circles; but the soldier had disappeared, and eventually, tired at last, she returned to her mother's house, and was grateful for the cocoa in the kitchen.

Davenant Road

I remember on Sunday morning I slipped out of the house while Mother was upstairs getting ready for church, and hurried down the street. I was myself dressed for church; that is to say, my hat, overcoat, gloves and purse were all dark brown. The street was empty, my shoes sounded loud on the pavement, and I wondered if any of the neighbours were watching me from the dark house windows. I had that feeling you have when you are very excited that someone is behind you, pursuing you; but I did not turn my head until I had reached the corner of the street. There, as I knew he would be, the one-legged man was sitting on the ground next to his sack full of Sunday papers and his cap full of coppers. I was so nervous and out of breath that for a moment I could not speak; then I said, 'Have you got a copy of the *World Messenger*, please?' This was the name of a popular Sunday paper which we did not take in – Mother only took the *Sunday Graphic*, and would have considered the *World Messenger* common, for it was full of football pools and horoscopes and competitions and scandalous news items. The man fumbled for a long time in his sack, and then he did produce a copy, saying it was the last one. I took two coppers from my purse and gave them to him; then I snatched the paper and went a little way back along the road. I was quite sick with excitement. I had intended not to open the paper until I was back in my room, but I could not wait and unfolded it clumsily standing there in the street. The wind blew it about and I had to hit the pages into position. I remember I was standing outside one of the many private hotels in our street; I could see through a window the edge of a table laid for Sunday lunch, and a table napkin folded in a green napkin ring.

At last I folded the paper at the 'Letters from Readers' column – and then I suddenly seemed to know for certain that what I was looking for would not be there. Muttering nervously to myself, I looked down the column until I noticed a very short letter printed under the heading 'Colourful!' Was that it? I read the letter through, and only after I had finished it did I fully realise that it was indeed the letter I had posted a week ago. This was what it said:

> Dear Sir,
>
> I thought it might interest you to know that at the office where I work the boss is called Mr Black, the two typists are called Miss White and Miss Green, and the office boy's name is Brown!
>
> Is this a record or can any of your readers beat it?

The letter was signed 'Miranda', and in square brackets under the signature was printed, 'Well, readers, can any of you tell of cases which beat Miranda's record? Ed.'

I folded the paper into a tiny square, went indoors and into my room, and put it away under my clothes in the chest of drawers.

At church Mother sang very loudly, but I only moved my lips and did not utter a sound. I never sit through a service without at some part of it suddenly being seized with a desire to scream. It is the thought of the shame and discomfort that would result from my scream that makes me long to more and more. I blush and sweat in my pew during the lessons, afraid that I may lose control at any moment, and shriek aloud, so that everybody in the church would turn and stare at me, shocked and startled. I have never done this, however, although going to church is always a torment for me; I think there must be some little brake in my mind, which works automatically and makes it physically impossible for me to do the disgraceful thing which I perversely long to do.

Anyway, that Sunday I had plenty to occupy my mind, and I sat through the service in a dream. It was the first time I had ever had anything printed in the papers, and for ages that had been my ambition. I had often thought of writing to one of those Advice Columns, but I had no problems about which to consult them, and it struck me as silly to invent one. Once I had written to the Information Bureau of a film magazine asking the date of Jeanette Macdonald's birthday, but the letter was neither printed nor answered. Then I thought of writing about the colour names, which was a good idea as my boss is called 'Mr Black', and I am a typist and my name is 'Miss White', which has always struck me as a strange coincidence. To make better best, I put in that about Green and Brown, which I had invented. I had chosen the *World Messenger* because it was not a paper Mother read, nor were they likely to read it at the office, and it would never have done if someone had noticed my letter, and said, 'Why, this must be from someone at our office!' I would have felt such a silly.

During church I thought of all the millions of people whom I did not know who were no doubt reading what I had written at that moment; and then I thought that of all the copies of the paper printed some must surely survive, and that perhaps in a year's time a man might come across that edition – it might be someone in Africa or China, you never know – and he would read my letter and say to himself, 'Well, that's a coincidence!'

After church as always Mother and I stood about and

265

chatted for a bit in the churchyard with the other people, and then we went home and had lunch together. I believe I behaved quite normally, but all the time I was thinking of the letter in the paper upstairs. When I went to my room after the meal and read it again, I had an odd feeling of disappointment, and felt rather flat. All the week before had been spent in looking forward to that day, and hoping that I would find my letter in the paper; and now that my wish had come true, the letter for some reason seemed very short and rather ridiculous. I remembered that, as a child, after longing for days for some parcel to arrive containing a present, I was not so much disappointed in the gift when it did at last arrive, as sorry that the excitement of waiting for it was over.

I usually spend Sundays with my friend, Mary Conners, who is another typist at the office. We had arranged to meet at three by the bandstand in the public gardens in the centre of the town. I had a little time to myself before that, so I lay on my bed and looked through the *World Messenger*. I came across the following item:

> There has been a further outbreak of anonymous letters in . . . (a London suburb was mentioned). The police say that they are on the track of the writer or writers of these poisonous epistles, and an arrest is expected shortly. The writing of anonymous letters is a particularly despicable and cowardly offence, and any person who may receive one is encouraged to inform the police immediately, and ignore the contents of the letter as they are usually pure fabrications.

As I had written my letter in such secrecy, I felt a strange sort of connection between myself and the writer of these anonymous letters who depended so much on secrecy for the success of his plans. I imagined him reading that bit about himself in the paper; and surely reading the words 'cowardly' and 'despicable' would give him a thrill, and the whole thing a sense of power? The police, the journalist, and the people to whom he had written – what, I wonder, *had* he written? – were all bewildered by him; he had the power to mystify them, make them wonder about him and fear him. And all by writing a few words on a piece of paper, slipping an envelope through a pillar box when no one was looking . . .

The band was not playing that afternoon, and Mary and I sat on a bench by the empty bandstand without finding anything much to say to each other. It was a dull day, and there were few people walking in the gardens. Suddenly Mary said, 'Oh, look! There's the Black Devil and his family!' Sure enough, there, walking towards us, was our boss, holding the arm of a small stout woman with an uninteresting face, wearing a woolly coat and a pixie hood. They were followed by two little girls with short dark hair. Mr Black himself wore a dark blue overcoat and a bowler hat. He had very black hair and a square face; his jaw, which was cleft, always looked as if it needed a shave – it was a sort of blue colour. That was one of the reasons why we girls at the office had christened him the Black Devil – it fitted in with his name, and also his sarcastic manner, which I think we all disliked. I shall never forget my first day at the office; I was nervous, and all thumbs. I had just got my diploma for typing from Miss Wells in the High Street, but they put me in front of a type of machine to which I was not accustomed. Something happened to the ribbon spool, and the ribbon came billowing out of the machine, making me and everything it touched inky. I could not get it back and it became all knotted and tangled. I was near tears, when who should come out of his office but Mr Black! He took one look at me, and said in that sarcastic voice of his, 'Ah, this damsel seems to be in distress. Can I be of any assistance?' Then he put it right in a few minutes while I stood by, feeling ever such a goose, and now and then trying to help but only getting in the way. Since that day I had never liked Mr Black. He was a man of thirty-odd, and he looked younger than his wife.

To go back to that Sunday in the Gardens. The Black family were still some way away from the bench where we sat when I felt Mary become alert; she was preparing to nod and smile at Mrs Black. I think the acquaintance between them was very slight, but Mary liked to make a lot of it, and many a time had she told me about the day when she went to tea at the Blacks' house, 'Polkerris', in Davenant Road, down near the Station. The houses in that street were semi-detached; they had garages, and short curving drives leading up to the front door – altogether more pleasant than the row of gloomy grey houses in which I lived. I had passed Polkerris several times, and had noticed that the front door, glimpsed between the laurels in the garden, had on it a design of the sun setting behind the sea, suggested by a few steel lines against frosted glass. Mary had told me that the names of the little girls were Hazel and Rosemary. These two children, as they walked behind their parents in the Garden, were playing some secret game with each other, pinching each other's arms, and then stifling their giggles with small fists covered by blue wool gloves.

Whether or not Mr and Mrs Black noticed Mary and myself sitting on the bench I shall never know, but anyway they walked straight past us without as much as a nod, their noses in the air. You would have thought that my boss would have deigned to recognise me outside office hours; and you would have expected Mrs Black to have spared Mary at least a smile after having asked her to tea at her house.

Mary's body relaxed, and she said, 'Well! The stuck-up things!'

I felt sorry for Mary, and I also felt that I had been slighted, as I had been sitting with Mary when she had been cut by Mrs Black. I thought it tactful not to speak for long on the subject, so after a bit I said, 'What about tea at the Regal?'

We did not feel like seeing the programme at the Regal after tea. There were two feature films, but from the advertisements outside the cinema I gathered that they were love stories, of the soppy variety. I do not care for that sort of picture any more, although I used to in my schooldays; and Mary only likes Gene Autry.

I left Mary at her mother's house, and then walked slowly home through the streets which form the outskirts of the town. It was late by now and evening was falling; the dull, dim light hurt my eyes, and made me feel uncomfortable, as though I needed a bath. The dusk seemed to penetrate into my clothes and I felt depressed. The smell that came from a small fish-and-chips shop made me shudder; but when I passed a public house, and saw a door open on a room empty but for a young man leaning up at the bar, I was tempted to go in. Not that I would have drunk a thing; spirits disagree with me; but it would have been nice to sit and listen to the wireless in the bar, which seemed to be broadcasting a better programme than I was ever able to get from our set in the lounge at home. A girl's voice followed me as I walked on down the street: 'How can I resist the sergeant-major . . .' I wanted to dance and skip all the way home, but I felt so tired and sad that I could only drag one foot after the other, and stare down at my blue shoes, the laces of which cut into my feet.

As I walked along, I heard a strange voice coming from some distance away, a sound of singing, cracked and mournful. It grew louder as I drew nearer home, and the evening became deeper and the cold more keen. It was a woman's voice, and this is what it sang:

There is a green hill far away
Without a city wall,
Where our dear Lord was crucified,
Who died to save us all.

My legs took me automatically nearer the house where I lived, but it seemed to me as though I were moving, without my own volition, towards the singer of this hymn. At length I turned a corner and stood looking down a long grey street at the other end of which our house was situated. A Salvation Army lass was standing a little way from me, quite alone, a collecting-box dangling from her arm while she rubbed her naked fingers together. She was singing this same hymn again and again in a cold, tuneless, hopeless voice, the kind of voice in which each member of a congregation in church sings the psalms, believing it to be indistinguishable in the noise made by the others.

There was a sixpenny piece in my overcoat pocket, and I dropped it into her box. She said, 'God bless you!' in between two verses, in a business-like voice; but I felt comforted, and a little of my sadness went away. I walked on down the street, now dark although illuminated faintly by occasional bead-shaded lamps shining through the thin curtains of the ground-floor windows. The woman's voice grew fainter as I went on, but now and then a high note would sound alone and sad above the others, a sort of wail in the deserted streets.

My bedroom at home is very small. Every day it strikes me as smaller than the day before. There are moments when the sound of Mother's breathing and continual swallowing gets on my nerves; when outside it is too cold or dark to sit in the Gardens, and when all the shops are shut and my friends busy; and then there is nowhere for me to be but in my room.

It is important to have something to think about, some-thing secret which not even your family knows. I suppose if I were the type of girl to fall in love, my thoughts would all the time be occupied by some young man; but I am not that sort. No, I like to think a lot about funny little things, so that when I meet a person with a superior smile on his face, I can think, 'Aha! I know something that you don't.' If I did not have these private secrets, I would be very lonely, and my life would be as empty as other people's. As a child I had many secrets; there was Miss Hopkins at school, and during the holidays there was the excitement of waiting for a letter from her. There was that time when I used to take half a crown from Mother's purse every week without her knowing, to buy sweets with; and there were the books I used to get from the Popular Library, books by Michael Arlen and Louis Bromfield, which I kept hidden as no one knew I was a subscriber. Recently this desire to write to the papers had taken hold of me, and I had thought of little else; I re-read my letter in the *World Messenger* that evening, and as I read the printed words I thought to myself, 'I wrote that. I invented those sentences.'

That night, in bed, I could not get the thought of Mr and Mrs Black and their two little daughters out of my head. When I thought of their rudeness to Mary, I blushed and felt hot, as though I had remembered one of those many bloomers I have made in public – silly things I have said which make people stare at me for a moment, and which afterwards at night I would give anything to take back. When I dozed off, the afternoon's scene in the gardens became muddled in my dreams, and the Black family became confused with words in my head, assuming some other meaning only understood by my slumbering brain, and fighting some obscure combat with one another. All the time I feared Mr Black's blue overcoat, the imagined texture of which mingled in my tired brain with the smooth white sheets to form a continuous humming noise in the room, smooth and sinister in my dream, infuriating me and driving me mad. I could not escape from it; it was a familiar nightmare. My open eyes detected little spots in the darkness, the room I stared at seemed far away, and the night like a dark photograph printed in a cheap newspaper. When I closed my eyes again I saw my boss's Brylcreemed head, the shiny, glossy hair, and the straight white scurfy parting cutting it unequally in two. I heard his scoffing voice, as plain as though he were talking near me, in my room.

At about midnight, I suddenly awoke from these troubled dreams and sat up in bed, excited, my heart beating fast. There must have been an idea hidden away at the back of my mind since the morning; at that moment it came to the surface, as though I had only then thought of it, or imagined it as a possibility. There is no use in writing excuses for what I did that night; the events of the day, as I look back on them now, seem to have been arranged by Fate in such an order as to make my decision almost inevitable. What I thought was this: it would be fun to write someone an anonymous letter of the kind of which I had read in the morning paper. And the person to whom I wished to write was Mrs Black, my boss's wife.

I felt an odd dislike for that woman, as well as for her husband; I did not wish to hurt her, but the idea of disquieting her in such a manner that she could not suspect that I was the cause of her disquiet, appealed to me.

I jumped out of bed and groped my way through the room to the door, where I switched on the light. I put on my dressing-gown and slippers and sat at my little writing-table. On the table was a pad of blue Basildon Bond notepaper, a red stampbook, and my Onoto fountain-pen with a platinum nib. As I sat there, staring dully at the watermarks on the sheet of paper in front of me, I had a brain wave. If, I reasoned, I wrote to Mrs Black and told her, as I intended to, that there was talk of her husband and another woman, how much I should lessen the chance of my authorship being discovered if I included myself in the accusation! I felt no guilt at the idea of writing an untruth; it was known for a fact at the office that Mr Black neglected his wife, and when I first worked there I used to notice him looking at me in a funny way. So, my tongue wetting my lips in my concentration, and clutching the pen so hard that the bump on my middle finger became covered in ink, I wrote the following, carefully, in block capitals:

> Dear Mrs Black,
>   I think you should know that for some time past your husband has been conducting an illicit liaison with Miss Edna White, who works at his office.
>
> Well wisher

I blotted it carefully, but too soon, so that the blue ink was scarcely discernible against the paper of the same colour; however, I did not feel up to writing a fair copy, so I sealed it in an envelope which I addressed to Mrs Desmond Black at the address which I knew to be hers, taking care to make the letters unlike the ones I usually form when writing in capitals.

After I had stuck on the stamp, I thought that I should never have the courage to send the letter, and was tempted to tear it up; but it seemed a shame to waste a stamp, and I knew that I could never bear to get back into bed knowing that the letter was unposted. I saw now that, while writing the letter, I had never really intended to send it; I had composed it with the care which one uses when playing a game, or drawing for one's own amusement; but now I felt a feverish haste and I began to dress, pulling on my satin blouse and my pleated brown skirt without thinking of what I was doing.

I stood outside in the street, shivering, the little white

square which was the envelope shaking in my hand. You will understand what a state I was in when I say that, only after I had walked a few paces towards the centre of the town, did I realise that I was still wearing my bedroom slippers . . .

I was going to post my letter at the GPO because I was smart enough to realise that if I posted it in the pillar box at the end of the street, it might eventually be traced to our district. The moon shone on the houses but did not mitigate their blackness, only lighting the streets and transforming them into gleaming canals along which my slippers made a slip slop noise which I felt must be audible in every bedroom beneath whose windows I passed. I saw no one, though at one moment, passing a dark telephone booth, I had a feeling that there was a man inside it, watching me through the glass, and I hastened my pace.

Soon I found myself in the High Street, which in the moonlight looked quite different from how I remembered it. It seemed much smaller than usual, like a toy street in a toy town. I noticed that the shops, whose windows seemed so large and inviting when open in the daytime, were merely the ground-floors of ordinary, small, and sometimes quite ramshackle houses. Devoid of people, the town was like a swimming pool drained of water; I walked along the middle of the broad street with the sensation of walking along a dry sea bed.

There were no blinds drawn across the big Post Office windows, and the moon's reflection shimmered in the glass. Oddly enough, the office where I worked was in the same building, on the floor above. Standing there in my bedroom slippers and with some curlers still in my hair, I really believed I was in a dream; so when I posted the letter, and heard it slide on to the base of the box, I merely felt a calm relief, and no guilt or apprehension. I was relieved that my indecision (which had been troubling me beneath the surface of my bewildered mind) could now no longer bother me; I had committed myself once and for all.

I walked home quickly, meeting no one, not even a policeman on his beat. Every day for weeks past, after five, I had made that journey from the office to my home; but that night, owing to the stillness in which I imagined I could discern the deep concerted breathing of all the sleepers in the town, and the absence of buses on the roads and people on the pavements, the distance seemed twice as long as it had ever done before. I entered the house without disturbing Mother and Gladys and as soon as I was back again in bed I fell asleep and this time did not dream.

The week that followed was the most exciting in my life. Every morning I walked to the office, with my heart in my mouth, as they say; but when I was there, I was surprised at how easy it was to appear as if I had nothing on my mind. I knew that Mrs Black was bound to receive the letter by the second post on Monday, and that night in bed I visualised the scene of its arrival at Polkerris. I saw Mr Black walk into the drawing-room, tired and cross after his day's work; and I could just picture his wife's face as she sat there, my letter on her lap, and looked up at him seriously. 'I want to speak to you, Desmond. Hazel and Rosemary, run outside and play for a bit, will you? Your father and I want to be alone.' I imagined the following conversation, certain to end in tears; the man shrugging his shoulders and trying to appear at his ease, the woman repeating again and again in a trembling voice. 'There's no smoke without fire, you know.'

On Tuesday I watched Mr Black closely, taking care to hide my interest lest it should betray me, and I noticed that he avoided me. I did not have to look far for the reason for this. Indeed, he scarcely spoke to me all through that long week. I kept a watch on the local paper, but found no mention of an anonymous letter; no doubt Mrs Black had not taken it to the police, and that implied that to some extent the letter had convinced her. I held my breath in horror when I speculated on what complications might result from my action. For some reason, I never considered writing another letter; I was content with the one, waiting impatiently for some indication of its effect, and covertly watching my boss for signs of his unease.

The one occasion on which Mr Black and I exchanged words that week was on the Thursday morning. He came out of his office, and straight up to where I was sitting.

'Oh, Miss White,' he said, looking over my head as was his custom, and with his hands in his pockets, 'I want you to take down a short letter for me.'

'Certainly,' I said, and though I was excited, I noticed with relief that my voice was calm.

He said he wished the letter to have his private address at the head of the page, as it was in fact a private letter. He asked me if I knew what the address was. I thought that this might be a trap of some sort, so I answered 'No'. Then I remembered that Mary, who was sitting a few feet away from me, had once told me where the Blacks lived, after she had been to tea there. I could see that she was listening with interest to our conversation, and although the inconsistency of my reply might never have struck her, I thought it better to be on the safe side, so I added in a nonchalant way, 'I believe I have been told, but I have forgotten.'

So he repeated the address, which I knew by heart, and after dictating a few lines, he took what I had typed for him, and went back into his office. Mary whispered to me 'You've been honoured, dear,' but I did not answer her.

In these days, every night I fell asleep wondering what would happen next, and woke up in the morning with the same thought in my mind. Mother noticed that I was dreamy, and thinking it might be my anaemia that was causing it, gave me a tonic to take. Nothing happened, however, until Saturday. I cannot say exactly for what I had been waiting, but what did occur was not as I had expected.

Mother had gone to the evening service, and as Saturday was Gladys's half-day, I was alone in the house. It was just beginning to grow dark but I had not yet drawn the blinds, although I knew that when this was done the lounge, which as always by this hour had become untidy and uncomfortable, would at once seem cosier. The sofa and chair covers needed tucking in and the morning papers lay scattered about the floor; the fire was low. I sat at the window and looked down the street, noticing that the inhabitants of the other houses had also not yet drawn their curtains; the street was studded by the pale lights of indoor lamps. I was tired and thinking about nothing. At that moment I was happy; I was enjoying the inactivity of my life, and if someone had come running up the street with the news that I had been left a fortune, or with a Hollywood contract for me in his hand, I would have been disturbed and annoyed that the peaceful order of my life must be altered. I very seldom felt like this. Usually I walked about in a strung-up mood, expecting something to happen at any moment. This had been particularly the case since I had posted my letter to Mrs Black, but that Saturday evening I was suffering from a reaction, and felt tired and interested in nothing but my lethargic sensations at that present moment. On the table in the middle of the room lay a green ticket; I was going to a whist drive that night in the Town Hall with Mary Conners.

There were few people walking in the street at that hour and so when I saw a figure turn the corner at the far end, near where I had met the Salvation Army lass that memorable Sunday, I watched its progress down the street, paying attention to it with half my mind. This man, who wore a dark blue overcoat and did not have a hat, walked slowly, with his shoulders raised and his hands in his pockets. Only as he passed 'Wychlea', a private hotel five doors from our house, did I recognise the overcoat as Mr Black's. I jumped up from the window seat and took a few paces back into the room, cold with excitement. My peaceful mood was shattered. Of course he was coming to see me; but I had no time to wonder what this visit might mean, and I stood quite still while his dark head passed the window, waiting for the door-bell to ring. Let him wait, I thought, when at last I heard the faint tinkle in the kitchen; but the second ring did not come and I ran into the hall, afraid that he might go away. Indeed, when I opened the door, he had already turned his back on it, and was descending the four steps to the pavement. If he had been already some way down the street I would have called him back, but as it was I just stood there in the open doorway while the cold of the evening penetrated into the house. He turned round quickly on hearing the door open and looked at me with his eyebrows raised and an embarrassed expression on his face.

'I thought you might be out,' he said.

I did not answer, but looked at him expectantly.

'I hope this isn't a bad time?' he said.

'Not at all,' I answered. 'But do come in, Mr Black. What am I thinking of, letting you stand out there? You must think I'm awfully ill-mannered. I'm afraid the drawing-room's very untidy. Mother is out. She will be so sorry to have missed you.'

I could think of no more nonsense to say at the moment, and we both stood silent in the lounge.

'Do sit down,' I said, suddenly.

He turned away from me.

'I've got something rather awkward to ask you,' he said.

I thought at once of the anonymous letter, but I could not in that minute realise the full implications of this interview, and I remained quite calm. I said 'Yes?' with just the right indication of a mystified desire to help him which would have been natural had his words come as a complete surprise to me.

'First, I had better show you this,' he said, and took from his overcoat pocket the letter which I had written to his wife. At first I did not recognise it, so altered did it appear after travelling through the post, and I even for a moment began to hope that I had been mistaken in the reason for his visit, and that it had to do with something quite different. 'My wife received this on Monday afternoon,' he added.

I took the envelope with a puzzled look, which I may have overdone, and I was relieved to notice that the writing on it did appear quite different from my own. I read the letter which had become very dirty and creased since I saw it last. As I did so, I realised with horror that on the table against which my visitor was leaning, there lay my Basildon Bond writing-pad, and also my fountain pen, for I had been meaning to write that evening to my cousin who lives in Hove.

When I had read the letter I could think of nothing to say, and there was a long silence. I was unconscious of my brain working at all, but what I did eventually say showed some subtlety. 'How perfectly horrible, Mr Black. You were quite right to show me this letter. Of course, you have explained to your wife how ridiculous it is – I mean what this horrible letter says?' Even this stumbling sentence, and the clumsy repetition of the word 'horrible' were unnatural and assumed by my brain with automatic cunning to deceive Mr Black.

'Such explanations were quite unnecessary, Miss White,' he said, and I noticed again how absurd it was that our names should complement each other in this way. He had said this with a return to his usual sarcastic manner, and I felt I wanted to slap his silly, big, conceited face.

'I hope you have told the police about it,' I said loudly.

'No, I did not want to do that. The letter is, as you say, ridiculous, and hasn't bothered either my wife or myself.'

Considering the contents of the letter, I thought this remark very rude. I said coldly, 'But the person who wrote it may write others, and may do other people some harm.'

'Yes, we thought about that. It really seemed more likely to have been written by someone who was unbalanced, and didn't mind whom he wrote to or what he wrote, than by someone with a personal grudge, don't you think?'

'Not at all. It might have been written by anyone.'

'I thought I ought to take steps to find out who wrote it, for your sake as well as for mine and my wife's, Miss White. But it seemed to me probable that it came from someone in the office, or someone connected with the office, because there can't be many outsiders who know that you are employed there – and it mentions you by name. So I tried to get to the bottom of the matter off my own bat, as it were.'

'I see.'

The fire was out now, and the room was getting dark; Mr Black and myself stood in it like two shadows with white faces whose features could scarcely be made out. I saw him move his arm, and it seemed to me as if he were taking another letter from his pocket. It was like a nightmare, and for a moment I thought we had gone back a few minutes in time, and were about to play the same scene all over again.

He handed me another piece of paper, saying, 'This is the result of my little bit of detective work.'

I had to turn on the light before I could read what was written on the paper, and I also put on my glasses which were lying by the lamp. I took a long time over this, and Mr Black stared out of the window, drumming his fingers on the table.

'Do you mind not doing that,' I said, and he stopped.

From that moment the whole nature of our interview altered. I recognised the paper as that on which I had typed the letter dictated by him on Thursday. I looked up at him as if to say, 'What does this mean?'

'You probably didn't notice just now,' he said, 'that the envelope which contained the anonymous letter had a misspelling of the address. It was the first thing my wife noticed, and we thought it would help us to find the sender. That letter I have just shown you misspells the address at the top of the page in the same way.'

With a terrible feeling of apprehension I looked at the address which I had typed on Thursday, and it seemed to be spelt correctly.

'But I typed this letter,' I said.

'Yes. I meant to test everyone in the office by getting them to spell the address, and I started off with you as you seemed to be the most likely person owing to your name being included in the letter.'

'You dared to suggest . . . you dared to try and trap me . . .' I began in a voice shaking with bitter anger. Then I said, 'But I can swear to you that I never wrote that letter. I don't know how you can imagine such a thing.' He did not answer, and I clutched at his sleeve. 'You must believe me that you have made a terrible mistake.' I noticed with misery that my voice contained the same high, queru-lous note that it had assumed years ago when I was a child and Mother had discovered that I had stolen money from her handbag. I felt the same as then; willing to swear anything to establish my innocence, and horrified and injured to find that I was not believed.

Still he did not answer, so I said, 'Anyhow, I don't see that it is spelt wrongly.'

'Yes, both times you spelt the word "Davenant" with the "e" and the "a" the wrong way round. You spelt it "Davanent".'

I saw that this was true. I was amazed that I had been unable to spell that word which I must have seen written down several times, while the other word in the address, 'Polkerris', a word with which I was quite unfamiliar and which was much harder to spell than 'Davenant', had apparently been spelt correctly.

'But anyone might have made that mistake,' I said.

'I don't think that is very likely. When I discovered this I did not know what to do, Miss White, but I decided to wait till the end of the week, and then come and ask you privately to discontinue work at the office. We shall, of course, say that it is your wish to resign. I may say that no one knows of this business except for my wife and myself. I have brought with me your salary for another month.'

'I would rather not accept it, thank you,' I said proudly.

'As you please.'

He turned round and began to leave the room. I realised suddenly what he must think of me, now that he knew I had written the letter. I called after him: 'You make me laugh, really you do, Mr Black. I don't know how you can have the conceit to imagine that I should bother to write about you. I really don't. Why ever should I? Tell me that.'

He turned round and smiled at me pityingly.

'That is not my affair,' he said.

I could only look at him then, and I believe I began to cry. He went out of the house, stumbling against the umbrella stand in the hall. I wanted to run after him and call him back, but I lacked the energy. I saw his head pass the window, but he did not look in at me. I ran to the window and watched him walk quickly away until I could not longer see him for the evening mist.

After that I felt very miserable. I had been so excited about that letter, and now my precious secret which had sustained me through evenings of depression was discovered, and I must appear ridiculous in other people's eyes. Besides, what would people say when I ceased to work at the office? Mother would be returning soon from the evening service, and I felt I could not bear to tell her that I had got the sack. What should I think about while waiting for her to come in? I felt that to go up to my bedroom, where the letter had been composed, and where I had spent so many happy hours waiting for the unknown outcome of my posting it, would be intolerable. Outside it was dark and cold. I tore up the whist-drive ticket, feeling that I was destroying a final link with my past sensations.

This despair was unlike anything I had known before. I could not get used to the idea that there was nothing at all that I could do to bring back the past with its feeling of safety and comparative content. The idea came to me to walk out of the house as I was, straight to the railway station, and there to buy a ticket to some distant place, it did not matter where, any village or small town the fare to which coincided with the money in my purse. There I would start a new life, away from Mother, Mary Conners and Mr Black, and all my old embarrassments. But I could not move. I sat in a kind of torpor waiting for Mother to return.

Tomorrow would be Sunday. I remembered how thrilled I had been about my letter to the *World Messenger* a week ago. Then I remembered the Editor's note: 'Well, readers, can any of you tell of cases which beat Miranda's record?' Tomorrow morning, if I bought a copy of the paper, perhaps I would find an answer to my letter.

This thought cheered me up a little.

Punctuality

When I got the sack from the office I told Mother I had resigned of my own accord, because I could not get on with the other girls.

'Well,' she said, 'and what do you propose to do now?'

'Have a little holiday.'

We were sitting in the lounge near the coal fire. Mother had just got back from the evening service, and she still wore her black overcoat with the fur collar and her black straw hat. Her face was hot and red and shiny under the lamp. She rolled up her knitting and put it on the table by her.

'And who, pray, is to keep you in pocket money?' she asked with assumed politeness, raising her eyebrows.

'I can soon get another job. I can start work again in about a fortnight.'

I picked up the local paper and opened it at the advertisements column. I read out the first one I saw. A young lady of refinement was needed, to sit at the cash desk of the café at the Regal cinema.

'The manageress is quite a friend of mine,' I said. 'I often go there for tea with Mary. I could get that job by raising my little finger.'

'And so,' Mother said in her whining voice, 'I spent all that money on getting you taught to type, so that you should end up behind a counter! And in a cinema, too!'

'I'm sick of typing,' I said, and walked out of the room.

That is how I started work at the Regal. Mrs Taylor, the manageress of the café, said she was pleased to have a girl with a good education at the cash desk, and she added that some of the waitresses were rather common, but I wasn't to take any notice of them. There was only one of them whom I got to be friendly with, Ruby, and she was a very nice refined girl indeed. I soon got into the way of my new life, and I came to enjoy my work at the café more than I had at the office.

Although the Regal was a big cinema, the café itself was small. There were three entrances: one from the kitchen, a hot poky place from which came a stuffy smell – waitresses were continually getting wedged together in the door; another for the public, at the top of a staircase leading from the foyer; and a third which led on to the balcony inside the auditorium. When this door was opened one could hear for a moment the noises made by the sound-track of the film then playing – an occasional shriek, or the sound of a car or train. One heard always in the café a humming noise, which came from the projection-room just above it: however, one did not notice this as it went on all the time.

The gold walls of the café were decorated with photographs of film stars, all taken some time ago. I sat under a picture of Loretta Young, boxed in by a waist-high wall, with my till and a wireless, which I turned on to amuse the customers whenever I could tune in to a good dance band. The pay was good, and the hours were not long – from four o'clock in the afternoon till ten. From the time we opened until six we had the tea rush; then an hour with practically no custom at all; and from seven onwards people trickled in for supper. We served only pots of tea, bread and butter, assorted cakes, and, for supper, such dishes as beans on toast, welsh rarebit, pilchards, and sometimes a fruit salad as a sweet. Ruby would lean up against the till, and sometimes Mary Conners, the girl I used to be friendly with at the office, would come in for a cup of tea by herself, and when she had finished we would have a chat. I always brought my library book with me (I got a lot of reading done this way), and a writing-pad and fountain-pen in case I felt like writing a letter.

The waitresses all wore green uniforms, but Mrs Taylor allowed me to wear mufti. We had few regular customers: most of them were, as Ruby put it, 'ships that pass in the night'. However, every evening Mr Tillett, the cinema organist, would come in at eight o'clock for a cup of tea and a welsh rarebit, before his turn at a quarter-past. He was a round, bald-headed little man, and always wore a white tie and tails, which looked very smart to the audience while he was playing, but near-to, in the café, seemed rather shabby. Sometimes we would get to chatting. Afterwards, if there were not many people in the café, I would open the door to the balcony, and stand there, at the very back of the theatre, watching Mr Tillett play the organ.

He was a little black speck in the distance, under a mauve spotlight, rolling about on his seat, and it seemed strange that he was responsible for the booming noise that filled the whole great theatre, and also that he was the same person who had sat near me a few minutes before. The words of the songs he played were projected on to the screen, and I would whisper them to myself in time to the music. I clapped loudly when he turned to bow to the audience and then disappeared spinning into the bowels of the theatre. The rest of the audience settled back more comfortably in their seats, looking forward to the big picture which was to follow, but I turned round and went back to my cash desk.

I began to feel as time went on, I don't know why, that Mr Tillett was playing especially for me. In a life like mine one gets used to a sort of routine, and I came to look forward to the moment when the clock hands pointed to eight o'clock and the organist walked into the café, on the stroke, for his evening refreshment.

It was fun to watch the strangers who came to the café, and wonder about them, and try to imagine what their lives were like. One afternoon (it was raining outside, I remember, and the first house had just finished) Ruby passed near me carrying a tea-tray, and whispered as she went by: 'My dear, look at Adolphe Menjou sitting at Number Eight!' Number Eight was a table at the other end of the room, in a corner. A man was sitting there by himself, having his tea. He was not really like Adolphe Menjou, but he had a distinguished, foreign air about him. His hair was dark but streaked with grey, very smooth and plastered near to his head with brilliantine. He wore a blue pin-stripe suit, and I liked the way his tie was knotted. He had more 'class' than any of the other people in the room. His face was thin and pale, and he had large sad eyes, which, from where I sat, seemed to be two black smudges in his face. I could see that he wore a ring on one finger.

I fell to thinking about him, and this made me absent-minded, so that one or two of the girls became quite short with me when I gave them the wrong change, and Ruby said: 'In a brown study?' I thought he must be a stranger in town, and no doubt was changing trains. I got it fixed in my head that he was a bachelor. Perhaps he came from the North.

Then my cash register got stuck. It had never happened before. I fiddled with it for a bit, and then, as ill-luck would have it, Mrs Taylor chose that moment to walk through the café. 'What's up, Edna?' she said.

'I think it's bust, Mrs Taylor.'

But it turned out that there was not much wrong with it, and Mrs Taylor soon put it right. Then she waddled off —

she was a fat woman, and wore spectacles. By the time I remembered about the man in the corner of the room, and looked to see what he was doing, he had gone away.

During the lull between six and seven, Ruby came up to me carrying a book. 'Look what somebody's left at Number Eight,' she said. 'I expect it belongs to Adolphe Menjou.'

I looked at it. It was an old copy of *A Tale of Two Cities*, nicely bound. This was one of my favourite books.

'What had I better do with it?' I said.

'Keep it here in case he comes back and claims it.'

I opened the book and looked at the fly-leaf. Written neatly in ink was the following name and address:

> Martin E. Hollingsworth,
> 10 Devon Crescent,
> N7

Meanwhile Ruby went on: 'My dear, he left a bob under the saucer — a change after the usual three-halfpence! I expect it was because he didn't have anything smaller, though, and didn't like to ask. Now, what have I done with Number Seven's receipt? Oh, drat! I must have left it in the kitchen. Dear, dear, my head will never save my heels.' She wandered off to the kitchen. I put the book in my handbag.

That evening I went to bed as soon as I got home, and looked through *A Tale of Two Cities*. I remembered how much I had enjoyed it when I had read it at school. I spent a long time looking at the signature in the beginning, and tried to imagine the man I had seen at the Regal writing it. I thought he had probably bought the book when still at school, and wondered what he had looked like then.

I decided to return the book to him; so, in the morning, I made a neat parcel of it, and enclosed the following note:

Dear Mr Hollingsworth,
I found this book yesterday at the Regal café, and am forwarding it to you at the address written inside it in the

hope that it will reach you safely. I know how sad it is to lose a book one is fond of.

It is strange I should be the finder, as *A Tale of Two Cities* happens to be an old favourite. Of all Dickens's works, it seems to me this is the best.

Hoping you recover it in good condition, I am,

Yours sincerely,

Edna White (Miss)

A few days later I was surprised to receive a very civil reply. Coming down to breakfast, I noticed an envelope on my plate. Mother, who had obviously inspected it, said: 'Who's your friend?' I did not deign to reply, although I had recognised the neat, well-educated handwriting as Mr Hollingsworth's, and simply slipped it into my cuff. Later I read it in the privacy of my room. This is what it said:

10 Devon Crescent, N7

Dear Miss White,

Very many thanks for your thoughtfulness in returning the errant *Tale*. I really do appreciate it. After grabbing a hasty cup of tea at the Regal while changing trains on my way to Town after a short holiday on the South Coast, I only noticed its absence when back in the railway-carriage – and have been cursing my carelessness ever since. The receipt of your parcel this morning, therefore, came as a delightful surprise and relief.

I am interested to hear you share my preference for the *Tale*. No doubt we have other tastes in common as well. Again, very many thanks, from

Yours very sincerely,

Martin E. Hollingsworth

I read this letter many times. The first time it seemed to me merely a formal acknowledgement of my letter to him, but on re-reading it I thought I saw more in it. The sentence, 'No doubt we have other tastes in common as well,' struck me as particularly significant, and seemed to hint that a reply was expected. At length I decided that Mr Hollingsworth would like me to continue the correspondence. Perhaps my letter had intrigued him: no doubt he would be pleased to receive another one from an unknown girl, whose face and figure he could imagine as he chose. There would be something romantic in a 'blind' correspondence between us, for he did not know that I had any more idea of his appearance than he had of mine.

I had not many friends, and my life with Mother was very lonely. I had often thought of answering one of those advertisements headed 'Lonely', which introduced one to a Pen Pal who shares one's tastes and hobbies. I had also at one time nearly joined a Ronald Colman Club which I had read about in *Picturegoer*: this would have involved a correspondence with another girl who was also mad about Colman, but then I went off film actors; and I hesitated to start writing to a fellow I had never seen – you never could tell, my Pen Pal might have turned out to be a most awful sight! As I had liked the look of Mr Hollingsworth that day at the Regal – something about him had appealed to my imagination, I felt he had a story attached to his past – and as I had the advantage of being to him a mysterious figure, I decided to write him another letter, in the hope of another answer.

I made many fair copies before finally sending one off, and in due course I received a reply. In this way Martin Hollingsworth and I started a friendship which lasted for some weeks. I came to live for his letters, to read them over and over, and kept them stored neatly, in chronological order, in a locked drawer. It was exciting, too, to compose my own: just as exciting as writing a novel or story, even though they were only for the eyes of one person. The days passed without their petty events making any impression on me; I lived in a dream, in a world apart; nothing Mother said could touch me; I sat at my cash desk at the Regal and looked at the other people in the room, thinking all the time: 'Ah! how little you know about me. How surprised you would be if you knew my secret!'

I shall give now the whole of the correspondence which followed on the two preliminary notes. Imagine me in the café, writing and reading the following letters, and hardly noticing the surrounding noise of dishes clattering in the kitchen; women talking over their tea about the shops and their children; the hum from the projection-room above; and the disjointed sounds of the films playing, over and over again, in the theatre.

Dear Mr Hollingsworth,

You may be surprised to hear from me again. But in your letter (received this morning) you say that you wonder whether we both have the same tastes. I have always been a serious girl and am very fond of reading. Once or twice I have tried my hand at writing, but so far without success, although once I sent a poem to a magazine, and although it was not accepted, the editor wrote me a very encouraging letter.

Skating and hockey are my favourite sports, but I do not get much of them now. If you have similar interests, no doubt you will let me know, and we might correspond? Because there are not many, as they say, 'congenial spirits' in this neighbourhood.

Yours sincerely,
Edna White

Dear Miss White,

I am intrigued – yes, definitely intrigued. I had hoped – hoped almost against hope – that my last letter to you might elicit a response. And when this morning your letter arrived saying so exactly what I had hoped it might say I thought to myself: 'I have made a new friend'. Thanks entirely to old Charles Dickens!

Tell me more about yourself – for you have not told me much. I feel there is more, much more to know about you. Have you perhaps a snap you could enclose in your next letter?

As to me – well, there is not much to say. I am a bachelor; I work in the City; I live with my married sister who runs a guest house. I, too, suffer from a lack of congenial spirits around me. Reading is a vice of mine, though I have never essayed to wield a pen myself. Do you belong to the Book of the Month Club?

I prefer golf to either of the sports you mention, and in my younger days was considered quite a dab at squash-rackets. I do not much care for the films, but am a regular theatregoer. Do you perhaps collect autographs?

Write to me again and tell me more.

Yours very sincerely,
Martin E. Hollingsworth

Dear Mr Hollingsworth,

Thank you for your letter. I have not a photo I can lay my hands on, but I can tell you that I am 25, and of medium height. My eyes are brown, and so is my hair – when I was 17 I could sit on it, but now it is bobbed.

I know a bit about handwriting, and can tell some things about you from yours which you have not told me yourself. You are very meticulous, almost finicky, generous to a fault, musical, artistic, proud, a bit touchy. Is that not correct?

I imagine you as tall, dark (perhaps a bit grey). You have large eyes, a thin sensitive face – a slim figure. How do I know all this? Aha! Call it intuition. By the way, what does the 'E' in your name stand for?

I live alone with my mother, my father having died when I was a mite. Mother is a dear, but rather old-fashioned in her views. She will not allow me to have any man friends, and even disapproves of my girl friends – for no reason at all. She does not let me go out much, so I have a dull life. Are you psychic?

Your letters are of great interest to me, and I look forward to them. Write again soon to

Your friend
Edna White

Dear (if I may make so free?) Edna,

Last night I dreamed about you. I was walking some-where in the country by a canal. It was evening. I came to a lock, and by the lock there was a little cottage with a light in the window. In my dream I knew that you were in the cottage. I waited and waited for you to come out, but nothing happened. Then you appeared at the window for a second – your face was pale and your hair hung long behind your back. You disappeared, and the light in the cottage was extinguished. I awoke with a start.

Write and tell me what my dream meant.

Martin

My second name is Edgar.

Dear Edgar (for I shall call you that),

I do not know the meaning of dreams, although I dream vividly myself. Mother says I live my whole life in a dream – I have always had a faraway look in my eye, as if a creature not quite of this world.

I have an idea. Every evening, at seven o'clock, think of me, because I will think of you and perhaps our thoughts will communicate across space. I have heard of cases of that happening.

Today is the birthday of my little niece, and I am going to tea with her. I love children. They are so gay and innocent.

Write and tell me of your daily doings, because even the littlest things have an interest. And remember to think of me at seven o'clock!

Edna

My dear Edna,

Last night, at seven, I concentrated with my eyes

closed, and it really seemed for a moment as though you were standing by me. I felt that if I opened my eyes, stretched out my hand, I should see you, touch you. But when I did, of course, all I saw was my little bedroom, empty but for me.

I had considered asking you if we might not arrange a meeting – but no, the time is not yet ripe! Some day perhaps – but for now, let us be contented with this strange spiritual communion, for you are nearer to me than any of my friends, although I have never seen your face. I will not write about trivial matters – they suffice as material for ordinary, everyday intercourse. To you I feel I can open my heart.

I was once very unhappy, when young. I loved a girl, and believed she loved me. Then I discovered that she had been false to me. This incident put me against the whole sex, and that is why I have remained single to this day.

Tell me, Edna, have you ever experienced the sweet agony of love?

. Edgar

My dear Edgar,

You ask me if I have ever been in love. The answer is yes, once. Of course, I do not count various silly schoolgirl crushes on teachers and actors: we all go through that phase! No, I have only been really in love once, and then it ended sadly. I have never breathed a word of it to anyone, but in you I feel I can confide. When I write to you I feel like a Catholic confessing: there are none of the barriers between us which are usually between human beings. We do away with pride, shame, embarrassment and so on – at last I can speak with safety about my love for Arthur Crawley.

Two years ago, when my Aunt Pearl, who had occupied the top room ever since Father's death, went to live at Eastbourne, Mother decided to let it to a stranger, as she missed Auntie's rent. The first person to answer our advert was a woman in her thirties, with brassy hair and a face covered in make-up. Well, Mother didn't fancy her, so she told her she had better try elsewhere. The next person who came along was Mr Crawley. Mother liked the look of him. I remember coming in one evening, and Mother saying: 'I've let the top room to such a pleasant-spoken young man. I think he'll make a nice friend for you, dear. He's upstairs now, having a shave.' Mother was always hunting about looking for what she called 'nice friends' for me, and they were usually pretty stuffy, so that put me against Mr Crawley. When he came down to supper I didn't think much of him. He was about thirty and looked delicate, but he was dressed neatly and I noticed that he had a nice tie-pin and cuff-links. (I always notice that sort of thing.) He had a job in town, something to do with the railway, but all the time he was with us, Mother and I never discovered exactly what it was.

After supper Mother played the piano, and we all three sang choruses – 'Love's Old Sweet Song', 'The Mountains of Mourne' and that sort of thing. When he had gone to bed, Mother said: 'You ought to be more civil to him, Edna.' I didn't reply. I could see Mother had taken a fancy to him.

He used to be out all day, and only appeared for supper, except at the weekends and then he usually went away. We would sit in the lounge for an hour in the evening, and then he would go to bed – every night punctually at the same time. His life was arranged in a routine which he never altered. So I never saw him alone. However, each morning I would do his room (Gladys, the maid, refused the extra work). I would make his bed, and indeed, I was often tempted not to make it properly, but just to straighten the counterpane, fluff out the pillow, and fold his pyjamas, because it was never much disarranged. His room was very tidy. He had one photograph – I think it must have been of his mother. His few clothes were always folded in the drawers, his extra pair of shoes always had trees in them. One book – from the town library – would be by his bed. (He never read novels, but seemed fond of biographies and travel.) I would wander round the little room touching his possessions, stand at the window and imagine him staring at the views of roofs which it commanded, and sometimes I would lay my head gently on his pillow. Oh, what a silly I was!

I don't know when it was I began to fall in love with him, as they say, for originally I had not been struck by him at all. I think Mother's hints and suggestions at first had a lot to do with it, though she soon dropped these and took it for granted that Arthur and I would not hit it off – I believe she wanted to think that. She always dominated the conversation in the evening.

He looked so seedy, I wanted to nurse him, feed him up, and make him well.

This went on for some months, and then came that terrible Saturday – a day I shall never forget. I had looked forward to it all the week – ever since Mother had told me she would be at the Missionary Sale in the Town Hall all afternoon, because Saturday was Arthur's day off, and I hoped I might have him to myself until teatime.

When Mother had gone, I sat at the window and waited for him to walk down the street. Soon I saw him coming; he passed the window. I heard the front door open. He looked into the lounge.

'Oh, hullo, Edna. Your mother out?'

'Yes.' I smiled at him.

'I'm just going to my room for a nap. I don't feel at all the thing. I'll be down for tea.'

He certainly did look poorly. I was very disappointed. I would not have my little chat with him after all. I had nothing to do with myself all afternoon, for I had told my girl friend, Mary, that I could not go with her to the pictures that day.

I wandered out into the street, for I felt that I could not stay in the house, or I would be sure to go up to the top room and do something silly. It was a lovely day. I felt lonely. I found myself at the station – perhaps I had gone there unknowing because I vaguely connected it with Arthur. It was as though I were out of my mind. The next thing I knew, I had taken a return ticket to Paddington and was sitting in a train. I thought the other people in the carriage looked at me oddly. I tried to get out again on to the platform, but at that moment the train started. It was a fast one, so now I should have to go to London. I thought even of pulling the communication cord, but then I sat back in my seat and tried to relax. I did feel a fool. Thank goodness, I didn't meet anyone I knew.

At Paddington I walked out through the white Bayswater streets, and into the park. I sat beside the water, and watched children and soldiers feed the birds.

Then I felt that I had to hear Arthur's voice or else I should go mad. I went to a telephone booth and put through a call home – for, as Mother and Gladys were out, he would probably answer. Luckily, I had the right amount of change to put in the box. I could hear the telephone ring in the hall at home. Then suddenly the ringing stopped; a loud voice said 'Hello': it was Mother, and she sounded in a bad temper; I hung up, shivering. She must have come home early, I thought. I returned to the station, and waited an hour for the next train back. I bought a copy of *Woman's Journal*, but could not read it.

When I got home, Mother was too fussed to ask where I had been, or to mention the telephone call which must have seemed funny to her. She had come back from the sale early, and had found Arthur ill in bed. The following day he developed pneumonia. For a fortnight she nursed him night and day (she would not let him be taken to hospital). Then he died. Mother cried for days. I think she must have loved him, too.

Only one person turned up for the funeral, a young man who had been at school with Arthur, Mr Robertson;

Arthur had been an orphan. Mother and I were the only other mourners. It was pathetic, and I felt silly at the funeral.

Later, without telling Mother, who would have been shocked, I went to consult a medium of whom Mary had told me, who lived in the outskirts of the town. The messages she gave me did not sound like Arthur at all, and I did not know what to think. But soon I stopped minding. I even grew to tolerate Mother's continual weeping and talking about him. She was always making such remarks as: 'I wish you had been more civil to the dear boy, Edna. He must have thought you very stand-offish.'

Of course, during his illness, I had never been allowed near his room. Mother took it all on herself. Doctor and Mr Robertson said she had done a wonderful job.

Soon Mother stopped mourning Arthur, and now I only look back on him with a feeling of depression. But sometimes, on a hot Saturday afternoon, I am filled with a feeling – not of love for him, but of a vague longing for something which he had seemed to symbolise.

What a long letter! I wonder if you will read it all. Forgive me if it has bored you.

Edna

My dear –

Business takes me near your home again on Friday next. Where and when can we meet?

Edgar

Picture postcard:

Meet me at 7.30 pm outside the Post Office in the High Street. Don't be late, as I have not much time.

E.W.

I arranged with Mrs Taylor to be free from seven onwards on Friday evening; she herself was going to take my place. I was very thrilled, but nervous too. I do not know which I feared most: that Edgar would turn out a disappointment to me, or that I would be one to him. We had both rather let ourselves go in our letters: would we be able to take up from where we left off, when confronted with each other in person?

Time on Friday moved very slowly. Everything seemed to be as if in a slow motion film; people appeared to take ages paying their bills, sipping their tea; even commonplace remarks about the weather fell heavily from Ruby's sluggish lips, and I longed to say to her: 'Get a move on, do!' Everyone I met had an air of being half-asleep: only I was alert, excited and apprehensive.

At last, at a quarter to seven, I could bear it no longer, and I slipped out of the empty café. I hastened to the Post Office, and as I reached it the clock struck seven. I still had half an hour to wait! It was raining and evening was starting, so that the street seemed misted, muffled and dim. I knew that I did not look my best in my mackintosh with its pixie cape; my face was shiny and the cold rain made my nose red. I had put on my best shoes in the morning, but now they were hidden by galoshes. How I wished I had chosen an indoor meeting-place!

I thought I should never live through the next half-hour. All sorts of dreary thoughts came into my mind. Suppose he never turned up? Suppose he had been playing a joke on me all along, and intended to blackmail me? Suppose he had been killed in a railway accident on the way? Soon it seemed impossible that the situation could be as I had imagined: had I perhaps dreamed the whole thing? And if, by great luck, he should arrive, what on earth would we talk about all evening? *And what would he think of me?*

This dreadful waiting was familiar to me because I am always early for appointments, even if it is only to meet Mary in the Gardens. I could not contemplate the idea that Edgar might be late: how could I bear to wait a second after half past seven? I regretted my impatience, and wished that I had stayed at the Regal until it had struck the half-hour, so that Edgar would have to wait for me.

There were several other people waiting nervously under the Post Office clock, and I guessed that they were also early for appointments. I noticed a girl of about my own age who was walking up and down, and continually looking at the time, and along the street. There was also a little man who resembled a clerk, wearing a mackintosh, with red hair and moustache and rabbity teeth. He had an evening paper, which he rolled up tight and offered to me: I thanked him and pretended to read it, but I could not concentrate. I stared for ages at an advertisement for lime juice, reading it again and again, but taking none of it in.

I did not know whether Edgar would come from the left or right, but as the station was on my left I faced that direction. At twenty five past seven I saw, with a feeling of relief and excitement, a tall, dark figure coming towards me through the rain, but as he approached, I realised that he was not Edgar, and yet still I hoped, why I do not know, that he would come up to me and, somehow, mysteriously, turn out to be my friend: I was afraid of admitting my full disappointment to myself. Then the other girl who was waiting ran to meet him; they kissed, and walked off arm-in-arm towards an ABC.

To prevent myself from thinking I looked up at the clock, and as I looked away I saw that the red-haired man, who was now standing alone with me, was looking into my face. We stared at each other for a moment, until he suddenly took off his hat (it was a dirty grey trilby) and said: 'Miss White?'

I answered yes automatically.

He held out his hand, after nervously pulling off a glove, and began to stutter: 'I am MMMMartin Hollings-worth . . .'

I realised the truth before he had finished the word Martin. I had taken it for granted that the copy of *A Tale of Two Cities* had belonged to the tall man whom I had noticed: now I saw that it must have been the property of this little clerk, who had sat at the same table earlier that evening, and whom I had not seen and could not remember, for he was indeed very insignificant. Many like him came into the café every day.

I kept my head. 'No,' I said. 'I am not Miss White — I thought you said Miss Wright. You must have made a mistake.' And I hurried away, while he was still stuttering an apology.

I felt sick with horror. This was the man to whom I had written those confidential letters! I hated him, and despised myself. I began to cry as I walked through the drizzle, by instinct returning to the café.

It was empty, and the yellow light hurt my eyes. I hung up my mackintosh and sat at the desk. I heard an actress in the film that was playing in the theatre call out shrilly: 'Help! Help!' That bit always came at a quarter to eight. I was grateful for my solitude. The wireless, turned down low, was muttering at my elbow, and I switched it off. I could hear the waitresses talking in the kitchen.

'Go on!'

'She did!'

'She never!'

'I tell you, she did!'

'Well, I never did!'

I was trying to stop myself from thinking of my recent experience, but I could not help whispering again and again to myself, 'How could I have made such a daft mistake?' as though confiding in somebody. At length I leant on my desk, with my head in my hands, and wept loudly, out of bitter shame and disappointment.

I do not know for how long I cried; however, I was

brought back to earth by a voice saying near me: 'Is anything the matter?' It was Mr Tillett, who had come into the café without my seeing him.

'It is a personal matter,' I said.

'Is there anything I can do?'

I blew my nose in the hankie which I keep under my desk, and smiled at him. 'I'm all right now,' I said. 'Please don't speak about it any more. I'm very ashamed of myself for giving way.'

'I was going to ask you, Miss White,' said Mr Tillett, 'if you would do me the honour of lunching with me one day next week?'

I was surprised to hear this. We arranged to meet on the following Monday at the Kardomah. He patted my shoulder, and left the room.

Then I felt better. It is funny how things cheer you up. Mr Tillett was no oil painting, but he was a gentlemanly sort of man. I decided to write to Martin Hollingsworth (the real Martin Hollingsworth, the seedy little clerk I had just left, not my Edgar, the man I had glimpsed for a moment weeks ago, whom I would never see again, who did not know that I existed), and say that I had been unable to keep the appointment owing to illness, and was leaving the town. I would say that Mother had found one of his letters, and that he must write no more, as she threatened to have the law on to him. He would never know that he had seen me at the Post Office.

I felt quite calm now. To fit my mood, as it were, the café was suddenly filled with the sound of beautiful organ music – Mr Tillett playing 'Ah! Sweet Mystery of Life!'

Temptation

On this hot Saturday afternoon, girls in cotton dresses and men in bright blue suits wandered arm-in-arm through the streets towards the swimming-baths, and children stopped every so often on the pavements to lick their ice-cream cones. A brass band played in the Public Gardens and the shops unfurled their awnings. The clock-face on the Town Hall glittered; the High Street was busy and the suburbs were still, for the people of the town had dutifully left their houses, forgoing their afternoon rests, to take their pleasure in the heavy, sticky air.

Edna, at a loss, ambled through the streets, walking like a child only on the squares of the pavements and trailing one hand along the railings which she passed. From her other hand dangled a shopping-bag containing her purse, a cauliflower and a tin of Vim. It was her afternoon off.

She stopped at a small bookshop, and looked in at the window where she saw spread-out copies of bright-covered magazines: *Psychology*, *Health and Strength*, *Graceful Poses*, *Film Frolics*. 'I wonder if they've got a *Picturegoer*,' she said to herself out loud, and turned through the door of the shop.

It was a box-like room of which three walls were lined from top to bottom with books, while the other consisted of the door and window. By the window stood a chair and table; on the table a till had been placed, and on the chair a fat, swarthy man was sitting, reading the *Daily Mirror*. He had hung his coat over the back of the chair and rolled up the sleeves of his collarless shirt. His yellow braces wrinkled over his fleshy chest and the top button of his trousers was open. Edna did not like the look of him at all.

She asked him if he had a copy of the magazine she wanted. Without looking up from his paper, the proprietor said 'Sorry,' and slightly shook his head.

Well! thought Edna. She decided to look round the shop. The sun shining through the window heightened the different colours of the books on the walls. The man paid no more attention to her.

She wandered round the room, now and then reaching or stooping for a volume which caught her fancy, reading a line or two, and then replacing it on the shelf. When she came upon an expurgated copy of *Lady Chatterley's Lover*, she automatically stretched out her hand towards it, but then stopped herself and stood still. What had she heard about this book, and why did its title intrigue her? She was aware of some mystery connected with it, some reason for hesitating before she inspected it. Then she remembered an incident in her childhood.

She must have been twelve or thirteen at the time. Her mother was entertaining a friend at tea. Edna recalled this friend's shocked voice: 'There she was, sitting up in bed, reading *Lady Chatterley's Lover*! "Wherever did you get that, young lady?" I said. "Jim gave it to me," she said. "You hand it over to me this minute, and be quick about it," I said. Disgraceful! They oughtn't to print such things, to find their way into the hands of young girls.'

Edna's mother said, 'What a thing! I wouldn't have it in the house.'

They had forgotten Edna, who interrupted: 'What is it about, then?'

The women looked alarmed. 'Never mind,' her mother

replied. 'It's nothing that would concern you.' And the friend added, 'Little pitchers have big ears.'

Standing in the shop, Edna also remembered that shortly after that conversation she had overheard two girls at school giggling over the same book. She often wondered about it then, and afterwards the name lodged itself in the back of her mind, still surrounded by an atmosphere of wickedness and fascination.

Now was her chance to explain and dispel that atmosphere. She must buy the book. It would be simple to conceal it from her mother, who no doubt would still disapprove of Edna reading it. However, she felt embarrassed at the thought of buying such a book from the unpleasant man sitting behind her.

She had been for some time trying to gather enough courage to pick out the novel and ask the proprietor its price, when she suddenly realised that her purse contained only a few pennies. She moved away, took another book in her hands and pretended to look at it, while her mind dealt with the problem. If she returned to the house for more money, her mother might waylay her; soon it would be closing-time, the shop would shut on Sunday, and she would be working all of the following week and unable to buy the book. By next Saturday it might be sold to someone else. The easiest thing to do was to steal it.

From then on she acted with instinctive cunning. Replacing the other book, whose title she had not noticed, with a gesture to imply, in case the man was watching her, that after all she had decided against it, she returned to her former position. She looked over her shoulder; the fat man was engrossed by a comic strip in his paper. Very quickly she reached for the book she wanted and slipped it into her shopping-bag between the Vim and the cauliflower. The shape of the bag was not much altered. Then she put up her hand, apparently to finger yet another book, and arranged the loosened volumes so that the absence of one should not be noticed. Again she glanced, in the airiest way possible, over her shoulder, but detected no move from the man.

Her instinct was to hurry at once with her booty from the shop, but she checked it. She forced herself to wander once more nonchalantly round the room, staring unseeing at the walls. At last, after what seemed to her an age, she turned at the door to say, 'Good afternoon' to the bookseller. For the first time he looked up at her. Did she imagine suspicion in his small dark eyes? 'Afternoon,' he mumbled, and turned back to the *Daily Mirror*. It struck her for a moment that there was something sinister in his lack of observation; he might have been all the time daring his customer to steal.

She did then hasten away. Walking as fast as she could without running, she moved blindly on through the crowded town. Her imagination, numbed during her theft, began to work again. Did the man have some check on every book in his shop; would he miss the D. H. Lawrence, remember her, set the police on her? Would she go to prison? Had he noticed, through the shop window, while she made her escape, a bulge in her leather shopping-bag which had not been there before? Was he following her at this moment? She hurried on.

She passed the deserted suburbs, the gasworks and the station, her lips moving in a torment of uncertainty, and eventually found herself outside the town. She halted, out of breath, and turned her head. No one was following her; a few people were strolling along the dusty road, come to breathe country air among the fields. Edna climbed over a stile, and took a path to where a stream ran between willows. Here she sat, and in the shade of a tree began to read her book.

She sat on until the air cooled and midges began to

worry her bare legs. She finished the book with her eyes aching, and a feeling of acute disappointment. She had not enjoyed it; after skipping impatiently, all the time expecting a passage of a revelatory salaciousness, she now felt dizzy and even cheated. Reading it too quickly, she had not always followed what she read. Nothing was satisfactorily explained.

Church bells were ringing in the town. Edna rose from the grass, and stretched her stiff limbs. She leant over the stream, and, after making sure that no one was near, she dropped the novel into the water. It sank into the muddy bed, and soon could not be seen. Glad to be rid of it, she knew that she need worry no longer, for even if the theft were discovered and suspicion fell on her, how could they prove it now?

Swinging her shopping-bag, her skirt stained by the grass on which she had lain, she walked slowly back through the green and yellow fields to the town.

It's Not Very Nice

'No,' said Mrs Lyddiard, 'I wouldn't be in Hitler's shoes now for all the tea in China.'

'Speaking perfectly frankly,' said Mrs Mitchell, 'I don't trust Stalin an inch. I wish I did, but I don't.'

Mrs Lyddiard sighed. 'Well, we must put our faith in Winston, as we did before.'

'And what do you think about it all, Agatha?' said Mrs Mitchell. 'You're the brainy one of the family.'

The two middle-aged women turned with angry expressions on their broad faces to the girl who was sitting in a dark corner of the room.

'I'm afraid I wasn't listening to your conversation,' said Agatha Lyddiard after a hesitant silence. Her mother and the visitor clicked their tongues, exchanged a look in the darkening drawing-room, and concentrated again on each other.

Outside the high bow window, which had a window-seat running along it between heavy dark green curtains, evening was slowly hiding the grey street with its porches, shrubberies and conservatories. Inside the room Agatha could hardly see the two women, the tall bead-shaded lamps standing here and there unlit like sentinels, the Japanese cabinet or the many small tables supporting bric-à-brac, although all these things were faintly illuminated by an electric fire in the draughty grate. The fire was made to resemble glowing coals, and flickered by artificial means. The tea tray had just been carried from the room.

Agatha was eighteen; she had brown hair which hung untidily, a good-looking face and a dumpy figure. She wore ankle-socks and a wool dress rather like a school tunic. She looked intelligent and resentful, and would have been attractive had she taken more trouble with her appearance. Her mother, a doctor's widow, was a large, bossy, and yet very feminine woman, with neat, greying hair and a white, pretty face. Her friend, Mrs Mitchell, was a less successful variant of the same type.

Agatha listened vaguely to the conversation, which, after touching on Mr Eden and the Princesses, turned from public figures to personal interests, such as the difficulty of getting 'staff', and the lack of a fourth at bridge in the neighbourhood. After a short literary interlude, during which the latest Daphne Du Maurier was discussed, the talk reverted to Agatha, although she herself was not addressed.

'What does Agatha find to do with herself all day?' asked Mrs Mitchell.

'She's waiting to be called up by the WAAFs.'

'Well, that will make a change for her. I do hope she's with a nice type of girl, they say that makes all the difference.'

'She had set her heart on Oxford, but of course in wartime one cannot pick and choose,' said Agatha's mother cheerfully.

'My Evelyn brought her commanding officer to tea with me the other day. A delightful woman. Evelyn has been very fortunate.'

Agatha restrained herself from interrupting the others; from assuring Mrs Mitchell that she did not want to go into the WAAF, and that she easily could have gone up to Oxford if her mother had approved. Such an interruption would only have convinced Mrs Mitchell that what she already suspected was true – Agatha was a 'highbrow'. This was a word which neither Mrs Mitchell nor Mrs Lyddiard used lightly, and, when they did, only in hushed tones, as though afraid that, if they were overheard, they might be involved in an action for slander. At last the conversation degenerated once more into a grumble, and the shortage of food, petrol, and, above all, servants, was examined in all its aspects with a hopelessly indignant, impotent and yet vaguely comforting thoroughness.

'I'm sure Beryl steals my face-powder. If I say anything, she threatens to leave. What can one do?'

'Exactly, what can one do?'

'I suppose I ought to be thankful to have *someone*. All the same, it's not very nice.'

'No, it's not very nice.'

Agatha got up from her seat with an effort. 'I'm going out now,' she said. 'I won't be in to dinner.'

'Might one make so bold as to enquire with whom you are dining?' asked Mrs Lyddiard, and Mrs Mitchell giggled.

'With Mary. Can you see the book I'm reading?'

Mrs Lyddiard picked up a volume and looked at its title with screwed-up eyes, and a patronising smile on her face. 'I suppose this is it, it certainly doesn't belong to me. Can you really understand French, or is it only show?'

Mrs Mitchell laughed politely and said, 'Oh, don't be killing, you know she understands French. After all, she's the latest from school.'

When Agatha left the room the others were talking about their schooldays, and complaining of the rustiness of their French. Agatha suspected that soon Mrs Mitchell would say, 'I thought Agatha was looking rather seedy at tea,' to which Mrs Lyddiard would reply, 'She's at a very difficult age. I shall miss her when she goes into the WAAF, but I expect it will make a new woman of her. It's all wrong she should be kicking her heels at home.'

Agatha put on her coat in the hall and hurried down the porch steps with the book of poems in her hand. At every window in the street she glimpsed a dim interior identical with the one she so gladly left behind. She walked towards the centre of the town, and stopped for a moment at the Repertory Theatre, which was just opening its doors, to look at the photographs of the actors which hung in the foyer. She stood opposite one which showed a thin, handsome face with straight fair hair, perfect for the young hero in almost any play. This was John Taylor, the youngest member of the company; Agatha was going to spend the evening with him, for he was not acting that night, but was to take the leading part in *The Vortex*, which would be playing the following week. Agatha stared at the photograph, and she knew that this anticipatory pleasure was greater than any she would feel in the company of the original. At last she combed her hair, pulled at her dress, and walked with controlled haste to a boarding-house in a street not far away. Had her mother and Mrs Mitchell seen her now, and noticed her guilty air, they would have been in a way satisfied, to find justification in their vague suspicions of Agatha's behaviour when she was supposed to be out with Mary.

Johnnie Taylor lived in a small room on the ground floor of the boarding-house. There was little room in it for anything but the narrow bed and enormous chest of drawers with which it was furnished, and the pattern on the wall-papers haunted his dreams and made them nightmares. Johnnie could have afforded better lodgings on the salary the theatre gave him, but he stayed here because the landlady had taken a fancy to him.

Agatha put her head round the door and said, 'Can I come in, Johnnie?' The room smelled of cigarette smoke, and she knew that the window had been closed all day. Johnnie lay on the bed wearing only a white shirt and grey trousers. In reality his appearance differed subtly from his photograph; he seemed on a smaller scale and his good looks were less conventional. His hair flopped from its parting in a smooth square over his forehead and one eye; he looked delicate. All his friends, including Agatha, pitied him, but with a safe sort of pity to which they could abandon themselves without fear of too great a demand on their emotions, for they knew that beneath Johnnie's apparent fragility there was a hard, tough core of self-sufficiency. Pity for a deserving object is not a pleasant feeling and people steel themselves against it; Johnnie inspired the other kind, and exploited it.

'Oh darling,' he said, a slight North-country accent perceptible in his stage voice which was modelled on Noel Coward's, 'I'd forgotten you were coming. I ought really to learn my part this evening.'

Agatha sat on his bed and smiled at him. 'Do you want me to go?'

'No, stay and cheer me up. Did you like the book?'

'Very much, I want to talk to you about it,' she said eagerly.

'Oh God, darling, *not* an intellectual discussion this evening, if you don't mind. I couldn't face it.'

Agatha dropped the French poems on the bed with such a hurt expression on her face that Johnnie had to turn away. He went on in a softer voice.

'I got a letter from Christopher this morning. It's made me so unhappy.'

He turned round to look at her again, critically, as though examining a picture. Agatha stared at the window with assumed unconcern, but one eyebrow was twitching nervously under his inspection.

'What have you done today?' Johnnie said suddenly.

'Nothing. Mrs Mitchell came to tea.'

'Who's Mrs Mitchell? Tell me about her.'

'Well, she has a dog called Keith Prowse.'

'How extraordinary. Why?'

'He's always sitting on the best chairs, she says, and

covering her cushions with black hairs,' Agatha explained in a dull voice. 'You see, it's a joke about the advertisement – You want the best seats, we have them.'

Johnnie laughed loudly. 'Oh, Agatha, what wonderful people you know. You are lucky.'

'They're not a bit wonderful really. They sound funny to you when I tell you about them, but you wouldn't think so if you lived with them.'

Johnnie took her hand and pressed it.

'It is nice to be with you, darling,' he said.

Agatha smiled at him happily and for some time they said nothing.

In spite of her wish to appear intelligent and sophisticated, Agatha's voice sounded now and then like a child's.

'Johnnie, if you could have one wish which would come true,' she said at last, with ingenuous eyes and a slightly self-conscious manner, 'what would you wish?'

'To be offered a good part in the West End, I suppose. Anything to get out of Rep.'

'But that's bound to come true soon.'

'No, never, probably. I'm such a bloody actor.'

'Oh, darling, I think you're wonderful, I think – '

'What would you wish?' Johnnie said quickly.

'To go away from here. That is, only if you are leaving.' He patted her hand and smiled absently at this. She went on, 'Oh, I suppose I should wish for mother to send me to Oxford instead of going into the WAAF.'

'God forbid, darling. I should hate you if you were an undergraduate. You're quite serious enough as it is. No, what you need is some terrific man to have a love affair with you. If I was only normal, I'd be just the person. Goodness, sweetie, you're blushing; you're red all the way from here' – he put his finger at the neck of her dress – 'to here' – and he touched her forehead. 'You are very virginal, aren't you?'

'Do you like that?'

'As long as you don't overdo it.'

'And do I overdo it?' Agatha asked very earnestly, leaning towards him. 'Do you think so, Johnnie?'

He jumped off the bed and began to put on his tie, socks, shoes and coat. 'I'm so hungry,' he said, 'let's go to our Milk Bar.'

It was quite dark outside now. They walked, arm-in-arm and singing softly, towards the Milk Bar where they usually ate. Although it was painted white all over, it was a dingy place, with an angry girl standing behind a wet, sloping counter. They sat on two high, uncomfortable stools and each ordered spaghetti pie and a strawberry shake.

'Do you remember when we first saw each other here?' said Agatha. 'What did you think when you saw me sitting here by myself?'

'I thought, what a beautiful girl, I should so like to make friends with her. What did you think when I spoke to you? Did you think I was making a pass at you?'

'Yes. I was very excited.'

'And were you disappointed when I didn't?'

'Oh *no*! How can you ask that?'

'We have a lovely friendship,' said Johnnie sadly, and, it seemed to Agatha, with no conviction in his voice. 'You're the only person in this place I can stand.'

'And you're *quite* the only person I can talk to,' said Agatha. 'I don't know anybody else who likes the same things as I do. You make all my other friends seem so boring. When I'm with you, I dread going back to the house and hearing Mother's conversation and never being able to talk about books and pictures and things, or laugh like we do sometimes. If it wasn't for you, I'd go mad.'

'What would your Mother and that wonderful Mrs Mitchell say if they could see you now?'

Agatha thought for a bit. 'Mother would probably say,

"You know, Agatha, really, it's not very nice, is it?" And Mrs Mitchell would repeat after her, "No, dear, it's not very nice."'

'And neither it is,' said Johnnie glumly.

A couple who had been sitting in silence at the bar now left the room, leaving Agatha and Johnnie alone with the waitress, who pulled a tattered book from behind the tea urn and began to read it, now and then glancing aggressively at her two customers as though she wished they would leave. Johnnie stared at his reflection in a mirror opposite him with a secretive look, giving the false impression of being absorbed in his thoughts. Agatha was not enjoying herself. She dared not talk naturally, for fear of being thought pretentious by Johnnie, and she was trying hard to think of something that might amuse him. The more desperately she searched for a sentence with which to break the terrible silence, the blanker her mind became, until, in a voice made unnatural by over-deliberation, she brought out, 'I went to a funeral yesterday.'

'Did you? Have you been to any more dances at the golf club? Let's go, darling, this place is getting me down. Have you any money on you, sweetie?' Agatha paid, and soon they were standing together outside the bar in the cold street.

'Listen,' said Johnnie. 'Would you think it awfully rude of me if I left you now? I've just remembered I promised to meet Tony at the Castle bar after the show tonight.'

'But, Johnnie, I've hardly been with you at all.'

'I know, but I really ought to meet Tony or he'll be furious, and there's no use in my bringing you too because you'd only be bored stiff.'

Agatha said in a trembling voice which she could not control, 'You hate being with me, don't you? I bore you.'

'Oh, for God's sake don't be difficult. You know I love you, Agatha, but I'm in an awful mood tonight and I can't help it. That letter upset me, and I know I shall be bloody in the play next week. Please understand.'

Agatha steeled herself against his pleading voice. 'You don't like me at all really. You only pretend to. You only see me at all because you want to be seen about with a girl occasionally instead of your awful men friends like Tony and Christopher.'

'Don't shout, do you want that woman in there to hear everything you say? And what a bitchy remark, Agatha,' said Johnnie in a genuinely shocked voice. 'You must be mad. Who is there to "see me about with you" anyway? You're so ashamed of me, you're so afraid your idiotic family will find out about me that we never go anywhere except to this squalid Milk Bar. If that's what you think I'll leave you now.'

He began to walk away, and Agatha called after him in an agonised voice.

He came back, put his hands on her shoulders, and said gently, 'It's all right darling. I know you didn't mean what you said and neither did I. Come round tomorrow evening and I may be in a better mood. I must fly now.' He gave her a long, careful kiss on the mouth and walked off once more, his head bent and his shoulders hunched.

Agatha's body had been tense during the kiss, but she relaxed as she watched him disappear. She nearly called after him, 'Do up your coat, or you'll catch cold,' but stopped herself as she knew this would irritate him, and be marked up against her in his mind for use in a later quarrel. Her evenings with Johnnie often ended like this; he kissed her, spoke to her kindly and affectionately, forgave her tactless outbursts, but still he conceded nothing. He always managed to do as he wished, to elude her completely, and yet make it appear as though she were in the wrong. Now Agatha longed to follow him, and could hardly bring herself to move in the opposite direction; at last she began to walk slowly towards her home. Soon she came to a traffic round-about in the middle of the town, and sat down on a bench beneath the War Memorial. She wanted to clear her confused brain, to check her steps which would lead her too soon to her mother's drawing-room.

Sitting in the dark, with the noises of the town going on round her, Agatha looked on her life in a detached way. She saw it as though from a great distance, and as if it had nothing to do with her. On one side, as it were, was her home life; here she saw herself bored and misunderstood. In contrast with this was the time she spent with Johnnie; she was never bored with him, but neither was she happy in his company. She loved him, but he defeated and frustrated her. During the day, with her family and the few friends of whom Mrs Lyddiard approved, Agatha seemed to exist only by looking forward to her next secret meeting with Johnnie; with him, she was saved from complete despair by the knowledge that behind her was her home and some form of security.

At moments like this, Agatha thought with a tremor of excitement of the possibility of suicide. Many times had her mind followed the same routine; what if she rose from her seat, and threw herself under the wheels of the car now coming down the High Street? For a second this seemed a frighteningly easy thing to do; then Agatha realised that it was out of the question, that even if her mind decided on the action, her body would not obey it. Next she imagined an attempted suicide, prevented at the last moment by something beyond her control. She saw herself lying in bed, injured, treated by everyone as a heroine; her mother would blame herself for her daughter's desperate behaviour and Johnnie would read of it in the papers and hurry to her side, white with anxiety. There, at last, would be a situation! After thinking of this for some time, Agatha began to feel sleepy and rather hungry, and decided to delay her suicide until the next day, and perhaps even abandon it altogether; she suddenly appreciated two great blessings of life, sleep and food.

At one time Agatha had comforted herself at such moments of depression by imagining unlikely successes for herself. 'Fever, the brilliant novel from the pen of a new young authoress, Agatha Lyddiard, has been acclaimed by all the critics as the book of the decade. We feel that Proust would have been proud to have written it.' 'Agatha Lyddiard, a new young actress, caused a sensation last night by her interpretation of Hedda Gabler. The greatest artist since Duse . . .' and so on. Now these dreams only depressed her by their futility.

Soon she began to feel that things were not so bad after all; she was seeing Johnnie tomorrow. She walked uphill towards the 'residential district' on the outskirts of the town. As she neared her home, she noticed that the drawing-room lamplight was glimmering feebly through the green curtains. In the hall, she was depressed once more by the smell of furniture polish and the sight of the wide, dark staircase; she was about to climb the latter, when she heard her mother calling from the drawing-room.

Mrs Lyddiard was sitting by the fire with a car rug over her knees and a book open on her lap. She was reading and knitting at the same time. She took off her spectacles and smiled at her daughter.

'Well, dear, did you enjoy yourself? How was Mary?'

'Very well,' said Agatha. She sat down and folded her hands patiently.

'I missed you this evening, darling,' said Mrs Lyddiard. 'I suppose I shall have to get used to dining alone. It will be rather beastly for me when you go away, but I mustn't be selfish. I've been thinking this evening, by myself, what a thin time you have of it here. There are so few people of your own age, and you really ought to know some young

318

men. I expect you'll go to air force dances, and perhaps you'll meet a nice type. Agatha,' she said, leaning forward and smiling, 'I want you to feel always that you can bring your friends home here, and be certain of a welcome. Background is so important for an unmarried girl.'

Dear Derek

Mrs Lyddiard had not seen her godson, Philip Hall, since his christening nineteen years ago. She had been able to follow his progress since then with tepid interest, for news of it filled the letters she received now and then from his mother, Lettice Hall, a friend of Mrs Lyddiard's youth whom she now never met. When one of these arrived, containing not only the latest bulletin (Philip had just finished his first year at Oxford), but also the request that the Lyddiards should put him up for the last week of the vac while Mrs Hall dealt with some vague domestic crisis, Mrs Lyddiard's first thought was, 'He might do for Agatha.'

Although Agatha spoke little of Philip before his arrival, she was looking forward to his visit. She had gathered from her mother – and to Agatha his being an Oxford undergraduate implied – that he was an intellectual. She thought of herself as artistic, and expected Philip to be better company than the dull young men who lived in the neighbourhood. She had learnt, however, always to prepare for disappointment, and so as a kind of mental insurance policy she discouraged herself from hoping too much of him, and whenever her mother said, 'He'll be company for you, dear,' she answered, 'I don't know, he may be frightfully boring, or pretentious, or something.'

People are always at a disadvantage arriving at a house, particularly a strange one, and even more so when they do not know that they are observed (although they may suspect this). Agatha had posted herself, on this longed-for morning, at the first-floor landing window, and when she saw Philip turn down the street, carrying two heavy suitcases, she was surprised to see him so young; she had forgotten that boys of nineteen seldom look mature. His face, which was not spotty, but looked as though it recently had been, was pale and broad, with handsome features. His brown hair was tousled. If Agatha felt disappointment at this first sight, it was not keen. His clothes were as she had expected: corduroy trousers, dark shirt, red tie and tweed jacket, and she found that they suited his tall figure.

Conscious of her mother restless in the drawing-room, near the window but not at it, Agatha hurried to her bedroom when the front door bell rang. She could well imagine Mrs Lyddiard's embarrassing welcome of her guest, and meant to give it a miss − ('The last time I saw you you were a toddler; isn't it fantastic? What sort of journey did you have? *How* is your dear mother? We *never* meet now . . . but you must be feeling fearfully grubby, let me show you your room.' Then, over her shoulder as she preceded him upstairs, 'We're a household of females, you know. I hope that doesn't alarm you!') Agatha had decided not to make her entrance until Beryl had beaten the gong for lunch. She knew that Philip had only the vaguest idea of what she would be like, and hoped to surprise him pleasantly, now that she saw from her secret observation of him that it would be worth trying. She felt slightly ridiculous, however, sitting firmly and unnaturally on her bed while she heard him unpacking in the room next to hers. She sat out his session in the bathroom, praying that her mother would not call her, and though the echo of the gong had long faded in the hall, she waited until he was safely back in the drawing-room, before she slowly walked downstairs.

*

Mrs Lyddiard ponderously replaced her empty green coffee-cup in its saucer. They were sitting in the drawing-room, all three feeling sleepy after an indigestible lunch. She rose heavily from her chair. With an expression of conscious tact, which Agatha hoped was not as obvious to Philip as it was to her, Mrs Lyddiard said, 'I've got to be off now to a Red Cross lecture. I'll be back for tea. So, Agatha, you must entertain Philip till then.'

Agatha looked distant; rather clumsily, Philip raced his hostess to the door, and just succeeded in opening it for her before she reached it. Alone together, the two young people were silent for what seemed to Agatha a long time.

She was pleased at last to see him notice a novel by Aldous Huxley which she had placed on a table that morning.

'I see you're an admirer of Huxley.'

Agatha had realised at lunch that Philip was shy of any enthusiasm, and so she altered the speech which she had prepared for this moment.

'His early ones amused me, but now I think he's getting rather tedious.'

She could not tell what he thought of this, but it seemed to her a foolproof remark.

Philip looked about him, more at his ease since Mrs Lyddiard's departure, and Agatha liked him for politely hiding the contempt which she imagined any intellectual must have for so hideous a room.

'I should imagine you don't have a very amusing time here,' he said sympathetically.

'No, it's very dull. Nothing to do but read or go to the cinema.'

'That's the case with so many people in this wretched war. One's youth is wasted. I shall be joining the army soon.'

'Do you enjoy it at Oxford?'

'Yes, on the whole, it's very pleasant.'

Agatha tried to find out about his life there, but he seemed to be more interested in her. She was horrified at how little she had to tell him about herself, and soon found herself magnifying the smallest incidents into 'stories' with which she hoped to amuse him. She made out that a young man, to whom she had actually only spoken once or twice at a party, had tried to make love to her, and enlarged on her imaginary difficulties in getting rid of him. 'For God's sake don't tell Mother,' she ended up, 'or she'd have kittens.'

'Yes, you must have a troop of admirers after you,' he said, sitting down next to her on a sofa.

'But they're so awfully dull, Philip,' she said, turning to him. 'Why Mother insists on remaining in this provincial place I can't imagine. Sometimes I think I'll write a book about it all.'

'You really ought to. You're lucky to have such good copy near at hand.'

They started to talk about books, and from then on any strain there might have been between them disappeared. Agatha's confidence returned; Philip was not, she decided, as clever as he thought himself, but she did not like him less for this. They discovered a mutual taste for jazz music, and Agatha played him her small selection of records.

'I hardly ever get a chance to put them on,' she said.

'You really must come and stay with us next summer,' he said. 'I've got some records you'd like. I wish to goodness I'd brought them with me, but I never thought I'd find an enthusiast here.'

'I suppose you thought I'd be madly boring.'

Unequal to this, he showed his embarrassment, and muttered, 'Of course not.'

'I'd simply love to come. I want to see your books, too.'

'I'll send you that book on Proust. Remind me before I leave.'

Herself reminded by this that he was supposed to be staying a week, Agatha said, 'I'm afraid you'll be terribly bored here.'

He smiled at her. 'Oh, we'll find some amusing things to do, I'm sure, Agatha.'

But even as he said this, she could see that her remark had taken effect, and wished that she had never uttered it.

Eventually he said, 'How long is it till tea?'

'Quarter of an hour. Are you starving?'

'No, but if you don't mind I think I'll go upstairs and dash off a letter. I should have written it yesterday.'

She watched him leave the room, and then began to gather up the gramophone records which were scattered over the floor. She was happy, even looking forward to Mrs Lyddiard's return from the lecture. Her interest in Philip had revived her affection for her mother; as soon as she knew herself appreciated by someone, she could forget the misunderstandings and boredom which up till then had seemed to permeate her home life.

After tea, Agatha left Mrs Lyddiard with Philip in the drawing-room, and went upstairs to do the black-out in the bedrooms. Her mother had irritated her at tea, repeating too often how nice it was for Agatha to have someone of her own age in the house at last, and also that it seemed only yesterday when Philip had been a baby in arms. Agatha sensed that Philip disliked having attention thus drawn to his youth; he was conscious, and proud, of sophistication.

The gloom of evening filled the landing; the Cries of London were dark smudges on the walls. She turned first of all into her own room. This had an empty, impersonal air about it, in spite of the dark wallpaper and solid furniture, for Agatha's occupation of it was indicated only by a novel by Virginia Woolf and a photograph of Gary Cooper on the dressing-table. She did not linger there.

Her mother's bedroom was a mass of photographs; the faces of many friends and relations, and, above all, her mother's own, snapped at every stage of its career, glared at Agatha when she switched on the light. The frames were ornate, with the exception of one containing a recent photograph of Agatha herself; this was plain, made of glass and steel, and the face inside it looked naked and immature. Having drawn the heavy curtains, Agatha, still for a moment, could just hear voices in the drawing-room below, and wondered what was being said.

The spare room was furnished like the others; the patterns on the wallpaper and china jug and basin were florid, the chest of drawers and wardrobe were menacing in the half-light. Philip had laid out his striped woollen pyjamas on the bed and his sponge bag dangled from the basin, but otherwise his luggage was still unpacked. Agatha noticed a stamped and addressed envelope on the dressing-table; picking it up with curiosity she saw that the flap had not yet been stuck. Unable to resist the temptation of learning more about the young man who was filling her thoughts, she carefully extracted the letter within. He had left her, she remembered, to 'dash this off before tea'. The notepaper was her mother's, with the address printed at the top. Beneath was written in neat classical handwriting,

Dear Derek,

You will wonder what I am doing at the above address. Well, I am staying a week with a godmother, in a Gothic revival villa in a very genteel suburb. The godmother, however, seems kind if a bit over-bearing, and the villa is comfortable in an old-fashioned sort of way. There is also a daughter, who seems intelligent, although much too intense – she has just reached the Aldous Huxley stage!

She's a year younger than me; rather beautiful, but her clothes are too arty, very Slade school, which is probably her intention. I feel I could do something here (I have just been tête-à-tête with her all afternoon, and the mother is always leaving us alone together), but the thought of a romantic friendship in this atmosphere is really too oppressive, so I shall probably keep her at bay. This sounds very conceited and unchivalrous, but I wouldn't write like this to anyone but you.

Will I see you at Oxford next term? I very much want to read you the last chapters of the book. I am rather pleased with them. Your opinion will be invaluable.

Must rush now, I have just realised that a terrible din which has been going on for some time is the maid beating the Indian gong for tea! Do write soon.

Philip

P.S. Better not write here, I doubt if I can stick it for a week. Write to Walton Street.

Agatha stood for a moment motionless after reading this. Then she quickly and carefully replaced the letter in the envelope, and when she was satisfied that her interference would not be noticed, she left the room.

Going downstairs, she met Philip coming up.

'Just going out to stretch my legs and post a letter,' he said as they passed each other. She joined her mother in the drawing-room.

'This is our first opportunity to discuss our guest,' said Mrs Lyddiard.

'Be careful, he might hear,' said Agatha in a low voice. She picked up her Huxley book, and then put it down again. They heard Philip run downstairs, and shut the front door behind him.

'He's a dear boy, don't you think?' said Mrs Lyddiard.

'Yes, he's rather nice.'

Mrs Lyddiard looked arch. 'Now, Agatha, tell me, honest injun, do you think he's attractive?'

Agatha turned to her mother, her eyes limpid, her expression puzzled.

'Attractive? No, I can't say I do. Of course, I suppose he might be to some people, in a puppyish sort of way. But after all, Mother, he is so very young.'

Iris Metcalfe

THE PIANO LESSON

This story begins at half past nine one summer morning, in the broad main street of a market town.

Outside the Town Hall at one end of the street there was a notice advertising a Whist Drive to take place there that evening, and another, recently printed at the offices of the *Norford Gazette*, which read: 'The Norford Amateur Dramatic and Operatic Society present two performances of *The Midshipmaid*, on July 10th and 17th at 7.0 p.m. in the Town Hall. Tickets to be obtained from Mrs Metcalfe, "Kalipur", Buckingham Road, and from the *Norford Gazette*, High Street.'

Women were walking along the pavements and in and out of the shops which had been open an hour: large red Woolworths, popular for the snack counter at the back of the shop where tasteless hard lumps of vanilla ice cream were sold, balanced at the top of wafer cones; its nearby rival, green Marks and Spencers; the blue front of the Violet Tea Rooms; the streamlined Court Hairdresser, with neat heads in the window advertising Evan Williams Shampoo and the Marcel Wave; black, gloomy Freeman Hardy & Willis, displaying behind a smooth window-pane a multitude of court shoes; Boots Cash Chemist, and the gay, monogrammic sign of W. H. Smith & Son dangling above a window in which were piled many copies of a new book with a local interest, called *Norford Rambles*.

Outside W. H. Smith's there stood a queue of people waiting for a bus. Some of them were altering their wrist-watches to the time told by the Church clock, which was, confusingly, ten minutes later than that on the clock of the Town Hall tower opposite. The bus appeared, a long red single-decker with its rows of jolting heads which, on entering the town, all turned outward to present to the pavements their pale, unrecognisable faces. The bus slowly circled the street, and then stopped reluctantly at the queue, in exactly the right position, so that the woman at the head of the queue found herself just at the entrance to the bus. This woman had to wait, with increasing impatience, while the former passengers climbed out.

The last two people to leave the bus were a little girl of eight and a middle-aged woman, her governess. Mary jumped out on to the pavement, but Miss Hunt took her time over the two steps, and then stood for a moment at the bottom, breathing heavily, as though she had just stepped from a dark room into one dazzlingly light.

'Don't be such a slowcoach, Miss Hunt,' said Mary. 'We've only got ten minutes to shop in before the lesson.'

She walked on impatiently, pushing past the other shoppers in the street, and the governess followed, moving with precision, while the bus filled with its new load and the driver and conductor disappeared into the Violet for a quick cup of coffee.

Miss Hunt's purchases took place in a small dark draper's shop in a street leading out of the High Street, uphill, towards the common. In its window stood two models, one of which represented a smiling woman with smooth brown hair, on whom was hung a green summer dress; its price dangled from one of the arched slim fingers, each carefully separated from the other. The second model was a schoolboy with red cheeks and sturdy legs; he wore a cap and blazer and grey trousers which reached below his knees.

Inside the shop one tired assistant waited behind the counter. Rolls of material were piled together, and some stuffs were draped against the white boxes which stood along the walls. The smell of the shop made Mary think of Miss Hunt's underclothes.

Miss Hunt bought some buttons, some hooks and eyes, some thin knitting needles and some material with a dark green pattern on a pale green background. The material, which was not for herself, but for her sister who lived in Reading, was measured out in yards by the assistant, cut, folded and covered to form a neat brown paper parcel with impressive competence.

Then Miss Hunt and Mary walked on up the hill, Miss Hunt with her parcels and Mary with a portfolio containing sheet music, for she had come into Norford to have her piano lesson.

The houses in Buckingham Road which faced the common (on which this morning a group of children were playing rounders) were detached, and each had a little garden and a garage shaded by laurels. Each had steps leading up to the front door, and a large window on the ground floor. They were built of grey stone; at the back, they each had a glass conservatory. One or two, larger than the others, were built so as to resemble miniature castles, with two square towers and little chinks in the stone which were the servants' windows. Most of them had some sign on the garden gate; one belonged to a doctor, another to a dentist; one was a school of typing and shorthand, and another the headquarters of the YWCA.

'Kalipur' had no sign on its gate. It belonged to Mrs Metcalfe, the widow of an assistant master at the public school just outside the town, and for which it was well known; she lived there with her daughter Iris, who was to give Mary her piano lesson.

Mary followed her governess through the gate of 'Kalipur' and along the crazy pavement in the middle of which was a chipped stone bird bath. On either side of the front door, and above it, were panes of stained glass. When the door was suddenly opened, just as Miss Hunt was reaching for the knocker, they could see that the sun shining through the fanlight lit part of the floor in the dark hall and coloured it, as oil does a puddle in the street.

Mrs Metcalfe had opened the door. She was a large, energetic woman, between fifty and sixty. She was pulling a shapeless hat down over her grey curls, beneath which swung green earrings. She was smoking a cigarette.

'Oh, good morning. Isn't it a heavenly day? Quite Godgiven. It seems a shame you should have to stuff indoors at the piano. I'll call Iris, I don't know where she's got to. Iris!' She sang this name, for Mrs Metcalfe had a contralto voice. 'I've just written a note to your mother,' she said to Mary. 'She's behind with her subscription to the Conservative Society. One has to pester people when one is held responsible. Just wait in the drawing-room till Iris comes down. Heaven knows what she's doing.' She walked out into the garden, calling up to a first-floor window, 'Iris, little Mary Stone is here, don't keep her waiting.' A faint voice could be heard from upstairs: 'Coming, Mummy.'

Miss Hunt put her parcels down on the umbrella stand in the hall beneath the barometer which hung on the wall. Mary removed her hat and gloves. Then they went into the drawing-room.

In spite of the big window, this room was dark and oppressive. It contained a heavy roll-top writing-table, on which were an inkstand, pens, a blotter, sealing-wax, a penwiper and several tradesmen's calendars. There were many photographs in the room, most of them school groups or portraits of pupils of the late Mr Metcalfe, presented to him on their leaving school. On them were written such inscriptions as 'To G.L.M. from P.H. 1924–30'. In the middle of the room there was a big table with magazines on it. There was a bookcase with glass doors which looked as if it were never opened; and, indeed, it never was, because the doors had been locked and the key mislaid. In one corner stood an old, upright piano, with yellow notes. A fringed shawl had been placed on the top, and on that there was a bowl of ferns. The music stand was bent sideways, forming a complicated zig-zag pattern; on either side of it projected a candlestick. Beside the piano was a music rack containing music neatly arranged.

While the two visitors stood in the drawing-room, they heard Mrs Metcalfe start up her two-seater which they later saw move slowly past the window. They could see her, a cigarette still in her mouth, leaning over the steering wheel and staring through the windscreen at the road.

Miss Hunt said in the restrained voice which she used in other people's houses, 'Why don't you start practising?' She looked about her with an air of disapproval.

Mary went over to the piano stool, which she adjusted to suit her own height. Then she took from her portfolio a book of music called 'Off we Go!' and, opening the piano, began to play a piece in it called 'Ronde'. She looked all the time at her hands, and never at the music, because she could not sight-read, and had to learn a piece by heart before she could play it at all. For some reason the tune which she knew so well sounded more professional and convincing on this piano than it did when Mary played it on the one at her home. When she pressed the loud pedal, she could hear it shift somewhere inside the instrument. Mary wondered why pianists did not play with the loud pedal on all the time.

Miss Metcalfe's system was to make her pupils practise one week the right-hand part of a piece, the next week the left-hand, and the third week the two together. Thus they all moved at an equal pace through 'Off we Go!' and the more advanced books which succeeded it. A friend of Mary's, who had started a fortnight before her, was therefore always one piece ahead of her, and Mary hoped that Susan would one day be ill, so that Mary would be able to catch her up, and perhaps even pass her in the steady race. At the moment Mary was the youngest, and most backward, of the pupils. At Miss Metcalfe's annual concert, when they performed to an audience consisting of their parents, Mary was always the first to play. This was the final week to be devoted to 'Ronde', and if the teacher was satisfied with Mary's performance, she was to start today on the right-hand part of the following tune, which was called 'Berceuse'.

It was rare for a piano lesson to be conducted at 'Kalipur'; Miss Metcalfe preferred to borrow her mother's car and visit her pupils, no doubt owing to the inferiority of her own piano. Today the car had been needed by Mrs Metcalfe, and so Mary had travelled the five miles from her house in the bus.

Miss Hunt selected a *Sporting and Dramatic* from the magazines on the table, and sat down stiffly on a leather armchair. She turned immediately to the Dramatic section, but then she realised that she had already seen this edition, and so she picked out a *Country Life* instead.

Iris Metcalfe came into the room, smiling apologetically. She was a tall woman of thirty, with a big white face and brown hair arranged in a nondescript manner. She wore a summer dress made of much the same material as that just bought by Miss Hunt for her sister; her arms were thin and pale, and the bare elbows wrinkled. Iris was usually seen in the company of her mother, whose personality was strong enough to obliterate Iris's altogether. When not with her mother, any sign of initiative on Iris's part, any individual movement or spontaneous sentence, was as surprising, and as endearing, as a child's remark whose influence cannot be easily traced.

Iris brought up a chair to the piano, and sat by while Mary played her piece. Mary was depressed by the smell of her teacher's clothes and hair, and the sight of her broad, clumsy hands which were suddenly nimble when at the piano.

While the lesson was in progress, Miss Hunt laid down her magazine, and after a pause began a conversation.

'Have you had any news of Mr Metcalfe?'

This referred to Iris's brother Alan, who was a year or two older than her; he had a stutter, and was abroad.

'Not for some time. Are you coming to the Drive tonight, Miss Hunt?'

Iris talked to Miss Hunt, watching Mary's fingers all the time, and occasionally interrupting the adult conversation to say, 'Not so much pedal, Mary,' or to groan humorously and grimace when the child struck a wrong note.

'I don't see how I'm to manage it,' answered Miss Hunt. 'I can get a bus to take me in, but I can't get a bus to take me back. Will you be there?'

'No, I've given up going, but Mummy's giving the prizes.'

'Oh, and what has she chosen?' asked Miss Hunt, with some hesitation, as though the question were an indelicate one; and so it may have been, for Iris answered with a careless air of deprecation, 'The men's prizes are all cigarettes, I believe. She's got rather a jolly Ladies' First Prize though; an ebony shoehorn, with glove stretchers to match. I tell her I'm tempted to play myself, just to try and win it! The Ladies' Second Prize is a pair of shoe trees. She's just gone out to see if she can get a suitable Consolation anywhere – a vase, we thought, or something of the sort.'

'How very nice.'

Mary, bored with the conversation, and wishing to attract attention, now struck an exaggerated discord; Iris said, 'Mary! You can't be concentrating. That sounded fearful.'

Mary found an opportunity to repeat a favourite catch phrase: 'Beg your pardon, Mrs Arden, there's a chicken in your garden.'

'I say, Miss Hunt, I shall have to buy a little bat, and hit her over the knuckles whenever she makes a mistake. She'd make far less then, I'm sure.'

Mary giggled, and her governess said crossly, 'She can play it correctly if she wants to, but she doesn't try.' Then, after waiting a little, she continued the interrupted conversation with Iris. 'The last time I came in to a Norford Drive, there were so many more ladies than men, that I had to play as a man, if you know what I mean. I obtained the highest score in the room, but of course I had to have the Men's First Prize – forty Gold Flake cigarettes, which were no good to me, as I don't smoke. However, I sent them to my brother, and he was very pleased with them.'

Mary, who had heard this story many times, was wondering what a Whist Drive could be like. She knew how to play Whist, but the word 'Drive' suggested something more exciting, and she longed to know exactly what it meant.

Miss Hunt continued, 'Oh, before I forget it, Mrs Stone asked me to ask you when and where the next rehearsal is.'

'Here, on Saturday afternoon; I do hope she turns up, and knows her part. I'm stage-managing, you know.'

'I'm sure we're all very much looking forward to the performance. They are always so amusing. It must be hard work.'

'Oh, there's masses to do. But I prefer it to acting.'

'I'm sorry you haven't a part.'

'Goodness,' said Iris, turning from the piano and pulling at the rings on her fingers, 'I can't act for toffee-apples.

What I do do keeps me busy enough. I have to get the play typed out, and send copies to everyone, with all their speeches marked in pencil. And I have to get hold of all the scenery, and see people turn up at rehearsals.'

Mary, who had turned her head away during this speech and had been picking her nose, now slipped off the stool and went up to Miss Hunt, whispering something in her ear.

'May I take her upstairs, Miss Metcalfe?'

'Of course. You know the way.'

Iris waited standing until they returned. The lesson was over. 'You must let us hear *you* before we leave,' said Miss Hunt.

So Iris sat down again at the piano and played a 'Song Without Words' while the governess tried to prevent Mary from fidgeting, and whispering, 'We'll miss the bus.'

When at last they were putting on their coats in the hall, they could smell food and hear the dining-room table being laid for lunch. The sound of Iris playing by herself followed them down Buckingham Road, and as they turned downhill they passed Mrs Metcalfe in her car, squinting ahead of her and clutching the steering wheel with determination.

THE GRAMOPHONE CLUB

The shops had shut for the lunch hour, but now they were opening again. Iris walked along the High Street to the Town Hall, which she entered by a side door. Tables, with four chairs at each, were set on the floor in preparation for the Whist Drive; they were covered in green baize, and on each had been placed a pack of cards and a marker with pencil attached. Iris knew well the formula of these enter-tainments; the chatter while at each table the hands were dealt, the hush while the cards were picked up and hastily

arranged, fanlike, in their suits, the sporadic talk and
laughter while the game was played. After each hand, the
winning man moved up (for every table was numbered, by
a chalk mark on the baize), the winning lady down, and the
losing couple stayed at the same table, only altering their
positions so that they no longer faced each other. The
proceeds of the Drive went to the Women's Institute, of
which Mrs Metcalfe was Treasurer, and Miriam Holmes,
Secretary.

Miriam was now standing on the stage in the hall, talking
to an electrician in a blue overall. She was arranging about
the lighting for *The Midshipmaid*, which she was producing, and in which she was taking the leading part. Miriam
was the daughter of a Norford housemaster; she was Iris's
greatest friend, and Iris admired her, because she ran the
local Pony Club, and had a hand in every club or Institute
formed in the town. Miriam was the same age as Iris, whom
she had known all her life; she had bright red hair and a
pale, freckled, face.

'I'll be with you in a moment, darling,' she called.

Iris sat down at one of the tables, and looked about the
hall. She had seen it arranged in many different ways; as
today, for a Whist Drive; as it would shortly be, with the
chairs in rows and facing the stage in front of which a
curtain would precariously be hung, for the amateur dra-
matics; and, as on every Saturday night, with the floor
cleared and the chairs along the walls, ready for the weekly
dance. On these occasions, the local band was hired, and sat
on the stage playing from seven o'clock till ten. They
advertised themselves as 'Bert Collins and his Boys, Playing
Music in the Modern Manner'. If the band had a previous
engagement, the man from Powell's Gramophone Shop
brought a radiogram to the hall, standing by it on the stage
and announcing each dance before playing one of his limited
supply of records. Iris imagined she could hear him now:

337

'Ladies and Gentlemen, take your partners for the Valeta!' Or the Paul Jones, the Tango, the Waltz, the Foxtrot and the Quickstep . . .

The electrician went away, and Miriam stepped down from the stage. 'Sorry to keep you . . .' she looked at her wrist-watch. 'We'll have to hurry, or we'll be late.'

Miriam picked up a pile of gramophone records which she had placed on one of the tables, and Iris followed her out of the hall. Miriam handed the records to Iris when they were outside, and turned round to lock the door behind her. Then she wriggled her shoulders under her cotton dress, and holding out her hands for the records said, 'Wouldn't it be nice to go for a swim today?'

They took a turning off the High Street, uphill, in the opposite direction to that leading up to the common, for the town lay in a valley. Miriam said, 'My dear, I'm counting on you to accompany my 'cello solo for the school concert.'

'Will there be many people this afternoon?'

'I doubt it. Some of the school are really awfully keen but it takes a lot of persuading to get them to try something new. Of course if nobody comes I shall have to give it up.'

'Tell me,' said Iris, 'have you met a new master called Mr Hill? Mother said at lunch that she'd asked him to tea today.'

'The Science man? My dear, yes, he's rather sweet. He came to dinner the other day, and sang. He's got a gorgeous voice.'

'That will give me something to talk to him about at tea.' Iris imagined herself saying later that afternoon, 'I hear you sing, Mr Hill.' 'How do you know that, Miss Metcalfe?' an agreeable tenor voice would enquire; and she would say, 'A little bird told me.' But no doubt Mrs Metcalfe would ask him to sing, before she had the chance.

They had now reached the outskirts of the town, where the school buildings began. Out of breath, they stopped for a moment to watch the bowling at the nets. A thin-haired master, wearing light grey flannels and a blue blazer with gold buttons, stood in the middle of a cricket field holding a bat and ball, surrounded by a widespread circle of school-boys.

'There's Daddy taking fielding-practice,' said Miriam.

The master sent the ball high up into the air; Iris watched it ascend, dizzy, until her eyes watered and she lost it; the fielders were standing tense, their heads upturned; suddenly the ball was again visible, descending fast; Iris jumped nervously as one of the fielders placed himself beneath it, hands cupped; the hands received it, and he jerked them back between his open knees, but the ball jumped out, fell and rolled along the ground. The other boys groaned and the master said crossly, 'What's the matter with you, Scho-field?' Schofield smiled uneasily.

'Come on,' said Miriam. She led Iris into the gymnasium.

The ropes were looped up and fastened to the handle-bars that stood along the walls, to leave the room clear. In one corner were gathered together two jumping-horses, some footballs, and a pile of long poles. Iris wondered what the poles were for. An electric radiogram stood at one end of the room, plugged into a light that hung from the ceiling. Round this were grouped two schoolboys and an elderly woman dressed in a uniform not unlike that of a hospital nurse.

'Matron,' shouted Miriam, in her irritatingly piercing voice, 'how splendid of you to come!'

'I heard there was to be music, Miss Holmes, and I never miss a concert if I can help it.'

'Is this everybody then?' asked Miriam.

One of the boys, who was very fat, said in a cultured voice, 'It's not a very good attendance, but alas, many who wanted to were unable to come. Schofield was mad keen – his aunt plays professionally, you know, she was on the wireless the other night – but he couldn't get out of fielding practice.'

'Oh dear. But four people is better than nothing.'

Iris glanced at the other boy, who was good-looking and wore a sulky, embarrassed expression. Then she looked through an open door near the gramophone, which led into a small room in which a PT instructor was punching a ball attached to the ceiling. The room was full of photographs of boxers and wrestlers. The instructor was small, and wore only a pair of blue trousers, secured by elastic round the waist, and tucked at the bottom into black boots. His muscular arms were covered with tattoo-marks. Suddenly he picked up a rugger ball, put it under his arms, and ran through the gymnasium and out of it, without looking at the others.

Matron sucked in her cheeks and looked round her with a smile. 'Where are we all to sit? Personally, I think the floor looks a bit hard.'

'Oh dear, there aren't any chairs. I never thought of that, wasn't I dippy? Could you two boys be poppets and run and secure us some form of seat? Anything would do, we can't afford to be choosy, but some deck chairs would be jolly if you could find any.'

'No sooner said than done. We won't be half a mo.'

Iris noticed a pile of hairy mats in one corner, the kind that are placed in front of a jumping-horse, for the jumper to land on. 'Couldn't we lie on those?' she said.

'Darling, what a brain wave. Let's drag them out.'

'Very luxurious and restful,' said Matron, uncertainly.

'A bit hairy,' said the fat boy. 'They're inclined to tickle but we might try.'

The boys dragged four of the mats into the middle of the room and put them side by side, facing the gramophone. Then the fat boy lay on one, resting his head on his hands. 'Very comfy,' he said.

'Splendid,' said Matron, sitting down gingerly. 'Yes, this will do splendidly.' Iris sat next to her, leaning on one elbow on which was soon imprinted the mat hairs' pattern. The good-looking boy lay down flat on her other side, staring up at the ceiling.

'Well,' said Miriam, 'now we can start.' She cleared her throat. 'The first record I've chosen is a Paul Robeson, because I know he's always popular. Singing,' she squinted at the label, 'the "Eriskay Love Lilt".'

'Wizard.'

Miriam switched on the gramophone, changed the needle, and started the record. Then, with exaggerated caution, she tiptoed back to the mats, and lowered herself to the ground, wincing slightly as the rough hairs touched her cotton dress. The fat boy listened with an expression of strained intelligence on his white, good-humoured face; Matron squatted by him, her mouth serene, her eyes preoccupied; Iris looked down at the other boy, who had closed his eyes. Suddenly she thought, 'How much younger he is than me.'

As a child, she had looked forward to the beginning of term with excitement, as it meant the presence of straw-hatted youths in the town, some of whom she knew. But she never knew one for longer than six years, as once they reached the interesting age of nineteen, and often sooner, they left the school and never came back. As a young girl this excitement had deepened to a more urgent sensation, for she had felt that her social life depended entirely on the schoolboys. Now she realised that for some time they had seemed children to her; she was the contemporary of the masters now, no longer that of the pupils. Iris felt sure that she would never get used to that idea.

The record ended. Miriam stayed motionless for a moment, as if still listening to the song; then she noticed that the needle was scratching on the inner circle of the record, and she rose to change it.

'What a voice,' said Matron, altering her uncomfortable position with relief.

'Do let's have the other side,' said the fat boy, his face gleaming with enjoyment.

'I don't know whether we have time. I want to get in the whole of the D minor concerto if I can before Abbers, and you don't want to be late for that. If we do have time, I'll play it at the end.'

'D minor concerto?' said Matron. 'I had heard a rumour that we were to have the Jupiter.'

'I hope you don't mind,' said Miriam, 'but I thought the D minor might be more popular.'

'Oh, delightful, but I must confess a soft spot for the Jupiter.'

Iris lay back and closed her eyes when the Mozart began. Her hip was just touching that of the good-looking boy; she checked an impulse to move, deciding to wait and see if he would. He did not, however, and soon she ceased to notice his proximity.

The sun shone through the high windows on to the smooth floorboards. Iris wondered which of her private imaginary scenes she would choose to accompany the music. She decided on her favourite.

There she was, sitting somewhere at the back of a crowded concert hall in Wigmore Street. She was clapping the conductor, (at first a shadowy figure, until she determined on his identity; today he would be Sir Malcolm Sargent). The orchestra had finished tuning up. There was an excited silence in the auditorium while Sir Malcolm walked towards the wings and held out his hands to someone lurking there. Faces stared at the stage and hands rustled programmes on laps. An old lady next to Iris put on her glasses and stared at her programme which she was holding upside down. 'What comes now?' she muttered. 'Mozart's piano concerto in D minor,' Iris whispered. 'Who's the soloist?' 'Look, there she is!' Sir Malcolm led on to the stage a tall girl in a white evening dress with neat brown hair and ear-rings like Mrs Metcalfe's. 'Isn't she good-looking?' said the old lady. 'Who is she?' 'Iris Metcalfe.' 'Ah, yes.' The Iris in the audience clapped loudly while the Iris on the stage bowed, with a smile, first to the spectators and then to Sir Malcolm. When the clapping stopped, moving deliberately and slowly, the soloist walked towards the enormous piano. She adjusted the stool and flexed her fingers. Then she exchanged a look, over her shoulder, with the conductor.

Lying on the mat in the gymnasium, Iris was excited by this imaginary scene. She was holding her breath and clenching her hands. What a moment! Then, returning to consciousness, she wondered: When will it happen? She opened her eyes and decided, Never. But that did not matter, for the scene took place in her imagination, no doubt far more pleasantly than it would in real life, every time she listened to a piano concerto. She had no regret, on waking up, that her dream was only a dream, for she knew that the dream was an improvement on actuality.

The last record over, Miriam said, 'I think we've time for the Robeson again, if you'd care to hear it.'

Iris rose. 'I must go home now,' she said in a shaking voice. 'I mustn't be late for tea. Don't get up,' she said to the boys who had made no move.

'Tomorrow morning for coffee at the Violet, don't forget,' said Miriam, turning to the gramophone.

Outside in the sun Iris blinked as she walked lightly downhill to the town.

TEA

When she reached 'Kalipur', out of breath and sweating after her hot walk, Iris noticed a green pork-pie hat, with a pheasant's feather stuck in the brim, hanging in the hall. She held her breath, and could distinguish a man's voice mingling with her mother's loud deep one in the conversation coming from the drawing-room. She went quickly into the room known as her father's study.

The bookshelves here contained a collection of Loeb classics and many old school books: Latin Primers, edited copies of *Julius Caesar* and *The Merchant of Venice*, Caesar's *Gallic War*. These were heavily marked in ink, and bore on their fly-leaves the names of the different schoolboys who had at various times owned them. Iris imagined she could smell in the study the tobacco which Mr Metcalfe had smoked, and, although he had been dead some years, it was still very much his room. It was here that, dribbling along his pipe-stem, a loose tweed mountain sunk in the swivel-chair behind his desk, he had received the group of boys who, every Thursday evening, had come stumbling out of the dark to be prepared, unwillingly, for Confirmation.

Iris stood in the study and wondered how she would make her entrance into the drawing-room. Somehow she must penetrate into the room – unless she went to bed with a headache? Her curiosity about Mr Hill, however, decided her against this. Should she slink in, creep in, stalk in, swing in, burst in . . .? Her mother's voice called angrily, 'Iris! What on earth are you doing?' She hurried out of the study repeating her usual obedient phrase, 'Coming, Mummy,' and found herself in the drawing-room before she realised it.

Her mother was sitting behind the teapot, opposite a man who clumsily rose from his chair when Iris came in.

'This is my daughter Iris, Mr Hill,' said Mrs Metcalfe in a bored way, as though she wished to get the introduction over as soon as possible. Iris held out her hand, staring at the stranger but, owing to a nervousness which she always felt on meeting someone new, unable to distinguish his features or receive any impression of his appearance. Mr Hill also held out his hand, but wide of Iris's, and as both leaned forward they missed each other, and nearly poked each other in the stomach. Iris giggled nervously, and there was an agitated movement of hands, until finally Mr Hill captured two of Iris's limp fingers and shook them heartily with a large red hand on which grew pale hairs.

'Sit down, Iris, and drink your tea. I'm afraid it's stewed, but that's your look out, if you must be late for meals.'

Iris sat down miserably, wishing that her mother would not treat her as though she were twenty years younger than she was. She found it difficult, when spoken to as a child of ten, not to answer in that character – sulkily, saucily or precociously – and thus appear ridiculous. Mrs Metcalfe, as though a tiresome interruption were now over, turned with a charming smile to her guest. Iris sipped her tea (which was indeed very dark, and tepid) and studied Mr Hill.

He was tall and thin, and wore a light-grey flannel suit, a white shirt and an Old Norfordian tie. His sandy hair appeared to be thick, as it was wiry and stood up in a wall above his white forehead, but in fact it was sparsely distributed over his head, and was already thinning at the crown. His face was pale and lightly freckled, and Iris suddenly noticed the beginnings of a soft moustache on his upper lip. He may have seen her look at it, for he said now, 'I have always been clean-shaven up to now, but on coming to Norford I decided I was altogether too mild-looking to keep a class in order, so I started this moustache in the hope of frightening the boys. I'm rather pleased with it,' he said stroking it with a slightly facetious air. 'I call it Bertram.'

Iris smiled, and her mother screamed out a laugh, saying, 'How perfectly priceless!'

'How do you like it at Norford?' Iris asked timidly. Her mother looked angry and embarrassed, as she often did when Iris spoke in public, giving the impression that her daughter was not quite all there, and might at any moment say something wild and obscene. She quickly interrupted, before Mr Hill could answer, and indeed before anyone could be sure that he had heard Iris's question, 'Isn't it splendid to think that the summer holidays will soon be here? Where do you go? When my husband was alive we always went to Switzerland, but since his death we have only visited friends in this country. It isn't the same as abroad.'

With a clatter Iris replaced her cup and saucer on the table. The presence of a stranger put her off her appetite. When people came to tea, she liked to eat nothing at the meal, but later to go into the kitchen and finish the dropscones by herself.

Mr Hill's pale grey eyes sparkled at his hostess's question, and he leant forward. 'Oh, I had a capital holiday a few years ago. An experience I shall never forget. I made a trek to the Passion Play at Oberammergau.'

Iris forgot her diffidence, and said with interest, 'It lasts for days, doesn't it? And they all wear their own beards?'

'Oh, yes, no one could possibly take offence at the presentation of,' he lowered his voice, 'our Lord on the stage, it is all so natural and reverent and moving.'

'Like *The Miracle*, or *Everyman*,' said Mrs Metcalfe.

'But Oberammergau is in a class by itself. Here, I have some photos.'

Mr Hill drew a wallet from his inside pocket, and from that some postcards of scenes from the passion play. The two women leant forward, breath held in reverence, and did not know what to say. Each felt that if the other had not been there, she would have said something suitable, interesting and original, and made a friend of the schoolmaster.

After a time Mr Hill tucked the photographs back into his pocket. He turned to Iris, who received his attention with a frightened face, and said, 'Your mother tells me that I am among a musical family.'

She answered in a little rush, accenting the wrong words like a foreigner and avoiding her mother's face on which she could imagine a gathering frown, 'Yes, Mummy sings awfully nicely.'

'And you play?'

'After a fashion.'

'Nonsense,' said Mrs Metcalfe. 'Don't be so modest, you know you play very well. Not first class, perhaps, not even second – you know your own limitations, but within them,' she said, turning to the man, 'she is quite an artist. We sent her to the Royal College when we saw she had talent.'

'I should love to hear you – if I might,' said Mr Hill humbly. Iris was thinking, 'If only Mummy were not here, I could talk about music, get his ideas on my favourite composers, and he would like me. But what I want to say comes out differently when she's there. Please God make her be called to the telephone.'

'Iris,' said Mrs Metcalfe (in a tone which implied, 'Here is your chance, at last, for heaven's sake wake up and take it'), 'why don't you accompany Mr Hill in a song?'

'You sing?' said Iris, with assumed surprise.

'Not today, alas. I've been laid up with a septic throat, so it's out of the question.'

'Play that charming sea thing – Macdowell, or whatever the man's name is,' continued Mrs Metcalfe, like an enormous engine which nothing can stop. 'Go on.'

'Oh, no Mummy, I'm sure Mr Hill wouldn't care for that.'

'Well, play something, child, Mr Hill doesn't want to

347

wait all night,' said Mrs Metcalfe, turning to the man with an amused, sympathetic expression.

'If Miss Metcalfe would rather not,' began the visitor, looking at his wrist-watch in evident embarrassment.

'Of course she wants to,' said Mrs Metcalfe sharply. 'What's the use of having a talent if you have to be begged and entreated to use it? It's mock modesty,' she said angrily, and then smiled, to show that she was not really angry, and added softly, 'That's all it is.'

In the following silence Iris found herself obliged to speak. 'I'd rather not play today,' she said, as firmly as she could. She had been ready, had indeed wanted to play to Mr Hill, but the long, embarrassing discussion had numbed, not only her fingers, but her whole body, so that she felt incapable of reaching the piano, let alone of playing it.

Mrs Metcalfe twitched her shoulders, and, avoiding looking at her daughter, turned to the schoolmaster with an apologetic expression, as though asking his forgiveness for her dog which had bitten him, and hoping that he would like her herself none the less after the incident, for which she had been only partly responsible.

Iris stood up. She longed to say something to Mr Hill, but through a strange wilfulness she ignored her hatred of her mother, which had been increasing during the last few minutes, and addressed her with an affectionate smile. 'Now I'm going to leave for Devizes,' she said.

Mr Hill looked surprised. 'You'll have a long journey in front of you,' he said.

Mrs Metcalfe shouted with laughter. 'Priceless! No, my dear man, Iris didn't mean what she said. It's a family joke. All the nicest families have family jokes, don't you think? I'm sure yours has. You see, my husband had an old Aunt Emma – she's been dead for years – but she was very deaf. One day she was in here and I had to go out, so I said to her, "Now, I'm going to leave you to your own devices."

After I'd gone, Gerald came in, and said "Where's Clarice, Aunt Emma?" And Aunt Emma said, "She's just left for Devizes!" You see, she hadn't heard me correctly.'

'So after that,' said Iris, 'whenever one of us goes off somewhere, we always say, "Now I'm going to leave for Devizes".'

After a short pause, Mr Hill said 'Capital!' and, throwing his head back and his legs out, and hitting his knee with his hand, laughed for a long time. It seemed to Iris that some of his laughter was false, and that he was not as amused as he pretended. She slipped out of the room before he had finished laughing. She walked slowly up the carpeted stairs, dragging her feet, and entered her own bedroom. She sat down on the brown and beige-striped counterpane which covered the narrow bed. Above the bed there hung, and had hung for twenty years, a flat cardboard spaniel, with 'Doggie' lettered in gold along the bottom. There were several calendars nailed to the fidgety wallpaper. The room was very neat, for Iris had a mania for tidiness, and hid every article she possessed in the chest of drawers; inside the drawers, however, all was confusion.

Some time ago, Iris had seen in a copy of a magazine called *Prediction*, lent to her by Miriam, the following advertisement:

Madame Marianne Robinson-Williams, Spiritual Medium. Numerology, psychometry, astrology, clairvoyance, Inspirational messages, herbs, faith healing. Send birth date and 5/- P.O. to 'Walhallah', 19, Devon Crescent, N.7.

Iris had sent the postal order, with a short note asking for a reading, and a week later had received a reply. She thought of it now, and searched in a drawer for the typewritten letter; when she found it, she sat on the bed and read it again, although she almost knew it by heart. This is what she read.

Dear Miss Metcalfe,

Many thanks for the letter and enclosure. Have carefully psychometrised your handwriting and cast your horoscope. A reading follows.

I should say you are of a highly inspirational tendency, surely sensitive and a bit nervy — liable to take offence and fly off the handle — resentful of interference, all up in the air — surely you seek expression artistically? In song or acting, no doubt have a talent for woodcuts, needlework, crochet or some such. Of a peculiarly sunny temperament — always merry and bright — should consort with others of cheery disposition, or folks out of the common — how shall I say? — a bit bohemian.

Marriage indicated not far off — should meet fiancé before Whitsun next — older man, grey hair, I should say of the 'distingué' type. Offspring are indicated — you love the kiddies and are a great favourite with them.

Oh, I get a whiff of sea air — would you be intending a holiday on the East Coast? I get a ginger gentleman much in your thoughts — oh, he does laugh a lot!

Message from the Other Side — get the name Muriel — do not despair — all will right itself — do not ponder your troubles but continue on the daily round with trust in Him who watches over you constantly — let your heart be high and sing 'Rock of Ages Cleft for Me'.

God bless you, dearie, and cheerio.

Marianne Robinson-Williams (Mme)

On first reading this letter Iris had been disappointed, recognising little in it that applied to her situation; but now she wondered whether she could identify the ginger gentleman with Mr Hill. Mr Hill was not, it is true, ginger, but he had sandy hair, and he had certainly laughed a lot about Devizes.

'Much in my thoughts . . . Well,' Iris thought, 'if that really is Mr Hill, there is no reason why all the rest, the grey-haired man and so on, should not come true.' She felt consoled by the letter, as she had not done till now, and put it back in the drawer with a feeling of mild excitement.

She heard the front door close, and moved quickly to the window where she watched Mr Hill, swinging his pork-pie hat, walk jauntily, and, it seemed to her, self-consciously, as though he knew she was watching him, down the garden path, and along Buckingham Road. She would have liked to have called out 'Goodbye' to him, and even opened her mouth to do so, but no words came, and she recognised the wish as one of many, which made up her life, and which she knew would for ever remain unfulfilled.

She stared out past the common at the sordid houses on the outskirts of Norford. Behind them round, irregular gasometers stood against the sky, and even further away, out in the country, a skeleton viaduct crested a hill. She watched a toy express creep along it noiselessly, bound for the Cornish Riviera, and wondered if the travellers, from the carriage windows, could notice the white speck which was her window in 'Kalipur'. One day she would take that train, and sit in a corner seat to see if her house was visible.

She heard her mother's heavy footsteps on the stairs. Ashamed of being discovered idling – for there was a chance that Mrs Metcalfe was coming into her room – Iris quickly left the window, and pretended to hunt in a drawer for something. Mrs Metcalfe did come into the room. She sat down on the bed, breathing heavily and fingering her earrings.

'Well,' she said, staring at her daughter's back, 'what became of you?'

'How do you mean?'

'I don't know what that poor youngster will think of you. You never said goodbye to him.'

'He wouldn't have noticed.'

'No, very likely he wouldn't. But, dear, you might have been more civil at tea. Weren't you feeling well?'

'I've got a headache. I came up to lie down.'

'I don't know why you don't pull yourself together when we have company. Not that it makes any difference to me. I speak for your own good, dear. But when I asked this young man to tea, I thought to myself, "Perhaps he will do as a friend for Iris." You don't have many friends, you know, dear.'

'I have all the friends I want.'

'Meaning that silly Miriam?' The mother shrugged her shoulders. 'Well, that's your affair. Far be it from me to interfere. But all the same I see no reason why you should bury your nose in your cup, mumble into your beard, and run from the room like a frightened schoolgirl. You can never hope to be happy if you . . .'

'I'm perfectly happy.'

'How can one be happy without friends? Look at me. Apart from you, dear, and Alan, I live for my friends now. And Alan, he was never any trouble, he was always a good mixer.'

'I don't want many friends, Mummy.'

'How can you hope to get married if you haven't any friends?'

'Oh, leave me alone.'

'No dear, when I see you mess up your life by your manner, which isn't the real you at all, I feel bound to correct you.'

'Well, what do you want me to do? Run up and kiss every man I meet?'

'Don't be cheap, Iris.'

'I'm quite all right, all I ask is to be let alone. There's a lot you don't know about me . . .'

'I suppose you mean,' said Mrs Metcalfe sarcastically, 'that you have some dark secret in your life, some great romance, eh?'

'What if I do?'

'No, my dear, that's too childish, there isn't much that gets past me.'

'Very well,' said Iris, 'if you prefer to think that . . .'

Iris left this sentence unfinished, and saw that she had disturbed her mother, who said, with eyebrows raised, 'I've always made a confidante of you, and I've naturally supposed that you tell me everything.'

'Don't let's talk about it any more. I've got a headache.'

'You want to be left alone with your secret, I suppose.'

'Yes.'

But Iris realised that her mother would never rest until she had found out for certain, either what the secret was, or that it did not exist. She foresaw an 'atmosphere' at dinner; a silence broken only by loud sipping of soup in the dining-room; pursed lips over knitting in the drawing-room after the meal.

'No,' she said, 'I haven't a secret romance. So you needn't worry about that.'

Mrs Metcalfe relaxed. 'Well, why the devil did you lead me to believe . . .? Oh, you're impossible! I can't say a few words in my own house without all this hullabaloo.'

'There wasn't any hullabaloo.'

'My dear, we're two lonely women, that's what we are, not as young as we were, and if we're going to quarrel when we're alone, God knows how we'll end up. Come on, my pet, kiss and make up.'

Iris kissed her coldly on the forehead. Mrs Metcalfe patted her shoulder, and chuckled.

'Well, all I can say is, thank God for my sense of humour. I don't know what I'd do without it. I've got a few chores to do before the shops shut, so I'll leave you with your headache. I'll be going to Smith's. What do you want out of the library?'

'See if they've got the latest Warwick Deeping.'

When Mrs Metcalfe had gone, Iris returned to the

window. She thought defiantly, 'There is something she doesn't know about. She doesn't know about the letter, and the grey-haired man. She doesn't know about that, and she never will.'

She saw her mother leave the house, carrying a leather shopping bag. Mrs Metcalfe moved slowly, waddling slightly as she walked. Some children, who had been playing on the common, paused in their game to watch her. When she started down Buckingham Road, one of them, a little boy wearing a big cap, with a button on the top of it, walked a few yards behind her, imitating her gait with exaggerated gestures, while the other children did not conceal their giggles. Iris could not bear to see her mother made ridiculous, and she moved away from the window.

Saturday

The town was so full on Saturday afternoon that the only place to have tea was at the café of the Elektra cinema. Its gold walls were decorated with pictures of film stars, all taken some time ago. From behind a door which led to the Circle inside the cinema the programme could be heard playing itself out fatalistically; it was the penultimate performance of the week.

The girl at the cash desk was reading a green Penguin book called *Mr Fortune, Please*. She was supposed to supply a loud radiogram beside her with records, for the amusement of the people taking tea at the café, but she had lazily adjusted it at Repeat, and an old recording of 'Rio Rita' played itself again and again, with a whining noise at the beginning. She found it easier to concentrate on her book to the accompaniment of one tune which she knew and liked, than to a disturbing variety which might distract her thoughts.

The six customers were served by an old waitress in a girlish uniform, who wore a green bow in her yellow hair. She brought the little girl and her governess, who had sat for a long time silent, a pot of tea and some assorted pastries. The child, whose name was Mary, wished that she were watching the film, having never seen real people on the screen, only Snow White and the Seven Dwarfs. A cat jumped on to the chair beside her, and she said affectedly and carefully to her governess, 'O! Look at the pretty pussy.'

Miss Hunt began to eat with a faraway look in her grey eyes. She had had a busy day shopping, and this moment was her first of relaxation. In ten minutes the crowded bus which she had to catch was going to leave from outside the cinema; she would really have liked to be watching the film herself, but she could not have taken her pupil. It was raining outside; Miss Hunt's purchases were heavy.

Two nuns, in their loose black clothes, with wicked spectacled faces, were also in the restaurant. They spoke to each other softly, and looked about them with sharp eyes. One was heard to say to the other in a high voice, '. . . it appears she went into the dining-room, ate the apple, and left the core on the side-board . . .' A man in a blue overall came through the curtained door from the cinema, and disappeared through another marked 'Private'.

A small soldier with very large eyes which gave him a sad appearance sat at a table, his heavy equipment beside him on the floor, eating the one-and-threepenny tea which he had ordered some time ago. This consisted of a pot of tea, beans on toast, and two slices of bread and margarine. He had been travelling all day, and still heard in his brain the bored voice of the girl who had announced the name of this station again and again through a megaphone as the train stopped. He was only in the town for an hour or two, and had that evening to continue his journey. Mary was staring at him with serious eyes, imagining herself giving up her seat to him in a railway carriage, because he was a soldier.

The soldier noticed at the next table to his a very tall girl; she wore no stockings, and the rain had made her ankles red. She tucked her hair delicately under her helmet-like hat with great strong hands which made the soldier imagine her capable of murder. Her face, too, had the hard, blurred look that one sees in newspaper photographs of murderesses at their trials; one imagined her covering it with a black sleeve to avoid the photographer's flare. Unconscious of what the soldier was thinking, but conscious of his presence, she took off her glasses which the steam from her tea had clouded, and with a sigh and a movement in her chair began to clean them with a strip of cloth provided for that purpose.

Miss Hunt took from her bag a letter from her brother, who was a missionary in Africa, and began to read it, after wiping round her pursed mouth with the handkerchief which she kept in her cuff. 'Mustn't read at table,' said Mary in a gay tone, but seeing that her pleasantry fell flat she adjusted her face to a serious expression and began to eat her éclair slowly with the oddly-shaped fork by her plate. Miss Hunt's brother had all the fascination for her of the unknown relation. That evening, when, tired and uncomfortable, she ate her supper of sodden cereals at the nursery table, Miss Hunt, she knew, would unscrew her fountain-pen, take the writing-pad mysteriously called 'Hieratica Bond' from the dresser drawer, and answer her brother's letter with compressed lips. The sound of a shriek came from the cinema, a maddening irritation to the little girl's curiosity, and the nuns left the room, having paid their bill at the cash desk, an imaginary crocodile of school-girls trooping behind them.

Somehow a conversation had arisen between the tall girl and the soldier; he was showing her his snapshots. 'This is my young lady,' he said, and she adjusted her glasses to look at a moon-faced, smiling girl, in a dress that reached to just above her ankles. 'I wanted her to have a Polyfoto, but it was too dear.' His sad eyes seemed to ask her to listen to him, because he had spoken to no one all day, and she leant forward on her sharp elbows with a smile on her face, while her fingers began to pull and pinch at her neck, and to lift her string of beads to her mouth, and to rub it nervously against her dry lips. The soldier then offered her a Player's

Weight, and after fiddling unsuccessfully for a time with his lighter, he lit their cigarettes. She smoked hers too fast, and half of it was soon a hard burning stretch of tobacco, not yet turned to ash.

Her tea finished, Mary opened and shut the small bag on her lap with gloved fingers. She had enjoyed her day in the drizzling town, avoiding the swirling gutters, spent in the huge draper's shop where the children were amused by someone dressed as Santa Claus and a Hornby train running furiously round and round a table, and in the crowded parlour of Miss Hunt's bearded friend who kept a school for typing and shorthand – the sound of typewriters in the next room, and the smell of the sweat of women, a smell which Miss Hunt knew well and accepted as part of her life. The child was sorry that the day was nearly over, for she looked upon it as a rare glimpse into the mysterious world inhabited by Miss Hunt and her kind – a world which was illustrated for Mary by the odd, old-fashioned advertisements which she sometimes saw on buses and at railway stations. Well-known phrases, such as 'Mazawattee Tea', 'Pullars of Perth', 'Peak Frean', seemed to have no meaning other than a secret one comprehensible only to Miss Hunt. She looked carefully at her governess who sat like an image in her blue tailor-made suit and white satin blouse; both were dreading the journey home in the bus. They knew from experience that they would be unable to sit down until almost at their country destination, when it was dark outside and every passenger but themselves had left the bus. They had that long stop to face at a village three miles from theirs where the moon shone on a white pool. Last of all there was the walk uphill from the bus stop to the house, Mary's stitch and Miss Hunt's headache solidified in the heavy Christmas parcels which they would be carrying. Mary knew that, as always after a tiring day, it would seem to her as she entered the house by the back way that she was seeing the familiar sight that she saw with dazzled eyes indoors under a different aspect, as the first impression of a place later to become well-known subtly differs from the one that is afterwards given and remembered.

Two women came into the café talking about the film.

'It's a dual role,' said one, 'she plays herself and her twin sister.'

'Yes, a psychological picture,' said the other.

Miss Hunt rose to pay her bill with a frown.

'It must be the end of the first house,' she said, but Mary could not think what she meant by this, and did not like to ask her.

As they left the room, the soldier went up to them with a parcel which Mary had left on her chair.

'You've forgotten this, Missy.' She said, 'O, thank you,' with a coy expression, and followed her governess who had not seen this incident.

In the Ladies' Cloakroom Miss Hunt spat on her handkerchief and rubbed it hard against her pupil's cheek, after tying Mary's sou'wester under her chin with a painful jerk. While she was doing this, the tall woman came in, and Miss Hunt bustled out, as though ashamed, or unwilling to let the little girl see this intruder. Alone in the cloakroom, the woman took off her hat and shook her hair away from her face. After washing her hands vigorously with the small strip of soap that remained, she looked with interest into the mirror above the basin. Beneath the glazed windows of the lavatory the six o'clock bus left with Miss Hunt and her parcels swaying inside it; the news began on the wireless in the restaurant, and in the cinema the organist, a fat little man in evening dress, spun up from underground in a mauve spotlight and bowed to the audience who clapped kindly. He then began to play old tunes whose words were projected on to the screen so that the audience could sing them. The girl looked at her own face in the glass because she had forgotten what she looked like; and she felt that she still did not know, that the reflection in the mirror had as little meaning to her as her own name when too often repeated. She went back to the café, and was surprised to find the soldier still there.

'It's nearly time for my train,' he said. 'Would you care to walk with me to the station?'

He was suddenly sorry to leave this town which had at first seemed so dreary.

They left the café together.

The Visitor

'Adam and Eve and Pinchme went down to the river to bathe; if Adam and Eve were drowned, who do you think was saved?'

'Pinchmenot!' shouted Mary.

'If frozen water's iced water, what is frozen ink?' Susan asked patiently.

'I stink,' said Mary, and then covered her face with her hands while her friend danced round her, screaming with triumph.

'Don't make so much noise,' called Miss Hunt, who was sitting on a garden seat a short way off, her work basket beside her. She was cutting out some brown paper patterns, with the ultimate aim of providing herself with a dress for the following summer much like the one she was now wearing. Its sleeves came to just above her elbows, its skirt to just below her knees; its neck was V-shaped, displaying a patch of her sun-burnt, freckled skin. Her hands busy with the scissors, Miss Hunt lifted her gentle eyes to watch the little girls playing on the sunny lawn at the back of the house.

Susan's fair hair had been cut short, and only covered half of her ears, so that the back of her neck had a naked look. Her stout body was shrouded in a tunic-like dress too big for her; her small eyes were hidden by steel-rimmed glasses, respectful consideration of which prevented her games with Mary from becoming too rough. Susan's shrill voice irritated Miss Hunt, who liked her least of her pupil's friends, and who was usually in a bad humour when Susan had been asked to tea.

Mary's knickers were made of the same material as her dress. Her thick, well-brushed hair hung below her shoulders; her large serious eyes implied a criticism of everything they saw. She was easily shocked, easily surprised, and easily impressed. She now stood on her hands, and for the fascinating moment before she fell over saw the house and her governess upside down.

Miss Hunt hurried towards her. 'Now you've ruined that frock,' she said.

Mary rose from the ground with dignity, staring with reproving eyes at the little patch of green which remained on her skirt. Susan, who knew that the whole performance had been for her benefit, watched in silence.

'It will soon come off,' said Mary.

At this moment a servant came out of the house and said to Miss Hunt with pointed lack of ceremony, 'Miss Mary's wanted in the drawing-room.'

'Run along then,' said Miss Hunt. 'You would choose that moment to fall over, wouldn't you? O dear, O dear, O dear.'

When Mary had followed the maid indoors, Susan sat on the garden seat, but all her attempts at conversation were snubbed by the governess's monosyllabic replies.

Mary knew that her mother had a visitor in the drawing-room; she had seen him arrive, in uniform and on a motor-bicycle, from the nursery window. She knocked with confidence at the door.

'Come in, darling,' called Mrs Stone.

Mary waited for a few seconds, and then opened the door a short way and squeezed through it. She shut it carefully, and remained with her hands on the knob.

'Come and say how-do-you-do, darling. You mustn't be shy,' said Mrs Stone in a voice which she took care to make natural. She was a pretty woman of thirty; her hair was arranged in curls at the top of her head. She smiled at her guest, an officer, who was sitting in a low chair with a whisky and soda on the ground beside him.

'Hullo, Mary,' he said.

Mary came slowly over to him and shook his hand, staring at him fascinated. He was embarrassed by her stare, and tried to make a joke of it by holding her hand for an unnecessarily long time.

'Come and sit by me on the sofa,' said Mrs Stone.

Mary obeyed, still staring at her mother's friend.

'Tell Tim what you've been doing today.'

All Mary's poise now left her. Suddenly shy, she wriggled her shoulders and squirmed on the sofa, digging her chin into her neck but still looking solemnly at Tim.

'You've got a little friend to tea, haven't you?'

'Yes,' said Mary in a low voice, overcoming a longing to turn her back on both the others and hide her face in the sofa.

'I know a trick which will make you laugh,' said the young man. He took an enormous white handkerchief from his pocket and wound it round his hand, making it look like some animal.

'I can do that,' said Mary in a voice which her acute and involuntary shyness filled with meaning.

'I bet you can't,' said Tim. 'Come over here and do it then.'

Her timing as subtle as an actress's, Mary went up to him and snatched the handkerchief from him.

'Don't stare at poor Tim so, darling,' said Mrs Stone. They watched the child in silence while she fumbled slowly with the handkerchief, breathing loudly. At last she threw it on the ground. 'I can't do it,' she said, smiling.

'Don't you like that handkerchief?' asked the man.

'Silly old handkerchief.'

Tim put his arm round Mary's waist and lifted her on to the arm of his chair.

'Don't encourage her to be silly,' said Mrs Stone.

'Won't you tell me what you've been doing today?' asked the young man, looking up at Mary's face.

She could no longer look at his, but without answering stared down at his chest, and began to fiddle with a button on his tunic.

'That button's very bright, isn't it?' he said. She continued to finger it, slowly smiling. 'I bet you couldn't polish it so bright.' She again wriggled her shoulders, and began to swing her legs, unfortunately knocking over his whisky and soda with her foot.

'Here, steady on,' said Tim, while Mrs Stone said crossly, 'O, look what you've done.'

'O,' said Mary, and covered her face with her hands.

'It doesn't matter, darling,' said her mother quickly, 'the glass isn't broken.'

Tim wiped up the spilt drink with his large handkerchief.

Mary pressed her hands hard against her face to stop herself from crying with shame.

'Give yourself another drink, Tim,' said Mrs Stone. 'Perhaps you'd better go back to Miss Hunt now, darling.'

'Goodbye, Mary,' said Tim, syphoning soda water into his glass. 'Don't go kicking over anything else now.' He clumsily tapped her under the chin.

'Goodbye,' said Mary.

She went out of the room looking at the ground, her hands behind her back, kicking out her feet in a careless way. She waited for a short time silently in the hall, hoping to overhear her mother or the officer say something about her. She had sometimes heard Mrs Stone say to a guest, 'Isn't she sweet?' after one of these short visits. She now heard them talk of other things, however, so she walked back thoughtfully to Susan and Miss Hunt.

Going to School

James and Mary Stone were to start school on the same day. Mary, who was nine years old, was going to a place called Field House, which was only twenty miles from her home; James, aged eight, to a well-known preparatory school fifty miles away. At first it had been arranged that Mr Stone should drive James here, and perhaps have a chat with Captain Jennings, the headmaster, before he left, while Mary and her mother travelled by train to the girls' school, where Mrs Stone might have a word with Matron; but James had cried so loudly, and had threatened so convincingly to throw himself from the window of the lavatory in which he had locked himself unless *he* was accompanied by his mother, that the plan had been reversed. So now Mr Stone and Mary sat opposite each other, alone in a dirty railway carriage with old photographs of bathers on the walls and thick china mugs containing brown remnants of tea under the seats. The train had no corridor, and stopped at even the smallest stations on their journey; sometimes it stopped in open country, for no reason at all. Mary was more assured than her father, who had dressed smartly for the occasion; he wore a dark suit, an Old Harrovian tie and a black Homburg hat. Mary wore a coat and skirt from Debenham and Freebody's and a hat to match pulled well down over her thick hair. She carried a bag which contained a comb, a mirror, and half a crown. She smiled politely at her father all the time, but he saw that she was nervous when she began to fidget, and to trace a profile on the misted window-pane beside her.

'I shouldn't do that, Mary, it's rather dirty.'

'Why?' she asked with curious eyes; then noticed that the finger of her woollen glove was stained. She effaced the drawing with her sleeve, and sat silent, thinking about her friend, Susan. They had had an emotional parting scene that morning, and had exchanged locks of hair. Susan was to go to another school, one exclusively for clergymen's daughters. Mary had slipped the thin, straw-coloured, straight bit of her friend's hair, tied by a blue ribbon, into her sponge bag which was now in the suitcase on the rack above her head. Mary sighed, and said for the second time, 'I wonder how Mummy and James are.'

'Yes, I wonder,' said her father. He lit a cigarette, removed a piece of tobacco from his lip, and looked out of the window, whistling softly. Both were conscious of something unsatisfactory about this journey; perhaps it was the fact that all the other girls were arriving on a later train from Paddington, and Mary knew that she would have to wait an hour at the station before driving with them to the school in a special charabanc. As these girls left the train, Mr Stone was to board it, and thus be transported back to his home station.

'Perhaps,' said Mary, 'it would be nice if I did take an Extra.'

'I thought you'd decided against it.'

'I might wait and see if all the other girls do.'

'Which would it be, Mary? Painting, music or dancing?'

She thought for a moment, then said, 'Dancing.'

'You'll only be able to dance with the other girls, you know.'

'Yes, of course. There won't be any boys at school.'

'But won't that be poor fun?'

'No, Father.' She laughed, and said conversationally, 'I

wonder if all the other girls will be bigger than me? Miss Hunt used to tell me I was tiny for my age. Poor Miss Hunt, she was very sad to go away.'

'I expect there will be some your size,' said Mr Stone, remembering the day when the governess had left sobbing in a taxi, and Mary, after one hour of depression, had been surprisingly 'good about it'.

'I wonder if the mistresses are decent. Miss Gough sounded awfully sweet on the phone. I wonder if I shall have a friend.'

'Won't it be fun when your best friend comes to stay with us in the hols?' said Mr Stone cleverly.

A new expression came to Mary's face. 'Yes, won't it? And won't it be fun when my report comes?'

'And mind it's a good one, my girl.'

Mary squirmed in her seat. 'Buck up, old train,' she said.

When they arrived, they found the station small and deserted, built two miles from the town at the end of a lane. As the train left them standing on the platform with Mary's trunk and suitcase, they noticed two big piles of luggage, one at each end of the station. They reverently examined the labels on one pile; the girls of Field House must have sent their trunks on in advance, all instinctively doing the same, and apparently the right thing. Mary read out the names on the labels in an awed voice.

'Muriel Clive, Heather Poole, Hazel Poole – they must be sisters – Shirley Hollis, Felicity Thorpe-Nicholson, crumbs, what a name!'

The other pile belonged to Greengates, a rival school, hated by Field House. 'They come back tomorrow, but they broke up a week after we did,' said Mary, who had this knowledge from a mysterious source and was speaking as though already of the school. A charabanc with 'Private' written on the front, empty but for the driver, jogged up the lane and stopped outside the station. The driver got out and stretched himself. Mary discovered a slot-machine under an advertisement for Brylcreem, and tried to work it with a penny borrowed from her father.

'O blow, it's bust,' she said, 'and I would so so like a Mintip.'

It was cold on the platform, and the girl clapped her hands and shook them up and down, trying to get warm. Mr Stone began to feel apprehensive, at the same time longing for and dreading the arrival of the train with the other girls on it. He was filled with affection for Mary, who ran up and down the roofless bridge over the line, living entirely for the moment. He thought sympathetically of his wife, who was probably having a difficult time with James, and said to himself with pride, 'It's going very well. We get on together, Mary and I.'

They went for a walk in the fields – for there was nowhere to have tea – and picked blackberries from the hedges. Later, the driver of the charabanc called to them, 'She's signalled.' Mr Stone glanced nervously at Mary, who took hold of his hand, and then immediately let it go. She had a concentrated expression on her face; her eyes stared as though just not weeping; she was sucking her under-lip, and all the time moving from one foot to the other. Her father was thinking, 'It will soon be over now'; he was thinking of himself, not of her. The train came into the station.

Several very tall girls stepped out, all surprisingly mature; one, Mr Stone noticed, was almost attractive. They fussed shrilly over their smart suitcases; many had brought golf clubs. A small woman, evidently a mistress, came up to Mary, glanced at Mr Stone, and told Mary, 'You must be Mary Stone.'

A girl with long fair plaits and big breasts who was passing said, 'That's the new bug.'

Mary grasped the mistress's hand; her father had never before seen her so ill at ease. She looked much smaller than the other girls, and altogether different.

The mistress said, 'Stay with me, dear,' and hurried off to talk to the driver.

Mr Stone climbed into the train, which gave no sign of leaving. He felt like an unwanted guest at a picnic; the girls ignored him, but Mary attracted some casual attention as she dumbly followed the mistress. The others talked to each other in a bullying way. 'O, don't be flabby!' they said, or 'O, don't be mouldy!' Mr Stone wondered if Mary would return after thirteen weeks using these unpleasant expressions.

The guard waved his flag. Mary said calmly to the mistress, 'Excuse me, please, I must say goodbye to my father.' She ran to the window of his carriage. 'Goodbye, darling,' he said, leaning out, 'the best of luck. Write and tell us how you get on. Be brave.' She could only look at him with agony suddenly in her eyes. She was frightened. He again said, with less conviction, 'Be brave.'

Mary seemed to want to fling herself into the carriage, into safety. The train began to leave the station with slow, silent jerks. Mr Stone wondered whether or not to kiss her; then decided that it might embarrass her. He saw her turn away with an angry face, and, listless and self-conscious, join the other girls who at first ignored her and then surrounded her with brutal curiosity as the train took him away.

Mrs Stone drove the grey Ford V8 through the flat country interlaced with tumbledown stone walls. Her son sat stiffly beside her, clutching his copy of *The Modern Boy* with clammy hands. His hair, cut short, jutted out in ridges; his eyes swam behind bent steel-rimmed spectacles; the straps of his knickerbockers hurt below his knees. Both he and his mother felt sick with dread. To whatever she said, he answered nervously, 'Yes, but . . .'

'Father and I are coming after three weeks. Captain Jennings said that was the earliest we could. Now, that isn't very long, is it, old boy?'

'Yes, but . . .' What he meant to say was, 'It is ages.'

Every now and then pretty Mrs Stone had to stop the car so that James could relieve himself behind a hedge. 'What will happen,' he said, suddenly desperate, as he climbed back into the warm car, 'if I want to do that in class?'

'I suppose you'll ask the master, and he'll let you go.'

'But suppose he won't let me?'

'Of course he will. Masters are quite kind, darling.'

'Father said they weren't.'

'Schools were different when he was a boy.' Mrs Stone was praying to God, 'Make it go off all right. Make him not cry.' But James was thinking, 'I wish the car would crash, and I was killed. No, not killed, but very badly hurt, and taken to hospital in an ambulance, and fussed over.' For the last few days, while his trunk was being packed and name-tapes being sewn on his clothes (his school number was 73, the lowest in the school), he had hoped to die before being delivered into the terrible unknown, and had several times thought of suicide; but he had always realised in time that there were left a few days, or hours in which the catastrophe for which he prayed might happen; an earthquake might swallow up the school, killing the Jenningses and all the masters.

'Look, there's an aerodrome,' said Mrs Stone. James would not look at it, but murmured, 'That means we must be nearly there.' An aeroplane flew low over their heads as they turned a corner, and saw the grey solid school-house standing beyond stretches of playing-fields with skeleton goal-posts and a wooden pavilion. This was James's last moment; thirteen weeks was for ever, too long to wait before resuming a life which, although not appreciated at the time, now seemed Heaven. His mother had told him often that the school was more like a private house than a school; he saw now that this was not true. It might have reminded other boys of their homes, but to James it was obviously an institution, for even at a distance it lacked the luxurious air of a hotel. He clasped his mother's tweed sleeve and said, 'Stop the car.'

'James,' she said sharply.

'Stop the car,' he said impatiently. The school had not been burnt to the ground as he had hoped; he was determined to go no nearer to it. 'I'm not going on,' he said, his voice shaking. He reached for the brake but Mrs Stone anticipated him, and the car stopped.

'Now, darling, you promised to be brave. Think how good Mary was, I'm sure she isn't making all this fuss.' Two cars passed them, driven by furred mothers and containing red-capped sons with round, beaming faces. Mrs Stone said desperately, 'Don't cry, James. For my sake.'

He was crying hopelessly, turned away from her. 'I'm not going. I can't bear it, I shall die.'

She whispered, 'Be a man. It's as bad for me as it is for you, darling, really it is. Here, use my hanky.'

He said, 'It's all *right* for you. You've at least got Father, but I shan't have anyone at all.'

'But everyone has to go to school.'

'I don't have to.'

'And you'll see me in three weeks.'

'I can't wait three weeks.' He said more calmly, 'You must come next Sunday.'

Mrs Stone remembered the headmaster's suspicious words: 'You know, we don't allow them to be taken out for the first three weeks. They must have time to settle down.

Parents are sometimes very unreasonable.' She said uncertainly, 'Will you go bravely if I promise?'

James turned towards her. 'You must swear,' he said, threateningly.

'I promise, darling.'

James shut his eyes and leant back, as he had done when at last persuaded to take the dentist's anaesthetic. His mother started the car again, feeling that by diplomacy she had saved her life. They turned up the drive, shaken by emotion and left almost comatose.

The house *did* have a deceptive appearance of being like any other house; but behind this façade, in which the Jenningses themselves lived, the school buildings were as drab as a prison. The boys and their parents were received in comfortable surroundings, but the children never saw these again; and after those first three weeks, so subtly calculated by Captain Jennings, hypnotised by school life they could only tell relieved mothers and proud fathers that they had enjoyed themselves. They came back for the holidays changed; their masters, impelled by an instinctive hatred of home and parents, had alienated them for ever from their natural backgrounds. This was to happen to James, but not until after weeks of suffering.

Parents and children were leaving their grand cars as though arriving at a party. The Jenningses stood on the porch; the Captain in plus-fours, with thick black eyebrows and moustache; his wife with frizzy fair hair, no eyebrows and face and hands heavily powdered. Near them a master, dressed in a baggy grey flannel suit, was moving about, smiling nervously. This was Mr Clarke, who had been shell-shocked in 1915 and made uneasy, effeminate gestures with his arms.

'How beautifully punctual you are, Mrs Stone,' said Mrs Jennings, laughing. They had met at race meetings. She patted James's head as he stood with his feet apart, red in the face and furious. 'Would you like to talk to Matron about James – or Stone as I ought to say now, oughtn't I? Some boys take Glucose, or Radio-Malt or things.'

'No, thank you, I don't think James needs anything.'

'I see you are going to be an ideal parent,' said Captain Jennings, jovially, but with a hint at menace, as though saying, 'Don't you dare be a fussy mother.' He hit James's round shoulders. 'Well, Stone, have you ever played football?'

Appalled at her son's silence, Mrs Stone heard herself say, 'Yes, he has played rugger with friends, haven't you?'

'Splendid,' said Captain Jennings, and turned away. His wife said, 'We play soccer here, but he'll soon learn.'

Other parents were leaving now, after kissing their children in a jolly way. Mr Clarke called out in a strange, high voice, 'Follow me, boys!'

'He'd better go to tea now,' said Mrs Jennings. 'Do you want to see the dormitories?' She whispered, 'It's wiser to leave them as soon as you can,' making an understanding grimace.

James said, 'I've had tea.'

'Run along, darling,' said Mrs Stone, 'I must go now if I want to be home before dark.' She bent to kiss him, but he did not kiss her, just saying loudly, 'Remember. Sunday.' Mrs Jennings, watching, pretended not to have heard this and said, 'The cat has got his tongue. I should follow the others, dear.'

James went off, skipping with false nonchalance, and disappeared round the corner of the house with Mr Clarke and some chattering boys who were also hiding their apprehension by an assumed assurance. Two of them were fighting each other behind the master's back, and one cried out 'Pax!' in a touchingly childish voice.

Mrs Stone did not watch him go. As she climbed into her car, dreading the lonely journey home, Captain Jennings came up to her, and said carelessly, 'You know our rule about three weeks, Mrs Stone?' She felt that he resented her being a woman and a mother, and began, 'I was just going to ask you if . . .' Before she could finish he said firmly, but pleasantly, 'We can never alter it, you know.'

'But if he is ill?'

'We have a sickroom, and the Matron is a trained nurse.'

She remembered, on her first visit to the school, a glimpse of the sickroom and clean, pyjamaed boys sitting up and drawing in bed.

'I see,' she said.

She could think of no more to say, and decided to consult her husband about her promise to James. She wondered sadly what her child was doing, how he was feeling, whether or not he could see her as she drove away from some strange window.

That evening, the house seemed unnaturally quiet. 'It's lonely without them, isn't it?' she said to her husband at dinner.

'I suppose we'll get used to it in time. Mary was marvellously plucky.'

'James was very upset, but I think he was all right when I left him.'

'Poor little chap. Did you speak to Captain Jennings?'

'Yes, he seemed quite nice.'

'I didn't see Miss Gough, thank God. These women terrify me.'

They were silent. Mr Stone was thinking, 'This is what it will be like when they are grown up, and have left home.' Mrs Stone was thinking of what James had said: 'You at least have Father, but I shan't have anyone at all.'

The Facts of Life

Through the big bow window of Captain Jennings's study he could see the skeleton goal-posts on the football field deserted now in summer, and beyond them the flimsy bungalow which two of the junior masters shared. Low grey stone walls intersected the flat country; not far off there were pine trees. When he turned from the window back into the room, it seemed to him that the green leather on the chairs was sweating in the heat, that the backs of his books on the shelves were melting, and that Vermeer's 'Girl with Earring', reproduced over his mantelpiece, had turned paler and drooped in her frame more than usual. It was the last day of term. Captain Jennings placed one large foot on his desk; then leant his elbow on his knee and his chin on his hand, while his other hand plunged and fidgeted in the pocket of his grey flannel trousers.

He was always embarrassed by these end-of-term talks with the leaving boys. All had gone well so far this afternoon; there now remained one more boy to see. Newton had not fitted in at Greenfields. Never bullied, he had at the same time never been popular with master or boy; indifferent both at games and work, he was yet by no means a dud; from the age of nine his unattractive face had suggested to Captain Jennings a wizened and disturbing sophistication unsuitable in a boy and impossible exactly to define. Captain Jennings's lips were moving beneath his thick black moustache in an automatic rehearsal of the scene he was about to act with Newton. When he heard a feeble knock on his door, he said 'Come in' rather louder and more abruptly than had been his intention.

Newton slid into the room, and as had done the other boys this afternoon, took an unnecessarily long time shutting the door behind him. He finally turned a blank, pallid face towards the master, and stood motionless, to attention, with an evident desire to impress which had an irritating effect.

'Oh, er, take a pew, old boy,' muttered Captain Jennings.

'Thank you, sir.' Newton sat down slowly.

'I'd like to have a little chat with you before we say goodbye tomorrow. Man to man, you understand, nothing in the nature of a lecture.'

'Yes, sir.'

The boy seemed bored. Captain Jennings went on, putting expression into his words, but not enough to make them sound spontaneous.

'This is always rather a sad occasion – at any rate Mrs Jennings and myself find it so – but of course for you it is a milestone in your life. Probably the first important one. How well I remember the last day at my own prepper!' He laughed. 'I had one of those funny lumps in the throat, you know the sort, that get you here.' Captain Jennings touched his collar. 'Silly, but there it was. Couldn't help it.'

'Yes, sir.'

'Nothing to be ashamed of, after all.'

'No, sir.'

'I've got a feeling – mind you I may be wrong – but I've a feeling that, taken all in all, you've been fairly happy here at Greenfields?'

'Oh, yes, sir.'

'Yes.' Captain Jennings's manner now changed; perhaps he was perplexed by Newton's over-phlegmatic replies. He continued gruffly: 'I know there is an idea going about the school that these last talks I have with the leaving boys are nothing but pi-jaws about sex. I shouldn't like you to run away with that idea. The fact is, once you chaps have reached this, er, stage in your life, I feel you need a few words of friendly advice. Of course you don't have to take it if you don't want to. I don't know how much you discuss with your own people – that's none of my business. You must realise that your life up till now has been rather, well, sheltered. I mean you've had a lot done for you here at Greenfields, and if you've made any little mistakes, they won't have had any serious consequences. But once you get to your public school, you'll be in a position to make or mar your whole future life yourself. Before I send you out into the world, as it were, there are a few little points I'd like to clear up with you. Do you compree so far?'

'Yes, sir.' Newton turned his attention from the window back to the schoolmaster.

'Now I'm sure you've got a few questions you'd like to ask me, Newton. Anything that's puzzled you, or bothered you in any way.'

'No, sir, I don't think so.'

'You don't have to feel embarrassed with me, you know. I mean, about sex, and all that rot.' There was a silence. 'I know, among fellows your age,' continued Captain Jennings, 'there's a good deal of rather futile giggling on that subject, smutty little jokes, and so on. Oh, I don't mean this personally, Newton; I've no idea what you've been told at home, and it's none of my business. But I am very keen to impress upon you that that particular attitude is really rather silly and childish. I know love sometimes seems awfully sloppy – at the cinema, for instance – often want to be sick myself when I go to the pictures. Nobody hates sentimentality more than I do. But I want you to realise, all ragging apart, that love can, and should, be a wonderful thing, a beautiful thing.'

'Yes, sir.'

Captain Jennings did not look at the boy; he seemed now to be talking to himself.

'The great thing is to look upon it in a healthy way. That is the key word – health. As long as you keep fit, you see things in their true proportion. I know some aspects of life can be pretty foul, but there's no reason you should ever have to bother your head over that, as long as you keep a healthy mind in a healthy body. I forget whether you have a sister, Newton?'

'No, sir, I haven't.'

'Well, we all have mothers, and if we want to be worthy of the name of gentlemen, we should think of women, and the love of man for woman, with the deepest respect.'

'Yes, sir.'

Captain Jennings coughed loudly, and the boy looked away self-consciously.

'When you get to your public school – Radley, isn't it? – there are a few things I want you to bear in mind. Choose your friends among the boys of your own age – there's bound to be some good fellows among them. If an older boy tries to pal up with you, don't pay any attention. And of course, when you get older yourself, you won't want to run around with any of the younger fellows. Oh, and it's always better that you don't make friends outside your own house. You must remember that a public school is said to be the world in miniature. You'll probably come into contact with a certain amount of tommy-rot while you're there, but you must remember that some boys won't have had your advantages, and you must pity them without having anything to do with them. Don't ever be afraid of sneaking if you stumble across anything you know to be wrong. You know that thing that goes, "I am the captain of my fate, the something of my soul" or something? Kipling, wasn't it, or one of those johnnies? I always think it's rather appropriate.'

'Yes, sir.'

'Yes.' There was another silence. Captain Jennings frowned down at his feet; Newton fidgeted in his chair, an expression of polite interest on his face. The master suddenly went on: 'I don't know what your people have planned for you later on, but it's possible that you'll go to the 'Varsity, as I did myself. You may find that a certain type of older woman will try to get hold of you. You don't want to get involved with anything like that.'

'No, sir.'

Captain Jennings looked at Newton, as if taking him in for the first time. The boy looked young for his thirteen years. 'Mind you, it's early days yet to be thinking of anything like that. But when the time comes, remember my advice, Newton; steer clear of older women. I don't want to depress you. After all, we're all part of Nature, when you come to think of it, and Nature can have her beautiful side. I mean, it's really pretty marvellous to think of a tree growing, and flowers, and even animals . . .' Captain Jennings's voice died away, as it met no response in his pupil. He began again: 'If you're lucky, when you've passed twenty, you'll meet a young lady in your own set, of about your own age, just as I met Mrs Jennings . . . And then, when you're in a position to think about getting married – but no doubt I've said enough.'

'Yes, sir.'

'You've got plenty of good times ahead of you yet. Games, comradeship . . . Certain there's nothing further you want to ask me?'

'I think that's all, sir.'

'Capital, capital.' Captain Jennings held out his hand. 'Goodbye, Newton, and Godspeed. Enjoy the holidays.'

'Thank you very much, sir. I hope you do too.'

'And drop me a line now and again. We'll send on the mag. Keep in touch, you know. We shall always be interested to hear of your doings. Goodbye, old boy.'

'Goodbye, sir.' Newton slipped his hand from the master's grip, and walked out of the study with the air of performing a difficult feat.

Captain Jennings stood still for some minutes, and then he too left the room. Instead of turning right, as the boy had done, down the dim passage that led to the classrooms, he swung open the green baize door to the left of his study. At once he was in a different atmosphere; here in the private part of the house his wife ruled, as he did in the bleak boys' quarters. The hall, a misleading façade designed to give parents the impression that they were leaving their sons in a home-from-home, was bright and fussy; prints were thick on the pale yellow walls, polish gleamed on the parquet. The drawing-room (into which no boy ever penetrated) was today full of flowers; the predominant colours here were pink, mauve and oyster-grey, and the room gave an impression of consisting entirely of satin. Captain Jennings found his wife curled up on a sofa, surrounded by tasselled cushions, reading the *Tatler*, and occasionally helping herself to a marshmallow from a box at her elbow.

Marjorie Jennings wore neither lipstick nor rouge, but her face was covered by thick powder, beneath which her lips thinned and her eyebrows disappeared altogether. Her hands were powdered too, while her frizzy pale hair looked as if it might have been. She smelt strongly of this powder, traces of which she often left behind her on chairs and sofas – a trail of dust. She smiled at him her understanding smile.

'Tired, Porker darling?'

He turned his back to the empty grate, stretching his legs as though he were warming them. 'Nearly finished.'

'I know. And then the nicest holidays of the year. I've written off to Keith Prowse for seats for Leslie Henson.'

This remark of his wife's immediately put Captain Jennings in a better temper. He suddenly longed for the delights of the summer holidays as intensely as any of his pupils. Matinees, race-meetings, garden-parties, picnics . . .

'Are we changing tonight?' asked Marjorie.

'I think so. I asked Fairman to dinner, and I expect he'll put on a black tie. He's made an awfully good start this term, you know. The boys respect him.'

'He did well in the war.'

'Yes, but that's not it. Look at Banks. Wonderful war record, but can't do a thing with his class. All over the shop, all over the shop.'

'We must have a talk about Matron.'

'Yes, darling, but later, later.' He went towards his wife and patted her hand. 'Better see how they're getting on at the nets. I'll see you at prayers.' Marjorie smiled at him again, and then reopened the *Tatler* as he left her.

As Captain Jennings walked in the sun to the cricket field, where Mr Banks was taking fielding practice, he smiled to himself; he had remembered another summer, nearly twenty years ago. He was in his second year at Oxford; Marjorie had been brought to tea in his rooms by her brother, another undergraduate. They had soon discovered that they shared the same ideas on many subjects . . . That night they had met again at a college dance; they found that they liked the same tunes. The next day he had taken her on the river, and they had played the gramophone. What was the name of that song they had both liked so much? He still had the record somewhere. Just by whistling it softly to himself, he could bring back the smell and texture of those days.

As he reached the nets, Captain Jennings remembered

the words, and the boys paused in their play, surprised to
hear the master suddenly sing out, loud and true,

> You're the cream in my coffee,
> You're the salt in my stew.
> You will always be
> My necessity,
> I'd be lost without you.

Sunday

Doris stood in her slip in her attic room before the small mirror dabbing Odorono on her armpits with a red brush. Too impatient to wait for it to dry, she tugged over her head a cotton dress and then pulled it down over her body catching her nose in the neck of the dress which wrinkled over her hips and stretched tight across her breasts. Her slip still showed beneath so she adjusted it clumsily at the shoulder-straps with two golden safety pins which she had been holding in her dry lips. She combed out her frizzy orange hair so that it stuck out in a solid mass behind her head like a veil in the wind, and then she squeezed her broad feet into a pair of high strapless shoes, of a wine colour to go with her dress. She had fat hairless legs and arms, but a slight red down could be seen from below on her upper lip. Her pig eyes looked lost without their glasses which she wore as seldom as possible. She felt in her bag to see that all its contents were safe; a white square inch of handkerchief, a flapjack with her lover's powdered photograph over the mirror, a ten shilling note four times folded and a crumpled Penguin book, as yet unread.

Red-faced Daphne awaited her in the porch, asleep in her perambulator. The muscles of her white limbs bulging with the strain the maid pushed the child up the dusty hill, closed and deserted on Sunday afternoon, and Daphne opened her eyes to look complacently at Doris's big face on which the sweat began to clot the yellow powder. Doris saw her auntie in brown as always at the window over the bookshop and lank-haired Muriel who worked there with her boy, a rating. 'Going to the pictures tonight?' 'Not on a day like this, it would be a crime.'

A lorryload of whistling soldiers passed slowly and Doris thought, that's a nice feller, the young one. She looked the other way as she passed the place where she knew was chalked on a red brick wall a vulgar drawing of Old Man Hitler, and by it had been for a long time the slogan Mosley Will Win, now methodically crossed out but not erased. Doris began to whistle, her mouth pursed to a mauve button, and thought, now what's that I'm whistling, it's been on my brain since Friday, and, silly, I can't call to mind its name. If I forget about it it will come to me suddenly, in the night or while I'm working, the name of it.

Daphne agitated her wrinkled arms in a worried and impotent way but Doris, who disliked her, took no notice. They reached the common high above the town and Doris sat on an empty seat and pushed the perambulator slowly up and down before her with her hand, so that the brown fringed hood hid Daphne from her sight. Behind her small boys and girls played cricket on the grass; a shock-haired schoolmaster headed a troop of red-capped boys out on a walk, shouting to them in a high voice now and then. Doris looked down the road at the town beneath her; she saw the house of her employers alone and squat by the black canal which crossed the town, and near it the yellow silent houseboat moored to the path by the lock. From where she sat the railway station was like a toy sold in the shops before the war with Hornby trains. It was a little way out of the town and now a short train shunted slowly backwards and forwards, sending out white smoke to evaporate in the fields and the cemetery near by. For ten minutes Doris thought about nothing.

Her brain said to her, Here comes Fred. He wore a bright

blue suit and was whistling, that tune her brain had been singing since Friday so now she said to herself, of course, The Whistler's Mother-in-Law.

'Hullo, Fred.'

This was not her day off, Wednesday, so her manner was strained. She made room for him on the seat uneasily because she did not want to make herself common like Muriel, on the common. She laughed at her private pun.

Silent Fred and she looked together now at the town, and her hand left the perambulator to rest in his. They noticed the gasworks in the slums of the town where they sometimes walked on her day off. Thinking of this she remembered girls in shabby dresses of bright colours too big for them who played complicated games with balls on the narrow pavements and did not make room for them to pass. A madwoman had croaked at them from an open doorway.

Fred's hair was shaved at the back as if he were in the Forces. Sometimes Doris wished that he was, but she knew that she had a lot to be grateful for. As he lived in the same town he had never had occasion to write her a letter, which she would have enjoyed in some ways more than his company; she thought of the letters girls had shown her written in blue ink on lined YMCA notepaper.

Fred worked in a bank and was not in the army because of his weak chest. He had a kind face with a worried expression, broad hips and small hands and feet. Doris's flashy way of dressing and painting seemed to bid for a more exciting fellow, but she was so ugly that she could be content with Fred. To him her frizzy hair, small eyes and tight white smile were pretty. Her hand which clasped his was threaded with soapy white lines, marks left by continual washing-up. It smelled of soap and her close-cut nails were dirty. Fred's hand was clean and manicured, and on one hairy finger he wore a ring. His creased shiny black shoes were no bigger than Doris's beside them, resting on the grass as though still in the shop beneath her naked blue-veined legs.

A child ran under the seat on which they were sitting and then away, frightened. Doris was thirsty. Daphne grimaced in her perambulator and howled for a time with desperate choking sobs. Fred and Doris sat together all the afternoon, their hips touching and her hand in Fred's on his crumpled blue serge lap.

Later the inhabitants of the town left their houses after resting, all at the same time, and climbed the hill sweating and gasping to queue outside the cinema on the common which opened late because it was Sunday. They wanted to escape from the heat outside into the stuffy, more restful atmosphere of the cinema where they could rest on velvet seats and stare wide-eyed at a flickering screen instead of with screwed-up eyes at dazzling colour and haze.

A party of girls in the ATS came laughing up the hill singing 'Bless 'Em All', led by a small stout woman with a pretty face powdered brown who sang in a loud high voice. They jerked their thumbs at passing cars but the cars ignored them, passing them with insulting acceleration while the small woman paused in her song to shout abuse at the drivers. A car did at last stop for them in front of the seat where Fred and Doris sat. Its driver, a bald man, said 'I've only room for four.' There were six girls.

'You go on, Titch,' they all said to the small one who was evidently a favourite.

'You get in, girls,' she answered. 'Me and my friend'll wait for the next one.'

'Buck up,' said the driver, who was wasting his petrol. Four climbed into the car and drove off in lower spirits leaving behind Titch and her friend who was tall and had a big pale face and shingled hair. The friend caught sight of Daphne.

'O, isn't he a duck?' she said. 'Come over here, Titch, isn't he a duck?' She looked at Fred. 'And isn't he like his dad too?'

Titch crossed the road and looked inside the perambulator. 'It's a girl,' said Doris with a consciously sweet expression and a slight frown.

'I bet you're ever so proud of her. What's her name?'

'Daphne.'

Daphne stared at them placidly. The two women looked at her for a time in admiring silence, and then Titch said, 'Come on, Lofty, we must be on our way.' They walked off with swinging strides like men.

'They thought she was our little girl,' said Doris after a moment's silence.

'Perhaps we will have a kid some day,' said Fred. 'When we're married.'

'O, don't be wet,' said Doris uncomfortably.

A dark aeroplane passed low over their heads, and on the ground its shadow moved quickly over the common. In the town Doris's auntie walked slowly with some other women to the evening service in the church opposite the town hall, outside which there was a notice advertising a dance on Wednesday, Alberto and his Mexican Mandoliers. A slight breeze caught the hood of Daphne's perambulator like a sail, and it began to roll down the hill unguided, with Doris's bag and the child in it as placid as before. Doris screamed, 'O, the pram,' and dumb Fred ran after it, his red tie flapping over his shoulder while Doris stumbled behind him. They ran some way down the hill after the pram, which moved madly, faster and faster until finally Fred caught up with it and stopped its progress, and Fred and Doris looked at each other panting and sweating, horrified at their adventure. Doris began to giggle guiltily and Daphne to bellow, realising late that something unusual had happened to her.

That evening Doris changed into a dark green dress and

stuck a white cap on her head. The sun shone through the laurel-shaded windows of the dining-room on the pale faces of Daphne's mother, Mrs Hollis, and Mrs Hollis's mother, Mrs Redman. With flushed face and suspended breath Doris removed the dirty plates from under their greedy mouths. They ignored her creaking shoes and the rustle of her dress when it stretched under her arms. Mrs Hollis ate her soup, cold meat and beetroot, and fruit salad with her mouth open and when she spoke her mother saw the food as a white mass behind her teeth. Mrs Redman was a large woman of slow movements. She ate with compressed lips and dared not speak for fear of betraying the wind in her voice. A fat black spaniel sat under the table, old and dying. There were yellow stains on the ceiling; the house was damp, as it was on the canal. Mrs Hollis said:

'Molly Homes heard from Cecil again last week, Mother, did I tell you? And her brother has been mentioned in despatches, they think. Remind me tomorrow to take Hester to the vet. Doris, has Hester had her dinner?'

'Yes.'

Mrs Hollis chuckled to herself. 'Sybil's expecting hers next month. Well, I hope it will be all right. It's the third time she's tried.'

Mrs Redman lifted her eyebrows in a silent question and her daughter formed answering words with her mouth without uttering them. '*Pas devant*,' she said, and Mrs Redman nodded wisely.

Mrs Hollis had tied up her hair neatly with a blue chiffon scarf and painted brown stockings on her legs. She touched her ear-rings in a distracted way, crossed her legs and lit a cigarette which she took from a pocket over her breast, screwing up her eyes as she did so and blowing the smoke out of her mouth and upwards by putting her lower lip outside her upper lip. This did not suit her as her teeth protruded slightly. She said:

'I went up to speak to one of the Italian prisoners working at Chapman's and the guard came up and said I wasn't allowed to. They seemed quite civil fellows. The Eyeteyes. I saw a little winter frock in Mason's window might do for Shirley. It was rather a pet, dear, but I should say worth the money.'

She yawned widely, making an unpleasant moaning sound at the back of her throat.

After dinner Doris went upstairs to turn down Mrs Hollis's bed. She could hear the wireless in the drawing-room play a selection from *The Student Prince*. She laid out the satin pyjamas which had the initials P.H. worked over a breast pocket. Then she critically inspected Mrs Hollis's make-up on the dressing-table, smearing her wrist with alternative samples of lipstick. Doris noticed a letter on the dressing-table, which she instinctively picked up and read.

My dearest Priscilla (otherwise know as Poppet),

By the time this reaches you I shall have arrived at where I am going. The voyage has been pleasant, but excruciatingly dull. There is a bloke on board I knew at school – Gerry Baker. I share a cabin with him and two other Majors, which is jolly. There is little to do but drink – and there is plenty of that, thank the Lord – and play cards, so as you can imagine we are all impatient to arrive and get cracking! I am also impatient for your first letter, my sweet, telling me how you are and all the gang. Gerry Baker has two daughters the same age as Shirley and Daphne which is a coincidence, isn't it? How are the little beauties, bless their hearts? Give them their daddy's love, if they remember him. I doubt if little Daphne will remember me when I return. How are Shirley's teeth?

Everyone on board is very sanguine about the war ending soon. I hope to God they are right. Jerry's going to get a kick in the pants he isn't expecting. Well, I know my little wife is keeping her chin up. The days are grey, but it won't be for long. And we both have happy memories, haven't we, to last us till we're together again? I know that I have.

I have no news to tell you, so I suppose I had better close now. Cheerio, old lady – and keep smiling.

With love from your devoted

Henry

There was a postscript to this letter which had been crossed out by the censor.

Doris then went into Mrs Redman's room. She put ready the old lady's night-dress which was kept in a fluffy case disguised as a rabbit beneath the many pillows on the bed, some pink mules of a dainty colour and design but a large size and a black dressing-gown with green dragons painted over it. The room was full of photographs, and on the table were some back numbers of *The Times* and four novels from the Times Book Club. Doris opened a drawer in the hope of finding a letter to read but discovered something much more interesting – a box of Black Magic chocolates which Mrs Redman must have been storing for some time.

The maid knew at once that she must steal them. The sweets would give her much more pleasure than anything could possibly give Mrs Redman. She undid the bodice of her dress and hid the box under her bosom; when she fastened again the hooks and eyes it stayed there firm. She walked calmly up to her attic and placed the chocolates in the bottom drawer of a large chest of drawers recently put there, beside an old copy of *Picturegoer* which had a picture of Irene Dunne on the cover.

That night, dressed in her white woollen pyjamas and sitting on her narrow bed, Doris opened the box of Black Magic and delightedly examined the little map on top of the chocolates which she had not seen for over a year. She picked out a Praline Paté, the chocolate which she knew she liked the least, and ate it, first sucking off the chocolate coating and then crunching the centre. After this she had to eat the whole lot.

Everyone in the house was now in bed. She heard outside in the street the noise of men coming out of the public houses which were closing. Doris pulled on her pink-flannel dressing-gown, embroidered at the sleeves and pockets with twisted white cord and tassels, and clutching the cardboard remains of her theft hurried downstairs to the kitchen. She burnt the empty box in the dying fire, stirring the embers with the crooked poker which she used so much in the daytime. A fat black beetle ran over her naked foot.

Back in bed Doris felt very sick. The night was hot and she pushed the bedclothes off her ill-made bed and lay almost naked, shaking and happy in wait for the sleep which she knew would come.

The Dancing Lesson

The soldier climbed the stairs to the top of the house, his heavy boots clattering on the stone. He stopped outside a door which had a green curtain drawn across it; on it was written, 'The Adair School of Ballroom Dancing. Private Lessons any Time.' There was also a photograph of a man and a smiling woman dancing together, holding each other at arms' length. From behind the door came the sound of Victor Sylvester's band playing 'Amapola'. The soldier went into the room, a large bleak studio with a skylight on which the evening rain was spattering. There were green chairs along the walls, a big clock and a gramophone near the door. In the middle of the room a girl and an Air Force officer were turning slowly, holding each other, and occasionally eyeing their reflection in the mirror on the wall. They ignored the newcomer who sat down and watched them.

The record came to an end, and the girl broke away from her partner, leaving him alone in the middle of the room, and went to the gramophone. She was small and thin, with black hair and a sharp, pretty face which she had powdered very white. She wore a tight black dress, a white artificial flower pinned to her shoulder, and high-heeled silver shoes. She said to the officer, who was now changing his shoes, 'When would you care to come again?' She recorded his answer in a book by the gramophone, and turned her attention to the soldier. He had arranged a course of lessons that morning, and as he had only a short time for them, she had offered to give him that day half an hour after the time when she normally closed the studio.

'Have you done any dancing before?'

'No.'

'We had better start with the quick-step, which is the simplest. Aren't you going to change your shoes?'

'I haven't brought any others.'

The girl frowned, and started 'Amapola'. He found it difficult to dance with her, because she was so much smaller than him. At first he was conscious of an amused audience in the last pupil, who soon left, after wishing the girl 'Good Evening'. She punctuated the lesson with instructions given in a bored voice: 'One two, three, and slide; one, two, three, and over; no, the left foot, not the right . . .' He felt humiliated when because of a mistake he had made they stopped, and had to start again. Her head came to his chest; his hand was hot on her thin shoulder-blades, and she pulled away from him with an almost vicious determination, her small legs moving automatically, followed by his clumsy, khaki ones. Often his boot trod on her toes, and although he apologised, she did not answer. Together they slid the round of the room, and then she put the same record on the gramophone again.

There soon arose a sense of hostility between them. He was too shy to laugh at his mistakes, and she made him realise, by an air of aggravated misery and bitter pathos, that but for him she would be now walking to her home, her tiring day of work finished. He felt both irritated by her, for she made him feel clumsy, and sorry for her, because she did look really ill. He could hardly bear to see their ridiculous reflection in the mirror, alone in the big room while the rain hit the glass above them, because it suggested that he was unwillingly torturing this conscientious little woman, who did not complain. The clock clicked after every minute, and he looked at it so often that the hands seemed to move unusually slowly.

His nervousness ended in disaster. A brutal stamp on her silver shoes unbalanced the teacher, and with an incredible loss of dignity she fell to the floor, and stayed there, her head turned away. He knelt down to help her up, and saw that she was crying. She said nothing, but made no effort to rise, and he guessed that she had hurt her ankle, and was waiting for the pain to subside. After miserable apologies, he said, 'Let me help you to a chair and it will soon pass off,' and put his arm round her thin shoulders. To his surprise, she yielded to his support; he sat down on his heels, and her head fell back on his shoulder, so that she looked up at him with sharp, weeping eyes. She had for him all the agonised pathos of smallness, and for a moment he wanted to hurt her more. He saw now that there were lines on her face, and noticed a white thread in her hair. He put his other arm round her, the rough khaki chafing the skin on her bony arms, and she began to cry more desperately, the cry of a child which follows the pause after sudden pain. Not embarrassed any more, he held her in his arms, uncomfortable on the hard floor, mirrored impersonally on the wall. Her head was pressed against his shoulder, her hollow throat against his chest, while he stared down at her neatly arranged hair, at the straight white parting which divided her head. Her nails, with their 'Natural' polish, were digging at his back, as one clenches one's hand to overcome the sense of pain. But it appeared that she had not sprained her ankle after all, for she rose slowly after the clock had clicked a minute, pulled down her dress, and went to the gramophone where she took a handkerchief from a black bag with silver clips. She blew her nose and dabbed at her face. The soldier's feet were numb, and he rose heavily. The record had come to an end.

'I'm sorry,' he said again.

She shut up her bag and looked at the clock. 'When would it suit you to come next?'

He helped her pull a cord which drew a blind across the skylight; together they fastened the door, and as they walked downstairs he rehearsed in his mind the suggestion to be made at the bottom that he should see her home; find out her name, and perhaps take her to the cinema in the evenings when they were both free.

The Town

There are certain parts of the town where a grey depression awaits the lonely traveller. One of these is the station buffet. It is to this sad place that he first goes, tired and hungry, on his arrival.

The door from the station to the buffet, which has the letters, 'Refreshments', cut from the dark blackout paper pasted on its glass so that at night the dim light from the room shines through and forms the word, is often stuck and discouragingly hard to open; inside there is a smell of sour tea and stale paste sandwiches. Tables are attached to the tiled floor. Behind the wet sloping counter a fat girl with huge white legs, wearing a black silk dress which hangs low in front and is hitched up over her behind, sells with a resentful air these sandwiches, hard as stone and piled up like a card castle beneath a glass dome. When asked for tea she pours a little off-white milk into a cracked china mug, indifferently washed and left to dry itself; then she adds an inch of tea which she draws from a steaming urn, and fills the cup with boiling water from another. She suspiciously slides in a few grains of sugar, and then stirs the mixture with a stained spoon tied by a piece of string to the ornate till, which is itself fastened to the counter. The tea tastes only of its heat and what sugar there is in it, and when it has been drunk a sediment of brown powder remains at the bottom of the mug. Along the wall behind the counter are wine-bottles containing coloured liquid and crisp empty cigarette cartons — all advertisements of non-existent wares. When there are any cigarettes, they are sold loose, and some slip from the waitress's fingers on to the counter, where they become sodden and are ruined. The clock has stopped at ten past ten, and its glass case is ajar.

Sometimes the waitress has a friend with her behind the counter, and then she can continue while serving with a story which she has been telling in instalments for several days. 'She didn't say anything to me at the *time* – no coffee, only tea. Beer the other end of the counter,' she says, although there is no one but herself to serve the beer at the other end of the counter, for her friend is obviously not expected to help her even when she is very busy. At a slack moment, bringing her hand down to squash an insect crawling up the till, she might tell a favoured customer, 'You know I couldn't keep from laughing this morning, when I came here I saw a big grey rat on the counter, big as that he was. He must have been at the sandwiches.' Then, over her shoulder, she replies in a softer voice to her friend's question, 'Ah, but that would be telling, wouldn't it?'

Mingling with the noise of the trains outside can be heard the polite, mysteriously ubiquitous voice of the woman who, apparently perched somewhere on the station roof, announces their departure and arrival, and tells passengers to 'hurry along to the bay, please, your train is waiting.' One of the workmen who comes to the buffet every morning before catching the six-thirty, wrapped in scarves and blowing on their hands, to buy a cup of tea from the waitress whose eyes are still sticky with sleep, is in love with the owner of the voice, and as he has never seen her imagines her to look like Dorothy Lamour.

In the evening the place is filled with the women porters who come in at eight o'clock laughing and joking for some beer. These are the only customers with whom the waitress is friendly; to any others she says, 'Haven't you anything smaller?', or 'Have you the extra halfpenny?', in a bored and offended voice which is meant to dissociate herself from her surroundings, and implies that all the time she is thinking of the glamorous life which she leads when away from the station. She knows that she sees people at a disadvantage, when they are fussed and apprehensive, and this gives her a low opinion of human life.

Outside the trains shriek and sigh. Tired women sit at the tables, luggage and children piled about them, sipping their tea – for drinking tea is often the most satisfactory physical experience that their lives can offer them. Its heat calms their nerves and its very tastelessness is comforting. Parting couples make stumbling conversation in the buffet, saying the same thing again and again but never admitting that they are longing for the train to arrive, and the parting to be over. They clutch at the present with an avidity that leaves them dumb and senseless. An enormous woman porter, twice the size of any of her male associates, leans over the bar and says grandly, 'I'll have twenty Woodies, Rita, and give me a pint.'

'Mild or bitter?' the waitress asks coyly.

'Either, so long as it's wet,' says the porter, and some people in the buffet laugh. The air gets thicker, and Rita more and more dazed and sick. Soon she will stumble home in her mackintosh, through the wet streets, to the soft bed that awaits her in a house by the railway line – for she does not escape the noise of trains even at night. Soon, also, it will be six o'clock; time for her to wash in a basin beneath a naked bulb, dress and return to the buffet where someone will be swilling the floor, muttering to herself. The days pass quickly and happily for Rita, and by now she does not notice the smell of tea and the noise of the trains; they have been absorbed by her senses, and she would only notice their absence.

Another place where life seems to be at its lowest ebb is

the lending library over the booksellers in the High Street. The books that line the walls have all been rebound by the library in brown covers, and their titles are printed in illegible gold lettering. Cardboard bookmarkers, covered with mysterious pencil marks, dangle from their backs. The more pencil marks that a book has on its cardboard extension, the more popular it proves itself to be. Only the newest books, available to a few subscribers who pay more than the others, have no markers, and sometimes have not yet been rebound so that they look more readable than the older, uniform volumes. These have been arranged in alphabetical order on the shelves by the single assistant, Miss Fraser, who is a small woman with frizzy pale hair and spectacles that look as if they hurt her. In summer the sun glitters on the backs of the novels as though it might melt them; there is a smell of leather in the library and Miss Fraser sits wilting in the stuffy room behind a desk on which she has placed a jar of flowers as limp as herself. Sometimes she is busy knitting bedsocks for herself with painfully thin steel needles; sometimes she sits idle, staring through the large bay window at the street, dabbing at her sharp nose with a small handkerchief which she keeps secured to her knee by the elastic strap of her knickers, and which therefore smells faintly of underclothes. At teatime she takes some bread and butter wrapped in tissue paper from the pocket of her check coat which hangs with her hat (either a pixie hood or a rabbi's cap) behind the door, and munches it slowly while crumbs fall between the pages of the books which she handles. Her fountain-pen has left two inky bumps on her middle and forefingers.

All day Miss Fraser's customers, who are mostly ladies in light-brown fur coats who live in the northern suburb of the town, stump up the broad staircase from the shop and fish their books from net shopping-bags, either with a reproachful air because they have not enjoyed their choice, or with patronising commendation because they have. They speak in low voices, as though at an oracle; and Miss Fraser is the goddess of the oracle, for they take it for granted that she has read every book in the library. 'Would I like this?' one might ask, doubtfully deciphering the title of a novel. 'I want something light but not trashy.' Miss Fraser answers with a frown, 'It's not as good as his others,' or, defiantly, 'Well, *I* liked it,' but she never gives away the fact that she does not read novels, or indeed anything, as reading makes her head ache, and that she is only interested in playing tennis, and tennis champions. She can tell, however, from a glance at a book, which of her customers it will please; and she can even successfully supply with amusement ladies whom she has never seen, invalids who do not leave their houses, but send out companions to Miss Fraser with long instructions written in spidery handwriting on scraps of paper. The librarian is conscious of her responsibility towards these, and sends them the new Warwick Deeping or Cecil Roberts with the air of a doctor prescribing a tonic wine. There is but one male subscriber, a Mr Young, who never asks Miss Fraser's advice, and is always wanting books that she has never heard of, or that are out of print; he seems to have joined the library owing to some mistake, and she respects him more than any other of her customers.

Miss Fraser despises readers of books, but rather admires the writers, for she thinks that they must be clever, not because they write anything of value, but because they can write at all. She knows how important it is for a novel to be long, and the longer a book is the more she admires its author for the purely physical feat of writing down so many words on so much paper. Miss Fraser feels that she conspires with the writers to dupe the readers and so her attitude to the latter is a mixture of contempt and apology. The ladies who visit her day after day respect her and are fond of her, but she pities them and if one of them asked her to tea on

Thursday she would not go. To please them, and to help business, she sometimes volunteers a scrap of information about her private life, so that a customer can ask while changing a book, 'How is your sister who was so poorly at Easter?' or 'Have you heard again from your brother in Kenya?' With instinctive art she exactly limits the extent of her personal relationship with the readers — she would always nod if surprised by one off duty at the Kardomah Café or buying slides at Marks and Spencers — but privately she classes herself apart from them, with the unseen writers, on a higher plane, the practiser of a fraud, the exploiter of the vice of reading.

As a young girl, Miss Fraser had wanted more than anything else to be another Betty Nuthall or Helen Wills Moody. Now, on summer Thursdays, she is able to change into a pleated white dress and stroll with her girl friend to the public courts, each balancing a box of balls marked Slazenger on their rackets which are screwed into triangular presses. She plays well; on these afternoons she is energetic, her face has a colour, and even her hair seems alive, but for the rest of the week she must wilt in her hot-house, her eyes dim, a sneer stamped on her face. 'What they really need here,' she thinks sadly, 'is a girl who is fond of reading', but she dare not leave her job as she might never find another. By now, however, she has come to think herself lucky to be able to do what she wants for a few hours every summer week.

Just as in the station buffet it is the depression caused by squalor that assails one, and in the lending library that of vegetable refinement, so in the Tudor Bar of the town's most expensive hotel does there come a moment when silence falls, time stops and the atmosphere is stale.

High, steel, immovable stools sit up at a streamlined bar. Until recently the room has been picturesque, as indicated by the name it still bears, but now it is modernised and gives the impression of an angular design in red and white. Small flamboyant girls, with hair sometimes an inky blue, sometimes a decorative pink or a dazzling yellow, but always piled high above their heads as though supported by a hidden construction of wire and cardboard, amuse their escorts in the RAF with a sullen gaiety. The barmaid appears to have powdered not only her face a dusty yellow, but also her hair and hands, and even her clothes and the Parma Violets sagging at her bosom. Every drink except for rum has run out, and its sickly smell fastens on the room and the people in it like hair oil on a plastered head.

Sometimes a husband and wife who are staying at the hotel penetrate into the bar, looking about them defiantly and moving self-consciously – for usually the residents look upon the bar as out of bounds, preferring to have their drinks brought to them by a waiter as they sit in one of the lounges. There, however, there is little to do but turn the pages of the *Morris Owner* until that magazine assumes a sickening familiarity; and as neither member of a married couple owes the other the politeness of conversation, towards the end of the evening boredom drives them into the bar. The woman immediately sits down, while the man sidles furtively up to the bar itself, now and then turning round to signal to his wife, who may ignore his signs, or answer them with a restrained nod. Eventually he returns balancing the glasses, carefully pushing them ahead of him through the crowd, and for the rest of the evening they sit and sip together, not looking at each other, unable to hide a feeling of superiority, and convinced that any remark they might make will be as embarrassingly audible to everyone in the noisy, smoky bar, as it would have been in the soporific, silent lounge where they really belong.

Just as a drunken bonhomie can suddenly change into a testy, quarrelsome misery, so the atmosphere in the bar, as the evening progresses, becomes less and less gay and careless, more and more bitter and hostile. Quarrels start between lovers, and between men who have never seen each other before. The barmaid has dark shadows under her eyes, and as the drink runs out appears to think that she is being blamed. The married couple want to go to bed, but each feels that if he or she suggests this, the other will be offended and the evening will be ruined. Only the red-faced drunk, who is found leaning on the bar each night, is happy and smiling, because he is now in a world where every face he sees, every word he happens to hear, assumes an exciting air of mystery; his brain is drowning and distressing reason has disappeared. Suddenly one of the lights is switched off; an airman shouts, a girl giggles, and everyone feels relieved. The fun has stopped, and the more enjoyable period of looking back on, thinking about and discussing that fun is beginning.

When you leave the bar at closing time, there is nothing to do but walk slowly past the lovers at each shop door in the High Street, down by the canal where cranes and gasometers in the mist caricature human forms, wondering what it would be like to spend the night, not in the bed to which you dread returning, but in the closed and empty Post Office or on the dance floor of the large Town Hall; and to hear the last buses at quarter past ten rock through the silent town, illuminated and sometimes containing ghostly shaking forms, seeming to make more noise than they do in the daytime.